PENGUIN POPULAR CLASSICS

GUYS AND DOLLS

BY DAMON RUNYON

DAMON RUNYON (1884–1946). A journalist and short-story writer, best remembered for his colourful tales of Broadway and for the distinctive style of his prose, commonly termed Runyonese.

Alfred Damon Runyon was born in 1884 at Manhattan, Kansas, the son of a printer. He grew up in Colorado and in his adolescence he wrote articles for the local newspapers. At the age of fourteen he enlisted in the Spanish–American War and served in the Philippines. He returned home in 1900 and worked on numerous newspapers in Colorado Springs, Denver and San Francisco, before getting the job of sportswriter for the New York *American* in 1911. During the First World War he became a war correspondent for the Hearst newspapers, with whom he continued as a columnist after the war. Runyon's stories are highly original and lively evocations of Broadway low-life and the New York sporting scene. They are light-hearted vignettes, peppered with Broadway slang and with 'types' rather than individuals, who have hearts of gold, but very little brain power. Initially collected in *Guys and Dolls* (1932), his other collections of stories include *Blue Plate Special* (1934) and *Take It Easy* (1938). He also wrote a comedy play, with Howard Lindsay, entitled *A Slight Case of Murder* (1935). Damon Runyon died in 1946.

Guys and Dolls is Runyon's most successful and enduringly popular work. It was the basis of J. L. Mankiewicz's famous musical film of 1955, starring Marlon Brando and Frank Sinatra.

PENGUIN POPULAR CLASSICS

GUYS AND DOLLS
& OTHER STORIES

DAMON RUNYON

PENGUIN BOOKS

PENGUIN BOOKS

Published by the Penguin Group
Penguin Books Ltd, 27 Wrights Lane, London w8 5tz, England
Penguin Books USA Inc., 375 Hudson Street, New York, New York 10014, USA
Penguin Books Australia Ltd, Ringwood, Victoria, Australia
Penguin Books Canada Ltd, 10 Alcorn Avenue, Toronto, Ontario, Canada m4v 3b2
Penguin Books (NZ) Ltd, 182–190 Wairau Road, Auckland 10, New Zealand

Penguin Books Ltd, Registered Offices: Harmondsworth, Middlesex, England

This selection first published 1956
Published in Penguin Popular Classics 1997
1 3 5 7 9 10 8 6 4 2

Printed in England by Clays Ltd, St Ives plc

CONTENTS

1 GUYS AND DOLLS

or The Idyll of Miss Sarah Brown

OF all the high players this country ever sees, there is no doubt but that the guy they call The Sky is the highest. In fact, the reason he is called The Sky is because he goes so high when it comes to betting on any proposition whatever. He will bet all he has, and nobody can bet any more than this.

His right name is Obadiah Masterson, and he is originally out of a little town in southern Colorado where he learns to shoot craps, and play cards, and one thing and another, and where his old man is a very well-known citizen, and something of a sport himself. In fact, The Sky tells me that when he finally cleans up all the loose scratch around his home town and decides he needs more room, his old man has a little private talk with him and says to him like this:

'Son,' the old guy says, 'you are now going out into the wide, wide world to make your own way, and it is a very good thing to do, as there are no more opportunities for you in this burg. I am only sorry,' he says, 'that I am not able to bank-roll you to a very large start, but,' he says, 'not having any potatoes to give you, I am now going to stake you to some very valuable advice, which I personally collect in my years of experience around and about, and I hope and trust you will always bear this advice in mind.

'Son,' the old guy says, 'no matter how far you travel, or how smart you get, always remember this: Some day, somewhere,' he says, 'a guy is going to come to you and show you a nice brand-new deck of cards on which the seal is never broken, and this guy is going to offer to bet you that the jack of spades will jump out of this deck and squirt cider in your ear. But, son,' the old guy says, 'do not bet him, for as sure as you do you are going to get an ear full of cider.'

Well, The Sky remembers what his old man says, and he is always very cautious about betting on such propositions as the jack of spades jumping out of a sealed deck of cards and squirting cider in his ear, and so he makes few mistakes as he goes along. In fact, the only real mistake The Sky makes is when he hits St Louis after leaving his old home town, and loses all his potatoes betting a guy St Louis is the biggest town in the world.

Now of course this is before The Sky ever sees any bigger towns, and he is never much of a hand for reading up on matters such as this. In fact, the only reading The Sky ever does as he goes along through life is in these Gideon Bibles such as he finds in the hotel rooms where he lives, for The Sky never lives anywhere else but in hotel rooms for years.

He tells me that he reads many items of great interest in these Gideon Bibles, and furthermore The Sky says that several times these Gideon Bibles keep him from getting out of line, such as the time he finds himself pretty much frozen-in over in Cincinnati, what with owing everybody in town except maybe the mayor from playing games of chance of one kind and another.

Well, The Sky says he sees no way of meeting these obligations and he is figuring the only thing he can do is to take a run-out powder, when he happens to read in one of these Gideon Bibles where it says like this:

'Better is it,' the Gideon Bible says, 'that thou shouldest not vow, than that thou shouldest vow and not pay.'

Well, The Sky says he can see that there is no doubt whatever but that this means a guy shall not welsh, so he remains in Cincinnati until he manages to wiggle himself out of the situation, and from that day to this, The Sky never thinks of welshing.

He is maybe thirty years old, and is a tall guy with a round kisser, and big blue eyes, and he always looks as innocent as a little baby. But The Sky is by no means as innocent as he looks. In fact, The Sky is smarter than three Philadelphia lawyers, which makes him very smart, indeed, and he is well established as a high player in New Orleans, and Chicago, and Los Angeles, and wherever else there is any action in the way of card-playing, or crap-shooting, or horse-racing, or betting on the baseball games, for The Sky is always moving around the country following the action.

But while The Sky will bet on anything whatever, he is more of a short-card player and a crap-shooter than anything else, and furthermore he is a great hand for propositions, such as are always coming up among citizens who follow games of chance for a living. Many citizens prefer betting on propositions to anything you can think of, because they figure a proposition gives them a chance to out-smart somebody, and in fact I know citizens who will sit up all night making up propositions to offer other citizens the next day.

A proposition may be only a problem in cards, such as what is the price against a guy getting aces back-to-back, or how often a pair of deuces will win a hand in stud, and then again it may be some very daffy proposition, indeed, although the daffier any proposition seems to be, the more some citizens like it. And no one ever sees The Sky when he does not have some proposition of his own.

The first time he ever shows up around this town, he goes to a baseball game at the Polo Grounds with several prominent citizens, and while he is at the ball game he buys himself a sack of Harry Stevens' peanuts, which he dumps in a side pocket of his coat. He is eating these peanuts all through the game, and after the game is over and he is walking across the field with the citizens, he says to them like this:

'What price,' The Sky says, 'I cannot throw a peanut from second base to the home plate?'

Well everybody knows that a peanut is too light for anybody to throw it this far, so Big Nig, the crap shooter, who always likes to have a little the best of it running for him, speaks as follows:

'You can have 3 to 1 from me, stranger,' Big Nig says.

'Two C's against six,' The Sky says, and then he stands on second base, and takes a peanut out of his pocket, and not only whips it to the home plate, but on into the lap of a fat guy who is still sitting in the grand stand putting the zing on Bill Terry for not taking Walker out of the box when Walker is getting a pasting from the other club.

Well, naturally, this is a most astonishing throw, indeed, but afterwards it comes out that The Sky throws a peanut loaded with lead, and of course it is not one of Harry Stevens' peanuts, either, as Harry is not selling peanuts full of lead at a dime a bag, with the price of lead what it is.

It is only a few nights after this that The Sky states another most unusual proposition to a group of citizens sitting in Mindy's restaurant when he offers to bet a C note that he can go down into Mindy's cellar and catch a live rat with his bare hands and everybody is greatly astonished when Mindy himself steps up and takes the bet, for ordinarily Mindy will not bet you a nickel he is alive.

But it seems that Mindy knows that The Sky plants a tame rat in the cellar, and this rat knows The Sky and loves him dearly, and will let him catch it any time he wishes, and it also seems that Mindy knows that one of his dish washers happens upon this rat, and not knowing it is tame, knocks it flatter than a pancake. So when The Sky goes down into the cellar and starts trying to catch a rat with his bare hands he is greatly surprised how inhospitable the rat turns out to be, because it is one of Mindy's personal rats, and Mindy is around afterwards saying he will lay plenty of 7 to 5 against even Strangler Lewis being able to catch one of his rats with his bare hands, or with boxing gloves on.

I am only telling you all this to show you what a smart guy The Sky is, and I am only sorry I do not have time to tell you about many other very remarkable propositions that he thinks up outside of his regular business.

It is well-known to one and all that he is very honest in every respect, and that he hates and despises cheaters at cards, or dice, and furthermore The Sky never wishes to play with any the best of it himself, or anyway not much. He will never take the inside of any situation, as many gamblers love to do, such as owning a gambling house, and having the percentage run for him instead of against him, for always The Sky is strictly a player, because he says he will never care to settle down in one spot long enough to become the owner of anything.

In fact, in all the years The Sky is drifting around the country, nobody ever knows him to own anything except maybe a bank roll, and when he comes to Broadway the last time, which is the time I am now speaking of, he has a hundred G's in cash money, and an extra suit of clothes, and this is all he has in the world. He never owns such a thing as a house, or an automobile, or a piece of jewellery. He never owns a watch, because The Sky says time means nothing to him.

Of course some guys will figure a hundred G's comes under the head of owning something, but as far as The Sky is concerned, money is nothing but just something for him to play with and the dollars may as well be doughnuts as far as value goes with him. The only time The Sky ever thinks of money as money is when he is broke, and the only way he can tell he is broke is when he reaches into his pocket and finds nothing there but his fingers.

Then it is necessary for The Sky to go out and dig up some fresh scratch somewhere, and when it comes to digging up scratch, The Sky is practically supernatural. He can get more potatoes on the strength of a telegram to some place or other than John D. Rockefeller can get on collateral, for everybody knows The Sky's word is as good as wheat in the bin.

Now one Sunday evening The Sky was walking along Broadway, and at the corner of Forty-ninth Street he comes upon a little bunch of mission workers who are holding a religious meeting, such as mission workers love to do of a Sunday evening, the idea being that they may round up a few sinners here and there, although personally I always claim the mission workers come out too early to catch any sinners on this part of Broadway. At such an hour the sinners are still in bed resting up from their sinning of the night before, so they will be in good shape for more sinning a little later on.

There are only four of these mission workers, and two of them are old guys, and one is an old doll, while the other is a young doll who is tootling on a cornet. And after a couple of ganders at this young doll, The Sky is a goner, for this is one of the most beautiful young dolls anybody ever sees on Broadway, and especially as a mission worker. Her name is Miss Sarah Brown.

She is tall, and thin, and has a first-class shape, and her hair is a light brown, going on blonde, and her eyes are like I do not know what, except that they are one-hundred-per-cent eyes in every respect. Furthermore, she is not a bad cornet player, if you like cornet players, although at this spot on Broadway she has to play against a scat band in a chop-suey joint near by, and this is tough competition, although at that many citizens believe Miss Sarah Brown will win by a large score if she only gets a little more support from one of the old guys with her who has a big bass drum, but does not pound it hearty enough.

Well, The Sky stands there listening to Miss Sarah Brown tootling on the cornet for quite a spell, and then he hears her make a speech in which she puts the blast on sin very good, and boosts religion quite some, and says if there are any souls around that need saving the owners of same may step forward at once. But no one steps forward, so The Sky comes over to Mindy's restaurant where many citizens are congregated, and starts telling us about Miss Sarah Brown. But of course we already know about Miss Sarah Brown, because she is so beautiful, and so good.

Furthermore, everybody feels somewhat sorry for Miss Sarah Brown, for while she is always tootling the cornet, and making speeches, and looking to save any souls that need saving, she never seems to find any souls to save, or at least her bunch of mission workers never gets any bigger. In fact, it gets smaller, as she starts out with a guy who plays a very fair sort of trombone, but this guy takes it on the lam one night with the trombone, which one and all consider a dirty trick.

Now from this time on, The Sky does not take any interest in anything but Miss Sarah Brown, and any night she is out on the corner with the other mission workers, you will see The Sky standing around looking at her, and naturally after a few weeks of this, Miss Sarah Brown must know The Sky is looking at her, or she is dumber than seems possible. And nobody ever figures

Miss Sarah Brown dumb, as she is always on her toes, and seems plenty able to take care of herself, even on Broadway.

Sometimes after the street meeting is over, The Sky follows the mission workers to their headquarters in an old storeroom around in Forty-eighth Street where they generally hold an indoor session, and I hear The Sky drops many a large coarse note in the collection box while looking at Miss Sarah Brown, and there is no doubt these notes come in handy around the mission, as I hear business is by no means so good there.

It is called the Save-a-Soul Mission, and it is run mainly by Miss Sarah Brown's grandfather, an old guy with whiskers, by the name of Arvide Abernathy, but Miss Sarah Brown seems to do most of the work, including tootling the cornet, and visiting the poor people around and about, and all this and that, and many citizens claim it is a great shame that such a beautiful doll is wasting her time being good.

How The Sky ever becomes acquainted with Miss Sarah Brown is a very great mystery, but the next thing anybody knows, he is saying hello to her, and she is smiling at him out of her one-hundred-per-cent eyes, and one evening when I happen to be with The Sky we run into her walking along Forty-ninth Street, and The Sky hauls off and stops her, and says it is a nice evening, which it is, at that. Then The Sky says to Miss Sarah Brown like this:

'Well,' The Sky says, 'how is the mission dodge going these days? Are you saving any souls?' he says.

Well, it seems from what Miss Sarah Brown says the soul-saving is very slow, indeed, these days.

'In fact,' Miss Sarah Brown says, 'I worry greatly about how few souls we seem to save. Sometimes I wonder if we are lacking in grace.'

She goes on up the street, and The Sky stands looking after her, and he says to me like this:

'I wish I can think of some way to help this little doll,' he says, 'especially,' he says, 'in saving a few souls to build up her mob at the mission. I must speak to her again, and see if I can figure something out.'

But The Sky does not get to speak to Miss Sarah Brown again, because somebody weighs in the sacks on him by telling her he is nothing but a professional gambler, and that he is a very undesirable character, and that his only interest in hanging around the mission is because she is a good-looking doll. So all of a sudden Miss Sarah Brown plays a plenty of chill for The Sky. Furthermore, she sends him word that she does not care to accept any more of his potatoes in the collection box, because his potatoes are nothing but ill-gotten gains.

Well, naturally, this hurts The Sky's feelings no little, so he quits standing around looking at Miss Sarah Brown, and going to the mission, and takes to mingling again with the citizens in Mindy's, and showing some interest in the affairs of the community, especially the crap games.

Of course the crap games that are going on at this time are nothing much, because practically everybody in the world is broke, but there is a head-and-head game run by Nathan Detroit over a garage in Fifty-second Street where there is occasionally some action, and who shows up at this crap game early one evening but The Sky, although it seems he shows up there more to find company than anything else.

In fact, he only stands around watching the play, and talking with other guys who are also standing around and watching, and many of these guys are very high shots during the gold rush, although most of them are now as clean as a jaybird, and maybe cleaner. One of these guys is a guy by the name of Brandy Bottle Bates, who is known from coast to coast as a high player when he has anything to play with, and who is called Brandy Bottle Bates because it seems that years ago he is a great hand for belting a brandy bottle around.

This Brandy Bottle Bates is a big, black-looking guy, with a large beezer, and a head shaped like a pear, and he is considered a very immoral and wicked character, but he is a pretty slick gambler, and a fast man with a dollar when he is in the money.

Well, finally The Sky asks Brandy Bottle why he is not playing and Brandy laughs, and states as follows:

'Why,' he says, 'in the first place I have no potatoes, and in the second place I doubt if it will do me much good if I do have any potatoes the way I am going the past year. Why,' Brandy Bottle says, 'I cannot win a bet to save my soul.'

Now this crack seems to give The Sky an idea, as he stands looking at Brandy Bottle very strangely, and while he is looking, Big Nig, the crap shooter, picks up the dice and hits three times hand-running, bing, bing, bing. Then Big Nig comes out on a six and Brandy Bottle Bates speaks as follows:

'You see how my luck is,' he says. 'Here is Big Nig hotter than a stove, and here I am without a bob to follow him with, especially,' Brandy says, 'when he is looking for nothing but a six. Why,' he says, 'Nig can make sixes all night when he is hot. If he does not make this six, the way he is, I will be willing to turn square and quit gambling forever.'

'Well, Brandy,' The Sky says, 'I will make you a proposition. I will lay you a G note Big Nig does not get his six. I will lay you a G note against nothing but your soul,' he says. 'I mean if Big Nig does not get his six, you are to turn square and join Miss Sarah Brown's mission for six months.'

'Bet!' Brandy Bottle Bates says right away, meaning the proposition is on, although the chances are he does not quite understand the proposition. All Brandy understands is The Sky wishes to wager that Big Nig does not make his six, and Brandy Bottle Bates will be willing to bet his soul a couple of times over on Big Nig making his six, and figure he is getting the best of it, at that, as Brandy has great confidence in Nig.

Well, sure enough, Big Nig makes the six, so The Sky weeds Brandy Bottle Bates a G note, although everybody around is saying The Sky makes a terrible over-lay of the natural price in giving Brandy Bottle a G against his soul. Furthermore, everybody around figures the chances are The Sky only wishes to give Brandy an opportunity to get in action, and nobody figures The Sky is on the level about trying to win Brandy Bottle Bates' soul, especially as The Sky does not seem to wish to go any further after paying the bet.

He only stands there looking on and seeming somewhat depressed as Brandy Bottle goes into action on his own account with the G note, fading other guys around the table with cash money. But Brandy Bottle Bates seems to figure what is in The Sky's mind pretty well, because Brandy Bottle is a crafty old guy.

It finally comes his turn to handle the dice, and he hits a couple of times, and then he comes out on a four, and anybody will tell you that a four is a very tough point to make, even with a lead pencil. Then Brandy Bottle turns to The Sky and speaks to him as follows:

'Well, Sky,' he says, 'I will take the odds off you on this one. I know you do not want my dough,' he says. 'I know you only want my soul for Miss Sarah Brown, and,' he says, 'without wishing to be fresh about it, I know why you want it for her. I am young once myself,' Brandy Bottle says. 'And you know if I lose to you, I will be over there in Forty-eighth Street in an hour pounding on the door, for Brandy always settles.

'But Sky,' he says, 'now I am in the money, and my price goes up. Will you lay me ten G's against my soul I do not make this four?'

'Bet!' The Sky says, and right away Brandy Bottle hits with a four.

Well, when word goes around The Sky is up at Nathan Detroit's crap game trying to win Brandy Bottle Bates' soul for Miss Sarah Brown, the excitement is practically intense. Somebody telephones Mindy's, where a large number of citizens are sitting around arguing about this and that, and telling one another how much they will bet in support of their arguments, if only they have something to bet, and Mindy himself is almost killed in the rush for the door.

One of the first guys out of Mindy's and up to the crap game is Regret, the horse player, and as he comes in Brandy Bottle is looking for a nine, and The Sky is laying him twelve G's against his soul that he does not make this nine, for it seems Brandy Bottle's soul keeps getting more and more expensive.

Well, Regret wishes to bet his soul against a G that Brandy Bottle gets his nine, and is greatly insulted when The Sky cannot figure his price any better than a double saw, but finally Regret accepts this price, and Brandy Bottle hits again.

Now many other citizens request a little action from The Sky, and if there is one thing The Sky cannot deny a citizen it is action, so he says he will lay them according to how he figures their word to join Miss Sarah Brown's mission if Brandy Bottle misses out, but about this time The Sky finds he has no more potatoes on him, being now around thirty-five G's loser, and he wishes to give markers.

But Brandy Bottle says that while ordinarily he will be pleased to extend The Sky this accommodation, he does not care to accept markers against his soul, so then The Sky has to leave the joint and go over to his hotel two or three blocks away, and get the night clerk to open his damper so The Sky can get the rest of his bank roll. In the meantime the crap game continues at Nathan Detroit's among the small operators, while the other citizens stand around and say that while they hear of many a daffy proposition in their time, this is the daffiest that ever comes to their attention, although Big Nig claims he hears of a daffier one, but cannot think what it is.

Big Nig claims that all gamblers are daffy anyway, and in fact he says if they are not daffy they will not be gamblers, and while he is arguing this matter back comes The Sky with fresh scratch, and Brandy Bottle Bates takes up where he leaves off, although Brandy says he is accepting the worst of it, as the dice have a chance to cool off.

Now the upshot of the whole business is that Brandy Bottle hits thirteen licks in a row, and the last lick he makes is on a ten, and it is for twenty G's against his soul, with about a dozen other citizens getting anywhere from one to five C's against their souls, and complaining bitterly of the price.

And as Brandy Bottle makes his ten, I happen to look at The Sky and I see him watching Brandy with a very peculiar expression on his face, and furthermore I see The Sky's right hand creeping inside his coat where I know he always packs a Betsy in a shoulder holster, so I can see something is wrong somewhere.

But before I can figure out what it is, there is quite a fuss at the door, and loud talking, and a doll's voice, and all of a sudden in bobs nobody else but Miss Sarah Brown. It is plain to be seen that she is all steamed up about something.

She marches right up to the crap table where Brandy Bottle

Bates and The Sky and the other citizens are standing, and one and all are feeling sorry for Dobber, the doorman, thinking of what Nathan Detroit is bound to say to him for letting her in. The dice are still lying on the table showing Brandy Bottle Bates' last throw, which cleans The Sky and gives many citizens the first means they enjoy in several months.

Well, Miss Sarah Brown looks at The Sky, and The Sky looks at Miss Sarah Brown, and Miss Sarah Brown looks at the citizens around and about, and one and all are somewhat dumbfounded, and nobody seems to be able to think of much to say, although The Sky finally speaks up as follows:

'Good evening,' The Sky says. 'It is a nice evening,' he says. 'I am trying to win a few souls for you around here, but,' he says, 'I seem to be about half out of luck.'

'Well,' Miss Sarah Brown says, looking at The Sky most severely out of her hundred-per-cent eyes, 'you are taking too much upon yourself. I can win any souls I need myself. You better be thinking of your own soul. By the way,' she says, 'are you risking your own soul, or just your money?'

Well, of course up to this time The Sky is not risking anything but his potatoes, so he only shakes his head to Miss Sarah Brown's question, and looks somewhat disorganized.

'I know something about gambling,' Miss Sarah Brown says, 'especially about crap games. I ought to,' she says. 'It ruins my poor papa and my brother Joe. If you wish to gamble for souls, Mister Sky, gamble for your own soul.'

Now Miss Sarah Brown opens a small black leather pocketbook she is carrying in one hand, and pulls out a two-dollar bill, and it is such a two-dollar bill as seems to have seen much service in its time, and holding up this deuce, Miss Sarah Brown speaks as follows:

'I will gamble with you, Mister Sky,' she says. 'I will gamble with you,' she says, 'on the same terms you gamble with these parties here. This two dollars against your soul, Mister Sky. It is all I have, but,' she says, 'it is more than your soul is worth.'

Well, of course anybody can see that Miss Sarah Brown is doing this because she is very angry, and wishes to make The Sky look small, but right away The Sky's duke comes from inside his coat, and he picks up the dice and hands them to her and speaks as follows:

'Roll them,' The Sky says, and Miss Sarah Brown snatches the dice out of his hand and gives them a quick sling on the table in such a way that anybody can see she is not a professional crap shooter, and not even an amateur crap shooter, for all amateur crap shooters first breathe on the dice, and rattle them good, and make remarks to them, such as 'Come on, baby!'

In fact, there is some criticism of Miss Sarah Brown afterwards on account of her haste, as many citizens are eager to string with her to hit, while others are just as anxious to bet she misses, and she does not give them a chance to get down.

Well, Scranton Slim is the stick guy, and he takes a gander at the dice as they hit up against the side of the table and bounce back, and then Slim hollers, 'Winner, winner, winner,' as stick guys love to do, and what is showing on the dice as big as life, but a six and a five, which makes eleven, no matter how you figure, so The Sky's soul belongs to Miss Sarah Brown.

She turns at once and pushes through the citizens around the table without even waiting to pick up the deuce she lays down when she grabs the dice. Afterwards a most obnoxious character by the name of Red Nose Regan tries to claim the deuce as a sleeper and gets the heave-o from Nathan Detroit, who becomes very indignant about this, stating that Red Nose is trying to give his joint a wrong rap.

Naturally, The Sky follows Miss Brown, and Dobber, the doorman, tells me as they are waiting for him to unlock the door and let them out, Miss Sarah Brown turns on The Sky and speaks to him as follows:

'You are a fool,' Miss Sarah Brown says.

Well, at this Dobber figures The Sky is bound to let one go, as this seems to be most insulting language, but instead of letting one go, The Sky only smiles at Miss Sarah Brown and says to her like this:

'Why,' The Sky says, 'Paul says "If any man among you seemeth to be wise in this world, let him become a fool, that he may be wise." I love you, Miss Sarah Brown,' The Sky says.

Well, now, Dobber has a pretty fair sort of memory, and he

says that Miss Sarah Brown tells The Sky that since he seems to know so much about the Bible, maybe he remembers the second verse of the Song of Solomon, but the chances are Dobber muffs the number of the verse, because I look the matter up in one of these Gideon Bibles, and the verse seems a little too much for Miss Sarah Brown, although of course you never can tell.

Anyway, this is about all there is to the story, except that Brandy Bottle Bates slides out during the confusion so quietly even Dobber scarcely remembers letting him out, and he takes most of The Sky's potatoes with him, but he soon gets batted in against the faro bank out in Chicago and the last anybody hears of him he gets religion all over again, and is preaching out in San Jose, so The Sky always claims he beats Brandy for his soul, at that.

I see The Sky the other night at Forty-ninth Street and Broadway, and he is with quite a raft of mission workers, including Mrs Sky, for it seems that the soul-saving business picks up wonderfully, and The Sky is giving a big bass drum such a first-class whacking that the scat band in the chop-suey joint can scarcely be heard. Furthermore, The Sky is hollering between whacks, and I never see a guy look happier, especially when Mrs Sky smiles at him out of her hundred-per-cent eyes. But I do not linger long, because The Sky gets a gander at me, and right away he begins hollering:

'I see before me a sinner of deepest dye,' he hollers. 'Oh, sinner, repent before it is too late. Join with us, sinner,' he hollers, 'and let us save your soul.'

Naturally, this crack about me being a sinner embarrasses me no little, as it is by no means true, and it is a good thing for The Sky there is no copper in me, or I will go to Mrs Sky, who is always bragging about how she wins The Sky's soul by out-playing him at his own game, and tell her the truth.

And the truth is that the dice with which she wins The Sky's soul, and which are the same dice with which Brandy Bottle Bates' wins all his potatoes, are strictly phony, and that she gets into Nathan Detroit's just in time to keep The Sky from killing old Brandy Bottle.

2 BLOOD PRESSURE

It is maybe eleven-thirty of a Wednesday night, and I am standing at the corner of Forty-eighth Street and Seventh Avenue, thinking about my blood pressure, which is a proposition I never before think much about.

In fact, I never hear of my blood pressure before this Wednesday afternoon when I go around to see Doc Brennan about my stomach, and he puts a gag on my arm and tells me that my blood pressure is higher than a cat's back, and the idea is for me to be careful about what I eat, and to avoid excitement, or I may pop off all of a sudden when I am least expecting it.

'A nervous man such as you with a blood pressure away up in the paint cards must live quietly,' Doc Brennan says. 'Ten bucks, please,' he says.

Well, I am standing there thinking it is not going to be so tough to avoid excitement the way things are around this town right now, and wishing I have my ten bucks back to bet it on Sun Beau in the fourth race at Pimlico the next day, when all of a sudden I look up, and who is in front of me but Rusty Charley.

Now if I have any idea Rusty Charley is coming my way, you can go and bet all the coffee in Java I will be somewhere else at once, for Rusty Charley is not a guy I wish to have any truck with whatever. In fact, I wish no part of him. Furthermore, nobody else in this town wishes to have any part of Rusty Charley, for he is a hard guy indeed. In fact, there is no harder guy anywhere in the world. He is a big wide guy with two large hard hands and a great deal of very bad disposition, and he thinks nothing of knocking people down and stepping on their kissers if he feels like it.

In fact, this Rusty Charley is what is called a gorill, because

23

he is known to often carry a gun in his pants pocket, and sometimes to shoot people down as dead as door-nails with it if he
does not like the way they wear their hats – and Rusty Charley
is very critical of hats. The chances are Rusty Charley shoots
many a guy in this man's town, and those he does not shoot he
sticks with his shiv – which is a knife – and the only reason he
is not in jail is because he just gets out of it, and the law does not
have time to think up something to put him back in again for.

Anyway, the first thing I know about Rusty Charley being in
my neighbourhood is when I hear him saying: 'Well, well, well,
here we are!'

Then he grabs me by the collar so it is no use of me thinking
of taking it on the lam away from there, although I greatly wish
to do so.

'Hello, Rusty,' I say, very pleasant. 'What is the score?'

'Everything is about even,' Rusty says. 'I am glad to see you,
because I am looking for company. I am over in Philadelphia for
three days on business.'

'I hope and trust that you do all right for yourself in Philly,
Rusty,' I say; but his news makes me very nervous, because I am
a great hand for reading the papers and I have a pretty good idea
what Rusty's business in Philly is. It is only the day before that I
see a little item from Philly in the papers about how Gloomy
Gus Smallwood, who is a very large operator in the alcohol
business there, is guzzled right at his front door.

Of course, I do not know that Rusty Charley is the party who
guzzles Gloomy Gus Smallwood, but Rusty Charley is in Philly
when Gus is guzzled, and I can put two and two together as well
as anybody. It is the same thing as if there is a bank robbery in
Cleveland, Ohio, and Rusty Charley is in Cleveland, Ohio, or
near there. So I am very nervous, and I figure it is a sure thing
my blood pressure is going up every second.

'How much dough do you have on you?' Rusty says. 'I am
plumb broke.'

'I do not have more than a couple of bobs, Rusty,' I say. 'I pay
a doctor ten bucks to-day to find out my blood pressure is very
bad. But of course you are welcome to what I have.'

'Well, a couple of bobs is no good to high-class guys like you and me,' Rusty says. 'Let us go to Nathan Detroit's crap game and win some money.'

Now, of course, I do not wish to go to Nathan Detroit's crap game; and if I do wish to go there I do not wish to go with Rusty Charley, because a guy is sometimes judged by the company he keeps, especially around crap games, and Rusty Charley is apt to be considered bad company. Anyway, I do not have any dough to shoot craps with, and if I do have dough to shoot craps with, I will not shoot craps with it at all, but will bet it on Sun Beau, or maybe take it home and pay off some of the overhead around my joint, such as rent.

Furthermore, I remember what Doc Brennan tells me about avoiding excitement, and I know there is apt to be excitement around Nathan Detroit's crap grame if Rusty Charley goes there, and maybe run my blood pressure up and cause me to pop off very unexpected. In fact, I already feel my blood jumping more than somewhat inside me, but naturally I am not going to give Rusty Charley any argument, so we go to Nathan Detroit's crap game.

This crap game is over a garage in Fifty-second Street this particular night, though sometimes it is over a restaurant in Forty-seventh Street, or in back of a cigar store in Forty-fourth Street. In fact, Nathan Detroit's crap game is apt to be anywhere, because it moves around every night, as there is no sense in a crap game staying in one spot until the coppers find out where it is.

So Nathan Detroit moves his crap game from spot to spot, and citizens wishing to do business with him have to ask where he is every night; and of course almost everybody on Broadway knows this, as Nathan Detroit has guys walking up and down, and around and about, telling the public his address, and giving out the password for the evening.

Well, Jack the Beefer is sitting in an automobile outside the garage in Fifty-second Street when Rusty Charley and I come along, and he says 'Kansas City,' very low, as we pass, this being the password for the evening; but we do not have to use any password whatever when we climb the stairs over the garage, because the minute Solid John, the doorman, peeks out through his peephole when we knock, and sees Rusty Charley with me, he opens up very quick indeed, and gives us a big castor-oil smile, for nobody in this town is keeping doors shut on Rusty Charley very long.

It is a very dirty room over the garage, and full of smoke, and the crap game is on an old pool table; and around the table, and packed in so close you cannot get a knitting-needle between any two guys with a mawl, are all the high shots in town, for there is plenty of money around at this time, and many citizens are very prosperous. Furthermore, I wish to say there are some very tough guys around the table, too, including guys who will shoot you in the head, or maybe the stomach, and think nothing whatever about the matter.

In fact, when I see such guys as Harry the Horse, from Brooklyn, and Sleepout Sam Levinsky, and Lone Louie, from Harlem, I know this is a bad place for my blood pressure, for these are very tough guys indeed, and are known as such to one and all in this town.

But there they are wedged up against the table with Nick the Greek, Big Nig, Grey John, Okay Okum, and many other high shots, and they all have big coarse G notes in their hands which they are tossing around back and forth as if these G notes are nothing but pieces of waste paper.

On the outside of the mob at the table are a lot of small operators who are trying to cram their fists in-between the high shots now and then to get down a bet, and there are also guys present who are called Shylocks, because they will lend you dough when you go broke at the table, on watches or rings, or maybe cuff-links, at very good interest.

Well, as I say, there is no room at the table for as many as one more very thin guy when we walk into the joint, but Rusty Charley lets out a big hello as we enter, and the guys all look around, and the next minute there is space at the table big enough not only for Rusty Charley but for me, too. It really is quite magical the way there is suddenly room for us when there is no room whatever for anybody when we come in.

'Who is the gunner?' Rusty Charley asks, looking all around.

'Why, you are, Charley,' Big Nig, the stick man in the game, says very quick, handing Charley a pair of dice, although afterward I hear that his pal is right in the middle of a roll trying to make nine when we step up to the table. Everybody is very quiet, just looking at Charley. Nobody pays any attention to me, because I am known to one and all as a guy who is just around, and nobody figures me in on any part of Charley, although Harry the Horse looks at me once in a way that I know is no good for my blood pressure, or for anybody else's blood pressure as far as this goes.

Well, Charley takes the dice and turns to a little guy in a derby hat who is standing next to him scrooching back so Charley will not notice him, and Charley lifts the derby hat off the little guy's head, and rattles the dice in his hand and chucks them into the hat and goes 'Hah!' like crap shooters always do when they are rolling the dice. Then Charley peeks into the hat and says 'Ten,' although he does not let anybody else look in the hat, not even me, so nobody knows if Charley throws a ten, or what.

But, of course, nobody around is going to up and doubt that Rusty Charley throws a ten, because Charley may figure it is the same thing as calling him a liar, and Charley is such a guy as is apt to hate being called a liar.

Now Nathan Detroit's crap game is what is called a head-and-head game, although some guys call it a fading game, because the guys bet against each other rather than against the bank, or house. It is just the same kind of game as when two guys get together and start shooting craps against each other, and Nathan Detroit does not have to bother with a regular crap table and a layout such as they have in gambling houses. In fact, about all Nathan Detroit has to do with the game is to find a spot, furnish the dice and take his percentage, which is by no means bad.

In such a game as this there is no real action until a guy is out on a point, and then the guys around commence to bet he makes this point, or that he does not make this point, and the odds in any country in the world that a guy does not make a ten with a pair of dice before he rolls seven, is 2 to 1.

Well, when Charley says he rolls ten in the derby hat nobody opens their trap, and Charley looks all around the table, and all of a sudden he sees Jew Louie at one end, although Jew Louie seems to be trying to shrink himself up when Charley's eyes light on him.

'I will take the odds for five C's,' Charley says, 'and Louie, you get it' – meaning he is letting Louie bet him $1,000 to $500 that he does not make his ten.

Now Jew Louie is a small operator at all times and more of a Shylock than he is a player, and the only reason he is up there against the table at all at this moment is because he moves up to lend Nick the Greek some dough; and ordinarily there is no more chance of Jew Louie betting a thousand to five hundred on any proposition whatever than there is of him giving his dough to the Salvation Army, which is no chance at all. It is a sure thing he will never think of betting a thousand to five hundred a guy will not make ten with the dice, and when Rusty Charley tells Louie he has such a bet, Louie starts trembling all over.

The others around the table do not say a word, and so Charley rattles the dice again in his duke, blows on them, and chucks them into the derby hat and says 'Hah!' But, of course, nobody can see in the derby hat except Charley, and he peeks in at the dice and says 'Five.' He rattles the dice once more and chucks them into the derby and says 'Hah!' and then after peeking into the hat at the dice he says 'Eight.' I am commencing to sweat for fear he may heave a seven in the hat and blow his bet, and I know Charley has no five C's to pay off with, although, of course, I also know Charley has no idea of paying off, no matter what he heaves.

On the next chuck, Charley yells 'Money!' – meaning he finally makes his ten, although nobody sees it but him; and he reaches out his hand to Jew Louie, and Jew Louie hands him a big fat G note, very, very slow. In all my life I never see a sadder-looking guy than Louie when he is parting with his dough. If Louie has any idea of asking Charley to let him see the dice in the hat to make sure about the ten, he does not speak about the matter, and as Charley does not seem to wish to show the ten around, nobody else says anything either, probably figuring Rusty Charley isn't a guy who is apt to let anybody question his word, especially over such a small matter as a ten.

'Well,' Charley says, putting Louie's G note in his pocket, 'I think this is enough for me to-night,' and he hands the derby hat back to the little guy who owns it and motions me to come on, which I am glad to do, as the silence in the joint is making my stomach go up and down inside me, and I know this is bad for my blood pressure. Nobody as much as opens his face from the time we go in until we start out, and you will be surprised how nervous it makes you to be in a big crowd with everybody dead still, especially when you figure it a spot that is liable to get hot any minute. It is only just as we get to the door that anybody speaks, and who is it but Jew Louie, who pipes up and says to Rusty Charley like this:

'Charley,' he says, 'do you make it the hard way?'

Well, everybody laughs, and we go on out, but I never hear myself whether Charley makes his ten with a six and a four, or with two fives – which is the hard way to make a ten with the dice – although I often wonder about the matter afterward.

I am hoping that I can now get away from Rusty Charley and go on home, because I can see he is the last guy in the world to have around a blood pressure, and, furthermore, that people may get the wrong idea of me if I stick around with him, but when I suggest going to Charley, he seems to be hurt.

'Why,' Charley says, 'you are a fine guy to be talking of quitting a pal just as we are starting out. You will certainly stay with me because I like company, and we will go down to Ikey the Pig's and play stuss. Ikey is an old friend of mine, and I owe him a complimentary play.'

Now, of course, I do not wish to go to Ikey the Pig's, because it is a place away downtown, and I do not wish to play stuss, because this is a game which I am never able to figure out myself, and, furthermore, I remember Doc Brennan says I ought to get a little sleep now and then; but I see no use in hurting Charley's feelings, especially as he is apt to do something drastic to me if I do not go.

So he calls a taxi, and we start downtown for Ikey the Pig's, and the jockey who is driving the short goes so fast that it makes my blood pressure go up a foot to a foot and a half from the way I feel inside, although Rusty Charley pays no attention to the speed. Finally I stick my head out of the window and ask the jockey to please take it a little easy, as I wish to get where I am going all in one piece, but the guy only keeps busting along.

We are at the corner of Nineteenth and Broadway when all of a sudden Rusty Charley yells at the jockey to pull up a minute, which the guy does. Then Charley steps out of the cab and says to the jockey like this:

'When a customer asks you to take it easy, why do you not be nice and take it easy? Now see what you get.'

And Rusty Charley hauls off and clips the jockey a punch on the chin that knocks the poor guy right off the seat into the street, and then Charley climbs into the seat himself and away we go with Charley driving, leaving the guy stretched out as stiff as a board. Now Rusty Charley once drives a short for a living himself, until the coppers get an idea that he is not always delivering his customers to the right address, especially such as may happen to be drunk when he gets them, and he is a pretty fair driver, but he only looks one way, which is straight ahead.

Personally, I never wish to ride with Charley in a taxicab under any circumstances, especially if he is driving, because he certainly drives very fast. He pulls up a block from Ikey the Pig's, and says we will leave the short there until somebody finds it and turns it in, but just as we are walking away from the short up steps a copper in uniform and claims we cannot park the short in this spot without a driver.

Well, Rusty Charley just naturally hates to have coppers give him any advice, so what does he do but peek up and down the street to see if anybody is looking, and then haul off and clout the copper on the chin, knocking him bow-legged. I wish to say I never see a more accurate puncher than Rusty Charley, because he always connects with that old button. As the copper tumbles, Rusty Charley grabs me by the arm and starts me running up a side street, and after we go about a block we dodge into Ikey the Pig's.

It is what is called a stuss house, and many prominent citizens of the neighbourhood are present playing stuss. Nobody seems any too glad to see Rusty Charley, although Ikey the Pig lets on he is tickled half to death. This Ikey the Pig is a short fat-necked guy who will look very natural at New Year's, undressed, and with an apple in his mouth, but it seems he and Rusty Charley are really old-time friends, and think fairly well of each other in spots.

But I can see that Ikey the Pig is not so tickled when he finds Charley is there to gamble, although Charley flashes his G note at once, and says he does not mind losing a little dough to Ikey just for old time's sake. But I judge Ikey the Pig knows he is never going to handle Charley's G note, because Charley puts it back in his pocket and it never comes out again even though Charley gets off loser playing stuss right away.

Well, at five o'clock in the morning, Charley is stuck one hundred and thirty G's, which is plenty of money even when a guy is playing on his muscle, and of course Ikey the Pig knows there is no chance of getting one hundred and thirty cents off of Rusty Charley, let alone that many thousands. Everybody else is gone by this time and Ikey wishes to close up. He is willing to take Charley's marker for a million if necessary to get Charley out, but the trouble is in stuss a guy is entitled to get back a percentage of what he loses, and Ikey figures Charley is sure to wish this percentage even if he gives a marker, and the percentage will wreck Ikey's joint.

Furthermore, Rusty Charley says he will not quit loser under such circumstances because Ikey is his friend, so what happens but Ikey finally sends out and hires a cheater by the name of Dopey Goldberg, who takes to dealing the game and in no time he has Rusty Charley even by cheating in Rusty Charley's favour.

Personally, I do not pay much attention to the play, but grab myself a few winks of sleep in a chair in a corner, and the rest seems to help my blood pressure no little. In fact, I am not noticing my blood pressure at all when Rusty Charley and I get out of Ikey the Pig's, because I figure Charley will let me go home and I can go to bed. But although it is six o'clock, and coming on broad daylight when we leave Ikey's, Charley is still full of zing, and nothing will do him but we must go to a joint that is called the Bohemian Club.

Well, this idea starts my blood pressure going again, because the Bohemian Club is nothing but a deadfall where guys and dolls go when there is positively no other place in town open, and it is run by a guy by the name of Knife O'Halloran, who comes from down around Greenwich Village and is considered a very bad character. It is well known to one and all that a guy is apt to lose his life in Knife O'Halloran's any night, even if he does nothing more than drink Knife O'Halloran's liquor.

But Rusty Charley insists on going there, so naturally I go with him; and at first everything is very quiet and peaceful, except that a lot of guys and dolls in evening clothes, who wind up there after being in the night clubs all night, are yelling in one corner of the joint. Rusty Charley and Knife O'Halloran are having a drink together out of a bottle which Knife carries in his pocket, so as not to get it mixed up with the liquor he sells his customers, and are cutting up old touches of the time when they run with the Hudson Dusters together, when all of a sudden in comes four coppers in plain clothes.

Now these coppers are off duty and are meaning no harm to anybody, and are only wishing to have a dram or two before going home, and the chances are they will pay no attention to Rusty Charley if he minds his own business, although of course they know who he is very well indeed and will take great pleasure in putting the old sleeve on him if they only have a few charges against him, which they do not. So they do not give him a tumble. But if there is one thing Rusty Charley hates it is a copper, and he starts eyeing them from the minute they sit down at a table, and by and by I hear him say to Knife O'Halloran like this:

'Knife,' Charley says, 'what is the most beautiful sight in the world?'

'I do not know, Charley,' Knife says. 'What is the most beautiful sight in the world?'

'Four dead coppers in a row,' Charley says.

Well, at this I personally ease myself over toward the door, because I never wish to have any trouble with coppers and especially with four coppers, so I do not see everything that comes off. All I see is Rusty Charley grabbing at the big foot which one of the coppers kicks at him, and then everybody seems to go into a huddle, and the guys and dolls in evening dress start squawking, and my blood pressure goes up to maybe a million.

I get outside the door, but I do not go away at once as anybody with any sense will do, but stand there listening to what is going on inside, which seems to be nothing more than a loud noise like ker-bump, ker-bump, ker-bump. I am not afraid there will be any shooting, because as far as Rusty Charley is concerned he is too smart to shoot any coppers, which is the worst thing a guy can do in this town, and the coppers are not likely to start any blasting because they will not wish it to come out that they are in a joint such as the Bohemian Club off duty. So I figure they will all just take it out in pulling and hauling.

Finally the noise inside dies down, and by and by the door opens and out comes Rusty Charley, dusting himself off here and there with his hands and looking very much pleased indeed, and through the door before it flies shut again I catch a glimpse of a lot of guys stretched out on the floor. Furthermore, I can still hear guys and dolls hollering.

'Well, well,' Rusty Charley says, 'I am commencing to think you take the wind on me, and am just about to get mad at you, but here you are. Let us go away from this joint, because they are making so much noise inside you cannot hear yourself think. Let us go to my joint and make my old woman cook us up some breakfast, and then we can catch some sleep. A little ham and eggs will not be bad to take right now.'

Well, naturally ham and eggs are appealing to me no little at this time, but I do not care to go to Rusty Charley's joint. As far as I am personally concerned, I have enough of Rusty Charley to do me a long, long time, and I do not care to enter into his home life to any extent whatever, although to tell the truth I am somewhat surprised to learn he has any such life. I believe I do once hear that Rusty Charley marries one of the neighbours' children, and that he lives somewhere over on Tenth Avenue in the Forties, but nobody really knows much about this, and everybody figures if it is true his wife must lead a terrible dog's life.

But while I do not wish to go to Charley's joint, I cannot very well refuse a civil invitation to eat ham and eggs, especially as Charley is looking at me in a very much surprised way because I do not seem so glad, and I can see that it is not everyone that he invites to his joint. So I thank him, and say there is nothing I will enjoy more than ham and eggs such as his old woman will cook for us, and by and by we are walking along Tenth Avenue up around Forty-fifth Street.

It is still fairly early in the morning, and business guys are opening up their joints for the day, and little children are skipping along the sidewalks going to school and laughing tee-hee, and old dolls are shaking bedclothes and one thing and another out of the windows of the tenement houses, but when they spot Rusty Charley and me everybody becomes very quiet indeed, and I can see that Charley is greatly respected in his own neighbourhood. The business guys hurry into their joints, and the little children stop skipping and tee-heeing and go tip-toeing along, and the old dolls yank in their noodles, and a great quiet comes to the street. In fact, about all you can hear is the heels of Rusty Charley and me hitting on the sidewalk.

There is an ice wagon with a couple of horses hitched to it standing in front of a store, and when he sees the horses Rusty Charley seems to get a big idea. He stops and looks the horses over very carefully, although as far as I can see they are nothing but horses, and big and fat, and sleepy-looking horses, at that. Finally Rusty Charley says to me like this:

'When I am a young guy,' he says, 'I am a very good puncher with my right hand, and often I hit a horse on the skull with my fist and knock it down. I wonder,' he says, 'if I lose my punch. The last copper I hit back there gets up twice on me.'

Then he steps up to one of the ice-wagon horses and hauls off and biffs it right between the eyes with a right-hand smack that does not travel more than four inches, and down goes old Mister Horse to his knees looking very much surprised indeed. I see many a hard puncher in my day including Dempsey when he really can punch, but I never see a harder punch than Rusty Charley gives this horse.

Well, the ice-wagon driver comes busting out of the store all heated up over what happens to his horse, but he cools out the minute he sees Rusty Charley, and goes on back into the store leaving the horse still taking a count, while Rusty Charley and I keep walking. Finally we come to the entrance of a tenement house that Rusty Charley says is where he lives, and in front of this house is a wop with a push-cart loaded with fruit and vegetables and one thing and another, which Rusty Charley tips over as we go into the house, leaving the wop yelling very loud, and maybe cussing us in wop for all I know. I am very glad, personally, we finally get somewhere, because I can feel that my blood pressure is getting worse every minute I am with Rusty Charley.

We climb two flights of stairs, and then Charley opens a door and we step into a room where there is a pretty little red-headed doll about knee high to a flivver, who looks as if she may just get out of the hay, because her red hair is flying around every which way on her head, and her eyes seem still gummed up with sleep. At first I think she is a very cute sight indeed, and then I see something in her eyes that tells me this doll, whoever she is, is feeling very hostile to one and all.

'Hello, tootsie,' Rusty Charley says. 'How about some ham and eggs for me and my pal here? We are all tired out going around and about.'

Well, the little red-headed doll just looks at him without saying a word. She is standing in the middle of the floor with one hand behind her, and all of a sudden she brings this hand, around, and what does she have in it but a young baseball bat, such as kids play ball with, and which cost maybe two bits; and the next thing I know I hear something go ker-bap, and I can see she smacks Rusty Charley on the side of the noggin with the bat.

Naturally I am greatly horrified at this business, and figure Rusty Charley will kill her at once, and then I will be in a jam for witnessing the murder and will be held in jail several years like all witnesses to anything in this man's town; but Rusty Charley only falls into a big rocking-chair in a corner of the room and sits there with one hand to his head, saying, 'Now hold on, tootsie,' and 'Wait a minute there, honey.' I recollect hearing him say, 'We have company for breakfast', and then the little red-headed doll turns on me and gives me a look such as I will always remember, although I smile at her very pleasant and mention it is a nice morning.

Finally she says to me like this:

'So you are the trambo who keeps my husband out all night, are you, you trambo?' she says, and with this she starts for me, and I start for the door; and by this time my blood pressure is all out of whack, because I can see Mrs Rusty Charley is excited more than somewhat. I get my hand on the knob and just then something hits me alongside the noggin, which I afterward figure must be the baseball bat, although I remember having a sneaking idea the roof caves in on me.

How I get the door open I do not know, because I am very dizzy in the head and my legs are wobbling, but when I think back over the situation I remember going down a lot of steps very fast, and by and by the fresh air strikes me, and I figure I am in the clear. But all of a sudden I feel another strange sensation back of my head and something goes plop against my noggin, and I figure at first that maybe my blood pressure runs up so high that it squirts out the top of my bean. Then I peek around over my shoulder just once to see that Mrs Rusty Charley is standing beside the wop peddler's cart snatching fruit and vegetables of one kind and another off the cart and chucking them at me.

But what she hits me with back of the head is not an apple, or a peach, or a rutabaga, or a cabbage, or even a casaba melon, but a brickbat that the wop has on his cart to weight down the paper sacks in which he sells his goods. It is this brickbat which makes a lump on the back of my head so big that Doc Brennan thinks it is a tumour when I go to him the next day about my stomach, and I never tell him any different.

'But,' Doc Brennan says, when he takes my blood pressure again, 'your pressure is down below normal now, and as far as it is concerned you are in no danger whatever. It only goes to show what just a little bit of quiet living will do for a guy,' Doc Brennan says. 'Ten bucks, please,' he says.

3   LONELY HEART

IT seems that one spring day, a character by the name of Nicely-Nicely Jones arrives in a ward in a hospital in the City of Newark, N.J., with such a severe case of pneumonia that the attending physician, who is a horse player at heart, and very absent-minded, writes 100, 40 and 10 on the chart over Nicely-Nicely's bed.

It comes out afterward that what the physician means is that it is 100 to 1 in his line that Nicely-Nicely does not recover at all, 40 to 1 that he will not last a week, and 10 to 1 that if he does get well he will never be the same again.

Well, Nicely-Nicely is greatly discouraged when he sees this price against him, because he is personally a chalk eater when it comes to price, a chalk eater being a character who always plays the short-priced favourites, and he can see that such a long shot as he is has very little chance to win. In fact, he is so discouraged that he does not even feel like taking a little of the price against him to show.

Afterward there is some criticism of Nicely-Nicely among the citizens around Mindy's restaurant on Broadway, because he does not advise them of this market, as these citizens are always willing to bet that what Nicely-Nicely dies of will be over-feeding and never anything small like pneumonia, for Nicely-Nicely is known far and wide as a character who dearly loves to commit eating.

But Nicely-Nicely is so discouraged that he does not as much as send them word that he is sick, let alone anything about the price. He just pulls the covers up over his head and lies there waiting for the finish and thinking to himself what a tough thing it is to pass away of pneumonia, and especially in Newark,

N.J., and nobody along Broadway knows of his predicament until Nicely-Nicely appears in person some months later and relates this story to me.

So now I will tell you about Nicely-Nicely Jones, who is called Nicely-Nicely because any time anybody asks him how he is feeling, or how things are going with him, he always says nicely, nicely, in a very pleasant tone of voice, although generally this is by no means the gospel truth, especially about how he is going.

He is a character of maybe forty-odd, and he is short, and fat, and very good-natured, and what he does for a livelihood is the best he can, which is an occupation that is greatly overcrowded at all times along Broadway.

Mostly, Nicely-Nicely follows the races, playing them whenever he has anything to play them with, but anyway following them, and the reason he finds himself in Newark, N.J., in the first place is because of a business proposition in connexion with the races. He hears of a barber in Newark, N.J., who likes to make a wager on a sure thing now and then, and Nicely-Nicely goes over there to tell him about a sure thing that is coming up at Pimlico the very next Tuesday.

Nicely-Nicely figures that the barber will make a wager on this sure thing and cut him in on the profits, but it seems that somebody else gets to the barber the week before with a sure thing that is coming up a Monday, and the barber bets on this sure thing, and the sure thing blows, and now the barber will have to shave half of Newark, N.J., to catch even.

Nicely-Nicely always claims that the frost he meets when he approaches the barber with his sure thing gives him a cold that results in the pneumonia I am speaking of, and furthermore that his nervous system is so disorganized by the barber chasing him nine blocks with a razor in his hand that he has no vitality left to resist the germs.

But at that it seems that he has enough vitality left to beat the pneumonia by so far the attending physician is somewhat embarrassed, although afterward he claims that he makes a mistake in chalking up the 100, 40 and 10 on Nicely-Nicely's chart. The attending physician claims he really means the character in the bed next to Nicely-Nicely, who passes away of lockjaw the second day after Nicely-Nicely arrives.

Well, while he is convalescing in the hospital of this pneumonia, Nicely-Nicely has a chance to do plenty of thinking, and what he thinks about most is the uselessness of the life he leads all these years, and how he has nothing to show for same except some high-class knowledge of race horses, which at this time is practically a drug on the market.

There are many other patients in the same ward with Nicely-Nicely, and he sees their ever-loving wives, and daughters, and maybe their sweet-peas visiting them, and hears their cheerful chatter, and he gets to thinking that here he is without chick or child, and no home to go to, and it just about breaks his heart.

He gets to thinking of how he will relish a soft, gentle, loving hand on his brow at this time, and finally he makes a pass at one of the nurses, figuring she may comfort his lonely hours, but what she lays on his brow is a beautiful straight right cross, and furthermore she hollers watch, murder, police, and Nicely-Nicely has to pretend he has a relapse and is in a delirium to avoid being mistreated by the internees.

As Nicely-Nicely begins getting some of his strength back, he takes to thinking, too, of such matters as food, and when Nicely-Nicely thinks of food it is generally very nourishing food, such as a nice double sirloin, smothered with chops, and thinking of these matters, and of hamburgers, and wiener schnitzel and goulash with noodles, and lamb stew, adds to his depression, especially when they bring him the light diet provided for invalids by the hospital.

He takes to reading to keep himself from thinking of his favourite dishes, and of his solitary life, and one day in a bundle of old magazines and newspapers that they give him to read, he comes upon a bladder that is called the *Matrimonial Tribune,* which seems to be all about marriage, and in this *Matrimonial Tribune* Nicely-Nicely observes an advertisement that reads as follows:

LONELY HEART

Widow of middle age, no children, cheerful companion, neat, excellent cook, owner of nice farm in Central New Jersey, wishes to meet home-loving gentleman of not more than fifty who need not necessarily be possessed of means but who will appreciate warm, tender companionship and pleasant home. Object, matrimony. Address Lonely Heart, this paper.

Well, Nicely-Nicely feels romance stirring in his bosom as he reads these lines, because he is never married, and has no idea that marriage is as described in this advertisement. So what does he do but write a letter to Lonely Heart in care of the *Matrimonial Tribune* stating that he is looking for a warm, tender companionship, and a pleasant home, and an excellent cook, especially an excellent cook, all his life, and the next thing he knows he is gazing into what at first seems to be an old-fashioned round cheese, but which he finally makes out as the face of a large Judy seated at his bedside.

She is anywhere between forty and fifty-five years of age, and she is as big and rawboned as a first baseman, but she is by no means a crow. In fact, she is rather nice-looking, except that she has a pair of eyes as pale as hens' eggs, and these eyes never change expression.

She asks Nicely-Nicely as many questions as an assistant district attorney, and especially if he has any money, and does he have any relatives, and Nicely-Nicely is able to state truthfully that he is all out of both, although she does not seem to mind. She wishes to know about his personal habits, and Nicely-Nicely says they are all good, but of course he does not mention his habit of tapping out any time a 4-to-5 shot comes along, which is as bad a habit as anybody can have, and finally she says she is well satisfied with him and will be pleased to marry him when he is able to walk.

She has a short, sharp voice that reminds Nicely-Nicely of a tough starter talking to the jockeys at the post, and she never seems to smile, and, take her all round, the chances are she is not such a character as Nicely-Nicely will choose as his ever-loving wife if he has the pick of a herd, but he figures that she is not bad for an off-hand draw.

So Nicely-Nicely and the Widow Crumb are married, and they go to live on her farm in Central New Jersey, and it is a very nice little farm, to be sure, if you care for farms, but it is ten miles from the nearest town, and in a very lonesome country, and furthermore there are no neighbours handy, and the Widow Crumb does not have a telephone or even a radio in her house.

In fact, about all she has on this farm are a couple of cows, and a horse, and a very old joskin with a chin whisker and rheumatism and a mean look, whose name seems to be Harley something, and who also seems to be the Widow Crumb's hired hand. Nicely-Nicely can see at once that Harley has no use for him, but afterward he learns that Harley has no use for anybody much, not even himself.

Well, it comes on supper-time the first night. Nicely-Nicely is there and he is delighted to observe that the Widow Crumb is making quite an uproar in the kitchen with the pots and pans, and this uproar is music to Nicely-Nicely's ears as by now he is in the mood to put on the hot meat very good, and he is wondering if the Widow Crumb is as excellent a cook as she lets on in her advertisement.

It turns out that she is even better. It turns out that she is as fine a cook as ever straddles a skillet, and the supper she spreads for Nicely-Nicely is too good for a king. There is round steak hammered flat and fried in a pan, with thick cream gravy, and hot biscuits, and corn on the cob, and turnip greens, and cottage-fried potatoes, and lettuce with hot bacon grease poured over it, and apple-pie, and coffee, and I do not know what all else, and Nicely-Nicely almost founders himself, because it is the first time since he leaves the hospital that he gets a chance to move into real food.

Harley, the old joskin, eats with them, and Nicely-Nicely notices that there is a fourth place set at the table, and he figures that maybe another hired hand is going to show up, but nobody appears to fill the vacant chair, and at first Nicely-Nicely is glad of it, as it gives him more room in which to eat.

But then Nicely-Nicely notices that the Widow Crumb loads the plate at the vacant place with even more food than she does any of the others, and all through the meal Nicely-Nicely keeps expecting someone to come in and knock off these victuals. Nobody ever appears, however, and when they are through eating, the Widow Crumb clears up the extra place the same as the others, and scrapes the food off the plate into a garbage pail.

Well, of course, Nicely-Nicely is somewhat perplexed by this proceeding, but he does not ask any questions, because where he comes from only suckers go around asking questions. The next morning at breakfast, and again at dinner, and in fact at every meal put on the table the extra place is fixed, and the Widow Crumb goes through the same performance of serving the food to this place, and afterward throwing it away, and while Nicely-Nicely commences thinking it is a great waste of excellent food, he keeps his trap closed.

Now being the Widow Crumb's husband is by no means a bad dodge, as she is anything but a gabby Judy, and will go all day long without saying more than a few words, and as Nicely-Nicely is a character who likes to chat this gives him a chance to do all the talking, although she never seems to be listening to him much. She seldom asks him to do any work, except now and then to help the old joskin around the barn, so Nicely-Nicely commences to figure this is about as soft a drop-in as anybody can wish.

The only drawback is that sometimes the Widow Crumb likes to sit on Nicely-Nicely's lap of an evening, and as he does not have much lap to begin with, and it is getting less every day under her feeding, this is quite a handicap, but he can see that it comes of her affectionate nature, and he bears up the best he can.

One evening after they are married several months, the Widow Crumb is sitting on what is left of Nicely-Nicely's lap, and she puts her arms around his neck, and speaks to him as follows:

'Nicely,' she says, 'do you love me?'

'Love you?' Nicely-Nicely says. 'Why, I love you like anything. Maybe more. You are a wonderful cook. How can I help loving you?' he says.

'Well,' the Widow Crumb says, 'do you ever stop to consider that if anything happens to you, I will be left here lone and lorn, because you do not have any means with which to provide for me after you are gone?'

'What do you mean after I am gone?' Nicely-Nicely says. 'I am not going anywhere.'

'Life is always a very uncertain proposition,' the Widow Crumb says. 'Who can say when something is apt to happen to you and take you away from me leaving me without a cent of life insurance?'

Naturally, Nicely-Nicely has to admit to himself that what she says is very true, and of course he never gives the matter a thought before, because he figures from the way the Widow Crumb feeds him that she must have some scratch of her own stashed away somewhere, although this is the first time the sub-ject of money is ever mentioned between them since they are married.

'Why,' Nicely-Nicely says, 'you are quite right, and I will get my life insured as soon as I get enough strength to go out and raise a few dibs. Yes, indeed,' Nicely-Nicely says, 'I will take care of this situation promptly.'

Well, the Widow Crumb says there is no sense in waiting on a matter as important as this, and that she will provide the money for the payment of the premiums herself, and for Nicely-Nicely to forget about going out to raise anything, as she cannot bear to have him out of her sight for any length of time, and then she gets to telling Nicely-Nicely what she is going to give him for breakfast, and he forgets about the insurance business.

But the next thing Nicely-Nicely knows, a thin character with a nose like a herring comes out from town, and there is another character with him who has whiskers that smell of corn whisky, but who seems to be a doctor, and in practically no time at all Nicely-Nicely's life is insured for five thousand dollars, with double indemnity if he gets used up by accident, and Nicely-Nicely is greatly pleased by this arrangement because he sees that he is now worth something for the first time in his career, although everybody on Broadway claims it is a terrible overlay by the insurance company when they hear the story.

Well, several months more go by, and Nicely-Nicely finds life on the farm very pleasant and peaceful as there is nothing much for him to do but eat and sleep, and he often finds himself wondering how he ever endures his old life, following the races and associating with the low characters of the turf.

He gets along first class with the Widow Crumb and never has a cross word with her, and he even makes friends with the old joskin, Harley, by helping him with his work, although Nicely-Nicely is really not fitted by nature for much work, and what he likes best at the farm is the eating and sleeping, especially the eating.

For a while he finds it difficult to get as much sleep as he requires, because the Widow Crumb is a great hand for staying up late reading books in their bedroom by kerosene lamp, and at the same time eating molasses candy which she personally manufactures, and sometimes she does both in bed, and the molasses candy bothers Nicely-Nicely no little until he becomes accustomed to it.

Once he tries reading one of her books to put himself to sleep after she dozes off ahead of him, but he discovers that it is all about nothing but spiritualism, and about parties in this life getting in touch with characters in the next world, and Nicely-Nicely has no interest whatever in matters of this nature, although he personally knows a character by the name of Spooks McGurk who claims to be a spiritualist, and who makes a nice thing of it in connexion with tips on the races, until a race-track fuzz catches up with him.

Nicely-Nicely never discusses the books with the Widow Crumb because in the first place he figures it is none of his business, and in the second place, the more she reads the better chance he has of getting to sleep before she starts snoring, because it seems that as a snorer the Widow Crumb is really all-America material, although of course Nicely-Nicely is too much of a gentleman to make an issue of this.

She gives him three meals every day, and every meal is better than the last, and finally Nicely-Nicely is as fat as a goose, and can scarcely wobble. But he notices that the Widow Crumb never once fails to set the fourth place that nobody ever fills, and furthermore he suddenly commences to notice that she always puts the best cuts of meat, and the best of everything else on the plate at this place, even though she throws it all away afterward.

Well, this situation preys on Nicely-Nicely's mind, as he cannot bear to see all this good fodder going to waste, so one morning he gets hold of old Harley and puts the siphon on him, because by this time Harley talks freely with Nicely-Nicely, although Nicely-Nicely can see that Harley is somewhat simple in spots and his conversation seldom makes much sense.

Anyway, he asks Harley what the Widow Crumb's idea is about the extra place at the table, and Harley says like this:

'Why,' he says, 'the place is for Jake.'

'Jake who?' Nicely-Nicely says.

'I do not recall his other name,' Harley says. 'He is her third or fourth husband, I do not remember which. Jake is the only one the Widow Crumb ever loves, although she does not discover this until after Jake departs. So,' Harley says, 'in memory of Jake she always sets his place at the table, and gives him the best she has. She misses Jake and wishes to feel that he is still with her.'

'What happens to Jake?' Nicely-Nicely says.

'Arsenic,' Harley says. 'Jake departs ten years ago.'

Well, of course, all this is news to Nicely-Nicely, and he becomes very thoughtful to be sure, because in all the time he is married to her the Widow Crumb does not crack to him about her other husbands, and in fact Nicely-Nicely has no idea there is ever more than one.

'What happens to the others?' he says. 'Do they depart the same as Jake?'

'Yes,' Harley says, 'they all depart. One by one. I remember Number Two well. In fact, you remind me of him. Carbon monoxide,' Harley says. 'A charcoal stove in his room. It is most ingenious. The coroner says Number Three commits suicide by hanging himself with a rope in the barn loft. Number Three is small and weak, and it is no trouble whatever to handle him.

'Then comes Jake,' Harley says, 'unless Jake is Number Three and the hanging item is Number Four. I do not remember exactly. But the Widow Crumb never employs arsenic or other matters of this nature again. It is too slow. Jake lingers for hours. Besides,' Harley says, 'she realizes it may leave traces if anybody happens to get nosy.

'Jake is a fine-looking character,' Harley says. 'But a ne'er-do-well. He is a plumber from Salt Lake City, Utah, and has a hearty laugh. He is always telling funny stories. He is a great eater, even better than you, and he loves beans the way the Widow Crumb cooks them, with bacon and tomatoes. He suffers no little from the arsenic. He gets it in his beans. Number Five comes upon a black widow spider in his bed. He is no good. I mean Number Five.'

Well, by this time, Nicely-Nicely is very thoughtful to be sure, because what Harley says is commencing to sound somewhat disquieting.

'Number Six steps on a plank in the doorway of the house that drops a two-hundred-pound keystone on his head,' Harley says. 'The Widow Crumb personally figures this out herself. She is very bright. It is like a figure-4 trap, and has to be very accurate. An inch one way or the other, and the stone misses Number Six. I remember he has a big wen on the back of his neck. He is a carpenter from Keokuk, Iowa,' Harley says.

'Why,' Nicely-Nicely says, 'do you mean to say that the Widow Crumb purposely arranges to use up husbands in the manner you describe?'

'Oh, sure,' Harley says. 'Why do you suppose she marries them? It is a good living to her because of the insurance,' he says, 'although,' he says, 'to show you how bright she is, she does not insure Number Five for a dime, so people can never say she is making a business of the matter. He is a total loss to her, but it quiets talk. I am wondering,' Harley says, 'what she will think up for you.'

Well, Nicely-Nicely now commences to wonder about this, too, and he hopes and trusts that whatever she thinks up it will not be a black widow spider, because if there is one thing Nicely-Nicely despises, it is insects. Furthermore, he does not approve of hanging, or of dropping weights on people.

After giving the matter much thought, he steps into the house and mentions to the Widow Crumb that he will like to pay a little visit to town, figuring that if he can get to town, she will never see him again for heel dust.

But he finds that the Widow Crumb is by no means in favour

of the idea of him visiting the town. In fact, she says it will bring great sorrow to her if he absents himself from her side more than two minutes, and moreover, she points out that it is coming on winter, and that the roads are bad, and she cannot spare the horse for such a trip just now.

Well, Nicely-Nicely says he is a fair sort of walker and, in fact, he mentions that he once walks from Saratoga Springs to Albany to avoid a bookmaker who claims there is a slight difference between them, but the Widow Crumb says she will not hear of him trying to walk to town because it may develop varicose veins in his legs.

In fact, Nicely-Nicely can see that the subject of his leaving the farm is very distasteful to her in every respect, and the chances are he will feel quite flattered by her concern for him if he does not happen to go into the house again a little later this same afternoon, and find her cleaning a double-barrelled shotgun.

She says she is thinking of going rabbit hunting, and wishes him to keep her company, saying it may take his mind off the idea of a visit to town; but she goes out of the room for a minute, and Nicely-Nicely picks up one of the shotgun shells she lays out on a table, and notices that it is loaded with buckshot.

So he tells her he guesses he will not go, as he is not feeling so good, and in fact he is not feeling so good, at that, because it seems that Nicely-Nicely is a rabbit hunter from infancy, and he never before hears of anyone hunting these creatures with buckshot. Then the Widow Crumb says all right, she will postpone her hunting until he feels better, but Nicely-Nicely cannot help noticing that she loads the shotgun and stands it in a corner where it is good and handy.

Well, Nicely-Nicely now sits down and gives this general situation some serious consideration, because he is now convinced that the Widow Crumb is unworthy of his companionship as a husband. In fact, Nicely-Nicely makes up his mind to take steps at his earliest convenience to sue her for divorce on the grounds of incompatibility, but in the meantime he has to think up a means of getting away from her, and while he is thinking of this phase of the problem, she calls him to supper.

It is now coming on dark, and she has the lamps lit and the table set when Nicely-Nicely goes into the dining-room, and a fire is going in the base burner, and usually this is a pleasant and comforting scene to Nicely-Nicely, but to-night he does not seem to find it as attractive as usual.

As he sits down at the table he notices that Harley is not present at the moment, though his place at the table is laid, and as a rule Harley is Johnny-at-the-rat-hole when it comes time to scoff, and moreover he is a pretty good doer, at that. The fourth place that nobody ever occupies is also laid as usual, and now that he knows who this place is for, Nicely-Nicely notes that it is more neatly laid than his own, and that none of the china at this place is chipped, and that the bread and butter, and the salt and pepper, and the vinegar cruet and the bottle of Worcestershire sauce are handier to it than to any other place, and naturally his feelings are deeply wounded.

Then the Widow Crumb comes out of the kitchen with two plates loaded with spare ribs and sauerkraut, and she puts one plate in front of Nicely-Nicely, and the other at Jake's place, and she says to Nicely-Nicely like this:

'Nicely,' she says, 'Harley is working late down at the barn, and when you get through with your supper, you go down and call him. But,' she says, 'go ahead and eat first.'

Then she returns to the kitchen, which is right next to the dining-room with a swinging door in between, and Nicely-Nicely now observes that the very choicest spare-ribs are on Jake's plate, and also the most kraut, and this is really more than Nicely-Nicely can bear, for if there is one thing he adores it is spare-ribs, so he gets to feeling very moody to be sure about this discrimination, and he turns to Jake's place, and in a very sarcastic tone of voice he speaks out loud as follows:

'Well,' he says, 'it is pretty soft for you, you big lob, living on the fat of the land around here.'

Now of course what Nicely-Nicely is speaking is what he is thinking, and he does not realize that he is speaking out loud until the Widow Crumb pops into the dining-room carrying a bowl of salad, and looking all around and about.

'Nicely,' she says, 'do I hear you talking to someone?'

Well, at first Nicely-Nicely is about to deny it, but then he takes another look at the choice spare-ribs on Jake's plate, and he figures that he may as well let her know that he is on to her playing Jake for a favourite over him, and maybe cure her of it, for by this time Nicely-Nicely is so vexed about the spare-ribs that he almost forgets about leaving the farm, and is thinking of his future meals, so he says to the Widow Crumb like this:

'Why, sure,' he says. 'I am talking to Jake.'

'Jake?' she says. 'What Jake?'

And with this she starts looking all around and about again, and Nicely-Nicely can see that she is very pale, and that her hands are shaking so that she can scarcely hold the bowl of salad, and there is no doubt but what she is agitated no little, and quite some.

'What Jake?' the Widow Crumb says again.

Nicely-Nicely points to the empty chair, and says:

'Why, Jake here,' he says. 'You know Jake. Nice fellow, Jake.'

Then Nicely-Nicely goes on talking to the empty chair as follows:

'I notice you are not eating much to-night, Jake,' Nicely-Nicely says. 'What is the matter, Jake? The food cannot disagree with you, because it is all picked out and cooked to suit you, Jake. The best is none too good for you around here, Jake,' he says.

Then he lets on that he is listening to something Jake is saying in reply, and Nicely-Nicely says is that so, and I am surprised, and what do you think of that, and tut-tut, and my-my, just as if Jake is talking a blue streak to him, although, of course, Jake is by no means present.

Now Nicely-Nicely is really only being sarcastic in this conversation for the Widow Crumb's benefit, and naturally he does not figure that she will take it seriously, because he knows she can see Jake is not there, but Nicely-Nicely happens to look at her while he is talking, and he observes that she is still standing with the bowl of salad in her hands, and looking at the empty chair with a most unusual expression on her face, and in fact, it is such an unusual expression that it makes Nicely-Nicely feel somewhat uneasy, and he readies himself up to dodge the salad bowl at any minute.

He commences to remember the loaded shotgun in the corner, and what Harley gives him to understand about the Widow Crumb's attitude towards Jake, and Nicely-Nicely is sorry he ever brings Jake's name up, but it seems that Nicely-Nicely now finds that he cannot stop talking to save his life with the Widow Crumb standing there with the unusual expression on her face, and then he remembers the books she reads in her bed at night, and he goes on as follows:

'Maybe the pains in your stomach are just indigestion, Jake,' he says. 'I have stomach trouble in my youth myself. You are suffering terribly, eh, Jake? Well, maybe a little of the old bicarb will help you, Jake. Oh,' Nicely-Nicely says, 'there he goes.'

And with this he jumps up and runs to Jake's chair and lets on that he is helping a character up from the floor, and as he stoops over and pretends to be lifting this character, Nicely-Nicely grunts no little, as if the character is very heavy, and the grunts are really on the level with Nicely-Nicely as he is now full of spare-ribs, because he never really stops eating while he is talking, and stooping is not easy for him.

At these actions the Widow Crumb lets out a scream and drops the bowl of salad on the floor.

'I will help you to bed, Jake,' he says. 'Poor Jake. I know your stomach hurts, Jake. There now, Jake,' he says, 'take it easy. I know you are suffering horribly, but I will get something for you to ease the pain. Maybe it is the sauerkraut,' Nicely-Nicely says.

Then when he seems to get Jake up on his legs, Nicely-Nicely pretends to be assisting him across the floor towards the bedroom and all the time he is talking in a comforting tone to Jake, although you must always remember that there really is no Jake.

Now, all of a sudden, Nicely-Nicely hears the Widow Crumb's voice, and it is nothing but a hoarse whisper that sounds very strange in the room, as she says like this:

'Yes,' she says, 'it is Jake. I see him. I see him as plain as day.'

Well, at this Nicely-Nicely is personally somewhat startled, and he starts looking around and about himself, and it is a good thing for Jake that Nicely-Nicely is not really assisting Jake or Jake will find himself dropped on the floor, as the Widow Crumb says:

'Oh, Jake,' she says, 'I am so sorry. I am sorry for you in your suffering. I am sorry you ever leave me. I am sorry for everything. Please forgive me, Jake,' she says. 'I love you.'

Then the Widow Crumb screams again and runs through the swinging door into the kitchen and out the kitchen door and down the path that leads to the barn about two hundred yards away, and it is plain to be seen that she is very nervous. In fact, the last Nicely-Nicely sees of her before she disappears in the darkness down the path, she is throwing her hands up in the air, and letting out little screams, as follows: eee-eee-eee, and calling out old Harley's name.

Then Nicely-Nicely hears one extra loud scream, and after this there is much silence, and he figures that now is the time for him to take his departure, and he starts down the same path towards the barn, but figuring to cut off across the fields to the road that leads to the town when he observes a spark of light bobbing up and down on the path ahead of him, and presently he comes upon old Harley with a lantern in his hand.

Harley is down on his knees at what seems to be a big, round hole in the ground, and this hole is so wide it extends clear across the path, and Harley is poking his lantern down the hole, and when he sees Nicely-Nicely, he says:

'Oh,' he says, 'there you are. I guess there is some mistake here,' he says. 'The Widow Crumb tells me to wait in the barn until after supper and she will send you out after me, and,' Harley says, 'she also tells me to be sure and remove the cover of this old well as soon as it comes on dark. And,' Harley says, 'of course, I am expecting to find you in the well at this time, but who is in there but the Widow Crumb. I hear her screech as she drops in. I judge she must be hastening along the path and forgets about telling me to remove the cover of the well,' Harley says. 'It is most confusing,' he says.

Then he pokes his lantern down the well again, and leans over and shouts as follows:

'Hello, down there,' Harley shouts. 'Hello, hello, hello.'

But all that happens is an echo comes out of the well like this: Hello. And Nicely-Nicely observes that there is nothing to be seen down the well but a great blackness.

'It is very deep, and dark, and cold down there,' Harley says. 'Deep, and dark, and cold, and half full of water. Oh, my poor baby,' he says.

Then Harley busts out crying as if his heart will break, and in fact he is so shaken by his sobs that he almost drops the lantern down the well.

Naturally Nicely-Nicely is somewhat surprised to observe these tears because personally he is by no means greatly distressed by the Widow Crumb being down the well, especially when he thinks of how she tries to put him down the well first, and finally he asks Harley why he is so downcast, and Harley speaks as follows:

'I love her,' Harley says. 'I love her very, very, very much. I am her Number One husband, and while she divorces me thirty years ago when it comes out that I have a weak heart, and the insurance companies refuse to give me a policy, I love her just the same. And now,' Harley says, 'here she is down a well.'

And with this he begins hollering into the hole some more, but the Widow Crumb never personally answers a human voice in this life again and when the story comes out, many citizens claim this is a right good thing, to be sure.

So Nicely-Nicely returns to Broadway, and he brings with him the sum of eleven hundred dollars, which is what he has left of the estate of his late ever-loving wife from the sale of the farm, and one thing and another, after generously declaring old Harley in for fifty per cent of his bit when Harley states that the only ambition he has left in life is to rear a tombstone to the memory of the Widow Crumb, and Nicely-Nicely announces that he is through with betting on horses, and other frivolity, and will devote his money to providing himself with food and shelter, and maybe a few clothes.

Well, the chances are Nicely-Nicely will keep his vow, too, but what happens the second day of his return, but he observes in the entries for the third race at Jamaica a horse by the name of Apparition, at 10 to 1 in the morning line, and Nicely-Nicely considers this entry practically a message to him, so he goes for his entire bundle on Apparition.

And it is agreed by one and all along Broadway who knows Nicely-Nicely's story that nobody in his right mind can possibly ignore such a powerful hunch as this, even though it loses, and Nicely-Nicely is again around doing the best he can.

4 A PIECE OF PIE

On Boylston Street, in the City of Boston, Mass., there is a joint where you can get as nice a broiled lobster as anybody ever slaps a lip over, and who is in there one evening partaking of this tidbit but a character by the name of Horse Thief and me.

This Horse Thief is called Horsey for short, and he is not called by this name because he ever steals a horse but because it is the consensus of public opinion from coast to coast that he may steal one if the opportunity presents.

Personally, I consider Horsey a very fine character, because any time he is holding anything he is willing to share his good fortune with one and all, and at this time in Boston he is holding plenty. It is the time we make the race meeting at Suffolk Down, and Horsey gets to going very good, indeed, and in fact he is now a character of means, and is my host against the broiled lobster.

Well, at a table next to us are four or five characters who all seem to be well-dressed, and stout-set, and red-faced, and prosperous-looking, and who all speak with the true Boston accent, which consists of many ah's and very few r's. Characters such as these are familiar to anybody who is ever in Boston very much, and they are bound to be politicians, retired cops, or contractors, because Boston is really quite infested with characters of this nature.

I am paying no attention to them, because they are drinking local ale, and talking loud, and long ago I learn that when a Boston character is engaged in aleing himself up, it is a good idea to let him alone, because the best you can get out of him is maybe a boff on the beezer. But Horsey is in there on the old Ear-ie, and very much interested in their conversation, and finally I listen myself just to hear what is attracting his attention, when one of the characters speaks as follows:

'Well,' he says, 'I am willing to bet ten thousand dollars that he can outeat anybody in the United States any time.'

Now at this, Horsey gets right up and steps over to the table and bows and smiles in a friendly way on one and all, and says:

'Gentlemen,' he says, 'pardon the intrusion, and excuse me for billing in, but,' he says, 'do I understand you are speaking of a great eater who resides in your fair city?'

Well, these Boston characters all gaze at Horsey in such a hostile manner that I am expecting any one of them to get up and request him to let them miss him, but he keeps on bowing and smiling, and they can see that he is a gentleman, and finally one of them says:

'Yes,' he says, 'we are speaking of a character by the name of Joel Duffle. He is without doubt the greatest eater alive. He just wins a unique wager. He bets a character from Bangor, Me., that he can eat a whole window display of oysters in this very restaurant, and he not only eats all the oysters but he then wishes to wager that he can also eat the shells, but,' he says, 'it seems that the character from Bangor, Me., unfortunately taps out on the first proposition and has nothing with which to bet on the second.'

'Very interesting,' Horsey says. 'Very interesting, if true, but,' he says, 'unless my ears deceive me, I hear one of you state that he is willing to wager ten thousand dollars on this eater of yours against anybody in the United States.'

'Your ears are perfect,' another of the Boston characters says. 'I state it, although,' he says, 'I admit it is a sort of figure of speech. But I state it all right,' he says, 'and never let it be said that a Conway ever pigs it on a betting proposition.'

'Well,' Horsey says, 'I do not have a tenner on me at the moment, but,' he says, 'I have here a thousand dollars to put up as a forfeit that I can produce a character who will outeat your party for ten thousand, and as much more as you care to put up.'

And with this, Horsey outs with a bundle of coarse notes and tosses it on the table, and right away one of the Boston characters, whose name turns out to be Carroll, slaps his hand on the money and says:

'Bet.'

Well, now this is prompt action to be sure, and if there is one thing I admire more than anything else, it is action, and I can see that these are characters of true sporting instincts and I commence wondering where I can raise a few dibs to take a piece of Horsey's proposition, because of course I know that he has nobody in mind to do the eating for his side but Nicely-Nicely Jones.

And knowing Nicely-Nicely Jones, I am prepared to wager all the money I can possibly raise that he can outeat anything that walks on two legs. In fact, I will take a chance on Nicely-Nicely against anything on four legs, except maybe an elephant, and at that he may give the elephant a photo finish.

I do not say that Nicely-Nicely is the greatest eater in all history, but what I do say is he belongs up there as a contender. In fact, Professor D, who is a professor in a college out West before he turns to playing the horses for a livelihood, and who makes a study of history in his time, says he will not be surprised but what Nicely-Nicely figures one-two.

Professor D says we must always remember that Nicely-Nicely eats under the handicaps of modern civilization, which require that an eater use a knife and fork, or anyway a knife, while in the old days eating with the hands was a popular custom and much faster. Professor D says he has no doubt that under the old rules Nicely-Nicely will hang up a record that will endure through the ages, but of course maybe Professor D overlays Nicely-Nicely somewhat.

Well, now that the match is agreed upon, naturally Horsey and the Boston characters begin discussing where it is to take place, and one of the Boston characters suggests a neutral ground, such as New London, Conn., or Providence, R.I., but Horsey holds out for New York, and it seems that Boston characters are always ready to visit New York, so he does not meet with any great opposition on this point.

They all agree on a date four weeks later so as to give the principals plenty of time to get ready, although Horsey and I know that this is really unnecessary as far as Nicely-Nicely is concerned, because one thing about him is he is always in condition to eat.

This Nicely-Nicely Jones is a character who is maybe five feet eight inches tall, and about five feet nine inches wide, and when he is in good shape he will weigh upward of two hundred and eighty-three pounds. He is a horse player by trade, and eating is really just a hobby, but he is undoubtedly a wonderful eater even when he is not hungry.

Well, as soon as Horsey and I return to New York, we hasten to Mindy's restaurant on Broadway and relate the bet Horsey makes in Boston, and right away so many citizens, including Mindy himself, wish to take a piece of the proposition that it is oversubscribed by a large sum in no time.

Then Mindy remarks that he does not see Nicely-Nicely Jones for a month of Sundays, and then everybody present remembers that they do not see Nicely-Nicely around lately, either, and this leads to a discussion of where Nicely-Nicely can be, although up to this moment if nobody sees Nicely-Nicely but once in the next ten years it will be considered sufficient.

Well, Willie the Worrier, who is a bookmaker by trade, is among those present, and he remembers that the last time he looks for Nicely-Nicely hoping to collect a marker of some years' standing, Nicely-Nicely is living at the Rest Hotel in West Forty-ninth Street, and nothing will do Horsey but I must go with him over to the Rest to make inquiry for Nicely-Nicely, and there we learn that he leaves a forwarding address away up on Morningside Heights in care of somebody by the name of Slocum.

So Horsey calls a short, and away we go to this address, which turns out to be a five-story walk-up apartment, and a card downstairs shows that Slocum lives on the top floor. It takes Horsey and me ten minutes to walk up the five flights as we are by no means accustomed to exercise of this nature, and when we finally reach a door marked Slocum, we are plumb tuckered out, and have to sit down on the top step and rest a while.

Then I ring the bell at this door marked Slocum, and who appears but a tall young Judy with black hair who is without doubt beautiful, but who is so skinny we have to look twice to see her, and when I ask her if she can give me any information about a party named Nicely-Nicely Jones, she says to me like this:

'I guess you mean Quentin,' she says. 'Yes,' she says, 'Quentin is here. Come in, gentlemen.'

So we step into an apartment, and as we do so a thin, sickly looking character gets up out of a chair by the window, and in a weak voice says good evening. It is a good evening, at that, so Horsey and I say good evening right back at him, very polite, and then we stand there waiting for Nicely-Nicely to appear, when the beautiful skinny young Judy says:

'Well,' she says, 'this is Mr Quentin Jones.'

Then Horsey and I take another swivel at the thin character, and we can see that it is nobody but Nicely-Nicely, at that, but the way he changes since we last observe him is practically shocking to us both, because he is undoubtedly all shrunk up. In fact, he looks as if he is about half what he is in his prime, and his face is pale and thin, and his eyes are away back in his head, and while we both shake hands with him it is some time before either of us is able to speak. Then Horsey finally says:

'Nicely,' he says, 'can we have a few words with you in private on a very important proposition?'

Well, at this, and before Nicely-Nicely can answer aye, yes or no, the beautiful skinny young Judy goes out of the room and slams a door behind her, and Nicely-Nicely says:

'My fiancée, Miss Hilda Slocum,' he says. 'She is a wonderful character. We are to be married as soon as I lose twenty pounds more. It will take a couple of weeks longer,' he says.

'My goodness gracious, Nicely,' Horsey says. 'What do you mean lose twenty pounds more? You are practically emaciated now. Are you just out of a sick bed, or what?'

'Why,' Nicely-Nicely says, 'certainly I am not out of a sick bed. I am never healthier in my life. I am on a diet. I lose eighty-three pounds in two months, and am now down to two hundred. I feel great,' he says. 'It is all because of my fiancée, Miss Hilda Slocum. She rescues me from gluttony and obesity, or anyway,' Nicely-Nicely says, 'this is what Miss Hilda Slocum calls it. My,

I feel good. I love Miss Hilda Slocum very much,' Nicely-Nicely says. 'It is a case of love at first sight on both sides the day we meet in the subway. I am wedged in one of the turnstile gates, and she kindly pushes on me from behind until I wiggle through. I can see she has a kind heart, so I date her up for a movie that night and propose to her while the newsreel is on. But,' Nicely-Nicely says, 'Hilda tells me at once that she will never marry a fat slob. She says I must put myself in her hands and she will reduce me by scientific methods and then she will become my ever-loving wife, but not before.

'So,' Nicely-Nicely says, 'I come to live here with Miss Hilda Slocum and her mother, so she can supervise my diet. Her mother is thinner than Hilda. And I surely feel great,' Nicely-Nicely says. 'Look,' he says.

And with this, he pulls out the waistband of his pants, and shows enough spare space to hide War Admiral in, but the effort seems to be a strain on him, and he has to sit down in his chair again.

'My goodness gracious,' Horsey says. 'What do you eat, Nicely?'

'Well,' Nicely-Nicely says, 'I eat anything that does not contain starch, but,' he says, 'of course everything worth eating contains starch, so I really do not eat much of anything whatever. My fiancée, Miss Hilda Slocum, arranges my diet. She is an expert dietician and runs a widely known department in a diet magazine by the name of *Let's Keep House*.'

Then Horsey tells Nicely-Nicely of how he is matched to eat against this Joel Duffle, of Boston, for a nice side bet, and how he has a forfeit of a thousand dollars already posted for appearance, and how many of Nicely-Nicely's admirers along Broadway are looking to win themselves out of all their troubles by betting on him, and at first Nicely-Nicely listens with great interest, and his eyes are shining like six bits, but then he becomes very sad, and says:

'It is no use, gentlemen,' he says. 'My fiancée, Miss Hilda Slocum, will never hear of me going off my diet even for a little while. Only yesterday I try to talk her into letting me have a little pumpernickel instead of toasted whole wheat bread, and she says if I even think of such a thing again, she will break our engagement. Horsey,' he says, 'do you ever eat toasted whole wheat bread for a month hand running? Toasted?' he says.

'No,' Horsey says. 'What I eat is nice, white French bread, and corn muffins, and hot biscuits with gravy on them.'

'Stop,' Nicely-Nicely says. 'You are eating yourself into an early grave, and, furthermore,' he says, 'you are breaking my heart. But,' he says, 'the more I think of my following depending on me in this emergency, the sadder it makes me feel to think I am unable to oblige them. However,' he says, 'let us call Miss Hilda Slocum in on an outside chance and see what her reactions to your proposition are.'

So we call Miss Hilda Slocum in, and Horsey explains our predicament in putting so much faith in Nicely-Nicely only to find him dieting, and Miss Hilda Slocum's reactions are to order Horsey and me out of the joint with instructions never to darken her door again, and when we are a block away we can still hear her voice speaking very firmly to Nicely-Nicely.

Well, personally, I figure this ends the matter, for I can see that Miss Hilda Slocum is a most determined character, indeed, and the chances are it does end it, at that, if Horsey does not happen to get a wonderful break.

He is at Belmont Park one afternoon, and he has a real good thing in a jump race, and when a brisk young character in a hard straw hat and eyeglasses comes along and asks him what he likes, Horsey mentions this good thing, figuring he will move himself in for a few dibs if the good thing connects.

Well, it connects all right, and the brisk young character is very grateful to Horsey for his information, and is giving him plenty of much-obliges, and nothing else, and Horsey is about to mention that they do not accept much-obliges at his hotel, when the brisk young character mentions that he is nobody but Mr McBurgle and that he is the editor of the *Let's Keep House* magazine, and for Horsey to drop in and see him any time he is around his way.

Naturally, Horsey remembers what Nicely-Nicely says about Miss Hilda Slocum working for this *Let's Keep House* magazine, and he relates the story of the eating contest to Mr

McBurgle and asks him if he will kindly use his influence with Miss Hilda Slocum to get her to release Nicely-Nicely from his diet long enough for the contest. Then Horsey gives Mr McBurgle a tip on another winner, and Mr McBurgle must use plenty of influence on Miss Hilda Slocum at once, as the next day she calls Horsey up at his hotel before he is out of bed, and speaks to him as follows:

'Of course,' Miss Hilda Slocum says, 'I will never change my attitude about Quentin, but,' she says, 'I can appreciate that he feels very bad about you gentlemen relying on him and having to disappoint you. He feels that he lets you down, which is by no means true, but it weighs upon his mind. It is interfering with his diet.

'Now,' Miss Hilda Slocum says, 'I do not approve of your contest, because,' she says, 'it is placing a premium on gluttony, but I have a friend by the name of Miss Violette Shumberger who may answer your purpose. She is my dearest friend from childhood, but it is only because I love her dearly that this friendship endures. She is extremely fond of eating,' Miss Hilda Slocum says. 'In spite of my pleadings, and my warnings, and my own example, she persists in food. It is disgusting to me but I finally learn that it is no use arguing with her.

'She remains my dearest friend,' Miss Hilda Slocum says, 'though she continues her practice of eating, and I am informed that she is phenomenal in this respect. In fact,' she says, 'Nicely-Nicely tells me to say to you that if Miss Violette Shumberger can perform the eating exploits I relate to him from hearsay she is a lily. Good-bye,' Miss Hilda Slocum says. 'You cannot have Nicely-Nicely.'

Well, nobody cares much about this idea of a stand-in for Nicely-Nicely in such a situation, and especially a Judy that no one ever hears of before, and many citizens are in favour of pulling out of the contest altogether. But Horsey has his thousand-dollar forfeit to think of, and as no one can suggest anyone else, he finally arranges a personal meet with the Judy suggested by Miss Hilda Slocum.

He comes into Mindy's one evening with a female character who is so fat it is necessary to push three tables together to give her room for her lap, and it seems that this character is Miss Violette Shumberger. She weighs maybe two hundred and fifty pounds, but she is by no means an old Judy, and by no means bad-looking. She has a face the size of a town clock and enough chins for a fire escape, but she has a nice smile and pretty teeth, and a laugh that is so hearty it knocks the whipped cream off an order of strawberry shortcake on a table fifty feet away and arouses the indignation of a customer by the name of Goldstein who is about to consume same.

Well, Horsey's idea in bringing her into Mindy's is to get some kind of line on her eating form, and she is clocked by many experts when she starts putting on the hot meat, and it is agreed by one and all that she is by no means a selling-plater. In fact, by the time she gets through, even Mindy admits she has plenty of class, and the upshot of it all is Miss Violette Shumberger is chosen to eat against Joel Duffle.

Maybe you hear something of this great eating contest that comes off in New York one night in the early summer of 1937. Of course eating contests are by no means anything new, and in fact they are quite an old-fashioned pastime in some sections of this country, such as the South and East, but this is the first big public contest of the kind in years, and it creates no little comment along Broadway.

In fact, there is some mention of it in the blats, and it is not a frivolous proposition in any respect, and more dough is wagered on it than any other eating contest in history, with Joel Duffle a 6 to 5 favourite over Miss Violette Shumberger all the way through.

This Joel Duffle comes to New York several days before the contest with the character by the name of Conway, and requests a meet with Miss Violette Shumberger to agree on the final details and who shows up with Miss Violette Shumberger as her coach and adviser but Nicely-Nicely Jones. He is even thinner and more peaked-looking than when Horsey and I see him last, but he says he feels great, and that he is within six pounds of his marriage to Miss Hilda Slocum.

Well, it seems that his presence is really due to Miss Hilda Slocum herself, because she says that after getting her dearest friend Miss Violette Shumberger into this jackpot, it is only fair to do all she can to help her win it, and the only way she can think of is to let Nicely-Nicely give Violette the benefit of his experience and advice.

But afterward we learn that what really happens is that this editor, Mr McBurgle, gets greatly interested in the contest, and when he discovers that in spite of his influence, Miss Hilda Slocum declines to permit Nicely-Nicely to personally compete, but puts in a pinch eater, he is quite indignant and insists on her letting Nicely-Nicely school Violette.

Furthermore we afterward learn that when Nicely-Nicely returns to the apartment on Morningside Heights after giving Violette a lesson, Miss Hilda Slocum always smells his breath to see if he indulges in any food during his absence.

Well, this Joel Duffle is a tall character with stooped shoulders, and a sad expression, and he does not look as if he can eat his way out of a tea shoppe, but as soon as he commences to discuss the details of the contest, anybody can see that he knows what time it is in situations such as this. In fact, Nicely-Nicely says he can tell at once from the way Joel Duffle talks that he is a dangerous opponent, and he says while Miss Violette Shumberger impresses him as an improving eater, he is only sorry she does not have more seasoning.

This Joel Duffle suggests that the contest consist of twelve courses of strictly American food, each side to be allowed to pick six dishes, doing the picking in rotation, and specifying the weight and quantity of the course selected to any amount the contestant making the pick desires, and each course is to be divided for eating exactly in half, and after Miss Violette Shumberger and Nicely-Nicely whisper together a while, they say the terms are quite satisfactory.

Then Horsey tosses a coin for the first pick, and Joel Duffle says heads, and it is heads, and he chooses, as the first course, two quarts of ripe olives, twelve bunches of celery, and four pounds of shelled nuts, all this to be split fifty-fifty between them. Miss Violette Shumberger names twelve dozen cherry-stone clams as the second course, and Joel Duffle says two gallons of Philadelphia pepper-pot soup as the third.

Well, Miss Violette Shumberger and Nicely-Nicely whisper together again, and Violette puts in two five-pound striped bass, the heads and tails not to count in the eating, and Joel Duffle names a twenty-two pound roast turkey. Each vegetable is rated as one course, and Miss Violette Shumberger asks for twelve pounds of mashed potatoes with brown gravy. Joel Duffle says two dozen ears of corn on the cob, and Violette replies with two quarts of lima beans. Joel Duffle calls for twelve bunches of asparagus cooked in butter, and Violette mentions ten pounds of stewed new peas.

This gets them down to the salad, and it is Joel Duffle's play, so he says six pounds of mixed green salad with vinegar and oil dressing, and now Miss Violette Shumberger has the final selection, which is the dessert. She says it is a pumpkin pie, two feet across, and not less than three inches deep.

It is agreed that they must eat with knife, fork or spoon, but speed is not to count, and there is to be no time limit, except they cannot pause more than two consecutive minutes at any stage, except in case of hiccoughs. They can drink anything, and as much as they please, but liquids are not to count in the scoring. The decision is to be strictly on the amount of food consumed, and the judges are to take account of anything left on the plates after a course, but not of loose chewings on bosom or vest up to an ounce. The losing side is to pay for the food, and in case of a tie they are to eat it off immediately on ham and eggs only.

Well, the scene of this contest is the second-floor dining-room of Mindy's restaurant, which is closed to the general public for the occasion, and only parties immediately concerned in the contest are admitted. The contestants are seated on either side of a big table in the centre of the room, and each contestant has three waiters.

No talking and no rooting from the spectators is permitted, but of course in any eating contest the principals may speak to each other if they wish, though smart eaters never wish to do this, as talking only wastes energy, and about all they ever say to each other is please pass the mustard.

About fifty characters from Boston are present to witness the contest, and the same number of citizens of New York are admitted, and among them is this editor, Mr McBurgle, and he is around asking Horsey if he thinks Miss Violette Shumberger is as good a thing as the jumper at the race track.

Nicely-Nicely arrives on the scene quite early, and his appearance is really most distressing to his old friends and admirers, as by this time he is shy so much weight that he is a pitiful scene, to be sure, but he tells Horsey and me that he thinks Miss Violette Shumberger has a good chance.

'Of course,' he says, 'she is green. She does not know how to pace herself in competition. But,' he says, 'she has a wonderful style. I love to watch her eat. She likes the same things I do in the days when I am eating. She is a wonderful character, too. Do you ever notice her smile?' Nicely-Nicely says.

'But,' he says, 'she is the dearest friend of my fiancée, Miss Hilda Slocum, so let us not speak of this. I try to get Hilda to come to see the contest, but she says it is repulsive. Well, anyway,' Nicely-Nicely says, 'I manage to borrow a few dibs, and am wagering on Miss Violette Shumberger. By the way,' he says, 'if you happen to think of it, notice her smile.'

Well, Nicely-Nicely takes a chair about ten feet behind Miss Violette Shumberger, which is as close as the judges will allow him, and he is warned by them that no coaching from the corners will be permitted, but of course Nicely-Nicely knows this rule as well as they do, and furthermore by this time his exertions seem to have left him without any more energy.

There are three judges, and they are all from neutral territory. One of these judges is a party from Baltimore, Md., by the name of Packard, who runs a restaurant, and another is a party from Providence, R.I., by the name of Croppers, who is a sausage manufacturer. The third judge is an old Judy by the name of Mrs Rhubarb, who comes from Philadelphia, and once keeps an actors' boarding-house, and is considered an excellent judge of eaters.

Well, Mindy is the official starter, and at 8.30 p.m. sharp, when there is still much betting among the spectators, he outs with his watch, and says like this:

'Are you ready, Boston? Are you ready, New York?'

Miss Violette Shumberger and Joel Duffle both nod their heads, and Mindy says commence, and the contest is on, with Joel Duffle getting the jump at once on the celery and olives and nuts.

It is apparent that this Joel Duffle is one of these rough-and-tumble eaters that you can hear quite a distance off, especially on clams and soups. He is also an eyebrow eater, an eater whose eyebrows go up as high as the part in his hair as he eats, and this type of eater is undoubtedly very efficient.

In fact, the way Joel Duffle goes through the groceries down to the turkey causes the Broadway spectators some uneasiness, and they are whispering to each other that they only wish the old Nicely-Nicely is in there. But personally, I like the way Miss Violette Shumberger eats without undue excitement, and with great zest. She cannot keep close to Joel Duffle in the matter of speed in the early stages of the contest, as she seems to enjoy chewing her food, but I observe that as it goes along she pulls up on him, and I figure this is not because she is stepping up her pace, but because he is slowing down.

When the turkey finally comes on, and is split in two halves right down the middle, Miss Violette Shumberger looks greatly disappointed, and she speaks for the first time as follows:

'Why,' she says, 'where is the stuffing?'

Well, it seems that nobody mentions any stuffing for the turkey to the chef, so he does not make any stuffing, and Miss Violette Shumberger's disappointment is so plain to be seen that the confidence of the Boston characters is somewhat shaken. They can see that a Judy who can pack away as much fodder as Miss Violette Shumberger has to date, and then beef for stuffing, is really quite an eater.

In fact, Joel Duffle looks quite startled when he observes Miss Violette Shumberger's disappointment, and he gazes at her with great respect as she disposes of her share of the turkey, and the mashed potatoes, and one thing and another in such a manner that she moves up on the pumpkin pie on dead even terms with him. In fact, there is little to choose between them at this point, although the judge from Baltimore is calling the attention of the other judges to a turkey leg that he claims Miss Violette Shumberger does not clean as neatly as Joel Duffle does his, but the other judges dismiss this as a technicality.

Then the waiters bring on the pumpkin pie, and it is without doubt quite a large pie, and in fact it is about the size of a manhole cover, and I can see that Joel Duffle is observing this pie with a strange expression on his face, although to tell the truth I do not care for the expression on Miss Violet Shumberger's face either.

Well, the pie is cut in two dead centre, and one half is placed before Miss Violet Shumberger and the other half before Joel Duffle, and he does not take more than two bites before I see him loosen his waistband and take a big swig of water, and thinks I to myself, he is now down to a slow walk, and the pie will decide the whole heat, and I am only wishing I am able to wager a little more dough on Miss Violette Shumberger. But about this moment, and before she as much as touches her pie, all of a sudden Violette turns her head and motions to Nicely-Nicely to approach her, and as he approaches, she whispers in his ear.

Now at this, the Boston character by the name of Conway jumps up and claims a foul and several other Boston characters join him in this claim, and so does Joel Duffle, although afterwards even the Boston characters admit that Joel Duffle is no gentleman to make such a claim against a lady.

Well, there is some confusion over this, and the judges hold a conference, and they rule that there is certainly no foul in the actual eating that they can see, because Miss Violette Shumberger does not touch her pie so far.

But they say that whether it is a foul otherwise all depends on whether Miss Violette Shumberger is requesting advice on the contest from Nicely-Nicely and the judge from Providence, R.I., wishes to know if Nicely-Nicely will kindly relate what passes between him and Violette so they may make a decision.

'Why,' Nicely-Nicely says, 'all she asks me is can I get her another piece of pie when she finishes the one in front of her.'

Now at this, Joel Duffle thrown down his knife, and pushes back his plate with all but two bites of his pie left on it, and says to the Boston characters like this:

'Gentlemen,' he says, 'I am licked. I cannot eat another mouthful. You must admit I put up a game battle, but,' he says, 'it is useless for me to go on against this Judy who is asking for more pie before she even starts on what is before her. I am almost dying as it is, and I do not wish to destroy myself in a hopeless effort. Gentlemen,' he says, 'she is not human.'

Well, of course this amounts to throwing in the old napkin and Nicely-Nicely stands up on his chair, and says:

'Three cheers for Miss Violette Shumberger!'

Then Nicely-Nicely gives the first cheer in person, but the effort overtaxes his strength, and he falls off the chair in a faint just as Joel Duffle collapses under the table, and the doctors at the Clinic Hospital are greatly baffled to receive, from the same address at the same time, one patient who is suffering from undernourishment, and another patient who is unconscious from over-eating.

Well, in the meantime, after the excitement subsides, and wagers are settled, we take Miss Violette Shumberger to the main floor in Mindy's for a midnight snack, and when she speaks of her wonderful triumph, she is disposed to give much credit to Nicely-Nicely Jones.

'You see,' Violette says, 'what I really whisper to him is that I am a goner. I whisper to him that I cannot possibly take one bite of the pie if my life depends on it, and if he has any bets down to try and hedge them off as quickly as possible.

'I fear,' she says, 'that Nicely-Nicely will be greatly disappointed in my showing, but I have a confession to make to him when he gets out of the hospital. I forget about the contest,' Violette says, 'and eat my regular dinner of pig's knuckles and sauerkraut an hour before the contest starts and,' she says, 'I have no doubt this tends to affect my form somewhat. So,' she says, 'I owe everything to Nicely-Nicely's quick thinking.'

It is several weeks after the great eating contest that I run into Miss Hilda Slocum on Broadway and it seems to me that she looks much better nourished than the last time I see her, and when I mention this she says:

'Yes,' she says, 'I cease dieting. I learn my lesson,' she says. 'I learn that male characters do not appreciate anybody who tries to ward off surplus tissue. What male characters wish is substance. Why,' she says, 'only a week ago my editor, Mr McBurgle, tells me he will love to take me dancing if only I get something on me for him to take hold of. I am very fond of dancing,' she says.

'But,' I say, 'what of Nicely-Nicely Jones? I do not see him around lately.'

'Why,' Miss Hilda Slocum says, 'do you not hear what this cad does? Why, as soon as he is strong enough to leave the hospital, he elopes with my dearest friend, Miss Violette Shumberger, leaving me a note saying something about two souls with but a single thought. They are down in Florida running a barbecue stand, and,' she says, 'the chances are, eating like seven mules.'

'Miss Slocum,' I says, 'can I interest you in a portion of Mindy's chicken fricassee?'

'With dumplings?' Miss Hilda Slocum says. 'Yes,' she says, 'you can. Afterwards I have a date to go dancing with Mr McBurgle. I am crazy about dancing,' she says.

5 BUTCH MINDS THE BABY

ONE evening along about seven o'clock I am sitting in Mindy's restaurant putting on the gefillte fish, which is a dish I am very fond of, when in come three parties from Brooklyn wearing caps as follows: Harry the Horse, Little Isadore, and Spanish John.

Now these parties are not such parties as I will care to have much truck with, because I often hear rumours about them that are very discreditable, even if the rumours are not true. In fact, I hear that many citizens of Brooklyn will be very glad indeed to see Harry the Horse, Little Isadore and Spanish John move away from there, as they are always doing something that is considered a knock to the community, such as robbing people, or maybe shooting or stabbing them, and throwing pineapples, and carrying on generally.

I am really much surprised to see these parties on Broadway, as it is well known that the Broadway coppers just naturally love to shove such parties around, but there they are in Mindy's, and there I am, so of course I give them a very large hello, as I never wish to seem inhospitable, even to Brooklyn parties. Right away they come over to my table and sit down, and Little Isadore reaches out and spears himself a big hunk of my gefillte fish with his fingers, but I overlook this, as I am using the only knife on the table.

Then they all sit there looking at me without saying anything, and the way they look at me makes me very nervous indeed. Finally I figure that maybe they are a little embarrassed being in a high-class spot such as Mindy's, with legitimate people around and about, so I say to them, very polite:

'It is a nice night.'

'What is nice about it?' asks Harry the Horse, who is a thin man with a sharp face and sharp eyes.

Well, now that it is put up to me in this way, I can see there is nothing so nice about the night, at that, so I try to think of something else jolly to say, while Little Isadore keeps spearing at my gefillte with his fingers, and Spanish John nabs one of my potatoes.

'Where does Big Butch live?' Harry the Horse asks.

'Big Butch?' I say, as if I never hear the name before in my life, because in this man's town it is never a good idea to answer any question without thinking it over, as some time you may give the right answer to the wrong guy, or the wrong answer to the right guy. 'Where does Big Butch live?' I ask them again.

'Yes, where does he live?' Harry the Horse says, very impatient. 'We wish you to take us to him.'

'Now wait a minute, Harry,' I say, and I am now more nervous than somewhat. 'I am not sure I remember the exact house Big Butch lives in, and furthermore I am not sure Big Butch will care to have me bringing people to see him, especially three at a time, and especially from Brooklyn. You know Big Butch has a very bad disposition, and there is no telling what he may say to me if he does not like the idea of me taking you to him.'

'Everything is very kosher,' Harry the Horse says. 'You need not be afraid of anything whatever. We have a business proposition for Big Butch. It means a nice score for him, so you take us to him at once, or the chances are I will have to put the arm on somebody around here.'

Well, as the only one around there for him to put the arm on at this time seems to be me, I can see where it will be good policy for me to take these parties to Big Butch especially as the last of my gefillte fish is just going down Little Isadore's gullet, and Spanish John is finishing up my potatoes, and is donking a piece of ryebread in my coffee, so there is nothing more for me to eat.

So I lead them over into West Forty-ninth Street, near Tenth Avenue, where Big Butch lives on the ground floor of an old brownstone-front house, and who is sitting out on the stoop but Big Butch himself. In fact, everybody in the neighbourhood is sitting out on the front stoops over there, including women and children, because sitting out on the front stoops is quite a custom in this section.

Big Butch is peeled down to his undershirt and pants, and he has no shoes on his feet, as Big Butch is a guy who loves his comfort. Furthermore, he is smoking a cigar, and laid out on the stoop beside him on a blanket is a little baby with not much clothes on. This baby seems to be asleep, and every now and then Big Butch fans it with a folded newspaper to shoo away the mosquitoes that wish to nibble on the baby. These mosquitoes come across the river from the Jersey side on hot nights and they seem to be very fond of babies.

'Hello, Butch,' I say, as we stop in front of the stoop.

'Sh-h-h!' Butch says, pointing at the baby, and making more noise with his shush than an engine blowing off steam. Then he gets up and tiptoes down to the sidewalk where we are standing, and I am hoping that Butch feels all right, because when Butch does not feel so good he is apt to be very short with one and all. He is a guy of maybe six feet two and a couple of feet wide, and he has big hairy hands and a mean look.

In fact, Big Butch is known all over this man's town as a guy you must not monkey with in any respect, so it takes plenty of weight off me when I see that he seems to know the parties from Brooklyn, and nods at them very friendly, especially at Harry the Horse. And right away Harry states a most surprising proposition to Big Butch.

It seems that there is a big coal company which has an office in an old building down in West Eighteenth Street, and in this office is a safe, and in this safe is the company pay-roll of twenty thousand dollars cash money. Harry the Horse knows the money is there because a personal friend of his who is the paymaster for the company puts it there late this very afternoon.

It seems that the paymaster enters into a dicker with Harry the Horse and Little Isadore and Spanish John for them to slug him while he is carrying the pay-roll from the bank to the office in the afternoon, but something happens that they miss connexions on the exact spot, so the paymaster has to carry the sugar on to the office without being slugged, and there it is now in two fat bundles.

Personally it seems to me as I listen to Harry's story that the paymaster must be a very dishonest character to be making deals to hold still while he is being slugged and the company's sugar taken away from him, but of course it is none of my business, so I take no part in the conversation.

Well, it seems that Harry the Horse and Little Isadore and Spanish John wish to get the money out of the safe, but none of them knows anything about opening safes, and while they are standing around over in Brooklyn talking over what is to be done in this emergency Harry suddenly remembers that Big Butch is once in the business of opening safes for a living.

In fact, I hear afterwards that Big Butch is considered the best safe-opener east of the Mississippi River in his day, but the law finally takes to sending him to Sing Sing for opening these safes, and after he is in and out of Sing Sing three different times for opening safes Butch gets sick and tired of the place, especially as they pass what is called the Baumes Law in New York, which is a law that says if a guy is sent to Sing Sing four times hand running, he must stay there the rest of his life, without any argument about it.

So Big Butch gives up opening safes for a living, and goes into business in a small way, such as running beer, and handling a little Scotch now and then, and becomes an honest citizen. Furthermore, he marries one of the neighbours' children over on the West Side by the name of Mary Murphy, and I judge the baby on this stoop comes of this marriage between Big Butch and Mary because I can see that it is a very homely baby, indeed. Still, I never see many babies that I consider rose geraniums for looks, anyway.

Well, it finally comes out that the idea of Harry the Horse and Little Isadore and Spanish John is to get Big Butch to open the coal company's safe and take the pay-roll money out, and they are willing to give him fifty per cent of the money for his bother, taking fifty per cent for themselves for finding the plant, and paying all the overhead, such as the paymaster, out of their bit, which strikes me as a pretty fair sort of deal for Big Butch. But Butch only shakes his head.

'It is old-fashioned stuff,' Butch says. 'Nobody opens pete boxes for a living any more. They makes the boxes too good, and they are all wired up with alarms and are a lot of trouble generally. I am in a legitimate business now and going along. You boys know I cannot stand another fall, what with being away three times already, and in addition to this I must mind the baby. My old lady goes to Mrs Clancy's wake to-night up in the Bronx, and the chances are she will be there all night, as she is very fond of wakes, so I must mind little John Ignatius Junior.'

'Listen, Butch,' Harry the Horse says, 'this is a very soft pete. It is old-fashioned, and you can open it with a toothpick. There are no wires on it, because they never put more than a dime in it before in years. It just happens they have to put the twenty G's in it to-night because my pal the paymaster makes it a point not to get back from the jug with the scratch in time to pay off to-day, especially after he sees we miss out on him. It is the softest touch you will ever know, and where can a guy pick up ten G's like this?'

I can see that Big Butch is thinking the ten G's over very seriously, at that, because in these times nobody can afford to pass up ten G's, especially a guy in the beer business, which is very, very tough just now. But finally he shakes his head again and says like this:

'No,' he says, 'I must let it go, because I must mind the baby. My old lady is very, very particular about this, and I dast not leave little John Ignatius Junior for a minute. If Mary comes home and finds I am not minding the baby she will put the blast on me plenty. I like to turn a few honest bobs now and then as well as anybody, but,' Butch says, 'John Ignatius Junior comes first with me.'

Then he turns away and goes back to the stoop as much as to say he is through arguing, and sits down beside John Ignatius Junior again just in time to keep a mosquito from carrying off one of John's legs. Anybody can see that Big Butch is very fond of this baby, though personally I will not give you a dime for a dozen babies, male and female.

Well, Harry the Horse and Little Isadore and Spanish John are very much disappointed, and stand around talking among themselves, and paying no attention to me, when all of a sudden Spanish John, who never has much to say up to this time, seems to have a bright idea. He talks to Harry and Isadore, and they get all pleasured up over what he has to say, and finally Harry goes to Big Butch.

'Sh-h-h-h!' Big Butch says, pointing to the baby as Harry opens his mouth.

'Listen, Butch,' Harry says in a whisper, 'we can take the baby with us, and you can mind it and work, too.'

'Why,' Big Butch whispers back, 'this is quite an idea indeed. Let us go into the house and talk things over.'

So he picks up the baby and leads us into his joint, and gets out some pretty fair beer, though it is needled a little, at that, and we sit around the kitchen chewing the fat in whispers. There is a crib in the kitchen, and Butch puts the baby in this crib, and it keeps on snoozing away first rate while we are talking. In fact, it is sleeping so sound that I am commencing to figure that Butch must give it some of the needled beer he is feeding us, because I am feeling a little dopey myself.

Finally Butch says that as long as he can take John Ignatius Junior with him he sees no reason why he shall not go and open the safe for them, only he says he must have five per cent more to put in the baby's bank when he gets back, so as to round himself up with his ever-loving wife in case of a beef from her over keeping the baby out in the night air. Harry the Horse says he considers this extra five per cent a little strong, but Spanish John, who seems to be a very square guy, says that after all it is only fair to cut the baby in if it is to be with them when making the score, and Little Isadore seems to think this is all right, too. So Harry the Horse gives in, and says five per cent it is.

Well, as they do not wish to start out until after midnight, and as there is plenty of time, Big Butch gets out some more needled beer, and then he goes looking for the tools with which he opens safes, and which he says he does not see since the day John Ignatius Junior is born and he gets them out to build the crib.

Now this is a good time for me to bid one and all farewell, and what keeps me there is something I cannot tell you to this day, because personally I never before have any idea of taking part in a safe opening, especially with a baby, as I consider such actions very dishonourable. When I come to think over things afterwards, the only thing I can figure is the needled beer, but I wish to say I am really very much surprised at myself when I find myself in a taxicab along about one o'clock in the morning with these Brooklyn parties and Big Butch and the baby.

Butch has John Ignatius Junior rolled up in a blanket, and John is still pounding his ear. Butch has a satchel of tools, and what looks to me like a big flat book, and just before we leave the house Butch hands me a package and tells me to be very careful with it. He gives Little Isadore a smaller package, which Isadore shoves into his pistol pocket, and when Isadore sits down in the taxi something goes wa-wa, like a sheep, and Big Butch becomes very indignant because it seems Isadore is sitting on John Ignatius Junior's doll, which says 'Mamma' when you squeeze it.

It seems Big Butch figures that John Ignatius Junior may wish something to play with in case he wakes up, and it is a good thing for Little Isadore that the mamma doll is not squashed so it cannot say 'Mamma' any more, or the chances are Little Isadore will get a good bust in the snoot.

We let the taxicab go a block away from the spot we are headed for in West Eighteenth Street, between Seventh and Eighth Avenues, and walk the rest of the way two by two. I walk with Big Butch carrying my package, and Butch is lugging the baby and his satchel and the flat thing that looks like a book. It is so quiet down in West Eighteenth Street at such an hour that you can hear yourself think, and in fact I hear myself thinking very plain that I am a big sap to be on a job like this, especially with a baby, but I keep going just the same, which shows you what a very big sap I am, indeed.

There are very few people in West Eighteenth Street when we get there, and one of them is a fat guy who is leaning against a building almost in the centre of the block, and who takes a walk for himself as soon as he sees us. It seems that this fat guy is the watchman at the coal company's office and is also a personal friend of Harry the Horse, which is why he takes the walk when he sees us coming.

It is agreed before we leave Big Butch's house that Harry the Horse and Spanish John are to stay outside the place as look-outs, while Big Butch is inside opening the safe, and that Little Isadore is to go with Butch. Nothing whatever is said by anybody about where I am to be at any time, and I can see that, no matter where I am, I will still be an outsider, but, as Butch gives me the package to carry, I figure he wishes me to remain with him.

It is no bother at all getting into the office of the coal company, which is on the ground floor, because it seems the watchman leaves the front door open, this watchman being a most obliging guy, indeed. In fact, he is so obliging that by and by he comes back and lets Harry the Horse and Spanish John tie him up good and tight, and stick a handkerchief in his mouth and chuck him in an areaway next to the office, so nobody will think he has anything to do with opening the safe in case anybody comes around asking.

The office looks out on the street, and the safe that Harry the Horse and Little Isadore and Spanish John wish Big Butch to open is standing up against the rear wall of the office facing the street windows. There is one little electric light burning very dim over the safe so that when anybody walks past the place outside, such as a watchman, they can look in through the window and see the safe at all times, unless they are blind. It is not a tall safe, and it is not a big safe, and I can see Big Butch grin when he sees it, so I figure this safe is not much of a safe, just as Harry the Horse claims.

Well, as soon as Big Butch and the baby and Little Isadore and me get into the office, Big Butch steps over to the safe and unfolds what I think is the big flat book, and what is it but a sort of screen painted on one side to look exactly like the front of a safe. Big Butch stands this screen up on the floor in front of the real safe, leaving plenty of space in between, the idea being that the screen will keep anyone passing in the street outside from seeing Butch while he is opening the safe, because when a man is opening a safe he needs all the privacy he can get.

Big Butch lays John Ignatius Junior down on the floor on the blanket behind the phony safe front and takes his tools out of the satchel and starts to work opening the safe, while Little Isadore and me get back in a corner where it is dark, because there is not room for all of us back of the screen. However, we can see what Big Butch is doing, and I wish to say while I never before see a professional safe-opener at work, and never wish to see another, this Butch handles himself like a real artist.

He starts drilling into the safe around the combination lock, working very fast and very quiet, when all of a sudden what happens but John Ignatius Junior sits up on the blanket and lets out a squall. Naturally this is most disquieting to me, and personally I am in favour of beaning John Ignatius Junior with something to make him keep still, because I am nervous enough as it is. But the squalling does not seem to bother Big Butch. He lays down his tools and picks up John Ignatius Junior and starts whispering, 'There, there, there, my itty oddleums. Da-dad is here.'

Well, this sounds very nonsensical to me in such a situation, and it makes no impression whatever on John Ignatius Junior. He keeps on squalling, and I judge he is squalling pretty loud because I see Harry the Horse and Spanish John both walk past the window and look in very anxious. Big Butch jiggles John Ignatius Junior up and down and keeps whispering baby talk to him, which sounds very undignified coming from a high-class safe-opener, and finally Butch whispers to me to hand him the package I am carrying.

He opens the package, and what is in it but a baby's nursing bottle full of milk. Moreover, there is a little tin stew pan, and Butch hands the pan to me and whispers to me to find a water tap somewhere in the joint and fill the pan with water. So I go stumbling around in the dark in a room behind the office and bark my shins several times before I find a tap and fill the pan. I take it back to Big Butch, and he squats there with the baby on one arm, and gets a tin of what is called canned heat out of the package, and lights this canned heat with his cigar lighter, and starts heating the pan of water with the nursing bottle in it.

Big Butch keeps sticking his finger in the pan of water while it is heating, and by and by he puts the rubber nipple of the nursing bottle in his mouth and takes a pull at it to see if the milk is warm enough, just like I see dolls who have babies do. Apparently the milk is okay, as Butch hands the bottle to John Ignatius Junior, who grabs hold of it with both hands, and starts sucking on the business end. Naturally he has to stop squalling, and Big Butch goes to work on the safe again, with John Ignatius Junior sitting on the blanket, pulling on the bottle and looking wiser than a treeful of owls.

It seems the safe is either a tougher job than anybody figures, or Big Butch's tools are not so good, what with being old and rusty and used for building baby cribs, because he breaks a couple of drills and works himself up into quite a sweat without getting anywhere. Butch afterwards explains to me that he is one of the first guys in this country to open safes without explosives, but he says to do this work properly you have to know the safes so as to drill to the tumblers of the lock just right, and it seems that this particular safe is a new type to him, even if it is old, and he is out of practice.

Well, in the meantime, John Ignatius Junior finishes his bottle and starts mumbling again, and Big Butch gives him a tool to play with, and finally Butch needs this tool and tries to take it away from John Ignatius Junior, and the baby lets out such a squawk that Butch has to let him keep it until he can sneak it away from him, and this causes more delay.

Finally Big Butch gives up trying to drill the safe open, and he whispers to us that he will have to put a little shot in it to loosen up the lock, which is all right with us, because we are getting tired of hanging around and listening to John Ignatius Junior's glug-glugging. As far as I am personally concerned, I am wishing I am home in bed.

Well, Butch starts pawing through his satchel looking for something and it seems that what he is looking for is a little bottle of some kind of explosive with which to shake the lock on the safe up some, and at first he cannot find this bottle, but finally he discovers that John Ignatius Junior has it and is gnawing at the cork, and Butch has quite a battle making John Ignatius Junior give it up.

Anyway, he fixes the explosive in one of the holes he drills near the combination lock on the safe, and then he puts in a fuse, and just before he touches off the fuse Butch picks up John Ignatius Junior and hands him to Little Isadore, and tells us to go into the room behind the office. John Ignatius Junior does not seem to care for Little Isadore, and I do not blame him, at that, because he starts to squirm around quite some in Isadore's arms and lets out a squall, but all of a sudden he becomes very quiet indeed, and, while I am not able to prove it, something tells me that Little Isadore has his hand over John Ignatius Junior's mouth.

Well, Big Butch joins us right away in the back room, and sound comes out of John Ignatius Junior again as Butch takes him from Little Isadore, and I am thinking that it is a good thing for Isadore that the baby cannot tell Big Butch what Isadore does to him.

'I put in just a little bit of a shot,' Big Butch says, 'and it will not make any more noise than snapping your fingers.'

But a second later there is a big whoom from the office, and the whole joint shakes, and John Ignatius laughs right out loud. The chances are he thinks it is the Fourth of July.

'I guess maybe I put in too big a charge,' Big Butch says, and then he rushes into the office with Little Isadore and me after him, and John Ignatius Junior still laughing very heartily for a small baby. The door of the safe is swinging loose, and the whole joint looks somewhat wrecked, but Big Butch loses no time in getting his dukes into the safe and grabbing out two big bundles of cash money, which he sticks inside his shirt.

As we go into the street Harry the Horse and Spanish John come running up much excited, and Harry says to Big Butch like this:

'What are you trying to do,' he says, 'wake up the whole town?'

'Well,' Butch says, 'I guess maybe the charge is too strong, at that, but nobody seems to be coming, so you and Spanish John walk over to Eighth Avenue, and the rest of us will walk to Seventh, and if you go along quiet, like people minding their own business, it will be all right.'

But I judge Little Isadore is tired of John Ignatius Junior's company by this time, because he says he will go with Harry the Horse and Spanish John, and this leaves Big Butch and John Ignatius Junior and me to go the other way. So we start moving, and all of a sudden two cops come tearing around the corner toward which Harry and Isadore and Spanish John are going. The chances are the cops hear the earthquake Big Butch lets off and are coming to investigate.

But the chances are, too, that if Harry the Horse and the other two keep on walking along very quietly like Butch tells them to, the coppers will pass them up entirely, because it is not likely that coppers will figure anybody to be opening safes with explosives in this neighbourhood. But the minute Harry the Horse sees the coppers he loses his nut, and he outs with the old equalizer and starts blasting away, and what does Spanish John do but get his out, too, and open up.

The next thing anybody knows, the two coppers are down on the ground with slugs in them, but other coppers are coming from every which direction, blowing whistles and doing a little blasting themselves, and there is plenty of excitement, especially when the coppers who are not chasing Harry the Horse and Little Isadore and Spanish John start poking around the neighbourhood and find Harry's pal, the watchman, all tied up nice and tight where Harry leaves him, and the watchman explains that some scoundrels blow open the safe he is watching.

All this time Big Butch and me are walking in the other direction toward Seventh Avenue, and Big Butch has John Ignatius in his arms, and John Ignatius is now squalling very loud indeed. The chances are he is still thinking of the big whoom back there which tickles him so and is wishing to hear some more whooms. Anyway, he is beating his own best record for squalling, and as we go walking along Big Butch says to me like this:

'I dast not run,' he says, 'because if any coppers see me running they will start popping at me and maybe hit John Ignatius

81

Junior, and besides running will joggle the milk up in him and make him sick. My old lady always warns me never to joggle John Ignatius Junior when he is full of milk.'

'Well, Butch,' I say, 'there is no milk in me, and I do not care if I am joggled up, so if you do not mind, I will start doing a piece of running at the next corner.'

But just then around the corner of Seventh Avenue toward which we are headed comes two or three coppers with a big fat sergeant with them, and one of the coppers, who is half-out of breath as if he has been doing plenty of sprinting, is explaining to the sergeant that somebody blows a safe down the street and shoots a couple of coppers in the getaway.

And there is Big Butch, with John Ignatius Junior in his arms and twenty G's in his shirt front and a tough record behind him, walking right up to them.

I am feeling very sorry, indeed, for Big Butch, and very sorry for myself, too, and I am saying to myself that if I get out of this I will never associate with anyone but ministers of the gospel as long as I live. I can remember thinking that I am getting a better break than Butch, at that, because I will not have to go to Sing Sing for the rest of my life, like him, and I also remember wondering what they will give John Ignatius Junior, who is still tearing off these squalls, with Big Butch saying, 'There, there, there, Daddy's itty woogleums.' Then I hear one of the coppers say to the fat sergeant:

'We better nail these guys. They may be in on this.'

Well, I can see it is good-bye to Butch and John Ignatius Junior and me, as the fat sergeant steps up to Big Butch, but instead of putting the arm on Butch, the fat sergeant only points at John Ignatius Junior and asks very sympathetic:

'Teeth?'

'No,' Big Butch says. 'Not teeth. Colic. I just get the doctor here out of bed to do something for him, and we are going to a drug store to get some medicine.'

Well, naturally I am very much surprised at this statement, because of course I am not a doctor, and if John Ignatius Junior has colic it serves him right, but I am only hoping they do not ask for my degree, when the fat sergeant says:

'Too bad. I know what it is. I got three of them at home. But,' he says, 'it acts more like it is teeth than colic.'

Then as Big Butch and John Ignatius Junior and me go on about our business I hear the fat sergeant say to the copper, very sarcastic:

'Yea, of course a guy is out blowing safes with a baby in his arms! You will make a great detective, you will!'

I do not see Big Butch for several days after I learn that Harry the Horse and Little Isadore and Spanish John get back to Brooklyn all right, except they are a little nicked up here and there from the slugs the coppers toss at them, while the coppers they clip are not damaged so very much. Furthermore, the chances are I will not see Big Butch for several years, if it is left to me, but he comes looking for me one night, and he seems to be all pleasured up about something.

'Say,' Big Butch says to me, 'you know I never give a copper credit for knowing any too much about anything, but I wish to say that this fat sergeant we run into the other night is a very, very smart duck. He is right about it being teeth that is ailing John Ignatius Junior, for what happens yesterday but John cuts his first tooth.'

6 BREACH OF PROMISE

ONE day a certain party by the name of Judge Goldfobber, who is a lawyer by trade, sends word to me that he wishes me to call on him at his office in lower Broadway, and while ordinarily I do not care for any part of lawyers, it happens that Judge Goldfobber is a friend of mine, so I go to see him.

Of course Judge Goldfobber is not a judge, and never is a judge, and he is 100 to 1 in my line against ever being a judge, but he is called Judge because it pleases him, and everybody always wishes to please Judge Goldfobber, as he is one of the surest-footed lawyers in this town, and beats more tough beefs for different citizens than seems possible. He is a wonderful hand for keeping citizens from getting into the sneezer, and better than Houdini when it comes to getting them out of the sneezer after they are in.

Personally, I never have any use for the professional services of Judge Goldfobber, as I am a law-abiding citizen at all times, and am greatly opposed to guys who violate the law, but I know the Judge from around and about for many years. I know him from around and about the night clubs, and other deadfalls, for Judge Goldfobber is such a guy as loves to mingle with the public in these spots, as he picks up much law business there, and sometimes a nice doll.

Well, when I call on Judge Goldfobber, he takes me into his private office and wishes to know if I can think of a couple of deserving guys who are out of employment, and who will like a job of work, and if so, Judge Goldfobber says, he can offer them a first-class position.

'Of course,' Judge Goldfobber says, 'it is not steady employment, and in fact it is nothing but piece-work, but the parties must be extremely reliable parties, who can be depended on in a pinch. This is out-of-town work that requires tact, and,' he says, 'some nerve.'

Well, I am about to tell Judge Goldfobber that I am no employment agent, and go on about my business, because I can tell from the way he says the parties must be parties who can be depended on in a pinch, that a pinch is apt to come up on the job at any minute, and I do not care to steer any friends of mine against a pinch.

But as I get up to go, I look out of Judge Goldfobber's window, and I can see Brooklyn in the distance beyond the river, and seeing Brooklyn I get to thinking of certain parties over there that I figure must be suffering terribly from the unemployment situation. I get to thinking of Harry the Horse, and Spanish John and Little Isadore, and the reason I figure they must be suffering from the unemployment situation is because if nobody is working and making any money, there is nobody for them to rob, and if there is nobody for them to rob, Harry the Horse and Spanish John and Little Isadore are just naturally bound to be feeling the depression keenly.

Anyway, I finally mention the names of these parties to Judge Goldfobber, and furthermore I speak well of their reliability in a pinch, and of their nerve, although I cannot conscientiously recommend their tact, and Judge Goldfobber is greatly delighted, as he often hears of Harry the Horse, and Spanish John and Little Isadore.

He asks me for their addresses, but of course nobody knows exactly where Harry the Horse and Spanish John and Little Isadore live, because they do not live anywhere in particular. However, I tell him about a certain spot in Clinton Street where he may be able to get track of them, and then I leave Judge Goldfobber for fear he may wish me to take word to these parties, and if there is anybody in this whole world I will not care to take word to, or to have any truck with in any manner, shape, or form, it is Harry the Horse, and Spanish John and Little Isadore.

Well, I do not hear anything more of the matter for several weeks, but one evening, when I am in Mindy's restaurant on Broadway enjoying a little cold borscht, which is a most refresh-

ing matter in hot weather such as is going on at the time, who
bobs up but Harry the Horse, and Spanish John and Little Isadore, and I am so surprised to see them that some of my cold
borscht goes down the wrong way, and I almost choke to death.

However, they seem quite friendly, and in fact Harry the
Horse pounds me on the back to keep me from choking, and
while he pounds so hard that he almost caves in my spine, I
consider it a most courteous action, and when I am able to talk
again, I say to him as follows:

'Well, Harry,' I say, 'it is a privilege and a pleasure to see you
again, and I hope and trust you will all join me in some cold
borscht, which you will find very nice, indeed.'

'No,' Harry says, 'we do not care for any cold borscht. We
are looking for Judge Goldfobber. Do you see Judge Goldfobber
round and about lately?'

Well, the idea of Harry the Horse and Spanish John and Little
Isadore looking for Judge Goldfobber sounds somewhat alarming to me, and I figure maybe the job Judge Goldfobber gives
them turns out bad and they wish to take Judge Goldfobber
apart, but the next minute Harry says to me like this:

'By the way,' he says, 'we wish to thank you for the job of
work you throw our way. Maybe some day we will be able to
do as much for you. It is a most interesting job,' Harry says,
'and while you are snuffing your cold borscht I will give you the
details, so you will understand why we wish to see Judge Goldfobber.'

It turns out [Harry the Horse says] that the job is not for
Judge Goldfobber personally, but for a client of his, and who is
this client but Mr Jabez Tuesday, the rich millionaire, who owns
the Tuesday string of one-arm joints where many citizens go for
food and wait on themselves. Judge Goldfobber comes to see us
in Brooklyn in person, and sends me to see Mr Jabez Tuesday
with a letter of introduction, so Mr Jabez Tuesday can explain
what he wishes me to do, because Judge Goldfobber is too smart
a guy to be explaining such matters to me himself.

In fact, for all I know maybe Judge Goldfobber is not aware
of what Mr Jabez Tuesday wishes me to do, although I am willing to lay a little 6 to 5 that Judge Goldfobber does not think

Mr Jabez Tuesday wishes to hire me as a cashier in any of his one-arm joints.

Anyway, I go to see Mr Tuesday at a Fifth Avenue hotel where he makes his home, and where he has a very swell layout of rooms, and I am by no means impressed with Mr Tuesday, as he hems and haws quite a bit before he tells me the nature of the employment he has in mind for me. He is a little guy, somewhat dried out, with a bald head, and a small mouser on his upper lip, and he wears specs, and seems somewhat nervous.

Well, it takes him some time to get down to cases, and tell me what is eating him, and what he wishes to do, and then it all sounds very simple, indeed, and in fact it sounds so simple that I think Mr Jabez Tuesday is a little daffy when he tells me he will give me ten G's for the job.

What Mr Tuesday wishes me to do is to get some letters that he personally writes to a doll by the name of Miss Amelia Bodkin, who lives in a house just outside Tarrytown, because it seems that Mr Tuesday makes certain cracks in these letters that he is now sorry for, such as speaking of love and marriage and one thing and another to Miss Amelia Bodkin, and he is afraid she is going to sue him for breach of promise.

'Such an idea will be very embarrassing to me,' Mr Jabez Tuesday says, 'as I am about to marry a party who is a member of one of the most high-toned families in this country. It is true,' Mr Tuesday says, 'that the Scarwater family does not have as much money now as formerly, but there is no doubt about its being very, very high-toned, and my fiancée, Miss Valerie Scarwater, is one of the high-tonedest of them all. In fact,' he says, 'she is so high-toned that the chances are she will be very huffy about anybody suing me for breach of promise, and cancel everything.'

Well, I ask Mr Tuesday what a breach of promise is, and he explains to me that it is when somebody promises to do something and fails to do this something, although of course we have a different name for a proposition of this nature in Brooklyn, and deal with it accordingly.

'This is a very easy job for a person of your standing,' Mr Tuesday says. 'Miss Amelia Bodkin lives all alone in her house the other side of Tarrytown, except for a couple of servants, and they are old and harmless. Now the idea is,' he says, 'you are not to go to her house as if you are looking for the letters, but as if you are after something else, such as her silverware, which is quite antique, and very valuable.

'She keeps the letters in a big inlaid box in her room,' Mr Tuesday says, 'and if you just pick up this box and carry it away along with the silverware, no one will ever suspect that you are after the letters, but that you take the box thinking it contains valuables. You bring the letters to me and get your ten G's,' Mr Tuesday says, 'and,' he says, 'you can keep the silverware, too. Be sure you get a Paul Revere teapot with the silverware,' he says. 'It is worth plenty.'

'Well,' I say to Mr Tuesday, 'every guy knows his own business best, and I do not wish to knock myself out of a nice soft job, but,' I say, 'it seems to me the simplest way of carrying on this transaction is to buy the letters off this doll, and be done with it. Personally,' I say, 'I do not believe there is a doll in the world who is not willing to sell a whole post-office full of letters for ten G's, especially in these times, and throw in a set of Shakespeare with them.'

'No, no,' Mr Tuesday says. 'Such a course will not do with Miss Amelia Bodkin at all. You see,' he says, 'Miss Bodkin and I are very, very friendly for a matter of maybe fifteen or sixteen years. In fact, we are very friendly, indeed. She does not have any idea at this time that I wish to break off this friendship with her. Now,' he says, 'if I try to buy the letters from her, she may become suspicious. The idea,' Mr Tuesday says, 'is for me to get the letters first, and then explain to her about breaking off the friendship, and make suitable arrangements with her afterwards.

'Do not get Miss Amelia Bodkin wrong,' Mr Tuesday says. 'She is an excellent person, but,' he says, 'you know the saying, "Hell hath no fury like a woman scorned". And maybe Miss Amelia Bodkin may figure I am scorning her if she finds out I am going to marry Miss Valerie Scarwater, and furthermore,' he says, 'if she still has the letters she may fall into the hands of unscrupulous lawyers, and demand a very large sum, indeed.

But,' Mr Tuesday says, 'this does not worry me half as much as the idea that Miss Valerie Scarwater may learn about the letters and get a wrong impression of my friendship with Miss Amelia Bodkin.'

Well, I round up Spanish John and Little Isadore the next afternoon, and I find Little Isadore playing klob with a guy by the name of Educated Edmund, who is called Educated Edmund because he once goes to Erasmus High School and is considered a very fine scholar, indeed, so I invite Educated Edmund to go along with us. The idea is, I know Educated Edmund makes a fair living playing klob with Little Isadore, and I figure as long as I am depriving Educated Edmund of a living for awhile, it is only courteous to toss something else his way. Furthermore, I figure as long as letters are involved in this proposition it may be a good thing to have Educated Edmund handy in case any reading becomes necessary, because Spanish John and Little Isadore do not read at all, and I read only large print.

We borrow a car off a friend of mine in Clinton Street, and with me driving we start for Tarrytown, which is a spot up the Hudson River, and it is a very enjoyable ride for one and all on account of the scenery. It is the first time Educated Edmund and Spanish John and Little Isadore ever see the scenery along the Hudson although they all reside on the banks of this beautiful river for several years at Ossining. Personally, I am never in Ossining, although once I make Auburn, and once Comstock, but the scenery in these localities is nothing to speak of.

We hit Tarrytown about dark, and follow the main drag through this burg, as Mr Tuesday tells me, until finally we come to the spot I am looking for, which is a little white cottage on a slope of ground above the river, not far off the highway. This little white cottage has quite a piece of ground around it, and a low stone wall, with a driveway from the highway to the house, and when I spot the gate to the driveway I make a quick turn, and what happens but I run the car slapdab into a stone gatepost, and the car folds up like an accordion.

You see, the idea is we are figuring to make this a fast stick-up job without any foolishness about it, maybe leaving any parties we come across tied up good and tight while we make a get-away, as I am greatly opposed to housebreaking, or sneak jobs, as I do not consider them dignified. Furthermore, they take too much time, so I am going to run the car right up to the front door when this stone post gets in my way.

The next thing I know, I open my eyes to find myself in a strange bed, and also in a strange bedroom, and while I wake up in many a strange bed in my time, I never wake up in such a strange bedroom as this. It is all very soft and dainty, and the only jarring note in my surroundings is Spanish John sitting beside the bed looking at me.

Naturally I wish to know what is what, and Spanish John says I am knocked snoring in the collision with the gatepost, although none of the others are hurt, and that while I am stretched in the driveway with the blood running out of a bad gash in my noggin, who pops out of the house but a doll and an old guy who seems to be a butler, or some such, and the doll insists on them lugging me into the house, and placing me in this bedroom.

Then she washes the blood off of me, Spanish John says, and wraps my head up and personally goes to Tarrytown to get a croaker to see if my wounds are fatal, or what, while Educated Edmund and Little Isadore are trying to patch up the car. So, Spanish John says, he is sitting there to watch me until she comes back, although of course I know what he is really sitting there for is to get first search of me in case I do not recover.

Well, while I am thinking all this over, and wondering what is to be done, in pops a doll of maybe forty odd, who is built from the ground up, but who has a nice, kind-looking pan, with a large smile, and behind her is a guy I can see at once is a croaker, especially as he is packing a little black bag, and has a grey goatee. I never see a nicer-looking doll if you care for middling-old dolls, although personally I like them young, and when she sees me with my eyes open, she speaks as follows:

'Oh,' she says, 'I am glad you are not dead, you poor chap. But,' she says, 'here is Doctor Diffingwell, and he will see how badly you are injured. My name is Miss Amelia Bodkin, and this is my house, and this is my own bedroom, and I am very, very sorry you are hurt.'

Well, naturally I consider this a most embarrassing situation, because here I am out to clip Miss Amelia Bodkin of her letters and her silverware, including her Paul Revere teapot, and there she is taking care of me in first-class style, and saying she is sorry for me.

But there seems to be nothing for me to say at this time, so I hold still while the croaker looks me over, and after he peeks at my noggin, and gives me a good feel up and down, he states as follows:

'This is a very bad cut,' he says. 'I will have to stitch it up, and then he must be very quiet for a few days, otherwise,' he says, 'complications may set in. It is best to move him to a hospital at once.'

But Miss Amelia Bodkin will not listen to such an idea as moving me to a hospital. Miss Amelia Bodkin says I must rest right where I am, and she will take care of me, because she says I am injured on her premises by her gatepost, and it is only fair that she does something for me. In fact, from the way Miss Amelia Bodkin takes on about me being moved, I figure maybe it is the old sex appeal, although afterwards I find out it is only because she is lonesome, and nursing me will give her something to do.

Well, naturally I am not opposing her idea, because the way I look at it, I will be able to handle the situation about the letters, and also the silverware, very nicely as an inside job, so I try to act even worse off than I am, although of course anybody who knows about the time I carry eight slugs in my body from Broadway and Fiftieth Street to Brooklyn will laugh very heartily at the idea of a cut on the noggin keeping me in bed.

After the croaker gets through sewing me up, and goes away, I tell Spanish John to take Educated Edmund and Little Isadore and go on back to New York, but to keep in touch with me by telephone, so I can tell them when to come back, and then I go to sleep, because I seem to be very tired. When I wake up later in the night, I seem to have a fever, and am really somewhat sick, and Miss Amelia Bodkin is sitting beside my bed swabbing my noggin with a cool cloth, which feels very pleasant, indeed.

I am better in the morning, and am able to knock over a little breakfast which she brings to me on a tray, and I am commencing to see where being an invalid is not so bad, at that, especially when there are no coppers at your bedside every time you open your eyes asking who does it to you.

I can see Miss Amelia Bodkin gets quite a bang out of having somebody to take care of, although of course if she knows who she is taking care of at this time, the chances are she will be running up the road calling for the gendarmes. It is not until after breakfast that I can get her to go and grab herself a little sleep, and while she is away sleeping the old guy who seems to be the butler is in and out of my room every now and then to see how I am getting along.

He is a gabby old guy, and pretty soon he is telling me all about Miss Amelia Bodkin, and what he tells me is that she is the old-time sweetheart of a guy in New York who is at the head of a big business, and very rich, and of course I know this guy is Mr Jabez Tuesday, although the old guy who seems to be the butler never mentions his name.

'They are together many years,' he says to me. 'He is very poor when they meet, and she has a little money, and establishes him in business, and by her management of this business, and of him, she makes it a very large business, indeed. I know, because I am with them almost from the start,' the old guy says. 'She is very smart in business, and also very kind, and nice, if anybody asks you.

'Now,' the old guy says, 'I am never able to figure out why they do not get married, because there is no doubt she loves him, and he loves her, but Miss Amelia Bodkin once tells me that it is because they are too poor at the start, and too busy later on to think of such things as getting married, and so they drift along the way they are, until all of a sudden he is rich. Then,' the old guy says, 'I can see he is getting away from her, although she never sees it herself, and I am not surprised when a few years ago he convinces her it is best for her to retire from active work, and move out to this spot.

'He comes out here fairly often at first,' the old guy says, 'but gradually he stretches the time between his visits, and now we do not see him once in a coon's age. Well,' the old guy says, 'it is just such a case as often comes up in life. In fact, I personally know of some others. But Miss Amelia Bodkin still thinks he loves her, and that only business keeps him away so much, so you can see she either is not as smart as she looks or is kidding herself. Well,' the old guy says, 'I will now bring you a little orange-juice, although I do not mind saying you do not look to me like a guy who drinks orange-juice as a steady proposition.'

Now I am taking many a gander around the bedroom to see if I can case the box of letters that Mr Jabez Tuesday speaks of, but there is no box such as he describes in sight. Then in the evening, when Miss Amelia Bodkin is in the room, and I seem to be dozing, she pulls out a drawer in the bureau, and hauls out a big inlaid box, and sits down at a table under a reading-lamp, and opens this box and begins reading some old letters. And as she sits there reading those letters, with me watching her through my eyelashes, sometimes she smiles, but once I see little tears rolling down her cheeks.

All of a sudden she looks at me, and catches me with my eyes wide open, and I can see her face turn red, and then she laughs, and speaks to me, as follows:

'Old love letters,' she says, tapping the box. 'From my old sweetheart,' she says. 'I read some of them every night of my life. Am I not foolish and sentimental to do such a thing?'

Well, I tell Miss Amelia Bodkin she is sentimental all right, but I do not tell her just how foolish she is to be letting me in on where she plants these letters, although of course I am greatly pleased to have this information. I tell Miss Amelia Bodkin that personally I never write a love-letter, and never get a love-letter, and in fact, while I hear of these propositions, I never even see a love-letter before, and this is all as true as you are a foot high. Then Miss Amelia Bodkin laughs a little, and says to me as follows:

'Why,' she says, 'you are a very unusual chap, indeed, not to know what a love-letter is like. Why,' she says, 'I think I will read you a few of the most wonderful love-letters in this world.

93

It will do no harm,' she says, 'because you do not know the writer, and you must lie there and think of me, not old and ugly, as you see me now, but as young, and maybe a little bit pretty.'

So Miss Amelia Bodkin opens a letter and reads it to me, and her voice is soft and low as she reads, but she scarcely ever looks at the letter as she is reading, so I can see she knows it pretty much by heart. Furthermore, I can see that she thinks this letter is quite a masterpiece, but while I am no judge of love-letters, because this is the first one I ever hear, I wish to say I consider it nothing but great nonsense.

'Sweetheart mine,' this love-letter says, 'I am still thinking of you as I see you yesterday standing in front of the house with the sunlight turning your dark brown hair to wonderful bronze. Darling,' it says, 'I love the colour of your hair. I am so glad you are not a blonde. I hate blondes, they are so emptyheaded, and mean, and deceitful. Also they are bad-tempered,' the letter says. 'I will never trust a blonde any farther than I can throw a bull by the tail. I never see a blonde in my life who is not a plumb washout,' it says. 'Most of them are nothing but peroxide, anyway. Business is improving,' it says. 'Sausage is going up. I love you now and always, my baby doll.'

Well, there are others worse than this, and all of them speak of her as sweetheart, or baby, or darlingest one, and also as loveykins, and precious, and angel, and I do not know what all else, and several of them speak of how things will be after they marry, and as I judge these are Mr Jabez Tuesday's letters, all right, I can see where they are full of dynamite for a guy who is figuring on taking a run-out powder on a doll. In fact, I say something to this general effect to Miss Amelia Bodkin, just for something to say.

'Why,' she says, 'what do you mean?'

'Well,' I say, 'documents such as these are known to bring large prices under certain conditions.'

Now Miss Amelia Bodkin looks at me a moment, as if wondering what is in my mind, and then she shakes her head as if she gives it up, and laughs and speaks as follows:

'Well,' she says, 'one thing is certain, my letters will never bring a price, no matter how large, under any conditions, even if anybody ever wants them. Why,' she says, 'these are my greatest treasure. They are my memories of my happiest days. Why,' she says, 'I will not part with these letters for a million dollars.'

Naturally I can see from this remark that Mr Jabez Tuesday makes a very economical deal with me at ten G's for the letters, but of course I do not mention this to Miss Amelia Bodkin as I watch her put her love-letters back in the inlaid box, and put the box back in the drawer of the bureau. I thank her for letting me hear the letters, and then I tell her good night, and I go to sleep, and the next day I telephone to a certain number in Clinton Street and leave word for Educated Edmund and Spanish John and Little Isadore to come and get me, as I am tired of being an invalid.

Now the next day is Saturday, and the day that comes after is bound to be Sunday, and they come to see me on Saturday, and promise to come back for me Sunday, as the car is now unravelled and running all right, although my friend in Clinton Street is beefing no little about the way his fenders are bent. But before they arrive Sunday morning, who is there ahead of them bright and early but Mr Jabez Tuesday in a big town car.

Furthermore, as he walks into the house, all dressed up in a cutaway coat, and a high hat, he grabs Miss Amelia Bodkin in his arms, and kisses her ker-plump right on the smush, which information I afterwards receive from the old guy who seems to be the butler. From upstairs I can personally hear Miss Amelia Bodkin crying more than somewhat, and then I hear Mr Jabez Tuesday speak in a loud, hearty voice as follows:

'Now, now, now, 'Mely,' Mr Tuesday says. 'Do not be crying, especially on my new white vest. Cheer up,' Mr Tuesday says, 'and listen to the arrangements I make for our wedding to-morrow, and our honeymoon in Montreal. Yes, indeed, 'Mely,' Mr Tuesday says, 'you are the only one for me, because you understand me from A to Izzard. Give me another big kiss, 'Mely, and let us sit down and talk things over.'

Well, I judge from the sound that he gets his kiss, and it is a very large kiss, indeed, with the cut-out open, and then I hear them chewing the rag at great length in the living-room downstairs. Finally I hear Mr Jabez Tuesday speak as follows:

'You know, 'Mely,' he says, 'you and I are just plain ordinary folks without any lugs, and,' he says, 'this is why we fit each other so well. I am sick and tired of people who pretend to be high-toned and mighty, when they do not have a white quarter to their name. They have no manners whatever. Why, only last night,' Mr Jabez Tuesday says, 'I am calling on a high-toned family in New York by the name of Scarwater, and out of a clear sky I am grossly insulted by the daughter of the house, and practically turned out in the street. I never receive such treatment in my life,' he says. ' 'Mely,' he says, 'give me another kiss, and see if you feel a bump here on my head.'

Of course, Mr Jabez Tuesday is somewhat surprised to see me present later on, but he never lets on he knows me, and naturally I do not give Mr Jabez any tumble whatever at the moment, and by and by Educated Edmund and Spanish John and Little Isadore come for me in the car, and I thank Miss Amelia Bodkin for her kindness to me, and leave her standing on the lawn with Mr Jabez Tuesday waving us good-bye.

And Miss Amelia Bodkin looks so happy as she snuggles up close to Mr Jabez Tuesday that I am glad I take the chance, which is always better than an even-money chance these days, that Miss Valerie Scarwater is a blonde, and send Educated Edmund to her to read her Mr Tuesday's letter in which he speaks of blondes. But of course I am sorry that this and other letters that I tell Educated Edmund to read to her heats her up so far as to make her forget she is a lady and causes her to slug Mr Jabez Tuesday on the bean with an 18-carat vanity case, as she tells him to get out of her life.

So [Harry the Horse says] there is nothing more to the story, except we are now looking for Judge Goldfobber to get him to take up a legal matter for us with Mr Jabez Tuesday. It is true Mr Tuesday pays us the ten G's, but he never lets us take the silverware he speaks of, not even the Paul Revere teapot, which he says is so valuable, and in fact when we drop around to Miss

Amelia Bodkin's house to pick up these articles one night not long ago, the old guy who seems to be the butler lets off a double-barrelled shotgun at us, and acts very nasty in general.

So [Harry says] we are going to see if we can get Judge Goldfobber to sue Mr Jabez Tuesday for breach of promise.

7 THE SNATCHING OF BOOKIE BOB

Now it comes on the spring of 1931, after a long hard winter, and times are very tough indeed, what with the stock market going all to pieces, and banks busting right and left, and the law getting very nasty about this and that, and one thing and another, and many citizens of this town are compelled to do the best they can.

There is very little scratch anywhere and along Broadway many citizens are wearing their last year's clothes and have practically nothing to bet on the races or anything else, and it is a condition that will touch anybody's heart.

So I am not surprised to hear rumours that the snatching of certain parties is going on in spots, because while snatching is by no means a high-class business, and is even considered somewhat illegal, it is something to tide over the hard times.

Furthermore, I am not surprised to hear that this snatching is being done by a character by the name of Harry the Horse, who comes from Brooklyn, and who is a character who does not care much what sort of business he is in, and who is mobbed up with other characters from Brooklyn such as Spanish John and Little Isadore, who do not care what sort of business they are in, either.

In fact, Harry the Horse and Spanish John and Little Isadore are very hard characters in every respect, and there is considerable indignation expressed around and about when they move over from Brooklyn into Manhattan and start snatching, because the citizens of Manhattan feel that if there is any snatching done in their territory, they are entitled to do it themselves.

But Harry the Horse and Spanish John and Little Isadore pay no attention whatever to local sentiment and go on the snatch on a pretty fair scale, and by and by I am hearing rumours of some very nice scores. These scores are not extra large scores, to be sure, but they are enough to keep the wolf from the door, and in fact from three different doors, and before long Harry the Horse and Spanish John and Little Isadore are around the race-tracks betting on the horses, because if there is one thing they are all very fond of, it is betting on the horses.

Now many citizens have the wrong idea entirely of the snatching business. Many citizens think that all there is to snatching is to round up the party who is to be snatched and then just snatch him, putting him away somewhere until his family or friends dig up enough scratch to pay whatever price the snatchers are asking. Very few citizens understand that the snatching business must be well organized and very systematic.

In the first place, if you are going to do any snatching, you cannot snatch just anybody. You must know who you are snatching, because naturally it is no good snatching somebody who does not have any scratch to settle with. And you cannot tell by the way a party looks or how he lives in this town if he has any scratch, because many a party who is around in automobiles, and wearing good clothes, and chucking quite a swell is nothing but the phonus bolonus and does not have any real scratch whatever.

So of course such a party is no good for snatching, and of course guys who are on the snatch cannot go around inquiring into bank accounts, or asking how much this and that party has in a safe-deposit vault, because such questions are apt to make citizens wonder why, and it is very dangerous to get citizens to wondering why about anything. So the only way guys who are on the snatch can find out about parties worth snatching is to make a connexion with some guy who can put the finger on the right party.

The finger guy must know the party he fingers has plenty of ready scratch to begin with, and he must also know that this party is such a party as is not apt to make too much disturbance about being snatched, such as telling the gendarmes. The party may be a legitimate party, such as a business guy, but he will have reasons why he does not wish it to get out that he is snatched, and the finger must know these reasons. Maybe the party is not leading the right sort of life, such as running around with blondes when he has an ever-loving wife and seven children in Mamaroneck, but does not care to have his habits known, as is apt to happen if he is snatched, especially if he is snatched when he is with a blonde.

And sometimes the party is such a party as does not care to have matches run up and down the bottom of his feet, which often happens to parties who are snatched and who do not seem to wish to settle their bill promptly, because many parties are very ticklish on the bottom of the feet, especially if the matches are lit. On the other hand, maybe the party is not a legitimate guy, such as a party who is running a crap game or a swell speakeasy, or who has some other dodge he does not care to have come out, and who also does not care about having his feet tickled.

Such a party is very good indeed for the snatching business, because he is pretty apt to settle without any argument. And after a party settles one snatching, it will be considered very unethical for anybody else to snatch him again very soon, so he is not likely to make any fuss about the matter. The finger guy gets a commission of twenty-five per cent of the settlement, and one and all are satisfied and much fresh scratch comes into circulation, which is very good for the merchants. And while the party who is snatched may know who snatches him, one thing he never knows is who puts the finger on him, this being considered a trade secret.

I am talking to Waldo Winchester, the newspaper scribe, one night and something about the snatching business comes up, and Waldo Winchester is trying to tell me that it is one of the oldest dodges in the world, only Waldo calls it kidnapping, which is a title that will be very repulsive to guys who are on the snatch nowadays. Waldo Winchester claims that hundreds of years ago guys are around snatching parties, male and female, and holding them for ransom, and furthermore Waldo Winchester says they even snatch very little children and Waldo states that it is all a very, very wicked proposition.

Well, I can see where Waldo is right about it being wicked to snatch dolls and little children, but of course no guys who are on the snatch nowadays will ever think of such a thing, because who is going to settle for a doll in these times when you can scarcely even give them away? As for little children, they are apt to be a great nuisance, because their mammas are sure to go running around hollering bloody murder about them, and furthermore little children are very dangerous, indeed, what with being apt to break out with measles and mumps and one thing and another any minute and give it to everybody in the neighbourhood.

Well, anyway, knowing that Harry the Horse and Spanish John and Little Isadore are now on the snatch, I am by no means pleased to see them coming along one Tuesday evening when I am standing at the corner of Fiftieth and Broadway, although of course I give them a very jolly hello, and say I hope and trust they are feeling nicely.

They stand there talking to me a few minutes, and I am very glad indeed that Johnny Brannigan, the strong-arm cop, does not happen along and see us, because it will give Johnny a very bad impression of me to see me in such company, even though I am not responsible for the company. But naturally I cannot haul off and walk away from this company at once, because Harry the Horse and Spanish John and Little Isadore may get the idea that I am playing the chill for them, and will feel hurt.

'Well,' I say to Harry the Horse, 'how are things going, Harry?'

'They are going no good,' Harry says. 'We do not beat a race in four days. In fact,' he says, 'we go overboard to-day. We are washed out. We owe every bookmaker at the track that will trust us, and now we are out trying to raise some scratch to pay off. A guy must pay his bookmaker no matter what.'

Well, of course this is very true, indeed, because if a guy does not pay his bookmaker it will lower his business standing quite some, as the bookmaker is sure to go around putting the blast on him, so I am pleased to hear Harry the Horse mention such honourable principles.

'By the way,' Harry says, 'do you know a guy by the name of Bookie Bob?'

Now I do not know Bookie Bob personally, but of course I know who Bookie Bob is, and so does everybody else in this town that ever goes to a race-track, because Bookie Bob is the biggest bookmaker around and about, and has plenty of scratch. Furthermore, it is the opinion of one and all that Bookie Bob will die with this scratch, because he is considered a very close guy with his scratch. In fact, Bookie Bob is considered closer than a dead heat.

He is a short fat guy with a bald head, and his head is always shaking a little from side to side, which some say is a touch of palsy, but which most citizens believe comes of Bookie Bob shaking his head 'No' to guys asking for credit in betting on the races. He has an ever-loving wife, who is a very quiet little old doll with grey hair and a very sad look in her eyes, but nobody can blame her for this when they figure that she lives with Bookie Bob for many years.

I often see Bookie Bob and his ever-loving wife eating in different joints along in the Forties, because they seem to have no home except an hotel, and many a time I hear Bookie Bob giving her a going-over about something or other, and generally it is about the price of something she orders to eat, so I judge Bookie Bob is as tough with his ever-loving wife about scratch as he is with everybody else. In fact, I hear him bawling her out one night because she has on a new hat which she says cost her six bucks, and Bookie Bob wishes to know if she is trying to ruin him with her extravagances.

But of course I am not criticizing Bookie Bob for squawking about the hat, because for all I know six bucks may be too much for a doll to pay for a hat, at that. And furthermore, maybe Bookie Bob has the right idea about keeping down his ever-loving wife's appetite, because I know many a guy in this town who is practically ruined by dolls eating too much on him.

'Well,' I say to Harry the Horse, 'if Bookie Bob is one of the bookmakers you owe, I am greatly surprised to see that you seem to have both eyes in your head, because I never before hear of Bookie Bob letting anybody owe him without giving him at least one of their eyes for security. In fact,' I say, 'Bookie Bob is such a guy as will not give you the right time if he has two watches.'

'No,' Harry the Horse says, 'we do not owe Bookie Bob. But,' he says, 'he will be owing us before long. We are going to put the snatch on Bookie Bob.'

Well, this is most disquieting news to me, not because I care if they snatch Bookie Bob or not, but because somebody may see me talking to them who will remember about it when Bookie Bob is snatched. But of course it will not be good policy for me to show Harry the Horse and Spanish John and Little Isadore that I am nervous, so I only speak as follows:

'Harry,' I say, 'every man knows his own business best, and I judge you know what you are doing. But,' I say, 'you are snatching a hard guy when you snatch Bookie Bob. A very hard guy, indeed. In fact,' I say, 'I hear the softest thing about him is his front teeth, so it may be very difficult for you to get him to settle after you snatch him.'

'No,' Harry the Horse says, 'we will have no trouble about it. Our finger gives us Bookie Bob's hole card, and it is a most surprising thing, indeed. But,' Harry the Horse says, 'you come upon many surprising things in human nature when you are on the snatch. Bookie Bob's hole card is his ever-loving wife's opinion of him.

'You see,' Harry the Horse says, 'Bookie Bob has been putting himself away with his ever-loving wife for years as a very important guy in this town, with much power and influence, although of course Bookie Bob knows very well he stands about as good as a broken leg. In fact,' Harry the Horse says, 'Bookie Bob figures that his ever-loving wife is the only one in the world who looks on him as a big guy, and he will sacrifice even his scratch, or anyway some of it, rather than let her know that guys have such little respect for him as to put the snatch on him. It is what you call psychology,' Harry the Horse says.

Well, this does not make good sense to me, and I am thinking to myself that the psychology that Harry the Horse really figures to work out nice on Bookie Bob is tickling his feet with matches, but I am not anxious to stand there arguing about it, and pretty soon I bid them all good evening, very polite, and take the wind, and I do not see Harry the Horse or Spanish John or Little Isadore again for a month.

In the meantime, I hear gossip here and there that Bookie Bob is missing for several days, and when he finally shows up again he gives it out that he is very sick during his absence, but I can put two and two together as well as anybody in this town and I figure that Bookie Bob is snatched by Harry the Horse and Spanish John and Little Isadore, and the chances are it costs him plenty.

So I am looking for Harry the Horse and Spanish John and Little Isadore to be around the race-track with plenty of scratch and betting them higher than a cat's back, but they never show up, and what is more I hear they leave Manhattan, and are back in Brooklyn working every day handling beer. Naturally this is very surprising to me, because the way things are running beer is a tough dodge just now, and there is very little profit in same, and I figure that with the scratch they must make off Bookie Bob, Harry the Horse and Spanish John and Little Isadore have a right to be taking things easy.

Now one night I am in Good Time Charley Bernstein's little speak in Forty-eighth Street, talking of this and that with Charley, when in comes Harry the Horse, looking very weary and by no means prosperous. Naturally I gave him a large hello, and by and by we get to gabbing together and I ask him whatever becomes of the Bookie Bob matter, and Harry the Horse tells me as follows:

Yes [Harry the Horse says], we snatch Bookie Bob all right. In fact, we snatch him the very next night after we are talking to you, or on a Wednesday night. Our finger tells us Bookie Bob is going to a wake over in his old neighbourhood on Tenth Avenue, near Thirty-eighth Street, and this is where we pick him up.

He is leaving the place in his car along about midnight, and of course Bookie Bob is alone as he seldom lets anybody ride with him because of the wear and tear on his car cushions, and Little

Isadore swings our flivver in front of him and makes him stop. Naturally Bookie Bob is greatly surprised when I poke my head into his car and tell him I wish the pleasure of his company for a short time, and at first he is inclined to argue the matter, saying I must make a mistake, but I put the old convincer on him by letting him peek down the snozzle of my John Roscoe.

We lock his car and throw the keys away, and then we take Bookie Bob in our car and go to a certain spot on Eighth Avenue where we have a nice little apartment all ready. When we get there I tell Bookie Bob that he can call up anybody he wishes and state that the snatch is on him and that it will require twenty-five G's, cash money, to take it off, but of course I also tell Bookie Bob that he is not to mention where he is or something may happen to him.

Well, I will say one thing for Bookie Bob, although everybody is always weighing in the sacks on him and saying he is no good – he takes it like a gentleman, and very calm and businesslike.

Furthermore, he does not seem alarmed, as many citizens are when they find themselves in such a situation. He recognizes the justice of our claim at once, saying as follows:

'I will telephone my partner, Sam Salt,' he says. 'He is the only one I can think of who is apt to have such a sum as twenty-five G's cash money. But,' he says, 'if you gentlemen will pardon the question, because this is a new experience to me, how do I know everything will be okay for me after you get the scratch?'

'Why,' I say to Bookie Bob, somewhat indignant, 'it is well known to one and all in this town that my word is my bond. There are two things I am bound to do,' I say, 'and one is to keep my word in such a situation as this, and the other is to pay anything I owe a bookmaker, no matter what, for these are obligations of honour with me.'

'Well,' Bookie Bob says, 'of course I do not know you gentlemen, and, in fact, I do not remember ever seeing any of you, although your face is somewhat familiar, but if you pay your bookmaker you are an honest guy, and one in a million. In fact,' Bookie Bob says, 'if I have all the scratch that is owing to me around this town, I will not be telephoning anybody for such a sum as twenty-five G's. I will have such a sum in my pants pocket for change.'

Now Bookie Bob calls a certain number and talks to somebody there but he does not get Sam Salt, and he seems much disappointed when he hangs up the receiver again.

'This is a very tough break for me,' he says. 'Sam Salt goes to Atlantic City an hour ago on very important business and will not be back until to-morrow evening, and they do not know where he is to stay in Atlantic City. And,' Bookie Bob says, 'I cannot think of anybody else to call up to get this scratch, especially anybody I will care to have know I am in this situation.'

'Why not call your ever-loving wife?' I say. 'Maybe she can dig up this kind of scratch.'

'Say,' Bookie Bob says, 'you do not suppose I am chump enough to give my ever-loving wife twenty-five G's, or even let her know where she can get her dukes on twenty-five G's belonging to me, do you? I give my ever-loving wife ten bucks per week for spending money,' Bookie Bob says, 'and this is enough scratch for any doll, especially when you figure I pay for her meals.'

Well, there seems to be nothing we can do except wait until Sam Salt gets back, but we let Bookie Bob call his ever-loving wife, as Bookie Bob says he does not wish to have her worrying about his absence, and tells her a big lie about having to go to Jersey City to sit up with a sick Brother Elk.

Well, it is now nearly four o'clock in the morning, so we put Bookie Bob in a room with Little Isadore to sleep, although, personally, I consider making a guy sleep with Little Isadore very cruel treatment, and Spanish John and I take turns keeping awake and watching out that Bookie Bob does not take the air on us before paying us off. To tell the truth, Little Isadore and Spanish John are somewhat disappointed that Bookie Bob agrees to settle so promptly, because they are looking forward to tickling his feet with great relish.

Now Bookie Bob turns out to be very good company when he wakes up the next morning, because he knows a lot of race-track stories and plenty of scandal, and he keeps us much interested at breakfast. He talks along with us as if he knows us all his life, and he seems very nonchalant indeed, but the chances are he will not be so nonchalant if I tell him about Spanish John's thought.

Well, about noon Spanish John goes out of the apartment and comes back with a racing sheet, because he knows Little Isadore and I will be wishing to know what is running in different spots although we do not have anything to bet on these races, or any way of betting on them, because we are overboard with every bookmaker we know.

Now Bookie Bob is also much interested in the matter of what is running, especially at Belmont, and he is bending over the table with me and Spanish John and Little Isadore, looking at the sheet, when Spanish John speaks as follows:

'My goodness,' Spanish John says, 'a spot such as this fifth race with Questionnaire at four to five is like finding money in the street. I only wish I have a few bobs to bet on him at such a price,' Spanish John says.

'Why,' Bookie Bob says, very polite, 'if you gentlemen wish to bet on these races I will gladly book to you. It is a good way to pass away the time while we are waiting for Sam Salt, unless you will rather play pinochle?'

'But,' I say, 'we have no scratch to play the races, at least not much.'

'Well,' Bookie Bob says, 'I will take your markers, because I hear what you say about always paying your bookmaker, and you put yourself away with me as an honest guy, and these other gentlemen also impress me as honest guys.'

Now what happens but we begin betting Bookie Bob on the different races, not only at Belmont, but at all the other tracks in the country, for Little Isadore and Spanish John and I are guys who like plenty of action when we start betting on the horses. We write out markers for whatever we wish to bet and hand them to Bookie Bob, and Bookie Bob sticks these markers in an inside pocket, and along in the late afternoon it looks as if he has a tumour on his chest.

We get the race results by phone off a poolroom down-town as fast as they come off, and also the prices, and it is a lot of fun, and Little Isadore and Spanish John and Bookie Bob and I are all little pals together until all the races are over and Bookie Bob takes out the markers and starts counting himself up.

It comes out then that I owe Bookie Bob ten G's, and Spanish John owes him six G's, and Little Isadore owes him four G's, as Little Isadore beats him a couple of races out west.

Well, about this time, Bookie Bob manages to get Sam Salt on the phone, and explains to Sam that he is to go to a certain safe-deposit box and get out twenty-five G's, and then wait until midnight and hire himself a taxicab and start riding around the block between Fifty-first and Fifty-second, from Eighth to Ninth avenues, and to keep riding until somebody flags the cab and takes the scratch off him.

Naturally Sam Salt understands right away that the snatch is on Bookie Bob, and he agrees to do as he is told, but he says he cannot do it until the following night because he knows there is not twenty-five G's in the box, and he will have to get the difference at the track the next day. So there we are with another day in the apartment and Spanish John and Little Isadore and I are just as well pleased because Bookie Bob has us hooked and we naturally wish to wiggle off.

But the next day is worse than ever. In all the years I am playing the horses I never have such a tough day, and Spanish John and Little Isadore are just as bad. In fact, we are all going so bad that Bookie Bob seems to feel sorry for us and often lays us a couple of points above the track prices, but it does no good. At the end of the day, I am in a total of twenty G's, while Spanish John owes fifteen, and Little Isadore fifteen, a total of fifty G's among the three of us. But we are never any hands to hold post-mortems on bad days, so Little Isadore goes out to a delicatessen store and lugs in a lot of nice things to eat, and we have a fine dinner, and then we sit around with Bookie Bob telling stories, and even singing a few songs together until time to meet Sam Salt.

When it comes on midnight Spanish John goes out and lays for Sam, and gets a little valise off of Sam Salt. Then Spanish John comes back to the apartment and we open the valise and the twenty-five G's are there okay, and we cut this scratch three ways.

Then I tell Bookie Bob he is free to go on about his business, and good luck to him, at that, but Bookie Bob looks at me as if he is very much surprised, and hurt, and says to me like this:

'Well, gentlemen, thank you for your courtesy, but what about the scratch you owe me? What about these markers? Surely, gentlemen, you will pay your bookmaker?'

Well, of course we owe Bookie Bob these markers, all right, and of course a man must pay his bookmaker, no matter what, so I hand over my bit and Bookie Bob puts down something in a little note-book that he takes out of his kick.

Then Spanish John and Little Isadore hand over their dough, too, and Bookie Bob puts down something more in the little note-book.

'Now,' Bookie Bob says, 'I credit each of your accounts with these payments, but you gentlemen still owe me a matter of twenty-five G's over and above the twenty-five I credit you with, and I hope and trust you will make arrangements to settle this at once because,' he says, 'I do not care to extend such accommodations over any considerable period.'

'But,' I say, 'we do not have any more scratch after paying you the twenty-five G's on account.'

'Listen,' Bookie Bob says, dropping his voice down to a whisper, 'what about putting the snatch on my partner, Sam Salt, and I will wait over a couple of days with you and keep booking to you, and maybe you can pull yourselves out. But of course,' Bookie Bob whispers, 'I will be entitled to twenty-five per cent of the snatch for putting the finger on Sam for you.'

But Spanish John and Little Isadore are sick and tired of Bookie Bob and will not listen to staying in the apartment any longer, because they say he is a jinx to them and they cannot beat him in any manner, shape, or form. Furthermore, I am personally anxious to get away because something Bookie Bob says reminds me of something.

It reminds me that besides the scratch we owe him, we forget to take out six G's two-fifty for the party who puts the finger on Bookie Bob for us, and this is a very serious matter indeed, because anybody will tell you that failing to pay a finger is considered a very dirty trick. Furthermore, if it gets around that you fail to pay a finger, nobody else will ever finger for you.

So [Harry the Horse says] we quit the snatching business because there is no use continuing while this obligation is outstanding against us, and we go back to Brooklyn to earn enough scratch to pay our just debts.

We are paying off Bookie Bob's IOU a little at a time, because we do not wish to ever have anybody say we welsh on a bookmaker, and furthermore we are paying off the six G's two-fifty commission we owe our finger.

And while it is tough going, I am glad to say our honest effort is doing somebody a little good, because I see Bookie Bob's ever-loving wife the other night all dressed up in new clothes and looking very happy, indeed.

And while a guy is telling me she is looking so happy because she gets a large legacy from an uncle who dies in Switzerland, and is now independent of Bookie Bob, I only hope and trust [Harry the Horse says] that it never gets out that our finger in this case is nobody but Bookie Bob's ever-loving wife.

8 THE BLOODHOUNDS OF BROADWAY

ONE morning along about four bells, I am standing in front of Mindy's restaurant on Broadway with a guy by the name of Regret, who has this name because it seems he wins a very large bet the year the Whitney filly, Regret, grabs the Kentucky Derby, and can never forget it, which is maybe because it is the only very large bet he ever wins in his life.

What this guy's real name is I never hear, and anyway names make no difference to me, especially on Broadway, because the chances are that no matter what name a guy has, it is not his square name. So, as far as I am concerned, Regret is as good a name as any other for this guy I am talking about, who is a fat guy, and very gabby, though generally he is talking about nothing but horses, and how he gets beat three dirty noses the day before at Belmont, or wherever the horses are running.

In all the years I know Regret he must get beat ten thousand noses, and always they are dirty noses, to hear him tell it. In fact, I never once hear him say he is beat a clean nose, but of course this is only the way horse-racing guys talk. What Regret does for a living besides betting on horses I do not know, but he seems to do pretty well at it, because he is always around and about, and generally well dressed, and with a lot of big cigars sticking up out of his vest pocket.

It is generally pretty quiet on Broadway along about four bells in the morning, because at such an hour the citizens are mostly in speakeasies, and night clubs, and on this morning I am talking about it is very quiet indeed, except for a guy by the name of Marvin Clay hollering at a young doll because she will not get into a taxicab with him to go to his apartment. But of course Regret and I do not pay much attention to such a scene, except that Regret remarks that the young doll seems to have more sense than you will expect to see in a doll loose on Broadway at four bells in the morning, because it is well known to one and all that any doll who goes to Marvin Clay's apartment either has no brains whatever, or wishes to go there.

This Marvin Clay is a very prominent society guy, who is a great hand for hanging out in night clubs, and he has plenty of scratch which comes down to him from his old man, who makes it out of railroads and one thing and another. But Marvin Clay is a most obnoxious character, being loud and ungentlemanly at all times, on account of having all this scratch, and being always very rough and abusive with young dolls such as work in night clubs, and who have to stand for such treatment from Marvin Clay because he is a very good customer.

He is generally in evening clothes, as he is seldom around and about except in the evening, and he is maybe fifty years old, and has a very ugly mugg, which is covered with blotches, and pimples, but of course a guy who has so much scratch as Marvin Clay does not have to be so very handsome, at that, and he is very welcome indeed wherever he goes on Broadway. Personally, I wish no part of such a guy as Marvin Clay, although I suppose in my time on Broadway I must see a thousand guys like him, and there will always be guys like Marvin Clay on Broadway as long as they have old men to make plenty of scratch out of railroads to keep them going.

Well, by and by Marvin Clay gets the doll in the taxicab, and away they go, and it is all quiet again on Broadway, and Regret and I stand there speaking of this and that, and one thing and another, when along comes a very strange-looking guy leading two very strange-looking dogs. The guy is so thin I figure he must be about two pounds lighter than a sack of wheats. He has a long nose, and a sad face, and he is wearing a floppy old black felt hat, and he has on a flannel shirt, and baggy corduroy pants, and a see-more coat, which is a coat that lets you see more hip pockets than coat.

Personally, I never see a stranger-looking guy on Broadway,

and I wish to say I see some very strange-looking guys on Broadway in my day. But if the guy is strange-looking, the dogs are even stranger-looking because they have big heads and jowls that hang down like an old-time faro bank dealer's, and long ears the size of bed sheets. Furthermore, they have wrinkled faces, and big, round eyes that seem so sad I half expect to see them bust out crying.

The dogs are a sort of black and yellow in colour, and have long tails, and they are so thin you can see their ribs sticking out of their hides. I can see at once that the dogs and the guy leading them can use a few Hamburgers very nicely, but then so can a lot of other guys on Broadway at this time, leaving out the dogs.

Well, Regret is much interested in the dogs right away, because he is a guy who is very fond of animals of all kinds, and nothing will do but he must stop the guy and start asking questions about what sort of dogs they are, and in fact I am also anxious to hear myself, because while I see many a pooch in my time I never see anything like these.

'They is bloodhounds,' the sad-looking guy says in a very sad voice, and with one of these accents such as Southern guys always have. 'They is man-tracking bloodhounds from Georgia.'

Now of course both Regret and me know what bloodhounds are because we see such animals chasing Eliza across the ice in *Uncle Tom's Cabin* when we are young squirts, but this is the first time either of us meet up with any bloodhounds personally, especially on Broadway. So we get to talking quite a bit to the guy, and his story is as sad as his face, and makes us both feel very sorry for him.

In fact, the first thing we know we have him and the bloodhounds in Mindy's and are feeding one and all big steaks, although Mindy puts up an awful squawk about us bringing the dogs in, and asks us what we think he is running, anyway. When Regret starts to tell him, Mindy says never mind, but not to bring any more Shetland ponies into his joint again as long as we live.

Well, it seems that the sad-looking guy's name is John Wangle, and he comes from a town down in Georgia where his uncle is the high sheriff, and one of the bloodhounds' name is Nip, and the other Tuck, and they are both trained from infancy to track down guys such as lags who escape from the county pokey, and bad niggers, and one thing and another, and after John Wangle gets the kinks out of his belly on Mindy's steaks, and starts talking good, you must either figure him a high-class liar, or the hounds the greatest man-trackers the world ever sees.

Now, looking at the dogs after they swallow six big sirloins apiece, and a lot of matzoths, which Mindy has left over from the Jewish holidays, and a job lot of goulash from the dinner bill, and some other odds and ends, the best I can figure them is hearty eaters, because they are now lying down on the floor with their faces hidden behind their ears, and are snoring so loud you can scarcely hear yourself think.

How John Wangle comes to be in New York with these bloodhounds is quite a story, indeed. It seems that a New York guy drifts into John's old home town in Georgia when the bloodhounds are tracking down a bad nigger, and this guy figures it will be a wonderful idea to take John Wangle and the dogs to New York and hire them out to the movies to track down the villains in the pictures. But when they get to New York, it seems the movies have other arrangements for tracking down their villains, and the guy runs out of scratch and blows away, leaving John Wangle and the bloodhounds stranded.

So here John Wangle is with Nip and Tuck in New York, and they are all living together in one room in a tenement house over in West Forty-ninth Street, and things are pretty tough with them, because John does not know how to get back to Georgia unless he walks, and he hears the walking is no good south of Roanoke. When I ask him why he does not write to his uncle, the high sheriff down there in Georgia, John Wangle says there are two reasons, one being that he cannot write, and the other that his uncle cannot read.

Then I ask him why he does not sell the bloodhounds, and he says it is because the market for bloodhounds is very quiet in New York, and furthermore if he goes back to Georgia without the bloodhounds his uncle is apt to knock his ears down. Anyway, John Wangle says he personally loves Nip and Tuck very dearly, and in fact he says it is only his great love for them that keeps him from eating one or the other and maybe both, the past week, when his hunger is very great indeed.

Well, I never before see Regret so much interested in any situation as he is in John Wangle and the bloodhounds, but personally I am getting very tired of them, because the one that is called Nip finally wakes up and starts chewing on my leg, thinking it is maybe more steak, and when I kick him in the snoot, John Wangle scowls at me, and Regret says only very mean guys are unkind to dumb animals.

But to show you that John Wangle and his bloodhounds are not so dumb, they come moseying along past Mindy's every morning after this at about the same time, and Regret is always there ready to feed them, although he now has to take the grub out on the sidewalk, as Mindy will not allow the hounds in the joint again. Naturally Nip and Tuck become very fond of Regret, but they are by no means as fond of him as John Wangle, because John is commencing to fat up very nicely, and the bloodhounds are also taking on weight.

Now what happens but Regret does not show up in front of Mindy's for several mornings hand running, because it seems that Regret makes a very nice score for himself one day against the horses, and buys himself a brand-new Tuxedo, and starts stepping out around the night clubs, and especially around Miss Missouri Martin's Three Hundred Club, where there are many beautiful young dolls who dance around with no more clothes on them than will make a pad for a crutch, and it is well known that Regret dearly loves such scenes.

Furthermore, I hear reports around and about of Regret becoming very fond of a doll by the name of Miss Lovey Lou, who works in Miss Missouri Martin's Three Hundred Club, and of him getting in some kind of a jam with Marvin Clay over this doll, and smacking Marvin Clay in the kisser, so I figure Regret is getting a little simple, as guys who hang around Broadway long enough are bound to do. Now, when John Wangle and Nip and Tuck come around looking for a hand-out, there is nothing much doing for them, as nobody else around Mindy's feels any great interest in bloodhounds, especially such interest as will cause them to buy steaks, and soon Nip and Tuck are commencing to look very sad again, and John Wangle is downcast more than somewhat.

It is early morning again, and warm, and a number of citizens are out in front of Mindy's as usual, breathing the fresh air, when along comes a police inspector by the name of McNamara, who is a friend of mine, with a bunch of plain-clothes coppers with him, and Inspector McNamara tells me he is on his way to investigate a situation in an apartment house over in West Fifty-fourth Street, about three blocks away, where it seems a guy is shot; and not having anything else to do, I go with them, although as a rule I do not care to associate with coppers, because it arouses criticism from other citizens.

Well, who is the guy who is shot but Marvin Clay, and he is stretched out on the floor in the living-room of his apartment in evening clothes, with his shirt front covered with blood, and after Inspector McNamara takes a close peek at him, he sees that Marvin Clay is plugged smack dab in the chest, and that he seems to be fairly dead. Furthermore, there seems to be no clue whatever to who does the shooting, and Inspector McNamara says it is undoubtedly a very great mystery, and will be duck soup for the newspapers, especially as they do not have a good shooting mystery for several days.

Well, of course all this is none of my business, but all of a sudden I happen to think of John Wangle and his bloodhounds, and it seems to me it will be a great opportunity for them, so I say to the Inspector as follows:

'Listen, Mac,' I say, 'there is a guy here with a pair of man-tracking bloodhounds from Georgia who are very expert in tracking down matters such as this, and,' I say, 'maybe they can track down the rascal who shoots Marvin Clay, because the trail must be hotter than mustard right now.'

Well, afterwards I hear there is much indignation over my suggestion, because many citizens feel that the party who shoots Marvin Clay is entitled to more consideration than being tracked with bloodhounds. In fact, some think the party is entitled to a medal, but this discussion does not come up until later.

Anyway, at first the Inspector does not think much of my idea, and the other coppers are very sceptical, and claim that the best way to do under the circumstances is to arrest everybody in sight and hold them as material witnesses for a month or so, but the trouble is there is nobody in sight to arrest at this time, except maybe me, and the Inspector is a broad-minded guy and finally he says all right, bring on the bloodhounds.

So I hasten back to Mindy's, and sure enough John Wangle and Nip and Tuck are out on the sidewalk peering at every passing face in the hope that maybe one of these faces will belong to Regret. It is a very pathetic sight, indeed, but John Wangle cheers up when I explain about Marvin Clay to him, and hurries back to the apartment house with me so fast that he stretches Nip's neck a foot, and is pulling Tuck along on his stomach half the time.

Well, when we get back to the apartment, John Wangle leads Nip and Tuck up to Marvin Clay, and they snuffle him all over, because it seems bloodhounds are quite accustomed to dead guys. Then John Wangle unhooks their leashes, and yells something at them, and the hounds begin snuffling all around and about the joint, with Inspector McNamara and the other coppers watching with great interest. All of a sudden Nip and Tuck go busting out of the apartment and into the street, with John Wangle after them, and all the rest of us after John Wangle. They head across Fifty-fourth Street back to Broadway, and the next thing anybody knows they are doing plenty of snuffling around in front of Mindy's.

By and by they take off up Broadway with their snozzles to the sidewalk, and we follow them very excited, because even the coppers now admit that it seems to be a sure thing they are red hot on the trail of the party who shoots Marvin Clay. At first Nip and Tuck are walking, but pretty soon they break into a lope, and there we are loping after them, John Wangle, the Inspector, and me, and the coppers.

Naturally, such a sight as this attracts quite some attention as we go along from any citizens stirring at this hour, and by and by milkmen are climbing down off their wagons, and scavenger guys are leaving their trucks standing where they are, and newsboys are dropping everything, and one and all joining in the chase, so by the time we hit Broadway and Fifty-sixth there is quite a delegation following the hounds with John Wangle in front, just behind Nip and Tuck, and yelling at them now and then as follows:

'Hold to it, boys!'

At Fifty-sixth the hounds turn east off Broadway and stop at the door of what seems to be an old garage, this door being closed very tight, and Nip and Tuck seem to wish to get through this door, so the Inspector and the coppers kick the door open, and who is in the garage having a big crap game but many prominent citizens of Broadway. Naturally, these citizens are greatly astonished at seeing the bloodhounds, and the rest of us, especially the coppers, and they start running every which way trying to get out of the joint, because crap shooting is quite illegal in these parts.

But the Inspector only says Ah-ha, and starts jotting down names in a note-book as if it is something he will refer to later, and Nip and Tuck are out of the joint almost as soon as they get in and are snuffling on down Fifty-sixth. They stop at four more doors in Fifty-sixth Street along, and when the coppers kick open these doors they find they are nothing but speakeasies, although one is a hop joint, and the citizens in these places are greatly put out by the excitement, especially as Inspector McNamara keeps jotting down things in his note-book.

Finally the Inspector starts glaring very fiercely at the coppers with us, and anybody can see that he is much displeased to find so much illegality going on in this district, and the coppers are starting in to hate Nip and Tuck quite freely, and one copper says to me like this:

'Why,' he says, 'these mutts are nothing but stool pigeons.'

Well, naturally, the noise of John Wangle's yelling, and the gabble of the mob following the hounds, makes quite a disturbance, and arouses many of the neighbours in the apartment houses and hotels in the side streets, especially as this is summer, and most everybody has their windows open.

In fact, we see many tousled heads poked out of windows, and hear guys and dolls inquiring as follows:

'What is going on?'

It seems that when word gets about that bloodhounds are tracking down a wrongdoer it causes great uneasiness all through the Fifties, and in fact I afterwards hear that three guys are taken to the Polyclinic suffering with broken ankles and severe bruises from hopping out of windows in the hotels we pass in the chase, or from falling off of fire-escapes.

Well, all of a sudden Nip and Tuck swing back into Seventh Avenue, and pop into the entrance of a small apartment house, and go tearing up the stairs to the first floor, and when we get there these bloodhounds are scratching vigorously at the door of Apartment B-2, and going woofle-woofle, and we are all greatly excited, indeed, but the door opens, and who is standing there but a doll by the name of Maud Milligan, who is well known to one and all as the ever-loving doll of Big Nig, the crap shooter, who is down in Hot Springs at this time taking the waters, or whatever it is guys take in Hot Springs.

Now, Maud Milligan is not such a doll as I will care to have any part of, being red-headed, and very stern, and I am glad Nip and Tuck do not waste any more time in her apartment than it takes for them to run through her living-room and across her bed, because Maud is commencing to put the old eye on such of us present as she happens to know. But Nip and Tuck are in and out of the joint before you can say cat, because it is only a two-room apartment, at that, and we are on our way down the stairs and back into Seventh Avenue again while Inspector McNamara is still jotting down something in his notebook.

Finally, where do these hounds wind up, with about four hundred citizens behind them, and everybody perspiring quite freely indeed from the exercise, but at the door of Miss Missouri Martin's Three Hundred Club, and the doorman, who is a guy by the name of Soldier Sweeney, tries to shoo them away, but Nip runs between the Soldier's legs and upsets him, and Tuck steps in the Soldier's eye in trotting over him, and most of the crowd behind the hounds tread on him in passing, so the old Soldier is pretty well flattened out at the finish.

Nip and Tuck are now more excited than somewhat, and are going zoople-zoople in loud voices as they bust into the Three

Hundred Club with John Wangle and the law, and all these citizens behind them. There is a very large crowd present and Miss Missouri Martin is squatted on the back of a chair in the middle of the dance floor when we enter, and is about to start her show when she sees the mob surge in, and at first she is greatly pleased because she thinks new business arrives, and if there is anything Miss Missouri Martin dearly loves, it is new business.

But before she can say hello, sucker, or anything else whatever, Nip runs under her chair, thinking maybe he is a dachshund, and dumps Miss Missouri Martin on the dance floor, and she lays there squawking no little, while the next thing anybody knows, Nip and Tuck are over in one corner of the joint, and are eagerly crawling up and down a fat guy who is sitting there with a doll alongside of him, and who is the fat guy but Regret!

Well, as Nip and Tuck rush at Regret he naturally gets up to defend himself, but they both hit him at the same time, and over he goes on top of the doll who is with him, and who seems to be nobody but Miss Lovey Lou. She is getting quite a squashing with Regret's heft spread out over her, and she is screaming quite some, especially when Nip lets out a foot of tongue and washes her make-up off her face, reaching for Regret. In fact, Miss Lovey Lou seems to be more afraid of the bloodhounds than she does of being squashed to death, for when John Wangle and I hasten to her rescue and pull her out from under Regret she is moaning as follows:

'Oh, do not let them devour me – I will confess.'

Well, as nobody but me and John Wangle seem to hear this crack, because everybody else is busy trying to split out Regret and the bloodhounds, and as John Wangle does not seem to understand what Miss Lovey Lou is mumbling about, I shove her off into the crowd, and on back into the kitchen, which is now quite deserted, what with all the help being out watching the muss in the corner, and I say to her like this:

'What is it you confess?' I say. 'Is it about Marvin Clay?'

'Yes,' she says. 'It is about him. He is a pig,' she says. 'I shoot him, and I am glad of it. He is not satisfied with what he does to me two years ago, but he tries his deviltry on my baby sister.

He has her in his apartment and when I find it out and go to get her, he says he will not let her go. So I shoot him. With my brother's pistol,' she says, 'and I take my baby sister home with me, and I hope he is dead, and gone where he belongs.'

'Well, now,' I say, 'I am not going to give you any argument as to where Marvin Clay belongs, but,' I say, 'you skip out of here and go on home, and wait until we can do something about this situation, while I go back and help Regret, who seems to be in a tough spot.'

'Oh, do not let these terrible dogs eat him up,' she says, and with this she takes the breeze and I return to the other room to find there is much confusion indeed, because it seems that Regret is now very indignant at Nip and Tuck, especially when he discovers that one of them plants his big old paw right on the front of Regret's shirt bosom, leaving a dirty mark. So when he struggles to his feet, Regret starts letting go with both hands, and he is by no means a bad puncher for a guy who does not do much punching as a rule. In fact, he flattens Nip with a right-hand to the jaw, and knocks Tuck plumb across the room with a left hook.

Well, poor Tuck slides over the slick dance floor into Miss Missouri Martin just as she is getting to her feet again, and bowls her over once more, but Miss Missouri Martin is also indignant by this time, and she gets up and kicks Tuck in a most unlady-like manner. Of course, Tuck does not know so much about Miss Martin, but he is pretty sure his old friend Regret is only playing with him, so back he goes to Regret with his tongue out, and his tail wagging, and there is no telling how long this may go on if John Wangle does not step in and grab both hounds, while Inspector McNamara puts the arm on Regret and tells him he is under arrest for shooting Marvin Clay.

Well, of course everybody can see at once that Regret must be the guilty party all right, especially when it is remembered that he once had trouble with Marvin Clay, and one and all present are looking at Regret in great disgust, and saying you can see by his face that he is nothing but a degenerate type.

Furthermore, Inspector McNamara makes a speech to Miss Missouri Martin's customers in which he congratulates John

Wangle and Nip and Tuck on their wonderful work in tracking down this terrible criminal and at the same time putting in a few boosts for the police department, while Regret stands there paying very little attention to what the Inspector is saying, but trying to edge himself over close enough to Nip and Tuck to give them the old foot.

Well, the customers applaud what Inspector McNamara says, and Miss Missouri Martin gets up a collection of over two C's for John Wangle and his hounds, not counting what she holds out for herself. Also the chef comes forward and takes John Wangle and Nip and Tuck back into the kitchen, and stuffs them full of food, although personally I will just as soon not have any of the food they serve in the Three Hundred Club.

They take Regret to the jail-house, and he does not seem to understand why he is under arrest, but he knows it has something to do with Nip and Tuck and he tries to bribe one of the coppers to put the bloodhounds in the same cell with him for awhile, though naturally the copper will not consider such a proposition. While Regret is being booked at the jail-house, word comes around that Marvin Clay is not only not dead, but the chances are he will get well, which he finally does, at that.

Moreover, he finally bails Regret out, and not only refuses to prosecute him but skips the country as soon as he is able to move, although Regret lays in the sneezer for several weeks, at that, never letting on after he learns the real situation that he is not the party who plugs Marvin Clay. Naturally, Miss Lovey Lou is very grateful to Regret for his wonderful sacrifice, and will no doubt become his ever-loving wife in a minute, if Regret thinks to ask her, but it seems Regret finds himself brooding so much over the idea of an ever-loving wife who is so handy with a Roscoe that he never really asks.

In the meantime, John Wangle and Nip and Tuck go back to Georgia on the dough collected by Miss Missouri Martin, and with a big reputation as man-trackers. So this is all there is to the story, except that one night I run into Regret with a suitcase in his hand, and he is perspiring very freely, although it is not so hot, at that, and when I ask him if he is going away, he says this is indeed his general idea. Moreover, he says he is going very far away. Naturally, I ask him why this is, and Regret says to me as follows:

'Well,' he says, 'ever since Big Nig, the crap shooter, comes back from Hot Springs, and hears how the bloodhounds track the shooter of Marvin Clay, he is walking up and down looking at me out of the corner of his eye. In fact,' Regret says, 'I can see that Big Nig is studying something over in his mind, and while Big Nig is a guy who is not such a fast thinker as others, I am afraid he may finally think himself to a bad conclusion.

'I am afraid,' Regret says, 'that Big Nig will think himself to the conclusion that Nip and Tuck are tracking me instead of the shooter, as many evil-minded guys are already whispering around and about, and that he may get the wrong idea about the trail leading to Maud Milligan's door.'

9 THE LILY OF ST PIERRE

THERE are four of us sitting in Good Time Charley Bernstein's little joint in Forty-eighth Street one Tuesday morning about four o'clock, doing a bit of quartet singing, very low, so as not to disturb the copper on the beat outside, a very good guy by the name of Carrigan, who likes to get his rest at such an hour.

Good Time Charley's little joint is called the Crystal Room, although of course there is no crystal whatever in the room, but only twelve tables, and twelve hostesses, because Good Time Charley believes in his customers having plenty of social life.

So he has one hostess to a table, and if there are twelve different customers, which is very seldom, each customer has a hostess to talk with. And if there is only one customer, he has all twelve hostesses to gab with and buy drinks for, and no customer can ever go away claiming he is lonesome in Good Time Charley's.

Personally, I will not give you a nickel to talk with Good Time Charley's hostesses, one at a time or all together, because none of them are anything much to look at, and I figure they must all be pretty dumb or they will not be working as hostesses in Good Time Charley's little joint. I happen to speak of this to Good Time Charley, and he admits that I may be right, but he says it is very difficult to get any Peggy Joyces for twenty-five bobs per week.

Of course I never buy any drinks in Good Time Charley's for hostesses, or anybody else, and especially for myself, because I am a personal friend of Good Time Charley's, and he will not sell me any drinks even if I wish to buy any, which is unlikely, as Good Time Charley figures that anybody who buys drinks in his place is apt to drink these drinks, and Charley does not care to see any of his personal friends drinking drinks in his place. If one of his personal friends wishes to buy a drink, Charley always sends him to Jack Fogarty's little speak down the street, and in fact Charley will generally go with him.

So I only go to Good Time Charley's to talk with him, and to sing in quartet with him. There are very seldom any customers in Good Time Charley's until along about five o'clock in the morning after all the other places are closed, and then it is sometimes a very hot spot indeed, and it is no place to sing in quartet at such hours, because everybody around always wishes to join in, and it ruins the harmony. But just before five o'clock it is okay, as only the hostesses are there, and of course none of them dast to join in our singing, or Good Time Charley will run them plumb out of the joint.

If there is one thing I love to do more than anything else, it is to sing in quartet. I sing baritone, and I wish to say I sing a very fine baritone, at that. And what we are singing – this morning I am talking about – is a lot of songs such as 'Little White Lies', and 'The Old Oaken Bucket', and 'My Dad's Dinner Pail', and 'Chloe', and 'Melancholy Baby', and I do not know what else, including 'Home, Sweet Home', although we do not go so good on this because nobody remembers all the words, and half the time we are all just going ho-hum-hum-ho-hum-hum, like guys nearly always do when they are singing 'Home, Sweet Home'.

Also we sing 'I Can't Give You Anything but Love, Baby', which is a very fine song for quartet singing, especially when you have a guy singing a nice bass, such as Good Time Charley, who can come in on every line with a big bum-bum, like this:

> *I can't give you anything but luh-huh-vuh,*
> *Bay-hay-bee!*
> ## BUM-BUM!

I am the one who holds these last words, such as love, and baby, and you can hear my fine baritone very far indeed, especially when I give a little extra roll like bay-hay-bay-BEE! Then when Good Time Charley comes in with his old bum-bum, it is worth going a long way to hear.

Well, naturally, we finally get around to torch songs, as guys who are singing in quartet are bound to do, especially at four o'clock in the morning, a torch song being a song which guys sing when they have the big burnt-up feeling inside themselves over a battle with their dolls.

When a guy has a battle with his doll, such as his sweetheart, or even his ever-loving wife, he certainly feels burnt up inside himself, and can scarcely think of anything much. In fact, I know guys who are carrying the torch to walk ten miles and never know they go an inch. It is surprising how much ground a guy can cover just walking around and about, wondering if his doll is out with some other guy, and everybody knows that at four o'clock in the morning the torch is hotter than at any other time of the day.

Good Time Charley, who is carrying a torch longer than anybody else on Broadway, which is nearly a year, or ever since his doll, Big Marge, gives him the wind for a rich Cuban, starts up a torch song by Tommy Lyman, which goes as follows, very, very slow, and sad:

> *Gee, but it's tough*
> *When the gang's gone home.*
> *Out on the corner*
> *You stand alone.*

Of course there is no spot in this song for Good Time Charley's bum-bum, but it gives me a great chance with my fine baritone, especially when I come to the line that says Gee, I wish I had my old gal back again.

I do not say I can make people bust out crying and give me money with this song like I see Tommy Lyman do in night clubs, but then Tommy is a professional singer, besides writing this song for himself, so naturally he figures to do a little better with it than me. But I wish to say it is nothing for me to make five or six of the hostesses in Good Time Charley's cry all over the joint when I hit this line about Gee, I wish I had my old gal back again, and making five or six hostesses out of twelve cry is a fair average anywhere, and especially Good Time Charley's hostesses.

Well, all of a sudden who comes popping into Good Time

Charley's by way of the front door, looking here and there, and around and about, but Jack O'Hearts, and he no sooner pokes his snozzle into the joint than a guy by the name of Louie the Lug, who is singing a very fair tenor with us, jumps up and heads for the back door.

But just as he gets to the door, Jack O'Hearts outs with the old equalizer and goes whangity-whang-whang at Louie the Lug. As a general proposition, Jack O'Hearts is a fair kind of a shot, but all he does to Louie the Lug is to knock his right ear off. Then Louie gets the back door open and takes it on the lam through an areaway, but not before Jack O'Hearts gets one more crack at him, and it is this last crack which brings Louie down half an hour later on Broadway, where a copper finds him and sends him to the Polyclinic.

Personally, I do not see Louie's ear knocked off, because by the second shot I am out the front door, and on my way down Forty-eighth Street, but they tell me about it afterwards.

I never know Jack O'Hearts is even mad at Louie, and I am wondering why he takes these shots at him, but I do not ask any questions, because when a guy goes around asking questions in this town people may get the idea he is such a guy as wishes to find things out.

Then the next night I run into Jack O'Hearts in Bobby's chop-house, putting on the hot meat, and he asks me to sit down and eat with him, so I sit down and order a hamburger steak, with plenty of onions, and while I am sitting there waiting for my hamburger, Jack O'Hearts says to me like this:

'I suppose,' he says, 'I owe you guys an apology for busting up your quartet when I toss those slugs at Louie the Lug?'

'Well,' I say, 'some considers it a dirty trick at that, Jack, but I figure you have a good reason, although I am wondering what it is.'

'Louie the Lug is no good,' Jack says.

Well, of course I know this much already, and so does everybody else in town for that matter, but I cannot figure what it has to do with Jack shooting off ears in this town for such a reason, or by and by there will be very few people left with ears.

'Let me tell you about Louie the Lug,' Jack O'Hearts says.

'You will see at once that my only mistake is I do not get my shots an inch to the left. I do not know what is the matter with me lately.'

'Maybe you are letting go too quick,' I say, very sympathetic, because I know how it annoys him to blow easy shots.

'Maybe,' he says. 'Anyway, the light in Charley's dump is no good. It is only an accident I get Louie with the last shot, and it is very sloppy work all around. But now I will tell you about Louie the Lug.'

*

It is back in 1924 [Jack O'Hearts says] that I go to St Pierre for the first time to look after some business matters for John the Boss, rest his soul, who is at this time one of the largest operators in high-grade merchandise in the United States, especially when it comes to Scotch. Maybe you remember John the Boss, and the heat which develops around and about when he is scragged in Detroit? John the Boss is a very fine character, and it is a terrible blow to many citizens when he is scragged.

Now if you are never in St Pierre, I wish to say you miss nothing much, because what is it but a little squirt of a burg sort of huddled up alongside some big rocks off Newfoundland, and very hard to get to, any way you go. Mostly you go there from Halifax by boat, though personally I go there in 1924 in John the Boss's schooner by the name of the *Maude*, in which we load a thousand cases of very nice merchandise for the Christmas trade.

The first time I see St Pierre I will not give you eight cents for the whole layout, although of course it is very useful to parties in our line of business. It does not look like much, and it belongs to France, and nearly all the citizens speak French, because most of them are French, and it seems it is the custom of the French people to speak French no matter where they are, even away off up yonder among the fish.

Well, anyway, it is on this trip to St Pierre in 1924 that I meet an old guy by the name of Doctor Armand Dorval, for what happens to me but I catch pneumonia, and it looks as if maybe I am a gone gosling, especially as there is no place in St Pierre where a guy can have pneumonia with any comfort. But this Doctor Armand Dorval is a friend of John the Boss, and he takes me into his house and lets me be as sick there as I please, while he does his best to doctor me up.

Now this Doctor Armand Dorval is an old Frenchman with whiskers, and he has a little granddaughter by the name of Lily, who is maybe twelve years old at the time I am talking about, with her hair hanging down her back in two braids. It seems her papa, who is Doctor Armand's son, goes out one day looking for cod on the Grand Banks when Lily is nothing but a baby, and never comes back, and then her mamma dies, so old Doc raises up Lily and is very fond of her indeed.

They live alone in the house where I am sick with this pneumonia, and it is a nice, quiet little house and very old-fashioned, with a good view of the fishing boats, if you care for fishing boats. In fact, it is the quietest place I am ever in in my life, and the only place I ever know any real peace. A big fat old doll who does not talk English comes in every day to look after things for Doctor Armand and Lily, because it seems Lily is not old enough to keep house as yet, although she makes quite a nurse for me.

Lily talks English very good, and she is always bringing me things, and sitting by my bed and chewing the rag with me about this and that, and sometimes she reads to me out of a book which is called *Alice in Wonderland*, and which is nothing but a pack of lies, but very interesting in spots. Furthermore, Lily has a big, blonde, dumb-looking doll by the name of Yvonne, which she makes me hold while she is reading to me, and I am very glad indeed that the *Maude* goes on back to the United States and there is no danger of any of the guys walking in on me while I am holding this doll, or they will think I blow my topper.

Finally, when I am able to sit up around the house of an evening I play checkers with Lily, while old Doctor Armand Dorval sits back in a rocking-chair, smoking a pipe and watching us, and sometimes I sing for her. I wish to say I sing a first-class tenor, and when I am in the war business in France with the Seventy-seventh Division I am always in great demand for singing a quartet. So I sing such songs to Lily as 'There's a Long, Long Trail', and 'Mademoiselle from Armentières', although of course when it comes to certain spots in this song I just go dum-dum-dee-dum and do not say the words right out.

By and by Lily gets to singing with me, and we sound very good together, especially when we sing the 'Long, Long Trail', which Lily likes very much, and even old Doctor Armand joins in now and then, although his voice is very terrible. Anyway, Lily and me and Doctor Armand become very good pals indeed, and what is more I meet up with other citizens of St Pierre and become friends with them, and they are by no means bad people to know, and it is certainly a nice thing to be able to walk up and down without being afraid every other guy you meet is going to chuck a slug at you, or a copper put the old sleeve on you and say that they wish to see you at headquarters.

Finally I get rid of this pneumonia and take the boat to Halifax, and I am greatly surprised to find that Doctor Armand and Lily are very sorry to see me go, because never before in my life do I leave a place where anybody is sorry to see me go.

But Doctor Armand seems very sad and shakes me by the hand over and over again, and what does Lily do but bust out crying, and the first thing I know I am feeling sad myself and wishing that I am not going. So I promise Doctor Armand I will come back some day to see him, and then Lily hauls off and gives me a big kiss right in the smush and this astonishes me so much that it is half an hour afterwards before I think to wipe it off.

Well, for the next few months I find myself pretty busy back in New York, what with one thing and another, and I do not have time to think much of Doctor Armand Dorval and Lily, and St Pierre, but it comes along the summer of 1925, and I am all tired out from getting a slug in my chest in the run-in with Jerk Donovan's mob in Jersey, for I am now in beer and have no more truck with the boats.

But I get to thinking of St Pierre and the quiet little house of Doctor Armand Dorval again, and how peaceful it is up there, and nothing will do but what I must pop off to Halifax, and pretty soon I am in St Pierre once more. I take a raft of things for Lily with me, such as dolls, and handkerchiefs, and perfume, and a phonograph, and also a set of razors for Doctor Armand, although afterwards I am sorry I take these razors because I remember the old Doc does not shave and may take them as a hint I do not care for his whiskers. But as it turns out the Doc finds them very useful in operations, so the razors are a nice gift after all.

Well, I spend two peaceful weeks there again, walking up and down in the daytime and playing checkers and singing with Lily in the evening, and it is tough tearing myself away, especially as Doctor Armand Dorval looks very sad again and Lily busts out crying, louder than before. So nearly every year after this I can hardly wait until I can get to St Pierre for a vacation, and Doctor Armand Dorval's house is like my home, only more peaceful.

Now in the summer of 1928 I am in Halifax on my way to St Pierre, when I run across Louie the Lug, and it seems Louie is a lammister out of Detroit on account of some job or other, and is broke, and does not know which way to turn. Personally, I always figure Louie a petty-larceny kind of guy, with no more moxie than a canary bird, but he always dresses well, and always has a fair line of guff, and some guys stand for him. Anyway, here he is in trouble, so what happens but I take him with me to St Pierre, figuring he can lay dead there until things blow over.

Well, Lily and old Doctor Armand Dorval are certainly glad to see me, and I am just as glad to see them, especially Lily, for she is now maybe sixteen years old and as pretty a doll as ever steps in shoe leather, what with her long black hair, and her big black eyes, and a million dollars' worth of personality. Furthermore, by this time she swings a very mean skillet, indeed, and gets me up some very tasty fodder out of fish and one thing and another.

But somehow things are not like they used to be at St Pierre with this guy Louie the Lug around, because he does not care for the place whatever, and goes roaming about very restless, and making cracks about the citizens, and especially the dolls, until one night I am compelled to tell him to keep his trap closed, although at that the dolls in St Pierre, outside of Lily, are no such lookers as will get Ziegfeld heated up.

But even in the time when St Pierre is headquarters for many citizens of the United States who are in the business of handling merchandise out of there, it is always sort of underhand that such citizens will never have any truck with the dolls at St Pierre. This is partly because the dolls at St Pierre never give the citizens of the United States a tumble, but more because we do not wish to get in any trouble around there, and if there is anything apt to cause trouble it is dolls.

Now I suppose if I have any brains I will see that Louie is playing the warm for Lily, but I never think of Lily as anything but a little doll with her hair in braids, and certainly not a doll such as a guy will start pitching to, especially a guy who calls himself one of the mob.

I notice Louie is always talking to Lily when he gets a chance, and sometimes he goes walking up and down with her, but I see nothing in this, because after all any guy is apt to get lonesome at St Pierre and go walking up and down with anybody, even a little young doll. In fact, I never see Louie do anything that strikes me as out of line, except he tries to cut in on the singing between Lily and me, until I tell him one tenor at a time is enough in any singing combination. Personally, I consider Louie the Lug's tenor very flat, indeed.

Well, it comes time for me to go away, and I take Louie with me, because I do not wish him hanging around St Pierre alone, especially as old Doctor Armand Dorval does not seem to care for him whatever, and while Lily seems as sad as ever to see me go I notice that for the first time she does not kiss me good-bye. But I figure this is fair enough, as she is now quite a young lady, and the chances are a little particular about who she kisses.

I leave Louie in Halifax and give him enough dough to go on to Denver, which is where he says he wishes to go, and I never see him again until the other night in Good Time Charley's. But almost a year later, when I happen to be in Montreal, I hear of him. I am standing in the lobby of the Mount Royal Hotel thinking of not much, when a guy by the name of Bob the Bookie, who is a hustler around the race-tracks, gets to talking to me and mentions Louie's name. It brings back to me a memory of my last trip to St Pierre, and I get to thinking that this is the longest stretch I ever go in several years without a visit there and of the different things that keep me from going.

I am not paying much attention to what Bob says, because he is putting the blast on Louie for running away from an ever-loving wife and a couple of kids in Cleveland several years before, which is something I do not know about Louie, at that. Then I hear Bob saying like this:

'He is an awful rat any way you take him. Why, when he hops out of here two weeks ago, he leaves a little doll he brings with him from St Pierre dying in hospital without a nickel to her name. It is a sin and a shame.'

'Wait a minute, Bob,' I say, waking up all of a sudden. 'Do you say a doll from St Pierre? What-for looking kind of a doll, Bob?' I say.

'Why,' Bob says, 'she is black-haired, and very young, and he calls her Lily, or some such. He is knocking around Canada with her for quite a spell. She strikes me as a t. b., but Louie's dolls always look this way after he has them a while. I judge,' Bob says, 'that Louie does not feed them any too good.'

Well, it is Lily Dorval, all right, but never do I see such a change in anybody as there is in the poor little doll I find lying on a bed in a charity ward in a Montreal hospital. She does not look to weigh more than fifty pounds, and her black eyes are sunk away back in her head, and she is in tough shape generally. But she knows me right off the bat and tries to smile at me.

I am in the money very good at this time, and I have Lily moved into a private room, and get her all the nurses the law allows, and the best croakers in Montreal, and flowers, and one thing and another, but one of the medicos tells me it is even money she will not last three weeks, and 7 to 5 she does not go a month. Finally Lily tells me what happens, which is the same thing that happens to a million dolls before and will happen to a million dolls again. Louie never leaves Halifax, but cons her into coming over there to him, and she goes because she loves him, for this is the way dolls are, and personally I will never have them any other way.

'But,' Lily whispers to me, 'the bad, bad thing I do is to tell poor old Grandfather I am going to meet you, Jack O'Hearts, and marry you, because I know he does not like Louie and will never allow me to go to him. But he loves you, Jack O'Hearts, and he is so pleased in thinking you are to be his son. It is wrong to tell Grandfather this story, and wrong to use your name, and to keep writing him all this time making him think I am your wife, and with you, but I love Louie, and I wish Grandfather to be happy because he is very, very old. Do you understand, Jack O'Hearts?'

Now of course all this is very surprising news to me, indeed, and in fact I am quite flabbergasted, and as for understanding it, all I understand is she got a rotten deal from Louie the Lug and that old Doctor Armand Dorval is going to be all busted up if he hears what really happens. And thinking about this nice old man, and thinking of how the only place I ever know peace and quiet is now ruined, I am very angry with Louie the Lug.

But this is something to be taken up later, so I dismiss him from my mind, and go out and get me a marriage licence and a priest, and have this priest marry me to Lily Dorval just two days before she looks up at me for the last time, and smiles a little smile, and then closes her eyes for good and all. I wish to say, however, that up to this time I have no more idea of getting myself a wife than I have of jumping out the window, which is practically no idea at all.

I take her body back to St Pierre myself in person, and we bury her in a little cemetery there, with a big fog around and about, and the siren moaning away very sad, and old Doctor Armand Dorval whispers to me like this:

'You will please to sing the song about the long trail, Jack O'Hearts.'

So I stand there in the fog, the chances are looking like a big sap, and I sing as follows:

> *There's a long, long trail a-winding*
> *Into the land of my dreams,*
> *Where the nightingale is singing,*
> *And the white moon beams.*

But I can get no farther than this, for something comes up in my throat, and I sit down by the grave of Mrs Jack O'Hearts, who was Lily Dorval, and for the first time I remember I bust out crying.

So [he says] this is why I say Louie the Lug is no good.

Well, I am sitting there thinking that Jack O'Hearts is right about Louie, at that, when in comes Jack's chauffeur, a guy by the name of Fingers, and he steps up to Jack and says, very low: 'Louie dies half an hour ago at the Polyclinic.'

'What does he say before he goes?' Jack asks.

'Not a peep,' Fingers says.

'Well,' Jack O'Hearts says, 'it is sloppy work, at that. I ought to get him the first crack. But maybe he had a chance to think a little of Lily Dorval.'

Then he turns to me and says like this:

'You guys need not feel bad about losing your tenor, because,' he says, 'I will be glad to fill in for him at all times.'

Personally I do not think Jack's tenor is as good as Louie the Lug's, especially when it comes to hitting the very high notes in such songs as 'Sweet Adeline', because he does not hold them long enough to let Good Time Charley in with his bum-bum.

But of course this does not go if Jack O'Hearts hears it, as I am never sure he does not clip Louie the Lug just to get a place in our quartet, at that.

10 PRINCESS O'HARA

Now of course Princess O'Hara is by no means a regular princess, and in fact she is nothing but a little red-headed doll, with plenty of freckles, from over in Tenth Avenue, and her right name is Maggie, and the only reason she is called Princess O'Hara is as follows:

She is the daughter of King O'Hara, who is hacking along Broadway with one of these old-time victorias for a matter of maybe twenty-five years, and every time King O'Hara gets his pots on, which is practically every night, rain or shine, he is always bragging that he has the royal blood of Ireland in his veins, so somebody starts calling him King, and this is his monicker as long as I can remember, although probably what King O'Hara really has in his veins is about ninety-eight per cent alcohol.

Well, anyway, one night about seven or eight years back, King O'Hara shows up on his stand in front of Mindy's restaurant on Broadway with a spindly-legged, little doll about ten years of age on the seat beside him, and he says that this little doll is nobody but his daughter, and he is taking care of her because his old lady is not feeling so good, and right away Last Card Louie, the gambler, reaches up and dukes the little doll and says to her like this:

'If you are the daughter of the King, you must be the princess,' Last Card Louie says. 'How are you, Princess?'

So from this time on, she is Princess O'Hara, and afterwards for several years she often rides around in the early evening with the King, and sometimes when the King has his pots on more than somewhat, she personally drives Goldberg, which is the King's horse, although Goldberg does not really need much driving as he knows his way along Broadway better than any-body. In fact, this Goldberg is a most sagacious old pelter, in-deed, and he is called Goldberg by the King in honour of a Jewish friend by the name of Goldberg, who keeps a delicates-sen store in Tenth Avenue.

At this time, Princess O'Hara is as homely as a mud fence, and maybe homelier, what with the freckles, and the skinny gambs, and a few buck teeth, and she does not weigh more than sixty pounds, sopping wet, and her red hair is down her back in pigtails, and she giggles if anybody speaks to her, so finally nobody speaks to her much, but old King O'Hara seems to think well of her, at that.

Then by and by she does not seem to be around with the King any more, and when somebody happens to ask about her, the King says his old lady claims the Princess is getting too grown-up to be shagging around Broadway, and that she is now going to public school. So after not seeing her for some years, every-body forgets that King O'Hara has a daughter, and in fact nobody cares a cuss.

Now King O'Hara is a little shrivelled-up old guy with a very red beezer, and he is a most familiar spectacle to one and all on Broadway as he drives about with a stove-pipe hat tipped so far over to one side of his noggin that it looks as if it is always about to fall off, and in fact the King himself is always tipped so far over to one side that it seems to be a sure thing that he is going to fall off.

The way the King keeps himself on the seat of his victoria is really most surprising, and one time Last Card Louie wins a nice bet off a gambler from St Louis by the name of Olive Street Oscar, who takes 8 to 5 off of Louie that the King cannot drive them through Central Park without doing a Brodie off the seat. But of course Louie is betting with the best of it, which is the way he always dearly loves to bet, because he often rides through Central Park with King O'Hara, and he knows the King never falls off, no matter how far over he tips.

Personally, I never ride with the King very much, as his vic-toria is so old I am always afraid the bottom will fall out from under me, and that I will run myself to death trying to keep up, because the King is generally so busy singing Irish come-all-yeez up on his seat that he is not apt to pay much attention to what his passengers are doing.

There are quite a number of these old victorias left in this town, a victoria being a low-neck, four-wheeled carriage with seats for four or five people, and they are very popular in the summer-time with guys and dolls who wish to ride around and about in Central Park taking the air, and especially with guys and dolls who may wish to do a little off-hand guzzling while taking the air.

Personally, I consider a taxicab much more convenient and less expensive than an old-fashioned victoria if you wish to get to some place, but of course guys and dolls engaged in a little off-hand guzzling never wish to get any place in particular, or at least not soon. So these victorias, which generally stand around the entrances to the Park, do a fair business in the summer-time, because it seems that no matter what conditions are, there are always guys and dolls who wish to do a little off-hand guzzling.

But King O'Hara stands in front of Mindy's because he has many regular customers among the citizens of Broadway, who do not go in for guzzling so very much, unless a case of guzzling comes up, but who love to ride around in the Park on hot nights just to cool themselves out, although at the time I am now speaking of, things are so tough with one and all along Broadway that King O'Hara has to depend more on strangers for his trade.

Well, what happens one night, but King O'Hara is seen approaching Mindy's, tipping so far over to one side of his seat that Olive Street Oscar, looking to catch even on the bet he loses before, is offering to take 6 to 5 off of Last Card Louie that this time the King goes plumb off, and Louie is about to give it to him, when the old King tumbles smack-dab into the street, as dead as last Tuesday, which shows you how lucky Last Card Louie is, because nobody ever figures such a thing to happen to the King, and even Goldberg, the horse, stops and stands looking at him very much surprised, with one hind hoof in the King's stovepipe hat. The doctors state that King O'Hara's heart just naturally hauls off and quits working on him, and afterwards Regret, the horse player, says the chances are the King probably suddenly remembers refusing a drink somewhere.

A few nights later, many citizens are out in front of Mindy's, and Big Nig, the crap shooter, is saying that things do not look the same around there since King O'Hara puts his checks back in the rack, when all of a sudden up comes a victoria that anybody can see is the King's old rattletrap, especially as it is being pulled by Goldberg.

And who is on the driver's seat, with King O'Hara's bunged-up old stovepipe hat sitting jack-deuce on her noggin, but a redheaded doll of maybe eighteen or nineteen with freckles all over her pan, and while it is years since I see her, I can tell at once that she is nobody but Princess O'Hara, even though it seems she changes quite some.

In fact, she is now about as pretty a little doll as anybody will wish to see, even with the freckles, because the buck teeth seem to have disappeared, and the gambs are now filled out very nicely, and so has the rest of her. Furthermore, she has a couple of blue eyes that are most delightful to behold, and a smile like six bits, and all in all, she is a pleasing scene.

Well, naturally, her appearance in this manner causes some comment, and in fact some citizens are disposed to criticize her as being unladylike, until Big Nig, the crap shooter, goes around among them very quietly stating that he will knock their ears down if he hears any more cracks from them, because it seems that Big Nig learns that when old King O'Hara dies, all he leaves in this world besides his widow and six kids is Goldberg, the horse, and the victoria, and Princess O'Hara is the eldest of these kids, and the only one old enough to work, and she can think of nothing better to do than to take up her papa's business where he leaves off.

After one peek at Princess O'Hara, Regret, the horse player, climbs right into the victoria, and tells her to ride him around the Park a couple of times, although it is well known to one and all that it costs two bobs per hour to ride in anybody's victoria, and the only dough Regret has in a month is a pound note that he just borrows off of Last Card Louie for eating money. But from this time on, the chances are Regret will be Princess

O'Hara's best customer if he can borrow any more pound notes, but the competition gets too keen for him, especially from Last Card Louie, who is by this time quite a prominent character along Broadway, and in the money, although personally I always say you can have him, as Last Card Louie is such a guy as will stoop to very sharp practice, and in fact he often does not wait to stoop.

He is called Last Card Louie because in his youth he is a great hand for riding the tubs back and forth between here and Europe and playing stud poker with other passengers, and the way he always gets much strength from the last card is considered quite abnormal, especially if Last Card Louie is dealing. But of course Last Card Louie no longer rides the tubs as this occupation is now very old-fashioned, and anyway Louie has more profitable interests that require his attention, such as a crap game, and one thing and another.

There is no doubt but what Last Card Louie takes quite a fancy to Princess O'Hara, but naturally he cannot spend all his time riding around in a victoria, so other citizens get a chance to patronize her now and then, and in fact I once take a ride with Princess O'Hara myself, and it is a very pleasant experience, indeed, as she likes to sing while she is driving, just as old King O'Hara does in his time.

But what Princess O'Hara sings is not Irish come-all-yeez but 'Kathleen Mavourneen', and 'My Wild Irish Rose', and 'Asthore' and other such ditties, and she has a loud contralto voice, and when she lets it out while driving through Central Park in the early hours of the morning, the birds in the trees wake up and go tweet-tweet, and the coppers on duty for blocks around stand still with smiles on their kissers, and the citizens who live in the apartment houses along Central Park West and Central Park South come to their windows to listen.

Then one night in October, Princess O'Hara does not show up in front of Mindy's, and there is much speculation among one and all about this absence, and some alarm, when Big Nig, the crap shooter, comes around and says that what happens is that old Goldberg, the horse, is down with colic, or some such, so there is Princess O'Hara without a horse.

Well, this news is received with great sadness by one and all, and there is some talk of taking up a collection to buy Princess O'Hara another horse, but nobody goes very far with this idea because things are so tough with everybody, and while Big Nig mentions that maybe Last Card Louie will be glad to do something large in this matter, nobody cares for this idea, either, as many citizens are displeased with the way Last Card Louie is pitching to Princess O'Hara, because it is well known that Last Card Louie is nothing but a wolf when it comes to young dolls, and anyway about now Regret, the horse player, speaks up as follows:

'Why,' Regret says, 'it is great foolishness to talk of wasting money buying a horse, even if we have any money to waste, when the barns up at Empire City are packed at this time with crocodiles of all kinds. Let us send a committee up to the track,' Regret says, 'and borrow a nice horse for Princess O'Hara to use until Goldberg is back on his feet again.'

'But,' I say to Regret, 'suppose nobody wishes to lend us a horse?'

'Why,' Regret says, 'I do not mean to ask anybody to lend us a horse. I mean let us borrow one without asking anybody. Most of these horse owners are so very touchy that if we go around asking them to lend us a horse to pull a hack, they may figure we are insulting their horses, so let us just get the horse and say nothing whatever.'

Well, I state that this sounds to me like stealing, and stealing is something that is by no means upright and honest, and Regret has to admit that it really is similar to stealing, but he says what of it, and as I do not know what of it, I discontinue the argument. Furthermore, Regret says it is clearly understood that we will return any horse we borrow when Goldberg is hale and hearty again, so I can see that after all there is nothing felonious in the idea, or anyway, not much.

But after much discussion, it comes out that nobody along Broadway seems to know anything about stealing a horse. There are citizens who know all about stealing diamond necklaces, or hot stoves, but when it comes to horses, everybody confesses themselves at a loss. It is really amazing the amount of ignorance there is on Broadway about stealing horses.

Then finally Regret has a bright idea. It seems that a rodeo is going on at Madison Square Garden at this time, a rodeo being a sort of wild west show with bucking bronchos, and cowboys, and all this and that, and Regret seems to remember reading when he is a young squirt that stealing horses is a very popular pastime out in the wild west.

So one evening Regret goes around to the Garden and gets to talking to a cowboy in leather pants with hair on them, and he asks this cowboy, whose name seems to be Laramie Pink, if there are any expert horse stealers connected with the rodeo. Moreover, Regret explains to Laramie Pink just why he wants a good horse stealer, and Pink becomes greatly interested and wishes to know if the loan of a nice bucking broncho, or a first-class cow pony will be of any assistance, and when Regret says he is afraid not, Laramie Pink says like this:

'Well,' he says, 'of course horse stealing is considered a most antique custom out where I come from, and in fact it is no longer practised in the best circles, but,' he says, 'come to think of it, there is a guy with this outfit by the name of Frying Pan Joe, who is too old to do anything now except mind the cattle, but who is said to be an excellent horse stealer out in Colorado in his day. Maybe Frying Pan Joe will be interested in your proposition,' Laramie Pink says.

So he hunts up Frying Pan Joe, and Frying Pan Joe turns out to be a little old pappy guy with a chin whisker, and a sad expression, and a wide-brimmed cowboy hat, and when they explain to him that they wish him to steal a horse, Frying Pan Joe seems greatly touched, and his eyes fill up with tears, and he speaks as follows:

'Why,' Frying Pan Joe says, 'your idea brings back many memories to me. It is a matter of over twenty-five years since I steal a horse, and the last time I do this it gets me three years in the calabozo. Why,' he says, 'this is really a most unexpected order, and it finds me all out of practice, and with no opportunity to get myself in shape. But,' he says, 'I will put forth my best efforts on this job for ten dollars, as long as I do not personally have to locate the horse I am to steal. I am not acquainted with the ranges hereabouts, and will not know where to go to find a horse.'

So Regret, the horse player, and Big Nig, the crap shooter, and Frying Pan Joe go up to Empire this very same night, and it turns out that stealing a horse is so simple that Regret is sorry he does not make the tenner himself, for all Frying Pan Joe does is to go to the barns where the horses live at Empire, and walk along until he comes to a line of stalls that do not seem to have any watchers around in the shape of stable hands at the moment. Then Frying Pan Joe just steps into a stall and comes out leading a horse, and if anybody sees him, they are bound to figure he has a right to do this, because of course not even Sherlock Holmes is apt to think of anybody stealing a horse around this town.

Well, when Regret gets a good peek at the horse, he sees right away it is not just a horse that Frying Pan Joe steals. It is Gallant Godfrey, one of the greatest handicap horses in this country, and the winner of some of the biggest stakes of the year, and Gallant Godfrey is worth twenty-five G's if he is worth a dime, and when Regret speaks of this, Frying Pan Joe says it is undoubtedly the most valuable single piece of horseflesh he ever steals, although he claims that once when he is stealing horses along the Animas River in Colorado, he steals two hundred horses in one batch that will probably total up more.

They take Gallant Godfrey over to Eleventh Avenue, where Princess O'Hara keeps Goldberg in a little stable that is nothing but a shack, and they leave Gallant Godfrey there alongside old Goldberg, who is groaning and carrying on in a most distressing manner, and then Regret and Big Nig shake hands with Frying Pan Joe and wish him good-bye.

So there is Princess O'Hara with Gallant Godfrey hitched up to her victoria the next night, and the chances are it is a good thing for her that Gallant Godfrey is a nice tame old dromedary, and does not mind pulling a victoria at all, and in fact he seems to enjoy it, although he likes to go along at a gallop instead of a slow trot, such as the old skates that pull these victorias usually employ.

And while Princess O'Hara understands that this is a borrowed horse, and is to be returned when Goldberg is well, nobody tells her just what kind of a horse it is, and when she gets Goldberg's harness on Gallant Godfrey his appearance changes so that not even the official starter is apt to recognize him if they come face to face.

Well, I hear afterwards that there is great consternation around Empire when it comes out that Gallant Godfrey is missing, but they keep it quiet as they figure he just wanders away, and as he is engaged in certain large stakes later on, they do not wish it made public that he is absent from his stall. So they have guys looking for him high and low, but of course nobody thinks to look for a high-class racehorse pulling a victoria.

When Princess O'Hara drives the new horse up in front of Mindy's, many citizens are anxious to take the first ride with her, but before anybody has time to think, who steps up but Ambrose Hammer, the newspaper scribe, who has a foreign-looking young guy with him, and Ambrose states as follows:

'Get in, Georges,' Ambrose says. 'We will take a spin through the Park and wind up at the Casino.'

So away they go, and from this moment begins one of the greatest romances ever heard of on Broadway, for it seems that the foreign-looking young guy that Ambrose Hammer calls Georges takes a wonderful liking to Princess O'Hara right from taw, and the following night I learn from Officer Corbett, the motor-cycle cop who is on duty in Central Park, that they pass him with Ambrose Hammer in the back seat of the Victoria, but with Georges riding on the driver's seat with Princess O'Hara.

And moreover, Officer Corbett states that Georges is wearing King O'Hara's old stovepipe hat, while Princess O'Hara is singing Kathleen Mavourneen in her loud contralto in such a way as nobody ever hears her sing before.

In fact, this is the way they are riding along a little later in the week, and when it is coming on four bells in the morning. But this time, Princess O'Hara is driving north on the street that is called Central Park West because it borders the Park on the west, and the reason she is taking this street is because she comes up Broadway through Columbus Circle into Central Park West, figuring to cross over to Fifth Avenue by way of the transverse at Sixty-sixth Street, a transverse being nothing but a roadway cut through the Park from Central Park West to the Avenue.

There are several of these transverses, and why they do not call them roads, or streets, instead of transverses, I do not know, except maybe it is because transverse sounds more fancy. These transverses are really like tunnels without any roofs, especially the one at Sixty-sixth Street, which is maybe a quarter of a mile long and plenty wide enough for automobiles to pass each other going in different directions, but once a car is in the transverse there is no way it can get out except at one end or the other. There is no such thing as turning off to one side anywhere between Central Park West and the Avenue, because the Sixty-sixth Street transverse is a deep cut with high sides, or walls.

Well, just as Princess O'Hara starts to turn Gallant Godfrey into the transverse, with the foreign-looking young guy beside her on the driver's seat, and Ambrose Hammer back in the cushions, and half-asleep, and by no means interested in the conversation that is going on in front of him, a big beer truck comes rolling along Central Park West, going very slow.

And of course there is nothing unusual in the spectacle of a beer truck at this time, as beer is now very legal, but just as this beer truck rolls alongside Princess O'Hara's victoria, a little car with two guys in it pops out of nowhere, and pulls up to the truck, and one of the guys requests the jockey of the beer truck to stop.

Of course Princess O'Hara and her passengers do not know at the time that this is one of the very first cases of histing a truckload of legal beer that comes off in this country, and that they are really seeing history made, although it all comes out later. It also comes out later that one of the parties committing this historical deed is nobody but a guy by the name of Fats O'Rourke, who is considered one of the leading characters over on the west side, and the reason he is histing this truckload of beer is by no means a plot against the brewing industry, but because it is worth several C's, and Fats O'Rourke can use several C's very nicely at the moment.

It comes out that the guy with him is a guy by the name of Joe the Blow Fly, but he is really only a fink in every respect, a fink being such a guy as is extra nothing, and many citizens are somewhat surprised when they learn that Fats O'Rourke is going around with finks.

Well, if the jockey of the beer truck does as he is requested without any shilly-shallying, all that will happen is he will lose his beer. But instead of stopping the truck, the jockey tries to keep right on going, and then all of a sudden Fats O'Rourke becomes very impatient and outs with the old thing, and gives it to the jockey as follows: Bang, bang.

By the time Fats O'Rourke lets go, The Fly is up on the seat of the truck and grabs the wheel just as the jockey turns it loose and falls back on the seat, and Fats O'Rourke follows The Fly up there, and then Fats O'Rourke seems to see Princess O'Hara and her customers for the first time, and he also realizes that these parties witness what comes off with the jockey, although otherwise Central Park West is quite deserted, and if anybody in the apartment houses along there hears the shots the chances are they figure it must be nothing but an automobile backfiring.

And in fact The Fly has the beer truck backfiring quite some at this moment as Fats O'Rourke sees Princess O'Hara and her customers, and only somebody who happens to observe the flashes from Fats O'Rourke's duke, or who hears the same buzzes that Princess O'Hara, and the foreign-looking young guy, and Ambrose Hammer hear, can tell that Fats is emptying that old thing at the victoria.

The chances are Fats O'Rourke will not mind anybody witnessing him histing a legal beer truck, and in fact he is apt to welcome their testimony in later years when somebody starts disputing his claim to being the first guy to hist such a truck, but naturally Fats does not wish to have spectators spying on him when he is giving it to somebody, as very often spectators are apt to go around gossiping about these matters, and cause dissension.

So he takes four cracks at Princess O'Hara and her customers, and it is a good thing for them that Fats O'Rourke is never much of a shot. Furthermore, it is a good thing for them that he is now out of ammunition, because of course Fats O'Rourke never figures that it is going to take more than a few shots to hist a legal beer truck, and afterwards there is little criticism of Fats' judgement, as everybody realizes that it is a most unprecedented situation.

Well, by now, Princess O'Hara is swinging Gallant Godfrey into the transverse, because she comes to the conclusion that it is no time to be loitering in this neighbourhood, and she is no sooner inside the walls of the transverse than she knows this is the very worst place she can go, as she hears a rumble behind her, and when she peeks back over her shoulder she sees the beer truck coming lickity-split, and what is more, it is coming right at the victoria.

Now Princess O'Hara is no chump, and she can see that the truck is not coming right at the victoria by accident, when there is plenty of room for it to pass, so she figures that the best thing to do is not to let the truck catch up with the victoria if she can help it, and this is very sound reasoning, indeed, because Joe the Blow Fly afterwards says that what Fats O'Rourke requests him to do is to sideswipe the victoria with the truck and squash it against the side of the transverse, Fats O'Rourke's idea being to keep Princess O'Hara and her customers from speaking of the transaction with the jockey of the truck.

Well, Princess O'Hara stands up in her seat, and tells Gallant Godfrey to giddap, and Gallant Godfrey is giddapping very nicely, indeed, when she looks back and sees the truck right at the rear wheel of the victoria, and coming like a bat out of what-is-this. So she grabs up her whip and gives Gallant Godfrey a good smack across the vestibule, and it seems that if there is one thing Gallant Godfrey hates and despises it is a whip. He makes a lunge that pulls the victoria clear of the truck, just as The Fly drives it up alongside the victoria and is bearing over for the squash, with Fats O'Rourke yelling directions at him, and from this lunge, Gallant Godfrey settles down to running.

While this is going on, the foreign-looking young guy is

standing up on the driver's seat of the victoria beside Princess O'Hara, whooping and laughing, as he probably figures it is just a nice, friendly little race. But Princess O'Hara is not laughing, and neither is Ambrose Hammer.

Now inside the next hundred yards, Joe the Blow Fly gets the truck up alongside again, and this time it looks as if they are gone goslings when Princess O'Hara gives Gallant Godfrey another smack with the whip, and the chances are Gallant Godfrey comes to the conclusion that Westrope is working on him in a stretch run, as he turns on such a burst of speed that he almost runs right out of his collar and leaves the truck behind by anyway a length and a half.

And it seems that just as Gallant Godfrey turns on, Fats O'Rourke personally reaches over and gives the steering-wheel of the beer truck a good twist, figuring that the squashing is now a cinch, and the next thing anybody knows the truck goes smack-dab into the wall with a loud kuh-boom, and turns over all mussed up, with beer kegs bouncing around very briskly, and some of them popping open and letting the legal beer leak out.

In the meantime, Gallant Godfrey goes tearing out of the transverse into Fifth Avenue and across Fifth Avenue so fast that the wheels of Princess O'Hara's victoria are scarcely touchin the ground, and a copper who sees him go past afterwards states that what Gallant Godfrey is really doing is flying, but personally I always consider this an exaggeration.

Anyway, Gallant Godfrey goes two blocks beyond Fifth Avenue before Princess O'Hara can get him to whoa-up, and there is still plenty of run in him, although by this time Princess O'Hara is plumb worn out, and Ambrose Hammer is greatly fatigued, and only the foreign-looking young guy seems to find any enjoyment in the experience, although he is not so jolly when he learns that the coppers take two dead guys out of the truck, along with Joe the Blow Fly, who lives just long enough to relate the story.

Fats O'Rourke is smothered to death under a stack of kegs of legal beer, which many citizens consider a most gruesome finish, indeed, but what kills the jockey of the truck is the bullet in his heart, so the smash-up of the truck does not make any difference to him one way or the other, although of course if he lives, the chances are his employers will take him to task for losing the beer.

I learn most of the details of the race through the transverse from Ambrose Hammer, and I also learn from Ambrose that Princess O'Hara and the foreign-looking young guy are suffering from the worst case of love that Ambrose ever witnesses, and Ambrose Hammer witnesses some tough cases of love in his day. Furthermore, Ambrose says they are not only in love but are planning to get themselves married up as quickly as possible.

'Well,' I say, 'I hope and trust this young guy is all right, because Princess O'Hara deserves the best. In fact,' I say, 'a Prince is not too good for her.'

'Well,' Ambrose says, 'a Prince is exactly what she is getting. I do not suppose you can borrow much on it in a hock shop in these times, but the title of Prince Georges Latour is highly respected over in France, although,' he says, 'I understand the proud old family does not have as many potatoes as formerly. But he is a nice young guy, at that, and anyway, what is money compared to love?'

Naturally, I do not know the answer to this, and neither does Ambrose Hammer, but the very same day I run into Princess O'Hara and the foreign-looking young guy on Broadway, and I can see the old love light shining so brightly in their eyes that I get to thinking that maybe money does not mean so much alongside of love, at that, although personally, I will take a chance on the money.

I stop and say hello to Princess O'Hara, and ask her how things are going with her, and she says they are going first class.

'In fact,' she says, 'it is a beautiful world in every respect. Georges and I are going to be married in a few days now, and are going to Paris, France, to live. At first I fear we will have a long wait, because of course I cannot leave my mamma and the rest of the children unprovided for. But,' Princess O'Hara says, 'what happens but Regret sells my horse to Last Card Louie for a thousand dollars, so everything is all right.

'Of course,' Princess O'Hara says, 'buying my horse is nothing but an act of great kindness on the part of Last Card Louie as my horse is by no means worth a thousand dollars, but I suppose Louie does it out of his old friendship for my papa. I must confess,' she says, 'that I have a wrong impression of Louie, because the last time I see him I slap his face thinking he is trying to get fresh with me. Now I realize it is probably only his paternal interest in me, and I am very sorry.'

Well, I know Last Card Louie is such a guy as will give you a glass of milk for a nice cow, and I am greatly alarmed by Princess O'Hara's statement about the sale, for I figure Regret must sell Gallant Godfrey, not remembering that he is only a borrowed horse and must be returned in good order, so I look Regret up at once and mention my fears, but he laughs and speaks to me as follows:

'Do not worry,' he says. 'What happens is that Last Card Louie comes around last night and hands me a G note and says to me like this: "Buy Princess O'Hara's horse off of her for me, and you can keep all under this G that you get it for."

'Well,' Regret says, 'of course I know that old Last Card is thinking of Gallant Godfrey, and forgets that the only horse that Princess O'Hara really owns is Goldberg, and the reason he is thinking of Gallant Godfrey is because he learns last night about us borrowing the horse for her. But as long as Last Card Louie refers just to her horse, and does not mention any names, I do not see that it is up to me to go into any details with him. So I get him a bill of sale for Princess O'Hara's horse, and I am waiting ever since to hear what he says when he goes to collect the horse and finds it is nothing but old Goldberg.'

'Well,' I say to Regret, 'it all sounds most confusing to me, because what good is Gallant Godfrey to Last Card Louie when he is only a borrowed horse, and is apt to be recognized anywhere except when he is hitched to a victoria? And I am sure Last Card Louie is not going into the victoria business.'

'Oh,' Regret says, 'this is easy. Last Card Louie undoubtedly sees the same ad. in the paper that the rest of us see, offering a reward of ten G's for the return of Gallant Godfrey and no questions asked, but of course Last Card Louie has no way of knowing that Big Nig is taking Gallant Godfrey home long before Louie comes around and buys Princess O'Hara's horse.'

Well, this is about all there is to tell, except that a couple of weeks later I hear that Ambrose Hammer is in the Clinic Hospital very ill, and I drop around to see him because I am very fond of Ambrose Hammer no matter if he is a newspaper scribe.

He is sitting up in bed in a nice private room, and he has on blue silk pyjamas with his monogram embroidered over his heart, and there is a large vase of roses on the table beside him, and a nice-looking nurse holding his hand, and I can see that Ambrose Hammer is not doing bad, although he smiles very feebly at me when I come in.

Naturally I ask Ambrose Hammer what ails him, and after he takes a sip of water out of a glass that the nice-looking nurse holds up to his lips, Ambrose sighs, and in a very weak voice he states as follows:

'Well,' Ambrose says, 'one night I get to thinking about what will happen to us in the transverse if we have old Goldberg hitched to Princess O'Hara's victoria instead of one of the fastest race-horses in the world, and I am so overcome by the thought that I have what my doctor claims is a nervous breakdown. I feel terrible,' Ambrose says.

11 ROMANCE IN THE ROARING FORTIES

ONLY a rank sucker will think of taking two peeks at Dave the Dude's doll, because while Dave may stand for the first peek, figuring it is a mistake, it is a sure thing he will get sored up at the second peek, and Dave the Dude is certainly not a man to have sored up at you.

But this Waldo Winchester is one hundred per cent sucker, which is why he takes quite a number of peeks at Dave's doll. And what is more, she takes quite a number of peeks right back at him. And there you are. When a guy and a doll get to taking peeks back and forth at each other, why, there you are indeed.

This Waldo Winchester is a nice-looking young guy who writes pieces about Broadway for the *Morning Item*. He writes about the goings-on in night clubs, such as fights, and one thing and another, and also about who is running around with who, including guys and dolls.

Sometimes this is very embarrassing to people who may be married and are running around with people who are not married, but of course Waldo Winchester cannot be expected to ask one and all for their marriage certificates before he writes his pieces for the paper.

The chances are if Waldo Winchester knows Miss Billy Perry is Dave the Dude's doll, he will never take more than his first peek at her, but nobody tips him off until his second or third peek, and by this time Miss Billy Perry is taking her peeks back at him and Waldo Winchester is hooked.

In fact, he is plumb gone, and being a sucker, like I tell you, he does not care whose doll she is. Personally, I do not blame him much, for Miss Billy Perry is worth a few peeks, especially when she is out on the floor of Miss Missouri Martin's Sixteen Hundred Club doing her tap dance. Still, I do not think the best tap-dancer that ever lives can make me take two peeks at her if I know she is Dave the Dude's doll, for Dave somehow thinks more than somewhat of his dolls.

He especially thinks plenty of Miss Billy Perry, and sends her fur coats, and diamond rings, and one thing and another, which she sends back to him at once, because it seems she does not take presents from guys. This is considered most surprising all along Broadway, but people figure the chances are she has some other angle.

Anyway, this does not keep Dave the Dude from liking her just the same, and so she is considered his doll by one and all, and is respected accordingly until this Waldo Winchester comes along.

It happens that he comes along while Dave the Dude is off in the Modoc on a little run down to the Bahamas to get some goods for his business, such as Scotch and champagne, and by the time Dave gets back Miss Billy Perry and Waldo Winchester are at the stage where they sit in corners between her numbers and hold hands.

Of course nobody tells Dave the Dude about this, because they do not wish to get him excited. Not even Miss Missouri Martin tells him, which is most unusual because Miss Missouri Martin, who is sometimes called 'Mizzoo' for short, tells everything she knows as soon as she knows it, which is very often before it happens.

You see, the idea is when Dave the Dude is excited he may blow somebody's brains out, and the chances are it will be nobody's brains but Waldo Winchester's, although some claim that Waldo Winchester has no brains or he will not be hanging around Dave the Dude's doll.

I know Dave is very, very fond of Miss Billy Perry, because I hear him talk to her several times, and he is most polite to her and never gets out of line in her company by using cuss words, or anything like this. Furthermore, one night when One-eyed Solly Abrahams is a little stewed up he refers to Miss Billy Perry as a broad, meaning no harm whatever, for this is the way many of the boys speak of the dolls.

But right away Dave the Dude reaches across the table and bops One-eyed Solly right in the mouth, so everybody knows from then on that Dave thinks well of Miss Billy Perry. Of course Dave is always thinking fairly well of some doll as far as this goes, but it is seldom he gets to bopping guys in the mouth over them.

Well, one night what happens but Dave the Dude walks into the Sixteen Hundred Club, and there in the entrance, what does he see but this Waldo Winchester and Miss Billy Perry kissing each other back and forth friendly. Right away Dave reaches for the old equalizer to shoot Waldo Winchester, but it seems Dave does not happen to have the old equalizer with him, not expecting to have to shoot anybody this particular evening.

So Dave the Dude walks over and, as Waldo Winchester hears him coming and lets go his strangle-hold on Miss Billy Perry, Dave nails him with a big right hand on the chin. I will say for Dave the Dude that he is a fair puncher with his right hand, though his left is not so good, and he knocks Waldo Winchester bow-legged. In fact, Waldo folds right up on the floor.

Well, Miss Billy Perry lets out a screech you can hear clear to the Battery and runs over to where Waldo Winchester lights, and falls on top of him squalling very loud. All anybody can make out of what she says is that Dave the Dude is a big bum, although Dave is not so big, at that, and that she loves Waldo Winchester.

Dave walks over and starts to give Waldo Winchester the leather, which is considered customary in such cases, but he seems to change his mind, and instead of booting Waldo around, Dave turns and walks out of the joint looking very black and mad, and the next anybody hears of him he is over in the Chicken Club doing plenty of drinking.

This is regarded as a very bad sign indeed, because while everybody goes to the Chicken Club now and then to give Tony Bertazzola, the owner, a friendly play, very few people care to do any drinking there, because Tony's liquor is not meant for anybody to drink except the customers.

Well, Miss Billy Perry gets Waldo Winchester on his pegs again, and wipes his chin off with her handkerchief, and by and by he is all okay except for a big lump on his chin. And all the time she is telling Waldo Winchester what a big bum Dave the Dude is, although afterwards Miss Missouri Martin gets hold of Miss Billy Perry and puts the blast on her plenty for chasing a two-handed spender such as Dave the Dude out of the joint.

'You are nothing but a little sap,' Miss Missouri Martin tells Miss Billy Perry. 'You cannot get the right time off this newspaper guy, while everybody knows Dave the Dude is a very fast man with a dollar.'

'But I love Mr Winchester,' says Miss Billy Perry. 'He is so romantic. He is not a bootlegger and a gunman like Dave the Dude. He puts lovely pieces in the paper about me, and he is a gentleman at all times.'

Now of course Miss Missouri is not in a position to argue about gentlemen, because she meets very few in the Sixteen Hundred Club and anyway, she does not wish to make Waldo Winchester mad as he is apt to turn around and put pieces in his paper that will be a knock to the joint, so she lets the matter drop.

Miss Billy Perry and Waldo Winchester go on holding hands between her numbers, and maybe kissing each other now and then, as young people are liable to do, and Dave the Dude plays the chill for the Sixteen Hundred Club and everything seems to be all right. Naturally we are all very glad there is no more trouble over the proposition, because the best Dave can get is the worst of it in a jam with a newspaper guy.

Personally, I figure Dave will soon find himself another doll and forget all about Miss Billy Perry, because now that I take another peek at her, I can see where she is just about the same as any other tap-dancer, except that she is red-headed. Tap-dancers are generally blackheads, but I do not know why.

Moosh, the doorman at the Sixteen Hundred Club, tells me Miss Missouri Martin keeps plugging for Dave the Dude with Miss Billy Perry in a quiet way, because he says he hears Miss Missouri Martin make the following crack one night to her: 'Well, I do not see any Simple Simon on your lean and linger.'

This is Miss Missouri Martin's way of saying she sees no diamond on Miss Billy Perry's finger, for Miss Missouri Martin is an old experienced doll, who figures if a guy loves a doll he will prove it with diamonds. Miss Missouri Martin has many diamonds herself, though how any guy can ever get himself heated up enough about Miss Missouri Martin to give her diamonds is more than I can see.

I am not a guy who goes around much, so I do not see Dave the Dude for a couple of weeks, but late one Sunday afternoon little Johnny McGowan, who is one of Dave's men, comes and says to me like this: 'What do you think? Dave grabs the scribe a little while ago and is taking him out for an airing!'

Well, Johnny is so excited it is some time before I can get him cooled out enough to explain. It seems that Dave the Dude gets his biggest car out of the garage and sends his driver, Wop Joe, over to the *Item* office where Waldo Winchester works, with a message that Miss Billy Perry wishes to see Waldo right away at Miss Missouri Martin's apartment on Fifty-ninth Street.

Of course this message is nothing but the phonus bolonus, but Waldo drops in for it and gets in the car. Then Wop Joe drives him up to Miss Missouri Martin's apartment, and who gets in the car there but Dave the Dude. And away they go.

Now this is very bad news indeed, because when Dave the Dude takes a guy out for an airing the guy very often does not come back. What happens to him I never ask, because the best a guy can get by asking questions in this man's town is a bust in the nose.

But I am much worried over this proposition, because I like Dave the Dude, and I know that taking a newspaper guy like Waldo Winchester out for an airing is apt to cause talk, especially if he does not come back. The other guys that Dave the Dude takes out for airings do not mean much in particular, but here is a guy who may produce trouble, even if he is a sucker, on account of being connected with a newspaper.

I know enough about newspapers to know that by and by the editor or somebody will be around wishing to know where Waldo Winchester's pieces about Broadway are, and if there are no pieces from Waldo Winchester, the editor will wish to know why. Finally it will get around to where other people will wish to know, and after a while many people will be running around saying: 'Where is Waldo Winchester?'

And if enough people in this town get to running around saying where is So-and-so, it becomes a great mystery and the newspapers hop on the cops and the cops hop on everybody, and by and by there is so much heat in town that it is no place for a guy to be.

But what is to be done about this situation I do not know. Personally, it strikes me as very bad indeed, and while Johnny goes away to do a little telephoning, I am trying to think up some place to go where people will see me, and remember afterwards that I am there in case it is necessary for them to remember.

Finally Johnny comes back, very excited, and says: 'Hey, the Dude is up at the Woodcock Inn on the Pelham Parkway, and he is sending out the word for one and all to come at once. Good Time Charley Bernstein just gets the wire and tells me. Something is doing. The rest of the mob are on their way, so let us be moving.'

But here is an invitation which does not strike me as a good thing at all. The way I look at it, Dave the Dude is no company for a guy like me at this time. The chances are he either does something to Waldo Winchester already, or is getting ready to do something to him which I wish no part of.

Personally, I have nothing against newspaper guys, not even the ones who write pieces about Broadway. If Dave the Dude wishes to do something to Waldo Winchester, all right, but what is the sense of bringing outsiders into it? But the next thing I know, I am in Johnny McGowan's roadster, and he is zipping along very fast indeed, paying practically no attention to traffic lights or anything else.

As we go busting out the Concourse, I get to thinking the situation over, and I figure that Dave the Dude probably keeps thinking about Miss Billy Perry, and drinking liquor such as they sell in the Chicken Club, until finally he blows his topper. The way I look at it, only a guy who is off his nut will think of taking a newspaper guy out for an airing over a doll, when dolls are a dime a dozen in this man's town.

Still, I remember reading in the papers about a lot of different guys who are considered very sensible until they get tangled up with a doll, and maybe loving her, and the first thing anybody knows they hop out of windows, or shoot themselves, or somebody else, and I can see where even a guy like Dave the Dude may go daffy over a doll.

I can see that little Johnny McGowan is worried, too, but he does not say much, and we pull up in front of the Woodcock Inn in no time whatever, to find a lot of other cars there ahead of us, some of which I recognize as belonging to different parties.

The Woodcock Inn is what is called a road house, and is run by Big Nig Skolsky, a very nice man indeed, and a friend of everybody's. It stands back a piece off the Pelham Parkway and is a very pleasant place to go to, what with Nig having a good band and a floor show with a lot of fair-looking dolls, and everything else a man can wish for a good time. It gets a nice play from nice people, although Nig's liquor is nothing extra.

Personally, I never go there much, because I do not care for road houses, but it is a great spot for Dave the Dude when he is pitching parties, or even when he is only drinking single-handed. There is a lot of racket in the joint as we drive up, and who comes out to meet us but Dave the Dude himself with a big hello. His face is very red, and he seems heated up no little, but he does not look like a guy who is meaning any harm to anybody, especially a newspaper guy.

'Come in, guys!' Dave the Dude yells. 'Come right in!'

So we go in, and the place is full of people sitting at tables, or out on the floor dancing, and I see Miss Missouri Martin with all her diamonds hanging from her in different places, and Good Time Charley Bernstein, and Feet Samuels, and Tony Bertazzola, and Skeets Bolivar, and Nick the Greek, and Rochester Red, and a lot of other guys and dolls from around and about.

In fact, it looks as if everybody from all the joints on Broadway are present, including Miss Billy Perry, who is all dressed up in white and is lugging a big bundle of orchids and so forth, and who is giggling and smiling and shaking hands and going on generally. And finally I see Waldo Winchester, the scribe, sitting at a ringside table all by himself, but there is nothing wrong with him as far as I can see. I mean, he seems to be all in one piece so far.

'Dave,' I say to Dave the Dude, very quiet, 'what is coming off here? You know a guy cannot be too careful what he does around this town, and I will hate to see you tangled up in anything, right now.'

'Why,' Dave says, 'what are you talking about? Nothing is coming off here but a wedding, and it is going to be the best wedding anybody on Broadway ever sees. We are waiting for the preacher now.'

'You mean somebody is going to be married?' I ask, being now somewhat confused.

'Certainly,' Dave the Dude says. 'What do you think? What is the idea of a wedding, anyway?'

'Who is going to be married?' I ask.

'Nobody but Billy and the scribe,' Dave says. 'This is the greatest thing I ever do in my life. I run into Billy the other night and she is crying her eyes out because she loves this scribe and wishes to marry him, but it seems the scribe has nothing he can use for money. So I tell Billy to leave it to me, because you know I love her myself so much I wish to see her happy at all times, even if she has to marry to be that way.

'So I frame this wedding party, and after they are married I am going to stake them a few G's so they can get a good running start,' Dave says. 'But I do not tell the scribe and I do not let Billy tell him as I wish it to be a big surprise to him. I kidnap him this afternoon and bring him out here and he is scared half to death thinking I am going to scrag him.

'In fact,' Dave says, 'I never see a guy so scared. He is still so scared nothing seems to cheer him up. Go over and tell him to shake himself together, because nothing but happiness for him is coming off here.'

Well, I wish to say I am greatly relieved to think that Dave intends doing nothing worse to Waldo Winchester than getting him married up, so I go over to where Waldo is sitting. He certainly looks somewhat alarmed. He is all in a huddle with himself, and he has what you call a vacant stare in his eyes. I can see that he is indeed frightened, so I give him a jolly slap on the back and I say: 'Congratulations, pal! Cheer up, the worst is yet to come!'

'You bet it is,' Waldo Winchester says, his voice so solemn I am greatly surprised.

'You are a fine-looking bridegroom,' I say. 'You look as if you are at a funeral instead of a wedding. Why do you not laugh ha-ha, and maybe take a dram or two and go to cutting up some?'

'Mister,' says Waldo Winchester, ' my wife is not going to care for me getting married to Miss Billy Perry.'

'Your wife?' I say, much astonished. 'What is this you are speaking of? How can you have any wife except Miss Billy Perry? This is great foolishness.'

'I know,' Waldo says, very sad. 'I know. But I got a wife just the same, and she is going to be very nervous when she hears about this. My wife is very strict with me. My wife does not allow me to go around marrying people. My wife is Lola Sapola, of the Rolling Sapolas, the acrobats, and I am married to her for five years. She is the strong lady who juggles the other four people in the act. My wife just gets back from a year's tour of the Interstate time, and she is at the Marx Hotel right this minute. I am upset by this proposition.'

'Does Miss Billy Perry know about this wife?' I ask.

'No,' he says. 'No. She thinks I am single-o.'

'But why do you not tell Dave the Dude you are already married when he brings you out here to marry you off to Miss Billy Perry?' I ask. 'It seems to me a newspaper guy must know it is against the law for a guy to marry several different dolls unless he is a Turk, or some such.'

'Well,' Waldo says, 'if I tell Dave the Dude I am married after taking his doll away from him, I am quite sure Dave will be very much excited, and maybe do something harmful to my health.'

Now there is much in what the guy says, to be sure. I am inclined to think, myself, that Dave will be somewhat disturbed when he learns of this situation, especially when Miss Billy

Perry starts in being unhappy about it. But what is to be done I do not know, except maybe to let the wedding go on, and then when Waldo is out of reach of Dave, to put in a claim that he is insane, and that the marriage does not count. It is a sure thing I do not wish to be around when Dave the Dude hears Waldo is already married.

I am thinking that maybe I better take it on the lam out of there, when there is a great row at the door and I hear Dave the Dude yelling that the preacher arrives. He is a very nice-looking preacher, at that, though he seems somewhat surprised by the goings-on, especially when Miss Missouri Martin steps up and takes charge of him. Miss Missouri Martin tells him she is fond of preachers, and is quite used to them, because she is twice married by preachers, and twice by justices of the peace, and once by a ship's captain at sea.

By this time one and all present, except maybe myself and Waldo Winchester, and the preacher and maybe Miss Billy Perry, are somewhat corned. Waldo is still sitting at his table looking very sad and saying 'Yes' and 'No' to Miss Billy Perry whenever she skips past him, for Miss Billy Perry is too much pleasured up with happiness to stay long in one spot.

Dave the Dude is more corned than anybody else, because he has two or three days' running start on everybody. And when Dave the Dude is corned I wish to say that he is a very unreliable guy as to temper, and he is apt to explode right in your face any minute. But he seems to be getting a great bang out of the doings.

Well, by and by Nig Skolsky has the dance floor cleared, and then he moves out on the floor a sort of arch of very beautiful flowers. The idea seems to be that Miss Billy Perry and Waldo Winchester are to be married under this arch. I can see that Dave the Dude must put in several days planning this whole proposition, and it must cost him plenty of the old do-re-mi, especially as I see him showing Miss Missouri Martin a diamond ring as big as a cough drop.

'It is for the bride,' Dave the Dude says. 'The poor loogan she is marrying will never have enough dough to buy her such a rock, and she always wishes a big one. I get it off a guy who brings it in from Los Angeles. I am going to give the bride away myself in person, so how do I act, Mizzoo? I want Billy to have everything according to the book.'

Well, while Miss Missouri Martin is trying to remember back to one of her weddings to tell him, I take another peek at Waldo Winchester to see how he is making out. I once see two guys go to the old warm squativoo up in Sing Sing, and I wish to say both are laughing heartily compared to Waldo Winchester at this moment.

Miss Billy Perry is sitting with him and the orchestra leader is calling his men dirty names because none of them can think of how 'Oh, Promise Me' goes, when Dave the Dude yells: 'Well, we are all set! Let the happy couple step forward!'

Miss Billy Perry bounces up and grabs Waldo Winchester by the arm and pulls him up out of his chair. After a peek at his face I am willing to lay 6 to 5 he does not make the arch. But he finally gets there with everybody laughing and clapping their hands, and the preacher comes forward, and Dave the Dude looks happier than I ever see him look before in his life as they all get together under the arch of flowers.

Well, all of a sudden there is a terrible racket at the front door of the Woodcock Inn, with some doll doing a lot of hollering in a deep voice that sounds like a man's, and naturally everybody turns and looks that way. The doorman, a guy by the name of Slugsy Sachs, who is a very hard man indeed, seems to be trying to keep somebody out, but pretty soon there is a heavy bump and Slugsy Sachs falls down, and in comes a doll about four feet high and five feet wide.

In fact, I never see such a wide doll. She looks all hammered down. Her face is almost as wide as her shoulders, and makes me think of a great big full moon. She comes in bounding-like, and I can see that she is all churned up about something. As she bounces in, I hear a gurgle, and I look around to see Waldo Winchester slumping down to the floor, almost dragging Miss Billy Perry with him.

Well, the wide doll walks right up to the bunch under the arch and says in a large bass voice: 'Which one is Dave the Dude?'

'I am Dave the Dude,' says Dave the Dude, stepping up. 'What do you mean by busting in here like a walrus and gumming up our wedding?'

'So you are the guy who kidnaps my ever-loving husband to marry him off to this little red-headed pancake here, are you?' the wide doll says, looking at Dave the Dude, but pointing at Miss Billy Perry.

Well now, calling Miss Billy Perry a pancake to Dave the Dude is a very serious proposition, and Dave the Dude gets very angry. He is usually rather polite to dolls, but you can see he does not care for the wide doll's manner whatever.

'Say, listen here,' Dave the Dude says, 'you better take a walk before somebody clips you. You must be drunk,' he says. 'Or daffy,' he says. 'What are you talking about, anyway?'

'You will see what I am talking about,' the wide doll yells. 'The guy on the floor there is my lawful husband. You probably frighten him to death, the poor dear. You kidnap him to marry this red-headed thing, and I am going to get you arrested as sure as my name is Lola Sapola, you simple-looking tramp!'

Naturally, everybody is greatly horrified at a doll using such language to Dave the Dude, because Dave is known to shoot guys for much less, but instead of doing something to the wide doll at once, Dave says: 'What is this talk I hear? Who is married to who? Get out of here!' Dave says, grabbing the wide doll's arm.

Well, she makes out as if she is going to slap Dave in the face with her left hand, and Dave naturally pulls his kisser out of the way. But instead of doing anything with her left, Lola Sapola suddenly drives her right fist smack-dab into Dave the Dude's stomach, which naturally comes forward as his face goes back.

I wish to say I see many a body punch delivered in my life, but I never see a prettier one than this. What is more, Lola Sapola steps in with the punch, so there is plenty on it.

Now a guy who eats and drinks like Dave the Dude does cannot take them so good in the stomach, so Dave goes 'oof', and sits down very hard on the dance floor, and as he is sitting there he is fumbling in his pants pocket for the old equalizer, so everybody around tears for cover except Lola Sapola, and Miss Billy Perry, and Waldo Winchester.

But before he can get his pistol out, Lola Sapola reaches down and grabs Dave by the collar and hoists him to his feet. She lets go her hold on him, leaving Dave standing on his pins, but teetering around somewhat, and then she drives her right hand to Dave's stomach a second time.

The punch drops Dave again, and Lola steps up to him as if she is going to give him the foot. But she only gathers up Waldo Winchester from off the floor and slings him across her shoulder like he is a sack of oats, and starts for the door. Dave the Dude sits up on the floor again and by this time he has the old equalizer in his duke.

'Only for me being a gentleman I will fill you full of slugs,' he yells.

Lola Sapola never even looks back, because by this time she is petting Waldo Winchester's head and calling him loving names and saying what a shame it is for bad characters like Dave the Dude to be abusing her precious one. It all sounds to me as if Lola Sapola thinks well of Waldo Winchester.

Well, after she gets out of sight, Dave the Dude gets up off the floor and stands there looking at Miss Billy Perry, who is out to break all crying records. The rest of us come out from under cover, including the preacher, and we are wondering how mad Dave the Dude is going to be about the wedding being ruined. But Dave the Dude seems only disappointed and sad.

'Billy,' he says to Miss Billy Perry, 'I am mighty sorry you do not get your wedding. All I wish for is your happiness, but I do not believe you can ever be happy with this scribe if he also has to have his lion tamer around. As Cupid I am a total bust. This is the only nice thing I ever try to do in my whole life, and it is too bad it does not come off. Maybe if you wait until he can drown her, or something —'

'Dave,' says Miss Billy Perry, dropping so many tears that she seems to finally wash herself right into Dave the Dude's arms, 'I will never, never be happy with such a guy as Waldo Winchester. I can see now you are the only man for me.'

'Well, well, well,' Dave the Dude says, cheering right up.

'Where is the preacher? Bring on the preacher and let us have our wedding anyway.'

I see Mr and Mrs Dave the Dude the other day, and they seem very happy. But you never can tell about married people, so of course I am never going to let on to Dave the Dude that I am the one who telephones Lola Sapola at the Marx Hotel, because maybe I do not do Dave any too much of a favour, at that.

12 MADAME LA GIMP

ONE night I am passing the corner of Fiftieth Street and Broadway, and what do I see but Dave the Dude standing in a doorway talking to a busted-down old Spanish doll by the name of Madame La Gimp. Or rather Madame La Gimp is talking to Dave the Dude, and what is more he is listening to her, because I can hear him say yes, yes, as he always does when he is really listening to anybody, which is very seldom.

Now this is a most surprising sight to me, because Madame La Gimp is not such an old doll as anybody will wish to listen to, especially Dave the Dude. In fact, she is nothing but an old haybag, and generally somewhat ginned up. For fifteen years, or maybe sixteen, I see Madame La Gimp up and down Broadway, or sliding along through the Forties, sometimes selling news-papers, and sometimes selling flowers, and in all these years I seldom see her but what she seems to have about half a heat on from drinking gin.

Of course, nobody ever takes the newspapers she sells, even after they buy them off of her, because they are generally yester-day's papers, and sometimes last week's, and nobody ever wants her flowers, even after they pay her for them, because they are flowers such as she gets off an undertaker over in Tenth Avenue, and they are very tired flowers, indeed.

Personally, I consider Madame La Gimp nothing but an old pest, but kind-hearted guys like Dave the Dude always stake her to a few pieces of silver when she comes shuffling along putting on the moan about her tough luck. She walks with a gimp in one leg, which is why she is called Madame La Gimp, and years ago I hear somebody say Madame La Gimp is once a Spanish dancer, and a big shot on Broadway, but that she meets up with an accident which puts her out of the dancing dodge, and that a busted romance makes her become a gin-head.

I remember somebody telling me once that Madame La Gimp is quite a beauty in her day, and has her own servants, and all this and that, but I always hear the same thing about every bum on Broadway, male and female, including some I know are bums, in spades, right from taw, so I do not pay any attention to these stories.

Still, I am willing to allow that maybe Madame La Gimp is once a fair looker, at that, and the chances are has a fair shape, because once or twice I see her when she is not ginned up, and has her hair combed, and she is not so bad-looking, although even then if you put her in a claiming race I do not think there is any danger of anybody claiming her out of it.

Mostly she is wearing raggedy clothes, and busted shoes, and her grey hair is generally hanging down her face, and when I say she is maybe fifty years old I am giving her plenty the best of it. Although she is Spanish, Madame La Gimp talks good English, and in fact she can cuss in English as good as anybody I ever hear, barring Dave the Dude.

Well, anyway, when Dave the Dude sees me as he is listening to Madame La Gimp, he motions me to wait, so I wait until she finally gets through gabbing to him and goes gimping away. Then Dave the Dude comes over to me looking much worried.

'This is quite a situation,' Dave says. 'The old doll is in a tough spot. It seems that she once has a baby which she calls by the name of Eulalie, being it is a girl baby, and she ships this baby off to her sister in a little town in Spain to raise up, because Madame La Gimp figures a baby is not apt to get much raising-up off of her as long as she is on Broadway. Well, this baby is on her way here. In fact,' Dave says, 'she will land next Saturday and here it is Wednesday already.'

'Where is the baby's papa?' I ask Dave the Dude.

'Well,' Dave says, 'I do not ask Madame La Gimp this, because I do not consider it a fair question. A guy who goes around this town asking where babies' papas are, or even who they are, is apt to get the name of being nosey. Anyway, this has nothing whatever to do with the proposition, which is that Madame La Gimp's baby, Eulalie, is arriving here.

'Now,' Dave says, 'it seems that Madame La Gimp's baby, being now eighteen years old, is engaged to marry the son of a very proud old Spanish nobleman who lives in this little town in Spain, and it also seems that the very proud old Spanish nobleman, and his ever-loving wife, and the son, and Madame La Gimp's sister, are all with the baby. They are making a tour of the whole world, and will stop over here a couple of days just to see Madame La Gimp.'

'It is commencing to sound to me like a movie such as a guy is apt to see at a midnight show,' I say.

'Wait a minute,' Dave says, getting impatient. 'You are too gabby to suit me. Now it seems that the proud old Spanish nobleman does not wish his son to marry any lob, and one reason he is coming here is to look over Madame La Gimp, and see that she is okay. He thinks that Madame La Gimp's baby's own papa is dead, and that Madame La Gimp is now married to one of the richest and most aristocratic guys in America.'

'How does the proud old Spanish nobleman get such an idea as this?' I ask. 'It is a sure thing he never sees Madame La Gimp, or even a photograph of her as she is at present.'

'I will tell you how,' Dave the Dude says. 'It seems Madame La Gimp gives her baby the idea that such is the case in her letters to her. It seems Madame La Gimp does a little scrubbing business around a swell apartment hotel in Park Avenue that is called the Marberry, and she cops stationery there and writes her baby in Spain on this stationery, saying this is where she lives, and how rich and aristocratic her husband is. And what is more, Madame La Gimp has letters from her baby sent to her care of the hotel and gets them out of the employees' mail.'

'Why,' I say, 'Madame La Gimp is nothing but an old fraud to deceive people in this manner, especially a proud old Spanish nobleman. And,' I say, 'this proud old Spanish nobleman must be something of a chump to believe a mother will keep away from her baby all these years, especially if the mother has plenty of dough, although of course I do not know just how smart a proud old Spanish nobleman can be.'

'Well,' Dave says, 'Madame La Gimp tells me the thing that makes the biggest hit of all with the proud old Spanish nobleman is that she keeps her baby in Spain all these years because she wishes her raised up a true Spanish baby in every respect until she is old enough to know what time it is. But I judge the proud old Spanish nobleman is none too bright, at that,' Dave says, 'because Madame La Gimp tells me he always lives in his little town which does not even have running water in the bathrooms.

'But what I am getting at is this,' Dave says. 'We must have Madame La Gimp in a swell apartment in the Marberry with a rich and aristocratic guy for a husband by the time her baby gets here, because if the proud old Spanish nobleman finds out Madame La Gimp is nothing but a bum, it is a hundred to one he will cancel his son's engagement to Madame La Gimp's baby and break a lot of people's hearts, including his son's.

'Madame La Gimp tells me her baby is daffy about the young guy, and he is daffy about her, and there are enough broken hearts in this town as it is. I know how I will get the apartment, so you go and bring me Judge Henry G. Blake for a rich and aristocratic husband, or anyway for a husband.'

Well, I know Dave the Dude to do many a daffy thing, but never a thing as daffy as this. But I know there is no use arguing with him when he gets an idea, because if you argue with Dave the Dude too much he is apt to reach over and lay his Sunday punch on your snoot, and no argument is worth a punch on the snoot, especially from Dave the Dude.

So I go out looking for Judge Henry G. Blake to be Madame La Gimp's husband, although I am not so sure Judge Henry G. Blake will care to be anybody's husband, and especially Madame La Gimp's after he gets a load of her, for Judge Henry G. Blake is a kind of classy old guy.

To look at Judge Henry G. Blake, with his grey hair, and his nose glasses, and his stomach, you will think he is very important people, indeed. Of course, Judge Henry G. Blake is not a judge, and never is a judge, but they call him Judge because he looks like a judge, and talks slow and puts in many long words, which very few people understand.

They tell me Judge Blake once has plenty of dough, and is quite a guy in Wall Street, and a high shot along Broadway, but he misses a few guesses at the market, and winds up without much dough, as guys generally do who miss guesses at the market. What Judge Henry G. Blake does for a living at this time nobody knows, because he does nothing much whatever, and yet he seems to be a producer in a small way at all times.

Now and then he makes a trip across the ocean with such as Little Manuel, and other guys who ride the tubs, and sits in with them on games of bridge, and one thing and another, when they need him. Very often when he is riding the tubs, Little Manuel runs into some guy he cannot cheat, so he has to call in Judge Henry G. Blake to outplay the guy on the level, although of course Little Manuel will much rather get a guy's dough by cheating him than by outplaying him on the level. Why this is, I do not know, but this is the way Little Manuel is.

Anyway, you cannot say Judge Henry G. Blake is a bum, especially as he wears good clothes, with a wing collar, and a derby hat, and most people consider him a very nice old man. Personally I never catch the judge out of line on any proposition whatever, and he always says hello to me, very pleasant.

It takes me several hours to find Judge Henry G. Blake, but finally I locate him in Derle's billiards-room playing a game of pool with a guy from Providence, Rhode Island. It seems the judge is playing the guy from Providence for five cents a ball, and the judge is about thirteen balls behind when I step into the joint, because naturally at five cents a ball the judge wishes the guy from Providence to win, so as to encourage him to play for maybe twenty-five cents a ball, the judge being very cute this way.

Well, when I step in I see the judge miss a shot anybody can make blindfold, but as soon as I give him the office I wish to speak to him, the judge hauls off and belts in every ball on the table, bingity-bing, the last shot being a bank that will make Al de Oro stop and think, because when it comes to pool, the old judge is just naturally a curly wolf.

Afterwards he tells me he is very sorry I make him hurry up this way, because of course after the last shot he is never going to get the guy from Providence to play him pool even for fun, and the judge tells me the guy sizes up as a right good thing, at that.

Now Judge Henry G. Blake is not so excited when I tell him what Dave the Dude wishes to see him about, but naturally he is willing to do anything for Dave, because he knows that guys who are not willing to do things for Dave the Dude often have bad luck. The judge tells me that he is afraid he will not make much of a husband because he tries it before several times on his own hook and is always a bust, but as long as this time it is not to be anything serious, he will tackle it. Anyway, Judge Henry G. Blake says, being aristocratic will come natural to him.

Well, when Dave the Dude starts out on any proposition, he is a wonder for fast working. The first thing he does is to turn Madame La Gimp over to Miss Billy Perry, who is now Dave's ever-loving wife which he takes out of tap-dancing in Miss Missouri Martin's Sixteen Hundred Club, and Miss Billy Perry calls in Miss Missouri Martin to help.

This is water on Miss Missouri Martin's wheel, because if there is anything she loves it is to stick her nose in other people's business, no matter what it is, but she is quite a help at that, although at first they have a tough time keeping her from telling Waldo Winchester, the scribe, about the whole cat-hop, so he will put a story in the *Morning Item* about it, with Miss Missouri Martin's name in it. Miss Missouri Martin does not believe in ever overlooking any publicity bets on the layout.

Anyway, it seems that between them Miss Billy Perry and Miss Missouri Martin get Madame La Gimp dolled up in a lot of new clothes, and run her through one of these beauty joints until she comes out very much changed, indeed. Afterwards I hear Miss Billy Perry and Miss Missouri Martin have quite a few words, because Miss Missouri Martin wishes to paint Madame La Gimp's hair the same colour as her own, which is a high yellow, and buy her the same kind of dresses which Miss Missouri Martin wears herself, and Miss Missouri Martin gets much insulted when Miss Billy Perry says no, they are trying to dress Madame La Gimp to look like a lady.

They tell me Miss Missouri Martin thinks some of putting the slug on Miss Billy Perry for this crack, but happens to remember just in time that Miss Billy Perry is now Dave the Dude's ever-loving wife, and that nobody in this town can put the slug on Dave's ever-loving wife, except maybe Dave himself.

Now the next thing anybody knows, Madame La Gimp is in a swell eight- or nine-room apartment in the Marberry, and the way this comes about is as follows: It seems that one of Dave the Dude's most important champagne customers is a guy by the name of Rodney B. Emerson, who owns the apartment, but who is at his summer home in Newport, with his family, or anyway with his ever-loving wife.

This Rodney B. Emerson is quite a guy along Broadway, and a great hand for spending dough and looking for laughs, and he is very popular with the mob. Furthermore, he is obligated to Dave the Dude, because Dave sells him good champagne when most guys are trying to hand him the old phonus bolonus, and naturally Rodney B. Emerson appreciates this kind of treatment.

He is a short, fat guy, with a round, red face, and a big laugh, and the kind of a guy Dave the Dude can call up at his home in Newport and explain the situation and ask for the loan of the apartment, which Dave does.

Well it seems Rodney B. Emerson gets a big bang out of the idea, and he says to Dave the Dude like this:

'You not only can have the apartment, Dave, but I will come over and help you out. It will save a lot of explaining around the Marberry if I am there.'

So he hops right over from Newport, and joins in with Dave the Dude, and I wish to say Rodney B. Emerson will always be kindly remembered by one and all for his co-operation, and nobody will ever again try to hand him the phonus bolonus when he is buying champagne, even if he is not buying it off of Dave the Dude.

Well, it is coming on Saturday and the boat from Spain is due, so Dave the Dude hires a big town car, and puts his own driver, Wop Sam, on it, as he does not wish any strange driver tipping off anybody that it is a hired car. Miss Missouri Martin is anxious to go to the boat with Madame La Gimp, and take her jazz band, the Hi Hi Boys, from her Sixteen Hundred Club with her to make it a real welcome, but nobody thinks much of this idea. Only Madame La Gimp and her husband, Judge Henry G. Blake, and Miss Billy Perry go, though the judge holds out for some time for Little Manuel, because Judge Blake says he wishes somebody around to tip him off in case there are any bad cracks made about him as a husband in Spanish, and Little Manuel is very Spanish.

The morning they go to meet the boat is the first time Judge Henry G. Blake gets a load of his ever-loving wife, Madame La Gimp, and by this time Miss Billy Perry and Miss Missouri Martin give Madame La Gimp such a going-over that she is by no means the worst looker in the world. In fact, she looks first-rate, especially as she is off gin and says she is off it for good.

Judge Henry G. Blake is really quite surprised by her looks, as he figures all along she will turn out to be a crow. In fact, Judge Blake hurls a couple of shots into himself to nerve himself for the ordeal, as he explains it, before he appears to go to the boat. Between these shots, and the nice clothes, and the good cleaning-up Miss Billy Perry and Miss Missouri Martin give Madame La Gimp, she is really a pleasant sight to the judge.

They tell me the meeting at the dock between Madame La Gimp and her baby is very affecting indeed, and when the proud old Spanish nobleman and his wife, and their son, and Madame La Gimp's sister, all go into action, too, there are enough tears around there to float all the battleships we once sink for Spain. Even Miss Billy Perry and Judge Henry G. Blake do some first-class crying, although the chances are the judge is worked up to the crying more by the shots he takes for his courage than by the meeting.

Still, I hear the old judge does himself proud, what with kissing Madame La Gimp's baby plenty, and duking the proud old Spanish nobleman, and his wife, and son, and giving Madame La Gimp's sister a good strong hug that squeezes her tongue out.

It turns out that the proud old Spanish nobleman has white sideburns, and is entitled Conde de Something, so his ever-loving wife is the Condesa, and the son is a very nice-looking quiet young guy any way you take him, who blushes every time anybody looks at him. As for Madame La Gimp's baby, she is as pretty as they come, and many guys are sorry they do not get Judge Henry G. Blake's job as stepfather, because he is able to take a kiss at Madame La Gimp's baby on what seems to be very small excuse. I never see a nicer-looking young couple, and anybody can see they are very fond of each other, indeed.

Madame La Gimp's sister is not such a doll as I will wish to have sawed off on me, and is up in the paints as regards to age, but she is also very quiet. None of the bunch talk any English, so Miss Billy Perry and Judge Henry G. Blake are pretty much outsiders on the way uptown. Anyway, the judge takes the wind as soon as they reach the Marberry, because the judge is now getting a little tired of being a husband. He says he has to take a trip out to Pittsburgh to buy four or five coal-mines, but will be back the next day.

Well, it seems to me that everything is going perfect so far, and that it is good judgement to let it lay as it is, but nothing will do Dave the Dude but to have a reception the following night. I advise Dave the Dude against this idea, because I am afraid something will happen to spoil the whole cat-hop, but he will not listen to me, especially as Rodney B. Emerson is now in town and is a strong booster for the party, as he wishes to drink some of the good champagne he has planted in his apartment.

Furthermore, Miss Billy Perry and Miss Missouri Martin are very indignant at me when they hear about my advice, as it seems they both buy new dresses out of Dave the Dude's bankroll when they are dressing up Madame La Gimp, and they wish to spring these dresses somewhere where they can be seen. So the party is on.

I get to the Marberry around nine o'clock and who opens the door of Madame La Gimp's apartment for me but Moosh, the door man from Miss Missouri Martin's Sixteen Hundred Club. Furthermore, he is in his Sixteen Hundred Club uniform, except he has a clean shave. I wish Moosh a hello, and he never raps to me but only bows, and takes my hat.

The next guy I see is Rodney B. Emerson in evening clothes, and the minute he sees me he yells out, 'Mister O. O. McIntyre'. Well, of course, I am not Mister O. O. McIntyre, and never put myself away as Mister O. O. McIntyre, and furthermore there is no resemblance whatever between Mister O. O. McIntyre and me, because I am a fairly good-looking guy, and I start to give Rodney B. Emerson an argument, when he whispers to me like this:

'Listen,' he whispers, 'we must have big names at this affair, so as to impress these people. The chances are they read the newspapers back there in Spain, and we must let them meet the folks they read about, so they will see Madame La Gimp is a real big shot to get such names to a party.'

Then he takes me by the arm and leads me to a group of people in a corner of the room, which is about the size of the Grand Central waiting-room.

'Mister O. O. McIntyre, the big writer!' Rodney B. Emerson says, and the next thing I know I am shaking hands with Mr and Mrs Conde, and their son, and with Madame La Gimp and her baby, and Madame La Gimp's sister, and finally with Judge Henry G. Blake, who has on a swallowtail coat, and does not give me much of a tumble. I figure the chances are Judge Henry G. Blake is getting a swelled head already, not to tumble up a guy who helps him get his job, but even at that I wish to say the old judge looks immense in his swallowtail coat, bowing and giving one and all the old castor-oil smile.

Madame La Gimp is in a low-neck black dress and is wearing a lot of Miss Missouri Martin's diamonds, such as rings and bracelets, which Miss Missouri Martin insists on hanging on her, although I hear afterwards that Miss Missouri Martin has Johnny Brannigan, the plain-clothes copper, watching these diamonds. I wonder at the time why Johnny is there, but figure it is because he is a friend of Dave the Dude's. Miss Missouri Martin is no sucker, even if she is kind-hearted.

Anybody looking at Madame La Gimp will bet you all the coffee in Java that she never lives in a cellar over in Tenth Avenue, and drinks plenty of gin in her day. She has her grey hair piled up high on her head, with a big Spanish comb in it, and she reminds me of a picture I see somewhere, but I do not remember just where. And her baby, Eulalie, in a white dress is about as pretty a little doll as you will wish to see, and nobody can blame Judge Henry G. Blake for copping a kiss off of her now and then.

Well, pretty soon I hear Rodney B. Emerson bawling, 'Mister Willie K. Vanderbilt', and in comes nobody but Big Nig, and Rodney B. Emerson leads him over to the group and introduces him.

Little Manuel is standing alongside Judge Henry G. Blake, and he explains in Spanish to Mr and Mrs Conde and the others that 'Willie K. Vanderbilt' is a very large millionaire, and Mr and Mrs Conde seem much interested, anyway, though naturally Madame La Gimp and Judge Henry G. Blake are jerry to Big Nig, while Madame La Gimp's baby and the young guy are interested in nobody but each other.

Then I hear 'Mister Al Jolson', and in comes nobody but Tony Bertazzola, from the Chicken Club, who looks about as much like Al as I do like O. O. McIntyre, which is not at all. Next comes 'the Very Reverend John Roach Straton', who seems to be Skeets Bolivar to me, then 'the Honourable Mayor James J. Walker', and who is it but Good Time Charley Bernstein.

'Mister Otto H. Kahn' turns out to be Rochester Red, and 'Mister Heywood Broun' is Nick the Greek, who asks me privately who Heywood Broun is, and gets very sore at Rodney B. Emerson when I describe Heywood Broun to him.

Finally there is quite a commotion at the door and Rodney B. Emerson announces 'Mister Herbert Bayard Swope' in an extra loud voice which makes everybody look around, but it is nobody but the Pale Face Kid. He gets me to one side, too, and wishes to know who Herbert Bayard Swope is, and when I explain to him, the Pale Face Kid gets so swelled up he will not speak to Death House Donegan, who is only 'Mister William Muldoon'.

Well, it seems to me they are getting too strong when they announce, 'Vice-President of the United States, the Honourable Charles Curtis', and in pops Guinea Mike, and I say as much to Dave the Dude, who is running around every which way looking after things, but he only says, 'Well, if you do not know it is Guinea Mike, will you know it is not Vice-President Curtis?'

But it seems to me all this is most disrespectful to our leading citizens, especially when Rodney B. Emerson calls, 'The

Honourable Police Commissioner, Mister Grover A. Whalen', and in pops Wild William Wilkins, who is a very hot man at this time, being wanted in several spots for different raps. Dave the Dude takes personal charge of Wild William and removes a rod from his pants pocket, because none of the guests are supposed to come rodded up, this being strictly a social matter.

I watch Mr and Mrs Conde, and I do not see that these names are making any impression on them, and I afterwards find out that they never get any newspapers in their town in Spain except a little local bladder which only prints the home news. In fact, Mr and Mrs Conde seem somewhat bored, although Mr Conde cheers up no little and looks interested when a lot of dolls drift in. They are mainly dolls from Miss Missouri Martin's Sixteen Hundred Club, and the Hot Box, but Rodney B. Emerson introduces them as 'Sophie Tucker', and 'Theda Bara', and 'Jeanne Eagles', and 'Helen Morgan', and 'Aunt Jemima', and one thing and another.

Well, pretty soon in comes Miss Missouri Martin's jazz band, the Hi Hi Boys, and the party commences getting up steam, especially when Dave the Dude gets Rodney B. Emerson to breaking out the old grape. By and by there is dancing going on, and a good time is being had by one and all, including Mr and Mrs Conde. In fact, after Mr Conde gets a couple of jolts of the old grape, he turns out to be a pretty nice old skate, even if nobody can understand what he is talking about.

As for Judge Henry G. Blake, he is full of speed, indeed. By this time anybody can see that the judge is commencing to believe that all this is on the level and that he is really entertaining celebrities in his own home. You put a quart of good grape inside the old judge and he will believe anything. He soon dances himself plumb out of wind, and then I notice he is hanging around Madame La Gimp a lot.

Along about midnight, Dave the Dude has to go out into the kitchen and settle a battle there over a crap game, but otherwise everything is very peaceful. It seems that 'Herbert Bayard Swope', 'Vice-President Curtis', and 'Grover Whalen' get a little game going, when 'the Reverend John Roach Straton' steps up and cleans them in four passes, but it seems they soon discover that 'the Reverend John Roach Straton' is using tops on them, which are very dishonest dice, and so they put the slug on 'the Reverend John Roach Straton' and Dave the Dude has to split them out.

By and by I figure on taking the wind, and I look for Mr and Mrs Conde to tell them good night, but Mr Conde and Miss Missouri Martin are still dancing, and Miss Missouri Martin is pouring conversation into Mr Conde's ear by the bucketful, and while Mr Conde does not savvy a word she says, this makes no difference to Miss Missouri Martin. Let Miss Missouri Martin do all the talking, and she does not care a whoop if anybody understands her.

Mrs Conde is over in a corner with 'Herbert Bayard Swope', or the Pale Face Kid, who is trying to find out from her by using hog Latin and signs on her if there is any chance for a good twenty-one dealer in Spain, and of course Mrs Conde is not able to make heads or tails of what he means, so I hunt up Madame La Gimp.

She is sitting in a darkish corner off by herself and I really do not see Judge Henry G. Blake leaning over her until I am almost on top of them, so I cannot help hearing what the judge is saying.

'I am wondering for two days,' he says, 'if by any chance you remember me. Do you know who I am?'

'I remember you,' Madame La Gimp says. 'I remember you – oh, so very well, Henry. How can I forget you? But I have no idea you recognize me after all these years.'

'Twenty of them now,' Judge Henry G. Blake says. 'You are beautiful then. You are still beautiful.'

Well, I can see the old grape is working first-class on Judge Henry G. Blake to make such remarks as this, although at that, in the half-light, with the smile on her face, Madame La Gimp is not so bad. Still, give me them carrying a little less weight for age.

'Well, it is all your fault,' Judge Henry G. Blake says. 'You go and marry that chile con carne guy, and look what happens!'

I can see there is no sense in me horning in on Madame La Gimp and Judge Henry G. Blake while they are cutting up old touches in this manner, so I think I will just say good-bye to the young people and let it go at that, but while I am looking for Madame La Gimp's baby, and her guy, I run into Dave the Dude.

'You will not find them here,' Dave says. 'By this time they are being married over at Saint Malachy's with my ever-loving wife and Big Nig standing up with them. We get the licence for them yesterday afternoon. Can you imagine a couple of young saps wishing to wait until they go plumb around the world before getting married?'

Well, of course, this elopement creates much excitement for a few minutes, but by Monday Mr and Mrs Conde and the young folks and Madame La Gimp's sister take a train for California to keep on going around the world, leaving us nothing to talk about but about old Judge Henry G. Blake and Madame La Gimp getting themselves married, too, and going to Detroit where Judge Henry G. Blake claims he has a brother in the plumbing business who will give him a job, although personally I think Judge Henry G. Blake figures to do a little booting on his own hook in and out of Canada. It is not like Judge Henry G. Blake to tie himself up to the plumbing business.

So there is nothing more to the story, except that Dave the Dude is around a few days later with a big sheet of paper in his duke and very, very indignant.

'If every single article listed here is not kicked back to the owners of the different joints in the Marberry that they are taken from by next Tuesday night, I will bust a lot of noses around this town,' Dave says. 'I am greatly mortified by such happenings at my social affairs, and everything must be returned at once. Especially,' Dave says, 'the baby grand piano that is removed from Apartment 9-D.'

13 A VERY HONOURABLE GUY

Off and on I know Feet Samuels a matter of eight or ten years, up and down Broadway, and in and out, but I never have much truck with him because he is a guy I consider no dice. In fact, he does not mean a thing.

In the first place, Feet Samuels is generally broke, and there is no percentage in hanging around brokers. The way I look at it, you are not going to get anything off a guy who has not got anything. So while I am very sorry for brokers, and am always willing to hope that they get hold of something, I do not like to be around them. Long ago an old-timer who knows what he is talking about says to me:

'My boy,' he says, 'always try to rub up against money, for if you rub up against money long enough, some of it may rub off on you.'

So in all the years I am around this town, I always try to keep in with the high shots and guys who carry these large coarse bank-notes around with them, and I stay away from small operators and chisellers and brokers. And Feet Samuels is one of the worst brokers in this town, and has been such as long as I know him.

He is a big heavy guy with several chins and very funny feet, which is why he is called Feet. These feet are extra large feet, even for a big guy, and Dave the Dude says Feet wears violin-cases for shoes. Of course this is not true, because Feet cannot get either of his feet in a violin-case, unless it is a case for a very large violin, such as a cello.

I see Feet one night in the Hot Box, which is a night club,

dancing with a doll by the name of Hortense Hathaway, who is in Georgie White's 'Scandals', and what is she doing but standing on Feet's feet as if she is on sled runners, and Feet never knows it. He only thinks the old gondolas are a little extra heavy to shove around this night, because Hortense is no invalid. In fact, she is a good rangy welterweight.

She has blonde hair and plenty to say, and her square monicker is Annie O'Brien, and not Hortense Hathaway at all. Furthermore, she comes from Newark, which is in New Jersey, and her papa is a taxi jockey by the name of Skush O'Brien, and a very rough guy, at that, if anybody asks you. But of course the daughter of a taxi jockey is as good as anybody else for Georgie White's 'Scandals' as long as her shape is okay, and nobody ever hears any complaint from the customers about Hortense on this proposition.

She is what is called a show girl, and all she has to do is to walk around and about Georgie White's stage with only a few light bandages on, and everybody considers her very beautiful, especially from the neck down, although personally I never care much for Hortense because she is very fresh to people. I often see her around the night clubs, and when she is in these deadfalls Hortense generally is wearing quite a number of diamond bracelets and fur wraps, and one thing and another, so I judge she is not doing bad for a doll from Newark, New Jersey.

Of course Feet Samuels never knows why so many other dolls besides Hortense are wishing to dance with him, but gets to thinking maybe it is because he has the old sex appeal, and he is very sore indeed when Henri, the head waiter at the Hot Box, asks him to please stay off the floor except for every tenth dance, because Feet's feet take up so much room when he is on the floor that only two other dancers can work out at the same time, it being a very small floor.

I must tell you more about Feet's feet, because they are very remarkable feet indeed. They go off at different directions under him, very sharp, so if you see Feet standing on a corner it is very difficult to tell which way he is going, because one foot will be headed one way, and the other foot the other way. In fact, guys around Mindy's restaurant often make bets on the proposition as to which way Feet is headed when he is standing still.

What Feet Samuels does for a living is the best he can, which is the same thing many other guys in this town do for a living. He hustles some around the race tracks and crap games and prize fights, picking up a few bobs here and there as a runner for the bookmakers, or scalping bets, or steering suckers, but he is never really in the money in his whole life. He is always owing and always paying off, and I never see him but what he is troubled with the shorts as regards to dough.

The only good thing you can say about Feet Samuels is he is very honourable about his debts, and what he owes he pays when he can. Anybody will tell you this about Feet Samuels, although of course it is only what any hustler such as Feet must do if he wishes to protect his credit and keep in action. Still, you will be surprised how many guys forget to pay.

It is because Feet's word is considered good at all times that he is nearly always able to raise a little dough, even off The Brain, and The Brain is not an easy guy for anybody to raise dough off of. In fact, The Brain is very tough about letting people raise dough off of him.

If anybody gets any dough off of The Brain he wishes to know right away what time they are going to pay it back, with certain interest, and if they say at five-thirty Tuesday morning, they better not make it five-thirty-one Tuesday morning, or The Brain will consider them very unreliable and never let them have any money again. And when a guy loses his credit with The Brain he is in a very tough spot indeed in this town, for The Brain is the only man who always has dough.

Furthermore, some very unusual things often happen to guys who get money off of The Brain and fail to kick it back just when they promise, such as broken noses and sprained ankles and other injuries, for The Brain has people around him who seem to resent guys getting dough off of him and not kicking it back. Still, I know of The Brain letting some very surprising guys have dough, because he has a bug that he is a wonderful judge of guys' characters, and that he is never wrong on them, although I must say that no guy who gets dough off of The Brain is more surprising than Feet Samuels.

The Brain's right name is Armand Rosenthal, and he is called The Brain because he is so smart. He is well known to one and all in this town as a very large operator in gambling, and one thing and another, and nobody knows how much dough The Brain has, except that he must have plenty, because no matter how much dough is around, The Brain sooner or later gets hold of all of it. Some day I will tell you more about The Brain, but right now I wish to tell you about Feet Samuels.

It comes on a tough winter in New York, what with nearly all hands who have the price going to Miami and Havana and New Orleans, leaving the brokers behind. There is very little action of any kind in town with the high shots gone, and one night I run into Feet Samuels in Mindy's, and he is very sad indeed. He asks me if I happen to have a finnif on me, but of course I am not giving finnifs to guys like Feet Samuels, and finally he offers to compromise with me for a deuce, so I can see things must be very bad with Feet for him to come down from five dollars to two.

'My rent is away overdue for the shovel and broom,' Feet says, 'and I have a hard-hearted landlady who will not listen to reason. She says she will give me the wind if I do not lay something on the line at once. Things are never so bad with me,' Feet says, 'and I am thinking of doing something very desperate.'

I cannot think of anything very desperate for Feet Samuels to do, except maybe go to work, and I know he is not going to do such a thing no matter what happens. In fact, in all the years I am around Broadway I never know any broker to get desperate enough to go to work.

I once hear Dave the Dude offer Feet Samuels a job riding rum between here and Philly at good wages, but Feet turns it down because he claims he cannot stand the open air, and anyway Feet says he hears riding rum is illegal and may land a guy in the pokey. So I know whatever Feet is going to do will be nothing difficult.

'The Brain is still in town,' I say to Feet. 'Why do you not put the lug on him? You stand okay with him.'

'There is the big trouble,' Feet says. 'I owe The Brain a C

note already, and I am supposed to pay him back by four o'clock Monday morning, and where I am going to get a hundred dollars I do not know, to say nothing of the other ten I must give him for interest.'

'What are you figuring on doing?' I ask, for it is now a Thursday, and I can see Feet has very little time to get together such a sum.'

'I am figuring on scragging myself,' Feet says, very sad. 'What good am I to anybody? I have no family and no friends, and the world is packing enough weight without me. Yes, I think I will scrag myself.'

'It is against the law to commit suicide in this man's town,' I say, 'although what the law can do to a guy who commits suicide I am never able to figure out.'

'I do not care,' Feet says. 'I am sick and tired of it all. I am especially sick and tired of being broke. I never have more than a few quarters to rub together in my pants pocket. Everything I try turns out wrong. The only thing that keeps me from scragging myself at once is the C note I owe The Brain, because I do not wish to have him going around after I am dead and gone saying I am no good. And the toughest thing of all,' Feet says, 'is I am in love. I am in love with Hortense.'

'Hortense?' I say, very much astonished indeed. 'Why, Hortense is nothing but a big —'

'Stop!' Feet says. 'Stop right here! I will not have her called a big boloney or whatever else big you are going to call her, because I love her. I cannot live without her. In fact,' Feet says, 'I do not wish to live without her.'

'Well,' I say, 'what does Hortense think about you loving her?'

'She does not know it,' Feet says. 'I am ashamed to tell her, because naturally if I tell her I love her, Hortense will expect me to buy her some diamond bracelets, and naturally I cannot do this. But I think she likes me more than somewhat, because she looks at me in a certain way. But,' Feet says, 'there is some other guy who likes her also, and who is buying her diamond bracelets and what goes with them, which makes it very tough on me. I do not know who the guy is, and I do not think Hortense cares for him so much, but naturally any doll must give serious consideration to a guy who can buy her diamond bracelets. So I guess there is nothing for me to do but scrag myself.'

Naturally I do not take Feet Samuels serious, and I forget about his troubles at once, because I figure he will wiggle out some way, but the next night he comes into Mindy's all pleasured up, and I figure he must make a scratch somewhere, for he is walking like a man with about sixty-five dollars on him.

But it seems Feet only has an idea, and very few ideas are worth sixty-five dollars.

'I am laying in bed thinking this afternoon,' Feet says, 'and I get to thinking how I can raise enough dough to pay off The Brain, and maybe a few other guys and my landlady, and leave a few bobs over to help bury me. I am going to sell my body.'

Well, naturally I am somewhat bewildered by this statement, so I ask Feet to explain, and here is his idea: He is going to find some doctor who wishes a dead body and sell his body to this doctor for as much as he can get, his body to be delivered after Feet scrags himself, which is to be within a certain time.

'I understand,' Feet says, 'that these croakers are always looking for bodies to practise on, and that good bodies are not easy to get nowadays.'

'How much do you figure your body is worth?' I ask.

'Well,' Feet says, 'a body as big as mine ought to be worth at least a G.'

'Feet,' I say, 'this all sounds most gruesome to me. Personally I do not know much about such a proposition, but I do not believe if doctors buy bodies at all that they buy them by the pound. And I do not believe you can get a thousand dollars for your body, especially while you are still alive, because how does a doctor know if you will deliver your body to him?'

'Why,' Feet says, very indignant, 'everybody knows I pay what I owe. I can give The Brain for reference, and he will okay me with anybody for keeping my word.'

Well, it seems to me that there is very little sense to what Feet Samuels is talking about, and anyway I figure that maybe he blows his topper, which is what often happens to brokers, so I pay no more attention to him. But on Monday morning, just before four o'clock, I am in Mindy's and what happens but in walks Feet with a handful of money, looking much pleased.

The Brain is also there at the table where he always sits facing the door so nobody can pop in on him without him seeing them first, because there are many people in this town that The Brain likes to see first if they are coming in where he is. Feet steps up to the table and lays a C note in front of The Brain and also a sawbuck, and The Brain looks up at the clock and smiles and says:

'Okay, Feet, you are on time.'

It is very unusual for The Brain to smile about anything, but afterwards I hear he wins two C's off of Manny Mandelbaum, who bets him Feet will not pay off on time, so The Brain has a smile coming.

'By the way, Feet,' The Brain says, 'some doctor calls me up to-day and asks me if your word is good, and you may be glad to know I tell him you are one hundred per cent. I put the okay on you because I know you never fail to deliver on a promise. Are you sick, or something?'

'No,' Feet says, 'I am not sick. I just have a little business deal on with the guy. Thanks for the okay.'

Then he comes over to the table where I am sitting, and I can see he still has money left in his duke. Naturally I am anxious to know where he makes the scratch, and by and by he tells me.

'I put over the proposition I am telling you about,' Feet says. 'I sell my body to a doctor over on Park Avenue by the name of Bodeeker, but I do not get a G for it as I expect. It seems bodies are not worth much right now because there are so many on the market, but Doc Bodeeker gives me four C's on thirty days' delivery.

'I never know it is so much trouble selling a body before,' Feet says. 'Three doctors call the cops on me when I proposition them, thinking I am daffy, but Doc Bodeeker is a nice old guy, and is glad to do business with me, especially when I give The Brain as reference. Doc Bodeeker says he is looking for a head shaped just like mine for years, because it seems he is a shark on heads. But,' Feet says, 'I got to figure out some way of scragging myself besides jumping out a window, like I plan, because Doc Bodeeker does not wish my head mussed up.'

'Well,' I say, 'this is certainly most ghastly to me and does not sound legitimate. Does The Brain know you sell your body?'

'No,' Feet says, 'Doc Bodeeker only asks him over the phone if my word is good, and does not tell him why he wishes to know, but he is satisfied with The Brain's okay. Now I am going to pay my landlady, and take up a few other markers here and there, and feed myself up good until it is time to leave this bad old world behind.'

But it seems Feet Samuels does not go to pay his landlady right away. Where he goes is to Johnny Crackow's crap game downtown, which is a crap game with a $500 limit where the high shots seldom go, but where there is always some action for a small operator. And as Feet walks into the joint it seems that Big Nig is trying to make four with the dice, and everybody knows that four is a hard point for Big Nig, or anybody else, to make.

So Feet Samuels looks on a while watching Big Nig trying to make four, and a guy by the name of Whitey offers to take two to one for a C note that Big Nig makes this four, which is certainly more confidence than I will ever have in Big Nig. Naturally Feet hauls out a couple of his C notes at once, as anybody must do who has a couple of C notes, and bets Whitey two hundred to a hundred that Big Nig does not make the four. And right away Big Nig outs with a seven, so Feet wins the bet.

Well, to make a long story short, Feet stands there for some time betting guys that other guys will not make four, or whatever it is they are trying to make with the dice, and the first thing anybody knows Feet Samuels is six G's winner, and has the crap game all crippled up. I see him the next night up in the Hot Box, and this big first baseman, Hortense, is with him, sliding around on Feet's feet, and a blind man can see that she has on at least three more diamond bracelets than ever before.

A night or two later I hear of Feet beating Long George McCormack, a high shot from Los Angeles, out of eighteen G's playing a card game that is called low ball, and Feet Samuels has no more licence to beat a guy like Long George playing low ball than I have to lick Jack Dempsey. But when a guy finally gets his rushes in gambling nothing can stop him for a while, and this is the way it is with Feet. Every night you hear of him winning plenty of dough at this or that.

He comes into Mindy's one morning, and naturally I move over to his table at once, because Feet is now in the money and is a guy anybody can associate with freely. I am just about to ask him how things are going with him, although I know they are going pretty good, when in pops a fierce-looking old guy with his face all covered with grey whiskers that stick out every which way, and whose eyes peek out of these whiskers very wild indeed. Feet turns pale as he sees the guy, but nods at him, and the guy nods back and goes out.

'Who is the Whiskers?' I ask Feet. 'He is in here the other morning looking around, and he makes people very nervous because nobody can figure who he is or what his dodge may be.'

'It is old Doc Bodeeker,' Feet says. 'He is around checking up on me to make sure I am still in town. Say, I am in a very hot spot one way and another.'

'What are you worrying about?' I ask. 'You got plenty of dough and about two weeks left to enjoy yourself before this Doc Bodeeker forecloses on you.'

'I know,' Feet says, very sad. 'But now I get this dough things do not look as tough to me as formerly, and I am very sorry I make the deal with the doctor. Especially,' Feet says, 'on account of Hortense.'

'What about Hortense?' I ask.

'I think she is commencing to love me since I am able to buy her more diamond bracelets than the other guy,' Feet says. 'If it is not for this thing hanging over me, I will ask her to marry me, and maybe she will do it, at that.'

'Well, then,' I say, 'why do you not go to old Whiskers and pay him his dough back, and tell him you change your mind about selling your body, although of course if it is not for Whiskers's buying your body you will not have all this dough.'

'I do go to him,' Feet says, and I can see there are big tears in his eyes. 'But he says he will not cancel the deal. He says he will not take the money back; what he wants is my body, because I have such a funny-shaped head. I offer him four times what he pays me, but he will not take it. He says my body must be delivered to him promptly on March first.'

'Does Hortense know about this deal?' I ask.

'Oh, no, no!' Feet says. 'And I will never tell her, because she will think I am crazy, and Hortense does not care for crazy guys. In fact, she is always complaining about the other guy who buys her the diamond bracelets, claiming he is a little crazy, and if she thinks I am the same way the chances are she will give me the breeze.'

Now this is a situation, indeed, but what to do about it I do not know. I put the proposition up to a lawyer friend of mine the next day, and he says he does not believe the deal will hold good in court, but of course I know Feet Samuels does not wish to go to court, because the last time Feet goes to court he is held as a material witness and is in the Tombs ten days.

The lawyer says Feet can run away, but personally I consider this a very dishonourable idea after The Brain putting the okay on Feet with old Doc Bodeeker, and anyway I can see Feet is not going to do such a thing as long as Hortense is around. I can see that one hair of her head is stronger than the Atlantic cable with Feet Samuels.

A week slides by, and I do not see so much of Feet, but I hear of him murdering crap games and short card players, and winning plenty, and also going around the night clubs with Hortense, who finally has so many bracelets there is no more room on her arms, and she puts a few of them on her ankles, which are not bad ankles to look at, at that, with or without bracelets.

Then goes another week, and it just happens I am standing in front of Mindy's about four-thirty one morning and thinking that Feet's time must be up and wondering how he makes out with old Doc Bodeeker, when all of a sudden I hear a ploppity-plop coming up Broadway, and what do I see but Feet Samuels running so fast he is passing taxis that are going thirty-five miles an hour like they are standing still. He is certainly stepping along.

There are no traffic lights and not much traffic at such an

hour in the morning, and Feet passes me in a terrible hurry. And about twenty yards behind him comes an old guy with grey whiskers, and I can see it is nobody but Doc Bodeeker. What is more, he has a big long knife in one hand, and he seems to be reaching for Feet at every jump with the knife.

Well, this seems to me a most surprising spectacle, and I follow them to see what comes of it, because I can see at once that Doc Bodeeker is trying to collect Feet's body himself. But I am not much of a runner, and they are out of my sight in no time, and only that I am able to follow them by ear through Feet's feet going ploppity-plop I will never trail them.

They turn east into Fifty-fourth Street off Broadway, and when I finally reach the corner I see a crowd half-way down the block in front of the Hot Box, and I know this crowd has something to do with Feet and Doc Bodeeker even before I get to the door to find that Feet goes on in while Doc Bodeeker is arguing with Soldier Sweeney, the door man, because as Feet passes the Soldier he tells the Soldier not to let the guy who is chasing him in. And the Soldier, being a good friend of Feet's, is standing the doc off.

Well, it seems that Hortense is in the Hot Box waiting for Feet, and naturally she is much surprised to see him come in all out of breath, and so is everybody else in the joint, including Henri, the head waiter, who afterwards tells me what comes off there, because you see I am out in front.

'A crazy man is chasing me with a butcher knife,' Feet says to Hortense. 'If he gets inside I am a goner. He is down at the door trying to get in.'

Now I will say one thing for Hortense, and this is she has plenty of nerve, but of course you will expect a daughter of Skush O'Brien to have plenty of nerve. Nobody ever has more moxie than Skush. Henri, the head waiter, tells me that Hortense does not get excited, but says she will just have a little peek at the guy who is chasing Feet.

The Hot Box is over a garage, and the kitchen windows look down into Fifty-fourth Street, and while Doc Bodeeker is arguing with Soldier Sweeney, I hear a window lift, and who looks out but Hortense. She takes one squint and yanks her head in quick, and Henri tells me afterwards she shrieks:

'My Lord, Feet! This is the same daffy old guy who sends me all the bracelets, and who wishes to marry me!'

'And he is the guy I sell my body to,' Feet says, and then he tells Hortense the story of his deal with Doc Bodeeker.

'It is all for you, Horty,' Feet says, although of course this is nothing but a big lie, because it is all for The Brain in the beginning. 'I love you, and I only wish to get a little dough to show you a good time before I die. If it is not for this deal I will ask you to be my ever-loving wife.'

Well, what happens but Hortense plunges right into Feet's arms, and gives him a big kiss on his ugly mush, and says to him like this:

'I love you too, Feet, because nobody ever makes such a sacrifice as to hock their body for me. Never mind the deal. I will marry you at once, only we must first get rid of this daffy old guy downstairs.'

Then Hortense peeks out of the window again and hollers down at old Doc Bodeeker. 'Go away,' she says. 'Go away, or I will chuck a moth in your whiskers, you old fool.'

But the sight of her only seems to make old Doc Bodeeker a little wilder than somewhat, and he starts struggling with Soldier Sweeney very ferocious, so the Soldier takes the knife away from the doc and throws it away before somebody gets hurt with it.

Now it seems Hortense looks around the kitchen for something to chuck out the window at old Doc Bodeeker, and all she sees is a nice new ham which the chef just lays out on the table to slice up for ham sandwiches. This ham is a very large ham, such as will last the Hot Box a month, for they slice the ham in their ham sandwiches very, very thin up at the Hot Box. Anyway, Hortense grabs up the ham and runs to the window with it and gives it a heave without even stopping to take aim.

Well, this ham hits the poor old Doc Bodeeker kerbowie smack dab on the noggin. The doc does not fall down, but he commences staggering around with his legs bending under him like he is drunk.

I wish to help him, because I feel sorry for a guy in such a spot as this, and what is more I consider it a dirty trick for a doll such as Hortense to slug anybody with a ham.

Well, I take charge of the old doc and lead him back down Broadway and into Mindy's, where I set him down and get him a cup of coffee and a Bismarck herring to revive him, while quite a number of citizens gather about him very sympathetic.

'My friends,' the old doc says finally, looking around, 'you see in me a broken-hearted man. I am not a crack-pot, although of course my relatives may give you an argument on this proposition. I am in love with Hortense. I am in love with her from the night I first see her playing the part of a sunflower in "Scandals". I wish to marry her, as I am a widower of long standing, but somehow the idea of me marrying anybody never appeals to my sons and daughters.

'In fact,' the doc says, dropping his voice to a whisper, 'sometimes they even talk of locking me up when I wish to marry somebody. So naturally I never tell them about Hortense, because I fear they may try to discourage me. But I am deeply in love with her and send her many beautiful presents, although I am not able to see her often on account of my relatives. Then I find out Hortense is carrying on with this Feet Samuels.

'I am desperately jealous,' the doc says, 'but I do not know what to do. Finally Fate sends this Feet to me offering to sell his body. Of course, I am not practising for years, but I keep an office on Park Avenue just for old times' sake, and it is to this office he comes. At first I think he is crazy, but he refers me to Mr Armand Rosenthal, the big sporting man, who assures me that Feet Samuels is all right.

'The idea strikes me that if I make a deal with Feet Samuels for his body as he proposes, he will wait until the time comes to pay his obligation and run away, and,' the doc says, 'I will never be troubled by his rivalry for the affections of Hortense again. But he does not depart. I do not reckon on the holding power of love.

'Finally in a jealous frenzy I take after him with a knife, figuring to scare him out of town. But it is too late. I can see now Hortense loves him in return, or she will not drop a scuttle of coal on me in his defence as she does.

'Yes, gentlemen,' the old doc says, 'I am broken-hearted. I also seem to have a large lump on my head. Besides, Hortense has all my presents, and Feet Samuels has my money, so I get the worst of it all around. I only hope and trust that my daughter Eloise, who is Mrs Sidney Simmons Bragdon, does not hear of this, or she may be as mad as she is the time I wish to marry the beautiful cigarette girl in Jimmy Kelley's.'

Here Doc Bodeeker seems all busted up by his feelings and starts to shed tears, and everybody is feeling very sorry for him indeed, when up steps The Brain, who is taking everything in.

'Do not worry about your presents and your dough,' The Brain says. 'I will make everything good, because I am the guy who okays Feet Samuels with you. I am wrong on a guy for the first time in my life, and I must pay, but Feet Samuels will be very, very sorry when I find him. Of course, I do not figure on a doll in the case, and this always makes quite a difference, so I am really not a hundred per cent wrong on the guy, at that.

'But,' The Brain says, in a very loud voice so everybody can hear, 'Feet Samuels is nothing but a dirty welsher for not turning in his body to you as per agreement, and as long as he lives he will never get another dollar or another okay off of me, or anybody I know. His credit is ruined for ever on Broadway.'

But I judge that Feet and Hortense do not care. The last time I hear of them they are away over in New Jersey where not even The Brain's guys dast to bother them on account of Skush O'Brien, and I understand they are raising chickens and children right and left, and that all of Hortense's bracelets are now in Newark municipal bonds, which I am told are not bad bonds, at that.

14 THE BRAIN GOES HOME

ONE night The Brain is walking me up and down Broadway in front of Mindy's Restaurant, and speaking of this and that, when along comes a red-headed raggedy doll selling apples at five cents per copy, and The Brain, being very fond of apples, grabs one out of her basket and hands her a five-dollar bill.

The red-headed raggedy doll, who is maybe thirty-odd and is nothing but a crow as far as looks are concerned, squints at the finnif, and says to The Brain like this:

'I do not have change for so much money,' she says, 'but I will go and get it in a minute.'

'You keep the change,' The Brain says, biting a big hunk out of the apple and taking my arm to start me walking again.

Well, the raggedy doll looks at The Brain again, and it seems to me that all of a sudden there are large tears in her eyes as she says:

'Oh, thank you, sir! Thank you, thank you, and God bless you, sir!'

And then she goes on up the street in a hurry, with her hands over her eyes and her shoulders shaking, and The Brain turns around very much astonished, and watches her until she is out of sight.

'Why, my goodness!' The Brain says. 'I give Doris Clare ten G's last night, and she does not make half as much fuss over it as this doll does over a pound note.'

'Well,' I say, 'maybe the apple doll needs a pound note more than Doris needs ten G's.'

'Maybe so,' The Brain says. 'And of course, Doris gives me much more in return than just an apple and a God bless me.

Doris gives me her love. I guess,' The Brain says, 'that love costs me about as much dough as any guy that ever lives.'

'I guess it does,' I say, and the chances are we both guess right, because off-hand I figure that if The Brain gets out on three hundred G's per year for love, he is running his love business very economically indeed, because it is well known to one and all that The Brain has three different dolls, besides an ever-loving wife.

In fact, The Brain is sometimes spoken of by many citizens as the 'Love King', but only behind his back, because The Brain likes to think his love affairs are a great secret to all but maybe a few, although the only guy I ever see in this town who does not know all about them is a guy who is deaf, dumb, and blind.

I once read a story about a guy by the name of King Solomon who lives a long time ago and who has a thousand dolls all at once, which is going in for dolls on a very large scale indeed, but I guarantee that all of King Solomon's dolls put together are not as expensive as any one of The Brain's dolls. The overhead on Doris Clare alone will drive an ordinary guy daffy, and Doris is practically frugal compared to Cynthia Harris and Bobby Baker.

Then there is Charlotte, who is The Brain's ever-loving wife and who has a society bug and needs plenty of coconuts at all times to keep her a going concern. I once hear The Brain tell Bobby Baker that his ever-loving wife is a bit of an invalid, but as a matter of fact there is never anything the matter with Charlotte that a few bobs will not cure, although of course this goes for nearly every doll in this world who is an invalid.

When a guy is knocking around Broadway as long as The Brain, he is bound to accumulate dolls here and there, but most guys accumulate one at a time, and when this one runs out on him, as Broadway dolls will do, he accumulates another, and so on, and so on, until he is too old to care about such matters as dolls, which is when he is maybe a hundred and four years old, although I hear of several guys who beat even this record.

But when The Brain accumulates a doll he seems to keep her accumulated, and none of them ever run out on him, and while this will be a very great nuisance to the average guy, it pleases

The Brain no little because it makes him think he has a very great power over dolls.

'They are not to blame if they fall in love with me,' The Brain says to me one night. 'I will not cause one of them any sorrow for all the world.'

Well, of course, it is most astonishing to me to hear a guy as smart as The Brain using such language, but I figure he may really believe it, because The Brain thinks very good of himself at all times. However, some guys claim that the real reason The Brain keeps all his dolls is because he is too selfish to give them away, although personally I will not take any of them if The Brain throws in a cash bonus, except maybe Bobby Baker.

Anyway, The Brain keeps his dolls accumulated, and furthermore he spends plenty of dough on them, what with buying them automobiles and furs and diamonds and swell places to live in – especially swell places to live in. One time I tell The Brain he will save himself plenty if he hires a house and bunches his dolls together in one big happy family, instead of having them scattered all over town, but The Brain says this idea is no good.

'In the first place,' he says, 'they do not know about each other, except Doris and Cynthia and Bobby know about Charlotte, although she does not know about them. They each think they are the only one with me. So if I corral them all together they will be jealous of each other over my love. Anyway,' The Brain says, 'such an arrangement will be very immoral and against the law. No,' he says, 'it is better to have them in different spots, because think of the many homes it gives to me to go to in case I wish to go home. In fact,' The Brain says, 'I guess I have more homes to go to than any other guy on Broadway.'

Well, this may be true, but what The Brain wants with a lot of different homes is a very great mystery on Broadway, because he seldom goes home, anyway, his idea in not going home being that something may happen in this town while he is at home that he is not in on. The Brain seldom goes anywhere in particular. He never goes out in public with any one of his dolls, except maybe once or twice a year with Charlotte, his ever-loving wife, and finally he even stops going with her because Doris Clare says it does not look good to Doris's personal friends.

The Brain marries Charlotte long before he becomes the biggest guy in gambling operations in the East, and a millionaire two or three times over, but he is never much of a hand to sit around home and chew the fat with his ever-loving wife, as husbands often do. Furthermore, when he is poor he has to live in a neighbourhood which is too far away for it to be convenient for him to go home, so finally he gets out of the habit of going there.

But Charlotte is not such a doll as cares to spend more than one or two years looking at the pictures on the wall, because it seems the pictures on her wall are nothing but pictures of cows in the meadows and houses covered with snow, so she does not go home any more than necessary, either, and has her own friends and is very happy indeed, especially after The Brain gets so he can send in right along.

I will say one thing about The Brain and his dolls: he never picks a crow. He has a very good eye for faces and shapes, and even Charlotte, his ever loving wife, is not a crow, although she is not as young as she used to be. As for Doris Clare, she is one of the great beauties on the Ziegfeld roof in her day, and while her day is by no means yesterday, or even the day before, Doris holds on pretty well in the matter of looks. Giving her a shade the best of it, I will say that Doris is thirty-two or -three, but she has plenty of zing left in her, at that, and her hair remains very blonde, no matter what.

In fact, The Brain does not care much if his dolls are blonde or brunette, because Cynthia Harris's hair is as black as the inside of a wolf, while Bobby Baker is betwixt and between, her hair being a light brown. Cynthia Harris is more of a Johnny-come-lately than Doris, being out of Mr Earl Carroll's 'Vanities', and I hear she first comes to New York as Miss Somebody in one of these beauty contests which she will win hands down if one of the judges does not get a big wink from a Miss Somebody Else.

Of course, Cynthia is doing some winking herself at this time, but it seems that she picks a guy to wink at thinking he is one of the judges, when he is nothing but a newspaperman and has no say whatever about the decision.

Well, Mr Earl Carroll feels sorry for Cynthia, so he puts her in the 'Vanities' and lets her walk around raw, and The Brain sees her, and the next thing anybody knows she is riding in a big foreign automobile the size of a rum chaser, and is chucking a terrible swell.

Personally, I always consider Bobby Baker the smartest of all The Brain's dolls, because she is just middling as to looks and she does not have any of the advantages of life like Doris Clare and Cynthia Harris, such as jobs on the stage where they can walk around showing off their shapes to guys such as The Brain. Bobby Baker starts off as nothing but a private secretary to a guy in Wall Street, and naturally she is always wearing clothes, or anyway, as many clothes as an ordinary doll wears nowadays, which is not so many, at that.

It seems that The Brain once has some business with the guy Bobby works for and happens to get talking to Bobby, and she tells him how she always wishes to meet him, what with hearing and reading about him, and how he is just as handsome and romantic-looking as she always pictures him to herself.

Now I wish to say I will never call any doll a liar, being at all times a gentleman, and for all I know, Bobby Baker may really think The Brain is handsome and romantic-looking, but personally I figure if she is not lying to him, she is at least a little excited when she makes such a statement to The Brain. The best you can give The Brain at this time is that he is very well dressed.

He is maybe forty years old, give or take a couple of years, and he is commencing to get a little bunchy about the middle, what with sitting down at card-tables so much and never taking any exercise outside of walking guys such as me up and down in front of Mindy's for a few hours every night. He has a clean-looking face, always very white around the gills, and he has nice teeth and a nice smile when he wishes to smile, which is never at guys who owe him dough.

And I will say for The Brain he has what is called personality. He tells a story well, although he is always the hero of any story he tells, and he knows how to make himself agreeable to dolls in many ways. He has a pretty fair sort of education, and while dolls such as Cynthia and Doris, and maybe Charlotte, too, will rather have a charge account at Cartier's than all the education in Yale and Harvard put together, it seems that Bobby Baker likes highbrow gab, so naturally she gets plenty of same from The Brain.

Well, pretty soon Bobby is riding around in a car bigger than Cynthia's, though neither is as big as Doris's car, and all the neighbours' children over in Flatbush, which is where Bobby hails from, are very jealous of her and running around spreading gossip about her, but keeping their eyes open for big cars themselves. Personally, I always figure The Brain lowers himself socially by taking up with a doll from Flatbush, especially as Bobby Baker soon goes in for literary guys, such as newspaper scribes and similar characters around Greenwich Village.

But there is no denying Bobby Baker is a very smart little doll, and in the four or five years she is one of The Brain's dolls, she gets more dough out of him than all the others put together, because she is always telling him how much she loves him, and saying she cannot do without him, while Doris Clare and Cynthia Harris sometimes forget to mention this more than once or twice a month.

Now what happens early one morning but a guy by the name of Daffy Jack hauls off and sticks a shiv in The Brain's left side. It seems that this is done at the request of a certain party by the name of Homer Swing, who owes The Brain plenty of dough in a gambling transaction, and who becomes very indignant when The Brain presses him somewhat for payment. It seems that Daffy Jack, who is considered a very good shiv artist, aims at The Brain's heart, but misses it by a couple of inches, leaving The Brain with a very bad cut in his side which calls for some stitching.

Big Nig, the crap shooter, and I are standing at Fifty-second Street and Seventh Avenue along about 2 a.m., speaking of not much, when The Brain comes stumbling out of Fifty-second Street, and falls in Big Nig's arms, practically ruining a brand-new topcoat which Big Nig pays sixty bucks for a few days back with the blood that is coming out of the cut. Naturally, Big Nig is indignant about this, but we can see that it is no time to be speaking to The Brain about such matters. We can see that The Brain is carved up quite some, and is in a bad way.

Of course, we are not greatly surprised at seeing The Brain in this condition, because for years he is practically no price around this town, what with this guy and that being anxious to do something or other to him, but we are never expecting to see him carved up like a turkey. We are expecting to see him with a few slugs in him, and both Big Nig and me are very angry to think that there are guys around who will use such instruments as a knife on anybody.

But while we are thinking it over, The Brain says to me like this:

'Call Hymie Weissberger, and Doc Frisch,' he says, 'and take me home.'

Naturally, a guy such as The Brain wishes his lawyer before he wishes his doctor, and Hymie Weissberger is The Brain's mouthpiece, and a very sure-footed guy, at that.

'Well,' I say, 'we better take you to a hospital where you can get good attention at once.'

'No,' The Brain says. 'I wish to keep this secret. It will be a bad thing for me right now to have this get out, and if you take me to a hospital they must report it to the coppers. Take me home.'

Naturally, I say which home, being somewhat confused about The Brain's homes, and he seems to study a minute as if this is a question to be well thought out.

'Park Avenue,' The Brain says finally, so Big Nig stops a taxicab, and we help The Brain into the cab and tell the jockey to take us to the apartment house on Park Avenue near Sixty-fourth where The Brain's ever-loving wife Charlotte lives.

When we get there, I figure it is best for me to go up first and break the news gently to Charlotte, because I can see what a shock it is bound to be to any ever-loving wife to have her husband brought home in the early hours of the morning all shivved up.

Well, the door man and the elevator guy in the apartment

house give me an argument about going up to The Brain's apartment, saying a blow out of some kind is going on there, but after I explain to them that The Brain is sick, they let me go. A big fat butler comes to the door of the apartment when I ring, and I can see there are many dolls and guys in evening clothes in the apartment, and somebody is singing very loud.

The butler tries to tell me I cannot see Charlotte, but I finally convince him it is best, so by and by she comes to the door, and a very pleasant sight she is, at that, with jewellery all over her. I stall around awhile, so as not to alarm her too much, and then I tell her The Brain meets with an accident and that we have him outside in a cab, and ask her where we shall put him.

'Why,' she says, 'put him in a hospital, of course. I am entertaining some very important people to-night, and I cannot have them disturbed by bringing in a hospital patient. Take him to a hospital, and tell him I will come and see him to-morrow and bring him some broth.'

I try to explain to her that The Brain does not need any broth, but a nice place to lie down in, but finally she gets very testy with me and shuts the door in my face, saying as follows:

'Take him to a hospital, I tell you. This is a ridiculous hour for him to be coming home, anyway. It is twenty years since he comes home so early.'

Then as I am waiting for the elevator, she opens the door again just a little bit and says:

'By the way, is he hurt bad?'

I say we do not know how bad he is hurt, and she shuts the door again, and I go back to the cab again, thinking what a heartless doll she is, although I can see where it will be very inconvenient for her to bust up her party, at that.

The Brain is lying back in the corner of the cab, his eyes half-closed, and by this time it seems that Big Nig stops the blood somewhat with a handkerchief, but The Brain acts somewhat weak to me. He sort of rouses himself when I climb in the cab, and when I tell him his ever-loving wife is not home he smiles a bit and whispers:

'Take me to Doris.'

Now Doris lives in a big apartment house away over on West

Seventy-second Street near the Drive, and I tell the taxi jockey to go there while The Brain seems to slide off into a doze. Then Big Nig leans over to me and says to me like this:

'No use taking him there,' Big Nig says. 'I see Doris going out to-night all dressed up in her ermine coat with this actor guy, Jack Walen, she is struck on. It is a very great scandal around and about the way they carry on. Let us take him to Cynthia,' Nig says. 'She is a very large-hearted doll who will be very glad to take him in.'

Now Cynthia Harris has a big suite of rooms that cost fifteen G's a year in a big hotel just off Fifth Avenue, Cynthia being a doll who likes to be downtown so if she hears of anything coming off anywhere she can get there very rapidly. When we arrive at the hotel I call her on the house 'phone and tell her I must see her about something very important, so Cynthia says for me to come up.

It is now maybe three-fifteen, and I am somewhat surprised to find Cynthia home, at that, but there she is, and looking very beautiful indeed in a négligée with her hair hanging down, and I can see that The Brain is no chump when it comes to picking them. She gives me a hello pleasant enough, but as soon as I explain what I am there for, her kisser gets very stern and she says to me like this:

'Listen,' she says, 'I got trouble enough around this joint, what with two guys getting in a fight over me at a little gathering I have here last night and the house copper coming in to split them out, and I do not care to have any more. Suppose it gets out that The Brain is here? What will the newspapers print about me? Think of my reputation!'

Well, in about ten minutes I can see there is no use arguing with her, because she can talk faster than I can, and mostly she talks about what a knock it will be to her reputation if she takes The Brain in, so I leave her standing at the door in her négligée, still looking very beautiful, at that.

There is now nothing for us to do but take The Brain to Bobby Baker, who lives in a duplex apartment in Sutton Place over by the East River, where the swells set up a colony of nice apartments in the heart of an old tenement-house neighbourhood, and as we are on our way there with The Brain lying back in the cab just barely breathing, I say to Big Nig like this:

'Nig,' I say, 'when we get to Bobby's, we will carry The Brain in without asking her first and just dump him on her so she cannot refuse to take him in, although,' I say, 'Bobby Baker is a nice little doll, and I am pretty sure she will do anything she can for him, especially,' I say, 'since he pays fifty G's for this apartment we are going to.'

So when the taxicab stops in front of Bobby's house, Nig and I take The Brain out of the cab and lug him between us up to the door of Bobby's apartment, where I ring the bell. Bobby opens the door herself, and I happen to see a guy's legs zip into a room in the apartment behind her, although of course there is nothing wrong in such a sight, even though the guy's legs are in pink pyjamas.

Naturally, Bobby is greatly astonished to see us with The Brain dangling between us, but she does not invite us in as I explain to her that The Brain is stabbed and that his last words are for us to take him to his Bobby. Furthermore, she does not let me finish my story which will be very sad indeed, if she keeps on listening.

'If you do not take him away from here at once,' Bobby says, before I am down to the pathetic part, 'I will call the cops and you guys will be arrested on suspicion that you know something about how he gets hurt.'

Then she slams the door on us, and we lug The Brain back down the stairs into the street, because all of a sudden it strikes us that Bobby is right, and if The Brain is found in our possession all stabbed up, and he happens to croak, we are in a very tough spot, because the cops just naturally love to refuse to believe guys like Big Nig and me, no matter what we say.

Furthermore, the same idea must hit the taxicab jockey after we lift The Brain out of the cab, because he is nowhere to be seen, and there we are away over by the East River in the early morning, with no other taxis in sight, and a cop liable to happen along any minute.

Well, there is nothing for us to do but get away from there, so Big Nig and I start moving, with me carrying The Brain's feet, and Big Nig his head. We get several blocks away from Sutton Place, going very slow and hiding in dark doorways when we hear anybody coming, and now we are in a section of tenement houses, when all of a sudden up out of the basement of one of these tenements pops a doll.

She sees us before we can get in a dark place, and she seems to have plenty of nerve for a doll, because she comes right over to us and looks at Big Nig and me, and then looks at The Brain, who loses his hat somewhere along the line, so his pale face is plain to be seen by even the dim street light.

'Why,' the doll says, 'it is the kind gentleman who gives me the five dollars for the apple – the money that buys the medicine that saves my Joey's life. What is the matter?'

'Well,' I say to the doll, who is still raggedy and still red-headed, 'there is nothing much the matter except if we do not get him somewhere soon, this guy will up and croak on us.'

'Bring him into my house,' she says, pointing to the joint she just comes out of. 'It is not much of a place, but you can let him rest there until you get help. I am just going over here to a drug store to get some more medicine for Joey, although he is out of danger now, thanks to this gentleman.'

So we lug The Brain down the basement steps with the doll leading the way, and we follow her into a room that smells like a Chinese laundry and seems to be full of kids sleeping on the floor. There is only one bed in the room, and it is not much of a bed any way you look at it, and there seems to be a kid in this bed, too, but the red-headed doll rolls this kid over to one side of the bed and motions us to lay The Brain alongside of the kid. Then she gets a wet rag and starts bathing The Brain's noggin.

He finally opens his eyes and looks at the red-headed raggedy doll, and she grins at him very pleasant. When I think things over afterward, I figure The Brain is conscious of much of what is going on when we are packing him around, although he does not say anything, maybe because he is too weak. Anyway, he turns his head to Big Nig, and says to him like this:

'Bring Weissberger and Frisch as quick as you can,' he says. 'Anyway, get Weissberger. I do not know how bad I am hurt, and I must tell him some things.'

Well, The Brain is hurt pretty bad, as it turns out, and in fact he never gets well, but he stays in the basement dump until he dies three days later, with the red-headed raggedy doll nursing him alongside her sick kid Joey, because the croaker, old Doc Frisch, says it is no good moving The Brain, and may only make him pop off sooner. In fact, Doc Frisch is much astonished that The Brain lives at all, considering the way we lug him around.

I am present at The Brain's funeral at Wiggins's Funeral Parlours, like everybody else on Broadway, and I wish to say I never see more flowers in all my life. They are all over the casket and knee-deep on the floor, and some of the pieces must cost plenty, the price of flowers being what they are in this town nowadays. In fact, I judge it is the size and cost of the different pieces that makes me notice a little bundle of faded red carnations not much bigger than your fist that is laying alongside a pillow of violets the size of a horse blanket.

There is a small card tied to the carnations, and it says on this card, as follows: 'To a kind gentleman', and it comes to my mind that out of all the thousands of dollars' worth of flowers there, these faded carnations represent the only true sincerity. I mention this to Big Nig, and he says the chances are I am right, but that even true sincerity is not going to do The Brain any good where he is going.

Anybody will tell you that for off-hand weeping at a funeral The Brain's ever-loving wife Charlotte does herself very proud indeed, but she is not one-two-seven with Doris Clare, Cynthia Harris, and Bobby Baker. In fact, Bobby Baker weeps so loud that there is some talk of heaving her out of the funeral altogether.

However, I afterwards hear that loud as they are at the funeral, it is nothing to the weep they all put on when it comes out that The Brain has Hymie Weissberger draw up a new will while he is dying and leaves all his dough to the red-headed raggedy doll, whose name seems to be O'Halloran, and who is the widow of a bricklayer and has five kids.

Well, at first all the citizens along Broadway say it is a wonderful thing for The Brain to do, and serves his ever-loving wife and Doris and Cynthia and Bobby just right; and from the way one and all speaks you will think they are going to build a monument to The Brain for his generosity to the red-headed raggedy doll.

But about two weeks after he is dead, I hear citizens saying the chances are the red-headed raggedy doll is nothing but one of The Brain's old-time dolls, and that maybe the kids are his and that he leaves them the dough because his conscience hurts him at the finish, for this is the way Broadway is. But personally I know it cannot be true, for if there is one thing The Brain never has it is a conscience.

15 SOCIAL ERROR

When Mr Ziegfeld picks a doll she is apt to be above the average when it comes to looks, for Mr Ziegfeld is by no means a chump at picking dolls. But when Mr Ziegfeld picks Miss Midgie Muldoon, he beats his own best record, or anyway ties it. I never see a better-looking doll in my life, although she is somewhat smaller than I like them. I like my dolls big enough to take a good hold on, and Miss Midgie Muldoon is only about knee-high to a Pomeranian. But she is very cute, and I do not blame Handsome Jack Maddigan for going daffy about her.

Now most any doll on Broadway will be very glad indeed to have Handsome Jack Maddigan give her a tumble, so it is very surprising to one and all when Miss Midgie Muldoon plays the chill for Handsome Jack, especially when you figure that Miss Midgie Muldoon is nothing but a chorus doll, while Handsome Jack is quite a high shot in this town. But one night in the Hot Box when Handsome Jack sends word to Miss Midgie Muldoon, by Miss Billy Perry, who is Dave the Dude's wife, that he will like to meet up with her, Miss Midgie Muldoon sends word back to Handsome Jack that she is not meeting up with tough guys.

Well, naturally this crack burns Handsome Jack up quite some. But Dave the Dude says never mind, and furthermore Dave says Miss Midgie Muldoon's crack serves Handsome Jack right for sitting around shooting off his mouth, and putting himself away as a tough guy, because if there is anything Dave hates it is a guy letting on he is tough, no matter how tough he really is, and Handsome Jack is certainly such a guy.

He is a big tall blond guy who comes up out of what they call Hell's Kitchen over on the West Side, and if he has a little more sense the chances are he will be as important a guy as Dave the Dude himself in time, instead of generally working for Dave, but Handsome Jack likes to wear very good clothes, and drink, and sit around a lot, and also do plenty of talking, and no matter how much dough he makes he never seems able to hold much of anything.

Personally, I never care to have any truck with Handsome Jack because he always strikes me as a guy who is a little too quick on the trigger to suit me, and I always figure the best you are going to get out of being around guys who are quick on the trigger is the worst of it, and so any time I see Handsome Jack I give him the back of my neck. But there are many people in this world such as Basil Valentine who love to be around these characters.

This Basil Valentine is a little guy who wears horn cheaters and writes articles for the magazines, and is personally a very nice little guy, and as harmless as a water snake, but he cannot have a whole lot of sense, or he will not be hanging out with Handsome Jack and other such characters.

If a guy hangs out with tough guys long enough he is apt to get to thinking maybe he is tough himself, and by and by other people may get the idea he is tough, and the first thing you know along comes some copper in plain clothes, such as Johnny Brannigan, of the strong-arm squad, and biffs him on the noggin with a blackjack just to see how tough he is. As I say, Basil Valentine is a very harmless guy, but after he is hanging out with Handsome Jack a while, I hear Basil talking very tough to a bus boy, and the chances are he is building himself up to talk tough to a waiter, and then maybe to a head waiter, and finally he may consider himself tough enough to talk tough to anybody.

I can show you many a guy who is supposed to be strictly legitimate sitting around with guys who are figured as tough guys, and why this is I do not know, but I am speaking to Waldo Winchester, the newspaper scribe, about the proposition one night, and Waldo Winchester, who is a half-smart guy in many respects, says it is what is called an underworld complex. Waldo Winchester says many legitimate people are much interested in the doings of tough guys, and consider them very romantic, and he says if I do not believe it look at all the junk the newspapers print making heroes out of tough guys.

Waldo Winchester says the underworld complex is a very common complex and that Basil Valentine has it, and so has Miss Harriet Mackyle, or she will not be all the time sticking her snoot into joints where tough guys hang out. This Miss Harriet Mackyle is one of these rich dolls who wears snaky-looking evening clothes, and has her hair cut like a boy's, with her ears sticking out, and is always around the night traps, generally with some guy with a little moustache, and a way of talking like an Englishman, and come to think of it I do see her in tough joints more than somewhat, saying hello to different parties such as nobody in their right minds will say hello to, including such as Red Henry, who is just back from Dannemora, after being away for quite a spell for taking things out of some-body's safe and blowing the safe open to take these things.

In fact, I see Miss Harriet Mackyle dancing one night in the Hearts and Flowers club, which is a very tough joint indeed, and who is she dancing with but Red Henry, and when I ask Waldo Winchester what he makes of this proposition, he says it is part of the underworld complex he is talking about. He says Miss Harriet Mackyle probably thinks it smart to tell her swell friends she dances with a safe-blower, although personally if I am going to dance with a safe-blower at all, which does not seem likely, I will pick me out a nicer safe-blower than Red Henry, because he is such a guy as does not take a bath since he leaves Dannemora, and he is back from Dannemora for several months.

One party who does not seem to have much of Waldo Win-chester's underworld complex as far as I can see is Miss Midgie Muldoon, because I never see her around any night traps except such as the Hot Box and the Sixteen Hundred club, which are considered very nice places, and reasonably safe for anybody who does not get too far out of line, and Miss Midgie Muldoon is always with very legitimate guys such as Buddy Donaldson, the song writer, or Walter Gumble, who plays the trombone in Paul Whiteman's band, or maybe sometimes with Paul Hawley, the actor.

Furthermore, when she is around such places, Miss Midgie Muldoon minds her own business quite a bit, and always looks right past Handsome Jack Maddigan, which burns Jack up all the more. It is the first time Handsome Jack ever runs into a doll who does not seem excited about him, and he does not know what to make of such a situation.

Well, what happens but Dave the Dude comes to me one day and says to me like this: 'Listen,' Dave says, 'this doll Miss Harriet Mackyle is one of my best customers for high-grade merchandise, and is as good as wheat in the bin, and she is asking a favour of me. She is giving a party Sunday night in her joint over on Park Avenue, and she wishes me to invite some of the mob, so go around and tell about a dozen guys to be there all dressed, and not get too fresh, because a big order of Scotch and champagne goes with the favour.'

Now such a party is by no means unusual, although generally it is some swell guy who gives it rather than a doll, and he gets Broadway guys to be there to show his pals what a mixer he is. Waldo Winchester says it is to give colour to things, though where the colour comes in I do not know, for Broadway guys, such as will go to a party like this, are apt to just sit around and say nothing, and act very gentlemanly, because they figure they are on exhibition like freaks, and the only way you can get them to such parties in the first place is through some such connexion as Miss Harriet Mackyle has with Dave the Dude.

Anyway, I go around and about and tell a lot of guys what Dave the Dude wishes them to do, and among others I tell Handsome Jack, who is tickled to death by the invitation, because if there is anything Jack loves more than anything else it is to be in a spot where he can show off some. Furthermore, Handsome Jack has a sneaking idea Miss Harriet Mackyle is red hot for him because she sometimes gives him the old eye when she sees him around the Sixteen Hundred club, and other spots, but then she does the same thing to Big Nig, and a lot of other guys I can mention, because that is just naturally the way Miss Harriet Mackyle is. But of course I do not speak of this to Handsome Jack. Basil Valentine is with Jack when I invite him, so I tell Basil to come along, too, because I do not wish him to think I am a snob.

It turns out that Basil is one of the very first guys to show up Sunday night at Miss Harriet Mackyle's apartment, where I am already on hand to help get in the Scotch and champagne, and to make Miss Harriet Mackyle acquainted with such of the mob as I invite, although I find we are about lost in the shuffle of guys with little moustaches, and dolls in evening clothes that leave plenty of them sticking out here and there. It seems everybody on Broadway is there, as well as a lot of Park Avenue, and Mr Ziegfeld is especially well represented, and among his people I see Miss Midgie Muldoon, although I have to stand on tiptoe to see her on account of the guys with little moustaches around her, and their interest in Miss Midgie Muldoon proves that they are not such saps as they look, even if they do wear little moustaches.

It is a very large apartment, and the first thing I notice is a big green parrot swinging in a ring hung from the ceiling in a corner of what seems to be the main room, and the reason I notice this parrot is because it is letting out a squawk now and then, and yelling different words, such as Polly wants a cracker. There are also a lot of canary birds hung around the joint, so I judge Miss Harriet Mackyle loves animals, as well as peculiar people, such as she has for guests.

I am somewhat surprised to see Red Henry all dressed up in evening clothes moving around among the guests. I do not invite Red Henry, so I suppose Miss Harriet Mackyle invites him, or he hears rumours of the party, and just crashes in, but personally I consider it very bad taste on Red Henry's part to show himself in such a spot, and so does everybody else that knows him, although he seems to be minding his own business pretty well.

Finally when the serious drinking is under way, and a good time is being had by one and all, Miss Harriet Mackyle comes over to me and says to me like this: 'Now tell me about your different friends, so I can tell my other guests. They will be thrilled to death meeting these bad characters.'

'Well,' I say, 'you see the little guy over there staring at you as if you are a ghost, or some such? Well, he is nobody but Bad Basil Valentine, who will kill you as quick as you can say scat, and maybe quicker. He is undoubtedly the toughest guy here to-night, or anywhere else in this man's town for that matter. Yes, ma'am, Bad Basil Valentine is one dead tough mug,' I say, 'although he is harmless-looking at this time. Bad Basil kills many a guy in his day. In fact, Miss Mackyle,' I say, 'Bad Basil can scarcely sleep good any night he does not kill some guy.'

'My goodness!' Miss Harriet Mackyle says, looking Basil over very carefully. 'He does not look so bad at first glance, although now that I examine him closely I believe I do detect a sinister gleam in his eye.'

Well, Miss Harriet Mackyle can hardly wait until she gets away from me, and the next I see of her she has Basil Valentine surrounded and is almost chewing his ear off as she gabs to him, and anybody can see that Basil is all pleasured up by this attention. In fact, Basil is snagged if ever I see a guy snagged, and personally I do not blame him, because Miss Harriet Mackyle may not look a million, but she has a couple, and you can see enough of her in her evening clothes to know that nothing about her is phony.

The party is going big along towards one o'clock when all of a sudden in comes Handsome Jack Maddigan with half a heat on, and in five minutes he is all over the joint, drinking everything that is offered him, and making a fast play for all the dolls, and talking very loud. He is sored up more than somewhat when he finds Miss Harriet Mackyle does not give him much of a tumble, because he figures she will be calling him on top the minute he blows in, but Miss Harriet Mackyle is too busy with Basil Valentine finding out from Basil how he knocks off six of Al Capone's mob out in Chicago one time when he is out there on a pleasure trip.

Well, while feeling sored up about Miss Harriet Mackyle passing him up for Basil Valentine, and not knowing how it comes Basil is in so stout with her, Handsome Jack bumps into Red Henry, and Red Henry makes some fresh crack to Jack about Basil moving in on him, which causes Handsome Jack to hit Red Henry on the chin, and knock him half into the lap of

Miss Midgie Muldoon, who is sitting in a chair with a lot of little moustaches around her.

Naturally this incident causes some excitement for a moment. But the way Miss Midgie Muldoon takes it is very surprising. She just sort of dusts Red Henry off her, and stands up no bigger than a demi-tasse, and looks Handsome Jack right in the eye very cool, and says: 'Ah, a parlour tough guy.' Then she walks away, leaving Handsome Jack with his mouth open, because he does not know up to this moment that Miss Midgie Muldoon is present.

Well, somebody heaves Red Henry out of the joint, and the party continues, but I see Handsome Jack wandering around looking very lonesome, and with not much speed left compared to what he brings in. Somehow I figure Handsome Jack is looking for Miss Midgie Muldoon, but she keeps off among the little moustaches, and finally Handsome Jack takes to belting the old grape right freely to get his zing back. He gets himself pretty well organized, and when he suddenly comes upon Miss Midgie Muldoon standing by herself for a moment, he is feeling very brisk indeed, and he says to her like this: 'Hello, Beautiful, are you playing the hard-to-get for me?' But Miss Midgie Muldoon only looks him in the eye again and says: 'Ah, the parlour tough guy! Go away, tough guy. I do not like tough guys.'

Well, this is not so encouraging when you come to think of it, but Handsome Jack is a guy who will never be ruled off for not trying with the dolls, and he is just about to begin giving her a little more work, when all of a sudden a voice goes 'Ha-ha-ha', and then it says: 'Hello, you fool!'

Now of course it is nothing but the parrot talking, and it says again: 'Ha-ha-ha. Hello, you fool!' Of course, the parrot, whose name turns out to be Polly, does not mean Handsome Jack, but of course Handsome Jack does not know the parrot does not mean him, and naturally he feels very much insulted. Furthermore, he has plenty of champagne inside him. So all of a sudden he outs with the old equalizer and lets go at Polly, and the next minute there are green feathers flying all over the joint, and poor old Mister, or maybe Missus, Polly is stretched out as dead as a doornail, and maybe deader.

Well, I never see a doll carry on like Miss Harriet Mackyle does when she finds out her Polly is a goner, and what she says to Handsome Jack is really very cutting and quite extensive, and the chances are Handsome Jack will finally haul off and smack Miss Harriet Mackyle in the snoot, only he realizes he is already guilty of a very grave social error in shooting the parrot, and he does not wish to make it any worse.

Anyway, Miss Midgie Muldoon is standing looking at Handsome Jack out of her great big round beautiful eyes with what Waldo Winchester, the scribe, afterwards tells me is plenty of scorn, and it looks to me as if Handsome Jack feels worse about Miss Midgie Muldoon's looks than he does about what Miss Harriet Mackyle is saying to him. But Miss Midgie Muldoon never opens her mouth. She just keeps looking at him for quite a spell, and then finally walks away, and it looks to me as if she is ready to bust out crying any minute, maybe because she feels sorry for Polly.

Well, naturally Handsome Jack's error busts up the party, because Miss Harriet Mackyle does not wish to take any chances on Handsome Jack starting in to pot her canaries, so we all go away leaving Miss Harriet Mackyle weeping over what she can find of Polly, and Basil Valentine crying with her, which I consider very chummy of Basil, at that.

A couple of nights later Basil comes into Mindy's restaurant, where I happen to be sitting with Handsome Jack, and anybody can tell that Basil is much worried about something.

'Jack,' he says, 'Miss Harriet Mackyle is very, very, very angry about you shooting Polly. In fact, she hates you, because Polly is a family heirloom.'

'Well,' Jack says, 'tell her I apologize, and will get her a new parrot as soon as I get the price. You know I am broke now. Tell her I am very sorry, although,' Jack says, 'her parrot has no right to call me a fool, and I leave this to everybody.'

'Miss Harriet Mackyle is after me every day to shoot you, Jack,' Basil says. 'She thinks I am a very tough guy, and that I will shoot anybody on short notice, and she wishes me to shoot you. In fact, she is somewhat displeased because I do not shoot you when you shoot poor Polly, but of course I explain to her I do not have a gun at the moment. Now Miss Harriet Mackyle says if I do not shoot you she will not love me, and I greatly wish to have Miss Harriet Mackyle love me, because I am practically daffy about her. So,' Basil says, 'I am wondering how much you will take to hold still and let me shoot you, Jack?'

'Why,' Handsome Jack says, very much astonished, 'you must be screwy.'

'Of course I do not mean to really shoot you, Jack,' Basil says. 'I mean to maybe shoot you with a blank cartridge, so Miss Harriet Mackyle will think I am shooting you sure enough, which will make her very grateful to me. I am thinking that maybe I can pay you one thousand five hundred dollars for such a job, although this sum represents nearly my life savings.'

'Why,' Handsome Jack says, 'your proposition sounds very reasonable, at that. I am just wondering where I can get hold of a few bobs to send Miss Midgie Muldoon a bar pin, or some such, and see if I cannot round myself up with her. She is still playing plenty of chill for me. You better make it two grand while you are about it.'

Well, Basil Valentine finally agrees to pay the two grand. Furthermore, Basil promises to put the dough up in advance with Dave the Dude, or some other reliable party, as this is rather an unusual business deal, and naturally Handsome Jack wishes to have his interests fully protected.

Well, the thing comes off a few nights later in the Hot Box, and it is all pretty well laid out in advance. It is understood that Basil is to bring Miss Harriet Mackyle into the Hot Box after regular hours when there are not apt to be any too many people around, and to find Handsome Jack there. Basil is to out with a gun and take a crack at Handsome Jack, and Handsome Jack is to let on he is hit, and Basil is to get Miss Harriet Mackyle out of the joint in the confusion.

Handsome Jack promises to lay low a few weeks afterwards so it will look as if he is dead, and Basil figures that in the meantime Miss Harriet Mackyle will be so grateful to him that she will love him very much indeed, and maybe marry him, which is really the big idea with Basil.

It is pretty generally known to one and all what is coming off, and quite a number of guys drift into the Hot Box during the night, including Dave the Dude, who seems to be getting quite a bang out of the situation. But who also bobs up very unexpectedly but Miss Midgie Muldoon with Buddy Donaldson, the song writer.

Handsome Jack is all upset by Miss Midgie Muldoon being there, but she never as much as looks at him. So Handsome Jack takes to drinking Scotch more than somewhat, and everybody commences to worry about whether he will hold still for Basil Valentine to shoot him, even with a blank cartridge. The Hot Box closes at three o'clock in the morning, and everybody is always turned out except the regulars. So by three-thirty there are only about a dozen guys and dolls in the joint when in comes Basil Valentine and Miss Harriet Mackyle.

Handsome Jack happens to be standing with his back to the door and not far from the table where Miss Midgie Muldoon and this Buddy Donaldson are sitting when Basil and Miss Harriet Mackyle come in, and right away Basil sings out, his voice wobbling no little: 'Handsome Jack Maddigan, your time has come!' At this Handsome Jack turns around, and there is Basil Valentine tugging a big rod out of the hind pocket of his pants.

The next thing anybody knows, there is a scream, and a doll's voice cries: 'Jack! Look out, Jack!' and out of her seat and over to Handsome Jack Maddigan bounces Miss Midgie Muldoon, and just as Basil finally raises the rod and turns it on, Miss Midgie Muldoon plants herself right in front of Jack and stretches out her arms on either side of her as if to shield him.

Well, the gun goes bingo in Basil's hand, but instead of falling like he is supposed to do, Handsome Jack stands there with his mouth open looking at Miss Midgie Muldoon, not knowing what to make of her jumping between him and the gun, and it is a good thing he does not fall, at that, because he is able to catch Miss Midgie Muldoon as she starts to keel over. At first we think maybe it is only a faint, but she has on a low-neck dress, and across her left shoulder there slowly spreads a red smear, and what is this red smear but blood, and as Handsome Jack grabs her she says to him like this: 'Hold me, dear, I am hurt.'

Now this is most unexpected, indeed, and is by no means a part of the play. Basil Valentine is standing by the door with the rod in his duke looking quite astonished, and making no move to get Miss Harriet Mackyle out of the joint as he is supposed to the minute he fires, and Miss Harriet Mackyle is letting out a few off-hand screams which are very piercing, and saying she never thinks that Basil will take her seriously and really plug anybody for her, although she also says she appreciates his thoughtfulness, at that.

You can see Basil is standing there wondering what goes wrong, when Dave the Dude, who is a fast thinker under all circumstances, takes a quick peek at Miss Midgie Muldoon, and then jumps across the room and nails Basil. 'Why,' Dave says to Basil, 'you are nothing but a rascal. You mean to kill him after all. You do not shoot a blank, you throw a slug, and you get Miss Midgie Muldoon with it in the shoulder.'

Well, Basil is a pretty sick-looking toad as Dave the Dude takes hold of him, and Miss Harriet Mackyle is putting on a few extra yips when Basil says: 'My goodness, Dave,' he says. 'I never know this gun is really loaded. In fact, I forget all about getting a gun of my own until the last minute, and am looking around for one when Red Henry comes along and says he will lend me his. I explain to him how the whole proposition is a joke, and tell him I must have blanks, and he kindly takes the lead out of the cartridges in front of my own eyes and makes them blank.'

'The chances are Red Henry works a quick change on you,' Dave the Dude says. 'Red Henry is very angry at Jack for hitting him on the chin.'

Then Dave takes the rod out of Basil's hand and breaks it open, and sure enough there are enough real slugs in it to sink a rowboat and no blanks whatever, which surprises Basil Valentine no little.

'Now,' Dave says, 'get away from here before Jack realizes

what happens, and keep out of sight until you hear from me, because if Miss Midgie Muldoon croaks it may cause some gossip. Furthermore,' Dave says, 'take this squawking doll with you.'

Well, you can see that Dave the Dude is pretty much steamed up, and he remains steamed up until it comes out that Miss Midgie Muldoon is only a little bit shot, and is by no means in danger of dying. We take her over to the Polyclinic Hospital, and a guy there digs the bullet out of her shoulder, and we leave her there with Handsome Jack holding her tight in his arms, and swearing he will never be tough again, but will get her a nice little home on Basil Valentine's two grand, and find himself a job, and take no more part in his old life, all of which seems to sound fair enough.

It is a couple of years before we hear of Miss Harriet Mackyle again, and then she is Mrs Basil Valentine, and is living in Naples over in Italy, and the people there are very much surprised because Mrs Basil Valentine never lets Mr Basil Valentine associate with guys over ten years old, and never lets him handle anything more dangerous than a niblick.

So this is about all there is to the story, except that when Handsome Jack Maddigan and Miss Midgie Muldoon stands up to be married by Father Leonard, Dave the Dude sizes them up for a minute, and then turns to me and says like this:

'Look,' Dave says, 'and tell me where does Miss Midgie Muldoon's shoulder come up to on Jack's left side.'

'Well,' I say, 'her shoulder comes just up to Jack's heart.'

'So you see,' Dave says, 'it is just as well for Jack she stops Basil's bullet, at that.'

16 UNDERTAKER SONG

Now this story I am going to tell you is about the game of football, a very healthy pastime for the young, and a great character builder from all I hear, but to get around to this game of football I am compelled to bring in some most obnoxious characters, beginning with a guy by the name of Joey Perhaps, and all I can conscientiously say about Joey is you can have him.

It is a matter of maybe four years since I see this Joey Perhaps until I notice him on a train going to Boston, Mass., one Friday afternoon. He is sitting across from me in the dining-car, where I am enjoying a small portion of baked beans and brown bread, and he looks over to me once, but he does not rap to me.

There is no doubt but what Joey Perhaps is bad company, because the last I hear of him he is hollering copper on a guy by the name of Jack Ortega, and as a result of Joey Perhaps hollering copper, this Jack Ortega is taken to the city of Ossining, N.Y., and placed in an electric chair, and given a very, very, very severe shock in the seat of his pants.

It is something about plugging a most legitimate business guy in the city of Rochester, N.Y., when Joey Perhaps and Jack Ortega are engaged together in a little enterprise to shake the guy down, but the details of this transaction are dull, sordid, and quite uninteresting, except that Joey Perhaps turns state's evidence and announces that Jack Ortega fires the shot which cools the legitimate guy off, for which service he is rewarded with only a small stretch.

I must say for Joey Perhaps that he looks good, and he is very well dressed, but then Joey is always particular about clothes, and he is quite a handy guy with the dolls in his day and, to tell the truth, many citizens along Broadway are by no means displeased when Joey is placed in the state institution, because they are generally pretty uneasy about their dolls when he is around.

Naturally, I am wondering why Joey Perhaps is on this train going to Boston, Mass., but for all I know maybe he is wondering the same thing about me, although personally I am making no secret about it. The idea is I am *en route* to Boston, Mass., to see a contest of skill and science that is to take place there this very Friday night between a party by the name of Lefty Ledoux and another party by the name of Pile Driver, who are very prominent middleweights.

Now ordinarily I will not go around the corner to see a contest of skill and science between Lefty Ledoux and Pile Driver, or anybody else, as far as that is concerned, unless they are using blackjacks and promise to hurt each other, but I am the guest on this trip of a party by the name of Meyer Marmalade, and I will go anywhere to see anything if I am a guest.

This Meyer Marmalade is really a most superior character, who is called Meyer Marmalade because nobody can ever think of his last name, which is something like Marmalodowski, and he is known far and wide for the way he likes to make bets on any sporting proposition, such as baseball, or horse races, or ice hockey, or contests of skill and science, and especially contests of skill and science.

So he wishes to be present at this contest in Boston, Mass., between Lefty Ledoux and Pile Driver to have a nice wager on Driver, as he has reliable information that Driver's manager, a party by the name of Koons, has both judges and the referee in the satchel.

If there is one thing Meyer Marmalade dearly loves, it is to have a bet on a contest of skill and science of this nature, and so he is going to Boston, Mass. But Meyer Marmalade is such a guy as loathes and despises travelling all alone, so when he offers to pay my expenses if I will go along to keep him company, naturally I am pleased to accept, as I have nothing on of importance at the moment, and, in fact, I do not have anything on of importance for the past ten years.

I warn Meyer Marmalade in advance that if he is looking to take anything off of anybody in Boston, Mass., he may as well remain at home, because everybody knows that statistics show that the percentage of anything being taken off of the citizens of Boston, Mass., is less *per capita* than anywhere else in the United States, especially when it comes to contests of skill and science, but Meyer Marmalade says this is the first time they ever had two judges and a referee running against the statistics, and he is very confident.

Well, by and by I go from the dining-car back to my seat in another car, where Meyer Marmalade is sitting reading a detective magazine, and I speak of seeing Joey Perhaps to him. But Meyer Marmalade does not seem greatly interested, although he says to me like this:

'Joey Perhaps, eh?' he says. 'A wrong gee. A dead wrong gee. He must just get out. I run into the late Jack Ortega's brother, young Ollie, in Mindy's restaurant last week,' Meyer Marmalade says, 'and when we happen to get to talking of wrong gees, naturally Joey Perhaps's name comes up, and Ollie remarks he understands Joey Perhaps is about due out, and that he will be pleased to see him some day. Personally,' Meyer Marmalade says, 'I do not care for any part of Joey Perhaps at any price.'

Now our car is loaded with guys and dolls who are going to Boston, Mass., to witness a large football game between the Harvards and the Yales at Cambridge, Mass., the next day, and the reason I know this is because they are talking of nothing else.

So this is where the football starts getting into this story.

One old guy that I figure must be a Harvard from the way he talks seems to have a party all his own, and he is getting so much attention from one and all in the party that I figure he must be a guy of some importance, because they laugh heartily at his remarks, and although I listen very carefully to everything he says he does not sound so very humorous to me.

He is a heavy-set guy with a bald head and a deep voice, and anybody can see that he is such a guy as is accustomed to plenty of authority. I am wondering out loud to Meyer Marmalade who the guy can be, and Meyer Marmalade states as follows:

'Why,' he says, 'he is nobody but Mr Phillips Randolph, who makes the automobiles. He is the sixth richest guy in this country,' Meyer says, 'or maybe it is the seventh. Anyway, he is pretty well up with the front runners. I spot his monicker on his suitcase, and then I ask the porter, to make sure. It is a great honour for us to be travelling with Mr Phillips Randolph,' Meyer says, 'because of him being such a public benefactor and having so much dough, especially having so much dough.'

Well, naturally everybody knows who Mr Phillips Randolph is, and I am surprised that I do not recognize his face myself from seeing it so often in the newspapers alongside the latest model automobile his factory turns out, and I am as much pleasured up as Meyer Marmalade over being in the same car with Mr Phillips Randolph.

He seems to be a good-natured old guy, at that, and he is having a grand time, what with talking, and laughing, and taking a dram now and then out of a bottle, and when old Crip McGonnigle comes gimping through the car selling his football souvenirs, such as red and blue feathers, and little badges and pennants, and one thing and another, as Crip is doing around the large football games since Hickory Slim is a two-year-old, Mr Phillips Randolph stops him and buys all of Crip's red feathers, which have a little white H on them to show they are for the Harvards.

Then Mr Phillips Randolph distributes the feathers around among his party, and the guys and dolls stick them in their hats, or pin them on their coats, but he has quite a number of feathers left over, and about this time who comes through the car but Joey Perhaps, and Mr Phillips Randolph steps out in the aisle and stops Joey and politely offers him a red feather, and speaks as follows:

'Will you honour us by wearing our colours?'

Well, of course, Mr Phillips Randolph is only full of good spirits, and means no harm whatever, and the guys and dolls in his party laugh heartily as if they consider his action very funny, but maybe because they laugh, and maybe because he is just naturally a hostile guy, Joey Perhaps knocks Mr Phillips Randolph's hand down, and says like this:

'Get out of my way,' Joey says. 'Are you trying to make a sucker out of somebody?'

Personally, I always claim that Joey Perhaps has a right to reject the red feather, because for all I know he may prefer a blue feather, which means the Yales, but what I say is he does not need to be so impolite to an old guy such as Mr Phillips Randolph, although of course Joey has no way of knowing at this time about Mr Phillips Randolph having so much dough.

Anyway, Mr Phillips Randolph stands staring at Joey as if he is greatly startled, and the chances are he is, at that, for the chances are nobody ever speaks to him in such a manner in all his life, and Joey Perhaps also stands there a minute staring back at Mr Phillips Randolph, and finally Joey speaks as follows:

'Take a good peek,' Joey Perhaps says. 'Maybe you will remember me if you ever see me again.'

'Yes,' Mr Phillips Randolph says, very quiet. 'Maybe I will. They say I have a good memory for faces. I beg your pardon for stopping you, sir. It is all in fun, but I am sorry,' he says.

Then Joey Perhaps goes on, and he does not seem to notice Meyer Marmalade and me sitting there in the car, and Mr Phillips Randolph sits down, and his face is redder than somewhat, and all the joy is gone out of him, and out of his party, too. Personally, I am very sorry Joey Perhaps comes along, because I figure Mr Phillips Randolph will give me one of his spare feathers, and I will consider it a wonderful keepsake.

But now there is not much more talking, and no laughing whatever in Mr Phillips Randolph's party, and he just sits there as if he is thinking, and for all I know he may be thinking that there ought to be a law against a guy speaking so disrespectfully to a guy with all his dough as Joey Perhaps speaks to him.

Well, the contest of skill and science between Lefty Ledoux and Pile Driver turns out to be something of a disappointment, and, in fact, it is a stinkeroo, because there is little skill and no science whatever in it, and by the fourth round the customers are scuffling their feet, and saying throw these bums out, and making other derogatory remarks, and furthermore it seems that this Koons does not have either one of the judges, or even as much as the referee, in the satchel, and Ledoux gets the duke by unanimous vote of the officials.

So Meyer Marmalade is out a couple of C's, which is all he can wager at the ringside, because it seems that nobody in Boston, Mass., cares a cuss about who wins the contest, and Meyer is much disgusted with life, and so am I, and we go back to the Copley Plaza Hotel, where we are stopping, and sit down in the lobby to meditate on the injustice of everything.

Well, the lobby is a scene of gaiety, as it seems there are a number of football dinners and dances going on in the hotel, and guys and dolls in evening clothes are all around and about, and the dolls are so young and beautiful that I get to thinking that this is not such a bad old world, after all, and even Meyer Marmalade begins taking notice.

All of a sudden, a very, very beautiful young doll who is about forty per cent in and sixty per cent out of an evening gown walks right up to us sitting there, and holds out her hand to me, and speaks as follows:

'Do you remember me?'

Naturally, I do not remember her, but naturally I am not going to admit it, because it is never my policy to discourage any doll who wishes to strike up an acquaintance with me, which is what I figure this doll is trying to do; then I see that she is nobody but Doria Logan, one of the prettiest dolls that ever hit Broadway, and about the same time Meyer Marmalade also recognizes her.

Doria changes no little since last I see her, which is quite some time back, but there is no doubt the change is for the better, because she is once a very rattle-headed young doll, and now she seems older, and quieter, and even prettier than ever. Naturally, Meyer Marmalade and I are glad to see her looking so well, and we ask her how are tricks, and what is the good word, and all this and that, and finally Doria Logan states to us as follows:

'I am in great trouble,' Doria says. 'I am in terrible trouble, and you are the first ones I see that I can talk to about it.'

Well, at this, Meyer Marmalade begins to tuck in somewhat, because he figures it is the old lug coming up, and Meyer Marmalade is not such a guy as will go for the lug from a doll unless he gets something more than a story. But I can see Doria Logan is in great earnest.

'Do you remember Joey Perhaps?' she says.

'A wrong gee,' Meyer Marmalade says. 'A dead wrong gee.'

'I not only remember Joey Perhaps,' I say, 'but I see him on the train to-day.'

'Yes,' Doria says, 'he is here in town. He hunts me up only a few hours ago. He is here to do me great harm. He is here to finish ruining my life.'

'A wrong gee,' Meyer Marmalade puts in again. 'Always a hundred per cent wrong gee.'

Then Doria Logan gets us to go with her to a quiet corner of the lobby, and she tells us a strange story, as follows, and also to wit :

It seems that she is once tangled up with Joey Perhaps, which is something I never know before, and neither does Meyer Marmalade, and, in fact, the news shocks us quite some. It is back in the days when she is just about sixteen and is in the chorus of Earl Carroll's Vanities, and I remember well what a standout she is for looks, to be sure.

Naturally, at sixteen, Doria is quite a chump doll, and does not know which way is south, or what time it is, which is the way all dolls at sixteen are bound to be, and she has no idea what a wrong gee Joey Perhaps is, as he is good-looking and young, and seems very romantic, and is always speaking of love and one thing and another.

Well, the upshot of it all is the upshot of thousands of other cases since chump dolls commence coming to Broadway, and the first thing she knows, Doria Logan finds herself mixed up with a very bad character, and does not know what to do about it.

By and by, Joey Perhaps commences mistreating her no little, and finally he tries to use her in some nefarious schemes of his, and of course everybody along Broadway knows that most of Joey's schemes are especially nefarious, because Joey is on the shake almost since infancy.

Well, one day Doria says to herself that if this is love, she has all she can stand, and she hauls off and runs away from Joey

Perhaps. She goes back to her people, who live in the city of Cambridge, Mass., which is the same place where the Harvards have their college, and she goes there because she does not know of any other place to go.

It seems that Doria's people are poor, and Doria goes to a business school and learns to be a stenographer, and she is working for a guy in the real estate dodge by the name of Poopnoodle, and doing all right for herself, and in the meantime she hears that Joey Perhaps gets sent away, so she figures her troubles are all over as far as he is concerned.

Now Doria Logan goes along quietly through life, working for Mr Poopnoodle, and never thinking of love, or anything of a similar nature, when she meets up with a young guy who is one of the Harvards, and who is maybe twenty-one years old, and is quite a football player, and where Doria meets up with this guy is in a drug store over a banana split.

Well, the young Harvard takes quite a fancy to Doria and, in fact, he is practically on fire about her, but by this time Doria is going on twenty, and is no longer a chump doll, and she has no wish to get tangled up in love again.

In fact, whenever she thinks of Joey Perhaps, Doria takes to hating guys in general, but somehow she cannot seem to get up a real good hate on the young Harvard, because, to hear her tell it, he is handsome, and noble, and has wonderful ideals.

Now as time goes on, Doria finds she is growing pale, and is losing her appetite, and cannot sleep, and this worries her no little, as she is always a first-class feeder, and finally she comes to the conclusion that what ails her is that she is in love with the young Harvard, and can scarcely live without him, so she admits as much to him one night when the moon is shining on the Charles River, and everything is a dead cold set-up for love.

Well, naturally, after a little off-hand guzzling, which is quite permissible under the circumstances, the young guy wishes her to name the happy day, and Doria has half a notion to make it the following Monday, this being a Sunday night, but then she gets to thinking about her past with Joey Perhaps, and all, and she figures it will be bilking the young Harvard to marry him unless she has a small talk with him first about Joey, because she is well aware that many young guys may have some objection to wedding a doll with a skeleton in her closet, and especially a skeleton such as Joey Perhaps.

But she is so happy she does not wish to run the chance of spoiling everything by these narrations right away, so she keeps her trap closed about Joey, although she promises to marry the young Harvard when he gets out of college, which will be the following year, if he still insists, because Doria figures that by then she will be able to break the news to him about Joey very gradually, and gently, and especially gently.

Anyway, Doria says she is bound and determined to tell him before the wedding, even if he takes the wind on her as a consequence, and personally I claim this is very considerate of Doria, because many dolls never tell before the wedding, or even after. So Doria and the young Harvard are engaged, and great happiness prevails, when, all of a sudden, in pops Joey Perhaps.

It seems that Joey learns of Doria's engagement as soon as he gets out of the state institution, and he hastens to Boston, Mass., with an inside coat pocket packed with letters that Doria writes him long ago, and also a lot of pictures they have taken together, as young guys and dolls are bound to do, and while there is nothing much out of line about these letters and pictures, put them all together they spell a terrible pain in the neck to Doria at this particular time.

'A wrong gee,' Meyer Marmalade says. 'But,' he says, 'he is only going back to his old shakedown dodge, so all you have to do is buy him off.'

Well, at this, Doria Logan laughs one of these little short dry laughs that go 'hah', and says like this:

'Of course he is looking to get bought off, but,' she says, 'where will I get any money to buy him off? I do not have a dime of my own, and Joey is talking large figures, because he knows my fiancé's papa has plenty. He wishes me to go to my fiancé and make him get the money off his papa, or he threatens to personally deliver the letters and pictures to my fiancé's papa.

'You can see the predicament I am in,' Doria says, 'and you can see what my fiancé's papa will think of me if he learns I am once mixed up with a blackmailer such as Joey Perhaps.

'Besides,' Doria says, 'it is something besides money with Joey Perhaps, and I am not so sure he will not double-cross me even if I can pay him his price. Joey Perhaps is very angry at me. I think,' she says, 'if he can spoil my happiness, it will mean more to him than money.'

Well, Doria states that all she can think of when she is talking to Joey Perhaps is to stall for time, and she tells Joey that, no matter what, she cannot see her fiancé until after the large football game between the Harvards and the Yales as he has to do a little football playing for the Harvards, and Joey asks her if she is going to see the game, and naturally she is.

And then Joey says he thinks he will look up a ticket speculator, and buy a ticket and attend the game himself, as he is very fond of football, and where will she be sitting, as he hopes and trusts he will be able to see something of her during the game, and this statement alarms Doria Logan no little, for who is she going with but her fiancé's papa, and a party of his friends, and she feels that there is no telling what Joey Perhaps may be up to.

She explains to Joey that she does not know exactly where she will be sitting, except that it will be on the Harvards' side of the field, but Joey is anxious for more details than this.

'In fact,' Doria says, 'he is most insistent, and he stands at my elbow while I call up Mr Randolph at this very hotel, and he tells me the exact location of our seats. Then Joey says he will endeavour to get a seat as close to me as possible, and he goes away.'

'What Mr Randolph?' Meyer says. 'Which Mr Randolph?' he says. 'You do not mean Mr Phillips Randolph, by any chance, do you?'

'Why, to be sure,' Doria says. 'Do you know him?'

Naturally, from now on Meyer Marmalade gazes at Doria Logan with deep respect, and so do I, although by now she is crying a little, and I am by no means in favour of crying dolls. But while she is crying, Meyer Marmalade seems to be doing some more thinking, and finally he speaks as follows:

'Kindly see if you can recall these locations you speak of.'

So here is where the football game comes in once more.

Only I regret to state that personally I do not witness this game, and the reason I do not witness it is because nobody wakes me up the next day in time for me to witness it, and the way I look at it, this is all for the best, as I am scarcely a football enthusiast.

So from now on the story belongs to Meyer Marmalade, and I will tell it to you as Meyer tells it to me.

It is a most exciting game [Meyer says]. The place is full of people, and there are bands playing, and much cheering, and more lovely dolls than you can shake a stick at, although I do not believe there are many lovelier present than Doria Logan.

It is a good thing she remembers the seat locations, otherwise I will never find her, but there she is surrounded by some very nice-looking people, including Mr Phillips Randolph, and there I am two rows back of Mr Phillips Randolph, and the ticket spec I get my seat off of says he cannot understand why everybody wishes to sit near Mr Phillips Randolph to-day when there are other seats just as good, and maybe better, on the Harvards' side.

So I judge he has other calls similar to mine for this location, and a sweet price he gets for it, too, and I judge that maybe at least one call is from Jocy Perhaps, as I see Joey a couple of rows on back up of where I am sitting, but off to my left on an aisle, while I am almost in a direct line with Mr Phillips Randolph.

To show you that Joey is such a guy as attracts attention, Mr Phillips Randolph stands up a few minutes before the game starts, peering around and about to see who is present that he knows, and all of a sudden his eyes fall on Joey Perhaps, and then Mr Phillips Randolph proves he has a good memory for faces, to be sure, for he states as follows:

'Why,' he says, 'there is the chap who rebuffs me so churlishly on the train when I offer him our colours. Yes,' he says, 'I am sure it is the same chap.'

Well, what happens in the football game is much pulling and hauling this way and that, and to and fro, between the Harvards and the Yales without a tally right down to the last five minutes of play, and then all of a sudden the Yales shove the football down to within about three-eighths of an inch of the Harvards' goal line.

At this moment quite some excitement prevails. Then the next thing anybody knows, the Yales outshove the Harvards, and now the game is over, and Mr Phillips Randolph gets up out of his seat, and I hear Mr Phillips Randolph say like this:

'Well,' he says, 'the score is not so bad as it might be, and it is a wonderful game, and,' he says, 'we seem to make one convert to our cause, anyway, for see who is wearing our colours.'

And with this he points to Joey Perhaps, who is still sitting down, with people stepping around him and over him, and he is still smiling a little smile, and Mr Phillips Randolph seems greatly pleased to see that Joey Perhaps has a big, broad crimson ribbon where he once wears his white silk muffler.

But the chances are Mr Phillips Randolph will be greatly surprised if he knows that the crimson ribbon across Joey's bosom comes of Ollie Ortega planting a short knife in Joey's throat, or do I forget to mention before that Ollie Ortega is among those present?

I send for Ollie after I leave you last night, figuring he may love to see a nice football game. He arrives by 'plane this morning, and I am not wrong in my figuring. Ollie thinks the game is swell.

Well, personally, I will never forget this game, it is so exciting. Just after the tally comes off, all of a sudden, from the Yales in the stand across the field from the Harvards, comes a long-drawn-out wail that sounds so mournful it makes me feel very sad, to be sure. It starts off something like Oh-oh-oh-oh-oh, with all the Yales Oh-oh-oh-oh-oh-ing at once, and I ask a guy next to me what it is all about.

'Why,' the guy says, 'it is the Yales' "Undertaker Song". They always sing it when they have the other guy licked. I am an old Yale myself, and I will now personally sing this song for you.'

And with this the guy throws back his head, and opens his mouth wide and lets out a yowl like a wolf calling to its mate.

Well, I stop the guy, and tell him it is a very lovely song, to be sure, and quite appropriate all the way around, and then I hasten away from the football game without getting a chance to say good-bye to Doria, although afterwards I mail her the package of letters and pictures that Ollie gets out of Joey Perhaps's inside coat pocket during the confusion that prevails when the Yales make their tally, and I hope and trust that she will think the crimson streaks across the package are just a little touch of colour in honour of the Harvards.

But the greatest thing about the football game (Meyer Marmalade says) is I win two C's off of one of the Harvards sitting near me, so I am now practically even on my trip.

17 LILLIAN

WHAT I always say is that Wilbur Willard is nothing but a very lucky guy, because what is it but luck that has him teetering along Forty-ninth Street one cold snowy morning when Lillian is mer-owing around the sidewalk looking for her mamma?

And what is it but luck that has Wilbur Willard all mulled up to a million, what with him having been sitting out a few seidels of Scotch with a friend by the name of Haggerty in an apartment over in Fifty-ninth Street? Because if Wilbur Willard is not mulled up he will see Lillian as nothing but a little black cat, and give her plenty of room, for everybody knows that black cats are terribly bad luck, even when they are only kittens.

But being mulled up like I tell you, things look very different to Wilbur Willard, and he does not see Lillian as a little black kitten scrabbling around in the snow. He sees a beautiful leopard because a copper by the name of O'Hara, who is walking past about then, and who knows Wilbur Willard, hears him say:

'Oh, you beautiful leopard!'

The copper takes a quick peek himself, because he does not wish any leopards running around his beat, it being against the law, but all he sees, as he tells me afterward, is this rumpot ham, Wilbur Willard, picking up a scrawny little black kitten and shoving it in his overcoat pocket, and he also hears Wilbur say:

'Your name is Lillian.'

Then Wilbur teeters on up to his room on the top floor of an old fleabag in Eighth Avenue that is called the Hotel de Brussels, where he lives quite a while, because the management does not mind actors, the management of the Hotel de Brussels being very broad-minded, indeed.

There is some complaint this same morning from one of Wilbur's neighbours, an old burlesque doll by the name of Minnie Madigan, who is not working since Abraham Lincoln is assassinated, because she hears Wilbur going on in his rooms about a beautiful leopard, and calls up the clerk to say that an hotel which allows wild animals is not respectable. But the clerk looks in on Wilbur and finds him playing with nothing but a harmless-looking little black kitten, and nothing comes of the old doll's beef, especially as nobody ever claims the Hotel de Brussels is respectable anyway, or at least not much.

Of course when Wilbur comes out from under the ether next afternoon he can see Lillian is not a leopard, and in fact Wilbur is quite astonished to find himself in bed with a little black kitten, because it seems Lillian is sleeping on Wilbur's chest to keep warm. At first Wilbur does not believe what he sees, and puts it down to Haggerty's Scotch, but finally he is convinced, and so he puts Lillian in his pocket, and takes her over to the Hot Box night club and gives her some milk, of which it seems Lillian is very fond.

Now where Lillian comes from in the first place of course nobody knows. The chances are somebody chucks her out of a window into the snow, because people are always chucking kittens, and one thing and another, out of windows in New York. In fact, if there is one thing this town has plenty of, it is kittens, which finally grow up to be cats, and go snooping around ash cans, and mer-owing on roofs, and keeping people from sleeping good.

Personally, I have no use for cats, including kittens, because I never see one that has any too much sense, although I know a guy by the name of Pussy McGuire who makes a first-rate living doing nothing but stealing cats, and sometimes dogs, and selling them to old dolls who like such things for company. But Pussy only steals Persian and Angora cats, which are very fine cats, and of course Lillian is no such cat as this. Lillian is nothing but a black cat, and nobody will give you a dime a dozen for black cats in this town, as they are generally regarded as very bad jinxes.

Furthermore, it comes out in a few weeks that Wilbur Willard can just as well name her Herman, or Sidney, as not, but Wilbur sticks to Lillian, because this is the name of his partner when he is in vaudeville years ago. He often tells me about Lillian Withington when he is mulled up, which is more often than somewhat, for Wilbur is a great hand for drinking Scotch, or rye, or bourbon, or gin, or whatever else there is around for drinking, except water. In fact, Wilbur Willard is a high-class drinking man, and it does no good to tell him it is against the law to drink in this country, because it only makes him mad, and he says to the dickens with the law, only Wilbur Willard uses a much rougher word than dickens.

'She is like a beautiful leopard,' Wilbur says to me about Lillian Withington. 'Black-haired, and black-eyed, and all ripply, like a leopard I see in an animal act on the same bill at the Palace with us once. We are headliners then,' he says, 'Willard and Withington, the best singing and dancing act in the country.

'I pick her up in San Antonia, which is a spot in Texas,' Wilbur says. 'She is not long out of a convent, and I just lose my old partner, Mary McGee, who ups and dies on me of pneumonia down there. Lillian wishes to go on the stage, and joins out with me. A natural-born actress with a great voice. But like a leopard,' Wilbur says. 'Like a leopard. There is cat in her, no doubt of this, and cats and women are both ungrateful. I love Lillian Withington. I wish to marry her. But she is cold to me. She says she is not going to follow the stage all her life. She says she wishes money, and luxury, and a fine home and of course a guy like me cannot give a doll such things.

'I wait on her hand and foot,' Wilbur says. 'I am her slave. There is nothing I will not do for her. Then one day she walks in on me in Boston very cool and says she is quitting me. She says she is marrying a rich guy there. Well, naturally it busts up the act and I never have the heart to look for another partner, and then I get to belting that old black bottle around, and now what am I but a cabaret performer?'

Then sometimes he will bust out crying, and sometimes I will cry with him, although the way I look at it, Wilbur gets a pretty fair break, at that, in getting rid of a doll who wishes things he cannot give her. Many a guy in this town is tangled up with a doll who wishes things he cannot give her, but who keeps him tangled up just the same and busting himself trying to keep her quiet.

Wilbur makes pretty fair money as an entertainer in the Hot Box, though he spends most of it for Scotch, and he is not a bad entertainer, either. I often go to the Hot Box when I am feeling blue to hear him sing Melancholy Baby, and Moonshine Valley and other sad songs which break my heart. Personally, I do not see why any doll cannot love Wilbur, especially if they listen to him sing such songs as Melancholy Baby when he is mulled up good, because he is a tall, nice-looking guy with long eyelashes, and sleepy brown eyes, and his voice has a low moaning sound that usually goes very big with the dolls. In fact, many a doll does do some pitching to Wilbur when he is singing in the Hot Box, but somehow Wilbur never gives them a tumble, which I suppose is because he is thinking only of Lillian Withington.

Well, after he gets Lillian, the black kitten, Wilbur seems to find a new interest in life, and Lillian turns out to be right cute, and not bad-looking after Wilbur gets her fed up good. She is blacker than a yard up a chimney, with not a white spot on her, and she grows so fast that by and by Wilbur cannot carry her in his pocket any more, so he puts a collar on her and leads her round. So Lillian becomes very well known on Broadway, what with Wilbur taking her many places, and finally she does not even have to be led around by Willard, but follows him like a pooch. And in all the Roaring Forties there is no pooch that cares to have any truck with Lillian, for she will leap aboard them quicker than you can say scat, and scratch and bite them until they are very glad indeed to get away from her.

But of course the pooches in the Forties are mainly nothing but Chows, and Pekes, and Poms, or little woolly white poodles, which are led around by blonde dolls, and are not fit to take their own part against a smart cat. In fact, Wilbur Willard is finally not on speaking terms with any doll that owns a pooch between Times Square and Columbus Circle, and they are all hoping that both Wilbur and Lillian will go lay down and die somewhere. Furthermore, Wilbur has a couple of battles with guys who also belong to the dolls, but Wilbur is no sucker in a battle if he is not mulled up too much and leg-weary.

After he is through entertaining people in the Hot Box, Wilbur generally goes around to any speakeasies which may still be open, and does a little off-hand drinking on top of what he already drinks down in the Hot Box, which is plenty, and although it is considered very risky in this town to mix Hot Box liquor with any other, it never seemed to bother Wilbur. Along towards daylight he takes a couple of bottles of Scotch over to his room in the Hotel de Brussels and uses them for a nightcap, so by the time Wilbur Willard is ready to slide off to sleep he has plenty of liquor of one kind and another inside him, and he sleeps pretty.

Of course nobody on Broadway blames Wilbur so very much for being such a rumpot, because they know about him loving Lillian Withington, and losing her, and it is considered a reasonable excuse in this town for a guy to do some drinking when he loses a doll, which is why there is so much drinking here, but it is a mystery to one and all how Wilbur stands off all this liquor without croaking. The cemeteries are full of guys who do a lot less drinking than Wilbur, but he never even seems to feel extra tough, or if he does he keeps it to himself and does not go around saying it is the kind of liquor you get nowadays.

He costs some of the boys around Mindy's plenty of dough one winter, because he starts in doing most of his drinking after hours in Good Time Charley's speakeasy, and the boys lay a price of four to one against him lasting until spring, never figuring a guy can drink very much of Good Time Charley's liquor and keep on living. But Wilbur Willard does it just the same, so everybody says the guy is naturally superhuman, and lets it go at that.

Sometimes Wilbur drops into Mindy's with Lillian following him on the look-out for pooches, or riding on his shoulder if the weather is bad, and the two of them will sit with us for hours chewing the rag about one thing and another. At such times Wilbur generally has a bottle on his hip and takes a shot now and then, but of course this does not come under the head of serious drinking with him. When Lillian is with Wilbur she always lays as close to him as she can get and anybody can see that she seems to be very fond of Wilbur, and that he is very fond of her, although he sometimes forgets himself and speaks of her as a beautiful leopard. But of course, this is only a slip of the tongue, and anyway if Wilbur gets any pleasure out of thinking Lillian is a leopard, it is nobody's business but his own.

'I suppose she will run away from me some day,' Wilbur says, running his hand over Lillian's back until her fur crackles. 'Yet, although I give her plenty of liver and catnip, and one thing and another, and all my affection, she will probably give me the shake. Cats are like women, and women are like cats. They are both very ungrateful.'

'They are both generally bad luck,' Big Nig, the crap shooter, says. 'Especially cats, and most especially black cats.'

Many other guys tell Wilbur about black cats being bad luck, and advise him to slip Lillian into the North River some night with a sinker on her, but Wilbur claims he already has all the bad luck in the world when he loses Lillian Withington, and that Lillian, the cat, cannot make it any worse, so he goes on taking extra good care of her, and Lillian goes on getting bigger and bigger, until I commence thinking maybe there is some St Bernard in her.

Finally I commence to notice something funny about Lillian. Sometimes she will be acting very loving towards Wilbur, and then again she will be very unfriendly to him, and will spit at him, and snatch at him with her claws, very hostile. It seems to me that she is all right when Willard is mulled up, but is as sad and fretful as he is himself when he is only a little bit mulled. And when Lillian is sad and fretful she makes it very tough indeed on the pooches in the neighbourhood of the Brussels.

In fact, Lillian takes to pooch-hunting, sneaking off when Wilbur is getting his rest, and running pooches bow-legged, especially when she finds one that is not on a leash. A loose pooch is just naturally cherry pie for Lillian.

Well, of course, this causes great indignation among the dolls who own the pooches, particularly when Lillian comes home one day carrying a Peke as big as she is herself by the scruff of the neck, and with a very excited blonde doll following her and yelling bloody murder outside Wilbur Willard's door when Lillian pops into Wilbur's room through a hole he cuts in the door for her, still lugging the Peke. But it seems that instead of being mad at Lillian and giving her a pasting for such goings on, Wilbur is somewhat pleased, because he happens to be still in a fog when Lillian arrives with the Peke, and is thinking of Lillian as a beautiful leopard.

'Why,' Wilbur says, 'this is devotion, indeed. My beautiful leopard goes off into the jungle and fetches me an antelope for dinner.'

Now of course there is no sense whatever to this, because a Peke is certainly not anything like an antelope, but the blonde doll outside Wilbur's door hears Wilbur mumble, and gets the idea that he is going to eat her Peke for dinner and the squawk she puts up is very terrible. There is plenty of trouble around the Brussels in chilling the blonde doll's beef over Lillian snagging her Peke, and what is more the blonde doll's ever-loving guy, who turns out to be a tough Ginney bootlegger by the name of Gregorio, shows up at the Hot Box the next night and wishes to put the slug on Wilbur Willard.

But Wilbur rounds him up with a few drinks and by singing Melancholy Baby to him, and before he leaves the Ginney gets very sentimental towards Wilbur, and Lillian, too, and wishes to give Wilbur five bucks to let Lillian grab the Peke again, if Lillian will promise not to bring it back. It seems Gregorio does not really care for the Peke, and is only acting quarrelsome to please the blonde doll and make her think he loves her dearly.

But I can see Lillian is having different moods, and finally I ask Wilbur if he notices it.

'Yes,' he says, very sad, 'I do not seem to be holding her love. She is getting very fickle. A guy moves on to my floor at the Brussels the other day with a little boy, and Lillian becomes very fond of this kid at once. In fact, they are great friends. Ah, well,' Wilbur says, 'cats are like women. Their affection does not last.'

I happen to go over to the Brussels a few days later to explain to a guy by the name of Crutchy, who lives on the same floor as Wilbur Willard, that some of our citizens do not like his face

and that it may be a good idea for him to leave town, especially
if he insists on bringing ale into their territory, and I see Lillian
out in the hall with a youngster which I judge is the kid Wilbur
is talking about. This kid is maybe three years old, and very
cute, what with black hair, and black eyes, and he is woolling
Lillian around the hall in a way that is most surprising, for
Lillian is not such a cat as will stand for much woolling around,
not even from Wilbur Willard.

I am wondering how anybody comes to take such a kid to a
joint like the Brussels, but I figure it is some actor's kid, and
that maybe there is no mamma for it. Later I am talking to
Wilbur about this, and he says:

'Well, if the kid's old man is an actor, he is not working at
it. He sticks close to his room all the time, and he does not allow
the kid to go anywhere but in the hall, and I feel sorry for the
little guy, which is why I allow Lillian to play with him.'

Now it comes on a very cold spell, and a bunch of us are sitting
in Mindy's along towards five o'clock in the morning when we
hear fire engines going past. By and by in comes a guy by the
name of Kansas, who is named Kansas because he comes from
Kansas, and who is a crap shooter by trade.

'The old Brussels is on fire,' this guy Kansas says.

'She is always on fire,' Big Nig says, meaning there is always
plenty of hot stuff going on around the Brussels.

About this time who walks in but Wilbur Willard, and anybody can see he is just naturally floating. The chances are he
comes from Good Time Charley's, and he is certainly carrying
plenty of pressure. I never see Wilbur Willard mulled up more.
He does not have Lillian with him, but then he never takes
Lillian to Good Time Charley's, because Charley hates cats.

'Hey, Wilbur,' Big Nig says, 'your joint, the Brussels, is on
fire.'

'Well,' Wilbur says, 'I am a little firefly, and I need a light.
Let us go where there is a fire.'

The Brussels is only a few blocks from Mindy's, and there is
nothing else to do just then, so some of us walk over to Eighth
Avenue with Wilbur teetering along ahead of us. The old shack
is certainly roaring good when we get in sight of it, and the

firemen are tossing water into it, and the coppers have the fire lines out to keep the crowd back, although there is not much of a crowd at such an hour in the morning.

'Is it not beautiful?' Wilbur Willard says, looking up at the flames. 'Is it not like a fairy palace all lighted up this way?'

You see, Wilbur does not realize the joint is on fire, although guys and dolls are running out of it every which way, most of them half dressed, or not dressed at all, and the firemen are getting out the life nets in case anybody wishes to hop out of the windows.

'It is certainly beautiful,' Wilbur says. 'I must get Lillian so she can see this.'

And before anybody has time to think, there is Wilbur Willard walking into the front door of the Brussels as if nothing happens. The firemen and the coppers are so astonished all they can do is holler at Wilbur, but he pays no attention whatever. Well, naturally everybody figures Wilbur is a gone gosling, but in about ten minutes he comes walking out of this same door through the fire and smoke as cool as you please, and he has Lillian in his arms.

'You know,' Wilbur says, coming over to where we are standing with our eyes popping out, 'I have to walk all the way up to my floor because the elevators seem to be out of commission. The service is getting terrible in this hotel. I will certainly make a strong beef to the management about it as soon as I pay something on my account.'

Then what happens but Lillian lets out a big mer-ow, and hops out of Wilbur's arms and skips past the coppers and the firemen with her back all humped up, and the next thing anybody knows she is tearing through the front door of the old hotel and making plenty of speed.

'Well, well,' Wilbur says, looking much surprised, 'there goes Lillian.'

And what does this daffy Wilbur Willard do but turn and go marching back into the Brussels again, and by this time the smoke is pouring out of the front doors so thick he is out of sight in a second. Naturally he takes the coppers and firemen by surprise, because they are not used to guys walking in and out of fires on them.

This time anybody standing around will lay you plenty of odds — two and a half and maybe three to one that Wilbur never shows up again, because the old Brussels is now just popping with fire and smoke from the lower windows, although there does not seem to be quite so much fire in the upper story. Everybody seems to be out of the joint, and even the firemen are fighting the blaze from the outside because the Brussels is so old and ramshackly there is no sense in them risking the floors.

I mean everybody is out of the joint except Wilbur Willard and Lillian, and we figure they are getting a good frying somewhere inside, although Feet Samuels is around offering to take thirteen to five for a few small bets that Lillian comes out okay, because Feet claims that a cat has nine lives and that is a fair bet at the price.

Well, up comes a swell-looking doll all heated up about something and pushing and clawing her way through the crowd up to the ropes and screaming until you can hardly hear yourself think, and about this same minute everybody hears a voice going ai-lee-hi-hee-hoo, like a Swiss yodeller, which comes from the roof of the Brussels, and looking up what do we see but Wilbur Willard standing up there on the edge of the roof, high above the fire and smoke, and yodelling very loud.

Under one arm he has a big bundle of some kind, and under the other he has the little kid I see playing in the hall with Lillian. As he stands up there going ai-lee-hi-hee-hoo, the swell-dressed doll near us begins yipping louder than Wilbur is yodelling, and the firemen rush over under him with a life net.

Wilbur lets go another ai-lee-hi-hee-hoo, and down he comes all spraddled out, with the bundle and the kid, but he hits the net sitting down and bounces up and back again for a couple of minutes before he finally settles. In fact, Wilbur is enjoying the bouncing, and the chances are he will be bouncing yet if the firemen do not drop their hold on the net and let him fall to the ground.

Then Wilbur steps out of the net, and I can see the bundle is a rolled-up blanket with Lillian's eyes peeking out of one end.

He still has the kid under the other arm with his head stuck out in front, and his legs stuck out behind, and it does not seem to me that Wilbur is handling the kid as careful as he is handling Lillian. He stands there looking at the firemen with a very sneering look, and finally he says:

'Do not think you can catch me in your net unless I wish to be caught. I am a butterfly, and very hard to overtake.'

Then all of a sudden the swell-dressed doll who is doing so much hollering, piles on top of Wilbur and grabs the kid from him and begins hugging and kissing it.

'Wilbur,' she says, 'God bless you, Wilbur, for saving my baby! Oh, thank you, Wilbur, thank you! My wretched husband kidnaps and runs away with him, and it is only a few hours ago that my detectives find out where he is.'

Wilbur gives the doll a funny look for about half a minute and starts to walk away, but Lillian comes wiggling out of the blanket, looking and smelling pretty much singed up, and the kid sees Lillian and begins hollering for her, so Wilbur finally hands Lillian over to the kid. And not wishing to leave Lillian, Wilbur stands around somewhat confused, and the doll gets talking to him, and finally they go away together, and as they go Wilbur is carrying the kid, and the kid is carrying Lillian, and Lillian is not feeling so good from her burns.

Furthermore, Wilbur is probably more sober than he ever is before in years at this hour in the morning, but before they go I get a chance to talk some to Wilbur when he is still rambling somewhat, and I make out from what he says that the first time he goes to get Lillian he finds her in his room and does not see hide or hair of the little kid and does not even think of him, because he does not know what room the kid is in, anyway, having never noticed such a thing.

But the second time he goes up, Lillian is sniffing at the crack under the door of a room down the hall from Wilbur's and Wilbur says he seems to remember seeing a trickle of something like water coming out of the crack.

'And,' Wilbur says, 'as I am looking for a blanket for Lillian, and it will be a bother to go back to my room, I figure I will get one out of this room. I try the knob but the door is locked, so I kick it in, and walk in to find the room full of smoke, and fire is shooting through the windows very lovely, and when I grab a blanket off the bed for Lillian, what is under the blanket but the kid?

'Well,' Wilbur says, 'the kid is squawking, and Lillian is mer-owing, and there is so much confusion generally that it makes me nervous, so I figure we better go up on the roof and let the stink blow off us, and look at the fire from there. It seems there is a guy stretched out on the floor of the room alongside an upset table between the door and the bed. He has a bottle in one hand, and he is dead. Well, naturally there is no percentage in lugging a dead guy along, so I take Lillian and the kid and go up on the roof, and we just naturally fly off like humming birds. Now I must get a drink,' Wilbur says, 'I wonder if anybody has anything on their hip?'

Well, the papers are certainly full of Wilbur and Lillian the next day, especially Lillian, and they are both great heroes.

But Wilbur cannot stand the publicity very long, because he never has any time to himself for his drinking, what with the scribes and the photographers hopping on him every few minutes wishing to hear his story, and to take more pictures of him and Lillian, so one night he disappears, and Lillian disappears with him.

About a year later it comes out that he marries his old doll, Lillian Withington-Harmon, and falls into a lot of dough, and what is more he cuts out the liquor and becomes quite a useful citizen one way and another. So everybody has to admit that black cats are not always bad luck, although I say Wilbur's case is a little exceptional because he does not start out knowing Lillian is a black cat, but thinking she is a leopard.

I happen to run into Wilbur one day all dressed up in good clothes and jewellery and chucking quite a swell.

'Wilbur,' I say to him, 'I often think how remarkable it is the way Lillian suddenly gets such an attachment for the little kid and remembers about him being in the hotel and leads you back there a second time to the right room. If I do not see this come off with my own eyes, I will never believe a cat has brains enough to do such a thing, because I consider cats extra dumb.'

'Brains nothing,' Wilbur says. 'Lillian does not have brains enough to grease a gimlet. And what is more, she has no more attachment for the kid than a jack rabbit. The time has come,' Wilbur says, 'to expose Lillian. She gets a lot of credit which is never coming to her. I will now tell you about Lillian, and nobody knows this but me.

'You see,' Wilbur says, 'when Lillian is a little kitten I always put a little Scotch in her milk, partly to help make her good and strong, and partly because I am never no hand to drink alone, unless there is nobody with me. Well, at first Lillian does not care so much for this Scotch in her milk, but finally she takes a liking to it, and I keep making her toddy stronger until in the end she will lap up a good big snort without any milk for a chaser, and yell for more. In fact, I suddenly realize that Lillian becomes a rumpot, just like I am in those days, and simply must have her grog, and it is when she is good and rummed up that Lillian goes off snatching Pekes, and acting tough generally.

'Now,' Wilbur says, 'the time of the fire is about the time I get home every morning and give Lillian her schnapps. But when I go into the hotel and get her the first time I forget to Scotch her up, and the reason she runs back into the hotel is because she is looking for her shot. And the reason she is sniffing at the kid's door is not because the kid is in there but because the trickle that is coming through the crack under the door is nothing but Scotch that is running out of the bottle in the dead guy's hand. I never mention this before because I figure it may be a knock to a dead guy's memory,' Wilbur says. 'Drinking is certainly a disgusting thing, especially secret drinking.'

'But how is Lillian getting along these days?' I ask Wilbur Willard.

'I am greatly disappointed in Lillian,' he says. 'She refuses to reform when I do, and the last I hear of her she takes up with Gregorio, the Ginney bootlegger, who keeps her well Scotched up all the time so she will lead his blonde doll's Peke a dog's life.'

18 DARK DOLORES

WALDO WINCHESTER, the newspaper scribe, is saying to me the other night up in the Hot Box that it is a very great shame that there are no dolls around such as in the old days to make good stories for the newspapers by knocking off guys right and left, because it seems that newspaper scribes consider a doll knocking off a guy very fine news indeed, especially if the doll or the guy belongs to the best people.

Then Waldo Winchester tells me about a doll by the name of Lorelei who hangs out in the Rhine River some time ago and stools sailors up to the rocks to get them wrecked, which I consider a dirty trick, although Waldo does not seem to make so much of it. Furthermore, he speaks of another doll by the name of Circe, who is quite a hand for luring guys to destruction, and by the time Waldo gets to Circe he is crying because there are no more dolls like her around to furnish news for the papers.

But of course the real reason Waldo is crying is not because he is so sorry about Circe. It is because he is full of the liquor they sell in the Hot Box, which is liquor that is apt to make anybody bust out crying on a very short notice. In fact, they sell the cryingest liquor in town up in the Hot Box.

Well, I get to thinking over these dolls Waldo Winchester speaks of, and, thinks I, the chances are Dolores Dark connects up with one of them away back yonder, and maybe with all of them for all I know, Dolores Dark being the name of a doll I meet when I am in Atlantic City with Dave the Dude the time of the big peace conference.

Afterwards I hear she is called Dark Dolores in some spots on account of her complexion but her name is really the other way around. But first I will explain how it is I am in Atlantic City with Dave the Dude the time of the big peace conference as follows:

One afternoon I am walking along Broadway thinking of not much, when I come on Dave the Dude just getting in a taxicab with a suit-case in his duke, and the next thing I know Dave is jerking me into the cab and telling the jockey to go to the Penn Station. This is how I come to be in Atlantic City the time of the big peace conference, although, of course, I have nothing to do with the peace conference, and am only with Dave the Dude to keep him company.

I am a guy who is never too busy to keep people company, and Dave the Dude is a guy who just naturally loves company. In fact, he hates to go anywhere, or be anywhere, by himself, and the reason is because when he is by himself Dave the Dude has nobody to nod him yes, and if there is one thing Dave is very, very fond of, it is to have somebody to nod him yes. Why it is that Dave the Dude does not have Big Nig with him I do not know, for Big Nig is Dave's regular nod-guy.

But I am better than a raw hand myself at nodding. In fact, I am probably as good a nod-guy as there is in this town, where there must be three million nod-guys, and why not, because the way I look at it, it is no bother whatever to nod a guy. In fact, it saves a lot of conversation.

Anyway, there I am in Atlantic City the time of the big peace conference, although I wish to say right now that if I know in advance who is going to be at this peace conference, or that there is going to be any peace conference, I will never be anywhere near Atlantic City, because the parties mixed up in it are no kind of associates for a nervous guy like me.

It seems this peace conference is between certain citizens of St Louis, such as Black Mike Marrio, Benny the Blond Jew, and Scoodles Shea, who all have different mobs in St Louis, and who are all ripping and tearing each other for a couple of years over such propositions as to who shall have what in the way of business privileges of one kind and another, including alky, and liquor, and gambling.

From what I hear there is plenty of shooting going on between these mobs, and guys getting topped right and left. Also there is much heaving of bombs, and all this and that, until finally the only people making any dough in the town are the undertakers, and it seems there is no chance of anybody cutting in on the undertakers, though Scoodles Shea tries.

Well, Scoodles, who is a pretty smart guy, and who is once in the war in France, finally remembers that when all the big nations get broke, and sick and tired of fighting, they hold a peace conference and straighten things out, so he sends word to Black Mike and Benny the Blond Jew that maybe it will be a good idea if they do the same thing, because half their guys are killed anyway, and trade is strictly on the bum.

It seems Black Mike and Benny think very well of this proposition, and are willing to meet Scoodles in a peace conference, but Scoodles, who is a very suspicious character, asks where they will hold this conference. He says he does not wish to hold any conference with Black Mike and Benny in St Louis, except maybe in his own cellar, because he does not know of any other place in St Louis where he will be safe from being guzzled by some of Black Mike's or Benny's guys, and he says he does not suppose Black Mike and Benny will care to go into his cellar with him.

So Scoodles Shea finally asks how about Atlantic City, and it seems this is agreeable to Black Mike because he has a cousin in Atlantic City by the name of Pisano that he does not see since they leave the old country.

Benny the Blond Jew says any place is okay with him as long as it is not in the State of Missouri, because, he says, he does not care to be seen anywhere in the state of Missouri with Black Mike and Scoodles, as it will be a knock to his reputation.

This seems to sound somewhat insulting, and almost busts up the peace conference before it starts, but finally Benny withdraws the bad crack, and says he does not mean the State of Missouri, but only St Louis, so the negotiations proceed, and they settle on Atlantic City as the spot.

Then Black Mike says some outside guy must sit in with them as a sort of umpire, and help them iron out their arguments, and Benny says he will take President Hoover, Colonel

Lindbergh, or Chief Justice Taft. Now of course this is great foolishness to think they can get any one of these parties, because the chances are President Hoover, Colonel Lindbergh and Chief Justice Taft are too busy with other things to bother about ironing out a mob war in St Louis.

So finally Scoodles Shea suggests Dave the Dude. Both Black Mike and Benny say Dave is okay, though Benny holds out for some time for at least Chief Justice Taft. So Dave the Dude is asked to act as umpire for the St Louis guys, and he is glad to do same, for Dave often steps into towns where guys are battling and straightens them out, and sometimes they do not start battling again for several weeks after he leaves town.

You see, Dave the Dude is friendly with everybody everywhere, and is known to one and all as a right guy, and one who always gives everybody a square rattle in propositions of this kind. Furthermore, it is a pleasure for Dave to straighten guys out in other towns, because the battling tangles up his own business interests in spots such as St Louis.

Now it seems that on their way to the station to catch a train for Atlantic City, Scoodles Shea and Black Mike and Benny decide to call on a young guy by the name of Frankie Farrone, who bobs up all of a sudden in St Louis with plenty of nerve, and who is causing them no little bother one way and another.

In fact, it seems that this Frankie Farrone is as good a reason as any other why Scoodles and Black Mike and Benny are willing to hold a peace conference, because Frankie Farrone is nobody's friend in particular and he is biting into all three wherever he can, showing no respect whatever to old-established guys.

It looks as if Frankie Farrone will sooner or later take the town away from them if they let him go far enough, and while each one of the three tries at different times to make a connexion with him, it seems he is just naturally a lone wolf, and wishes no part of any of them. In fact, somebody hears Frankie Farrone say he expects to make Scoodles Shea and Black Mike and Benny jump out of a window before he is through with them, but whether he means one window or three different windows he does not say.

So there is really nothing to be done about Frankie Farrone but to call on him, especially as the three are now together, because the police pay no attention to his threats and make no move to protect Scoodles and Black Mike and Benny, the law being very careless in St Louis at this time.

Of course, Frankie Farrone has no idea Scoodles and Black Mike and Benny are friendly with each other, and he is probably very much surprised when they drop in on him on their way to the station. In fact, I hear there is a surprised look still on his face when they pick him up later.

He is sitting in a speak-easy reading about the Cardinals losing another game to the Giants when Scoodles Shea comes in the front door, and Black Mike comes in the back door, and Benny the Blond Jew slides in through a side entrance, it being claimed afterwards that they know the owner of the joint and get him to fix it for them so they will have no bother about dropping in on Frankie Farrone sort of unsuspected like.

Well, anyway, the next thing Frankie Farrone knows he has four slugs in him, one from Scoodles Shea, one from Benny, and two from Black Mike, who seems to be more liberal than the others. The chances are they will put more slugs in him, only they leave their taxi a block away with the engine running and they know the St Louis taxi jockeys are terrible for jumping the meter on guys who keep them waiting.

So they go on to catch their train, and they are all at the Ritz Hotel in Atlantic City when Dave the Dude and I get there, and they have a nice layout of rooms looking out over the ocean, for these are high-class guys in every respect, and very good spenders.

They are sitting around a table with their coats off playing pinochle and drinking liquor when Dave and I show up, and right away Black Mike says: 'Hello, Dave! Where do we find the tomatoes?'

I can see at once that this Black Mike is a guy who has little bringing up, or he will not speak of dolls as tomatoes, although, of course, different guys have different names for dolls, such as broads, and pancakes, and cookies, and tomatoes, which I claim are not respectful.

This Black Mike is a Guinea, and not a bad-looking Guinea at that, except for a big scar on one cheek.

Benny the Blond Jew is a tall, pale guy, with soft, light-coloured hair and blue eyes, and if I do not happen to know that he personally knocks off about nine guys I will consider him as harmless a looking guy as I ever see. Scoodles Shea is a big, red-headed muzzler with a lot of freckles and a big grin all over his kisser.

They are all maybe thirty-odd, and wear coloured silk shirts with soft collars fastened with gold pins, and Black Mike and Scoodles Shea are wearing diamond rings and wrist-watches. Unless you know who they are, you will never figure them to be gorills, even from St Louis, although at the same time the chances are you will not figure them to be altar boys unless you are very simple-minded.

They seem to be getting along first-rate together, which is not surprising, because it will be considered very bad taste indeed for guys such as these from one town to go into another town and start up any heat. It will be regarded as showing no respect whatever for the local citizens.

Anyway, Atlantic City is never considered a spot for anything but pleasure, and even guys from Philly who may be mad at each other, and who meet up in Atlantic City, generally wait until they get outside the city limits before taking up any arguments.

Well, it seems that not only Black Mike wishes to meet up with some dolls, but Scoodles Shea and Benny are also thinking of such, because the first two things guys away from home think of are liquor and dolls, although personally I never give these matters much of a tumble.

Furthermore, I can see that Dave the Dude is not so anxious about them as you will expect, because Dave is now married to Miss Billy Perry, and if Miss Billy Perry hears that Dave is having any truck with liquor and dolls, especially dolls, it is apt to cause gossip around his house.

But Dave figures he is a sort of host in this territory, because the others are strangers to Atlantic City, and important people where they come from, so we go down to Joe Goss's joint, which is a big cabaret just off the Boardwalk, and in no time there are half a dozen dolls of different shapes and sizes from Joe Goss's chorus, and also several of Joe Goss's hostesses, for Joe Goss gets many tired business men from New York among his customers, and there is nothing a tired business man from New York appreciates more than a lively hostess. Furthermore, Joe Goss himself is sitting with us as a mark of respect to Dave the Dude.

Black Mike and Scoodles and Benny are talking with the dolls and dancing with them now and then, and a good time is being had by one and all, as far as I can see, including Dave the Dude after he gets a couple of slams of Joe Goss's liquor in him and commences to forget about Miss Billy Perry. In fact, Dave so far forgets about Miss Billy Perry that he gets out on the floor with one of the dolls, and dances some, which shows you what a couple of slams of Joe Goss's liquor will do to a guy.

Most of the dolls are just such dolls as you will find in a cabaret, but there is one among them who seems to be a hostess, and whose name seems to be Dolores, and who is a lily for looks. It is afterwards that I find out her other name is Dark, and it is Dave the Dude who afterwards finds out that she is called Dark Dolores in spots.

She is about as good a looker as a guy will wish to clap an eye on. She's tall and limber, like a buggy whip, and she has hair as black as the ace of spades, and maybe blacker, and all smooth and shiny. Her eyes are black and as big as doughnuts, and she has a look in them that somehow makes me think she may know more than she lets on, which I afterwards find out is very true indeed.

She does not have much to say, and I notice she does not drink, and does not seem to be so friendly with the other dolls, so I figure her a fresh-laid one around there, especially as Joe Goss himself does not act as familiar towards her as he does towards most of his dolls, although I can see him give her many a nasty look on account of her passing up drinks.

In fact, nobody gives her much of a tumble at all at first because guys generally like gabby dolls in situations such as this. But finally I notice that Benny the Blond Jew is taking his peeks at her, and I figure it is because he has better judgement than the others, although I do not understand how Dave the Dude can overlook such a bet, because no better judge of dolls ever lives than Dave the Dude.

But even Benny does not talk to Dolores or offer to dance with her, and at one time when Joe Goss is in another part of the joint chilling a beef from some customer about a check, or maybe about the liquor, which calls for at least a mild beef, and the others are out on the floor dancing, Dolores and I are left alone at the table.

We sit there quite a spell with plenty of silence between us, because I am never much of a hand to chew the fat with dolls, but finally, not because I wish to know or care a whoop, but just to make small talk, I ask how long she is in Atlantic City.

'I get here this afternoon, and go to work for Mr Goss just this very night,' she says. 'I am from Detroit.'

Now I do not ask her where she is from, and her sticking in this information makes me commence to think that maybe she is a gabby doll after all, but she dries up and does not say anything else until the others come back to the table.

Now Benny the Blond Jew moves into a chair alongside Dolores, and I hear him say:

'Are you ever in St Louis? Your face is very familiar to me.'

'No,' she says. 'I am from Cleveland. I am never in St Louis in my life.'

'Well,' Benny says, 'you look like somebody I see before in St Louis. It is very strange, because I cannot believe it possible for there to be more than one wonderful beautiful doll like you.'

I can see Benny is there with the old stuff when it comes to carrying on a social conversation, but I am wondering how it comes this Dolores is from Detroit with me and from Cleveland with him. Still, I know a thousand dolls who cannot remember off-hand where they are from if you ask them quick.

By and by Scoodles Shea and Black Mike notice Benny is all tangled in conversation with Dolores, which makes them take a second peek at her, and by this time they are peeking through plenty of Joe Goss's liquor, which probably makes her look ten times more beautiful than she is really is. And I wish to say that any doll ten times more beautiful than Dolores is nothing but a dream.

Anyway, before long Dolores is getting much attention from Black Mike and Scoodles, as well as Benny, and the rest of the dolls finally take the wind, because nobody is giving them a tumble any more. And even Dave the Dude begins taking dead aim at Dolores until I remind him that he must call up Miss Billy Perry, so he spends the next half-hour in a phone booth explaining to Miss Billy Perry that he is in his hotel in the hay, and that he loves her very dearly.

*

Well, we are in Joe Goss's joint until five o'clock a.m., with Black Mike and Scoodles and Benny talking to Dolores and taking turns dancing with her, and Dave the Dude is plumb wore out, especially as Miss Billy Perry tells him she knows he is a liar and a bum, as she can hear an orchestra playing 'I Get So Blue When It Rains', and for him to just wait until she sees him. Then we take Dolores and go to Childs's restaurant on the Boardwalk and have some coffee, and finally all hands escort her to a little flea-bag in North Caroline Avenue where she says she is stopping.

'What are you doing this afternoon, beautiful one?' asks Benny the Blond Jew as we are telling her good night, even though it is morning, and at this crack Black Mike and Scoodles Shea look at Benny, very, very cross.

'I am going bathing in front of the Ritz,' she says. 'Do some of you boys wish to come along with me?'

Well, it seems that Black Mike and Scoodles and Benny all think this is a wonderful idea, but it does not go so big with Dave the Dude or me. In fact, by this time, Dave the Dude and me are pretty sick of Dolores.

'Anyway,' Dave says, 'we must start our conference this afternoon and get through with it, because my ever-loving doll is already steaming, and I have plenty of business to look after in New York.'

*

But the conference does not start this afternoon, or the next night, or the next day, or the next day following, because in the afternoons Black Mike and Scoodles and Benny are in the ocean with Dolores and at night they are in Joe Goss's joint, and in between they are taking her riding in rolling chairs on the Boardwalk, or feeding her around the different hotels.

No one guy is ever alone with her as far as I can see, except when she is dancing with one in Joe Goss's joint, and about the third night they are so jealous of each other they all try to dance with her at once.

Well, naturally even Joe Goss complains about this because it makes confusion on his dance floor, and looks unusual. So Dolores settles the proposition, by not dancing with anybody, and I figure this is a good break for her, as no doll's dogs can stand all the dancing Black Mike and Scoodles and Benny wish to do.

The biggest rolling chair on the Boardwalk only takes in three guys or two guys and one doll, or, what is much better, one guy and two dolls, so when Dolores is in a rolling chair with a guy sitting on each side of her the other walks alongside the chair, which is a peculiar sight, indeed.

How they decide the guy who walks I never know, but I suppose Dolores fixes it. When she is in bathing in the ocean Black Mike and Scoodles and Benny all stick so close to her that she is really quite crowded at times.

I doubt if even Waldo Winchester, the scribe, who hears of a lot of things, ever hears of such a situation as this with three guys all daffy over the same doll, and guys who do not think any too well of each other to begin with. I can see they are getting more and more hostile towards each other over her, but when they are not with Dolores they stick close to each other for fear one will cop a sneak, and get her to himself.

I am very puzzled, because Black Mike and Scoodles and Benny do not get their rods out and start a shooting match among themselves over her, but I find that Dave the Dude makes them turn in their rods to him the second day because he does not care to have them doing any target practice around Atlantic City.

So they cannot start a shooting match among themselves if they wish, and the reason they do not put the slug on each other is because Dolores tells them she hates tough guys who go around putting the slug on people. So they are gentlemen, bar a few bad cracks passing among them now and then.

*

Well, it comes on a Friday, and there we are in Atlantic City since a Monday and nothing stirring on the peace conference as yet, and Dave the Dude is very much disgusted indeed.

All night Friday and into Saturday morning we are in Joe Goss's, and personally I can think of many other places I will rather be. To begin with, I never care to be around gorills when they are drinking, and when you take gorills who are drinking and get them all crazy about the same doll, they are apt to turn out to be no gentlemen any minute.

I do not know who it is who suggests a daybreak swimming party, because I am half asleep, and so is Dave the Dude, but I hear afterwards it is Dolores. Anyway, the next thing anybody knows we are out on the beach, and Dolores and Black Mike and Scoodles Shea and Benny the Blond Jew are in their bathing suits and the dawn is touching up the old ocean very beautiful.

Of course, Dave the Dude and me are not in bathing suits, because in the first place neither of us is any hand for going in bathing, and in the second place, if we are going in bathing, we will not go in bathing at such an hour. Furthermore, as far as I am personally concerned, I hope I am never in a bathing suit if I will look no better in it than Black Mike, while Scoodles Shea is no Gene Tunney in regards to shape. Benny the Blond Jew is the only one who looks human, and I do not give him more than sixty-five points.

Dave the Dude and me stand around watching them, and mostly we are watching Dolores. She is in a red bathing suit with a red rubber cap over her black hair, and while most dolls in bathing suits hurt my eyes, she is still beautiful. I will always claim she is the most beautiful thing I ever see, bar Blue Larkspur, and of course Blue Larkspur is a racehorse and not a doll. I am very glad that Miss Billy Perry is not present to see the look in Dave the Dude's eyes as he watches Dolores in her bathing suit, for Miss Billy Perry is quick to take offence.

When she is in the water Dolores slides around like a big beautiful red fish. You can see she loves it. The chances are I can swim better on my back than Black Mike or Scoodles Shea can on their stomachs, and Benny the Blond Jew is no Gertrude Ederle, but, of course, I am allowing for them being well loaded with Joe Goss's liquor, and a load of Joe Goss's liquor is not apt to float well anywhere.

*

Well, after they paddle around in the ocean a while, Dolores and her three Romeos lay out on the sand, and Dave the Dude and me are just figuring on going to bed, when all of a sudden we see Dolores jump up and start running for the ocean with Black Mike and Benny head-and-head just behind her, and Scoodles Shea half a length back.

She tears into the water, kicking it every which way until she gets to where it is deep, when she starts to swim, heading for the open sea. Black Mike and Scoodles Shea and Benny the Blond Jew are paddling after her like blazes. We can see it is some kind of a chase, and we stand watching it. We can see Dolores's little red cap bouncing along over the water like a rubber ball on a sidewalk, with Black Mike and Scoodles and Benny staggering along behind her, for Joe Goss's liquor will make a guy stagger on land or sea.

She is away ahead of them at first, but then she seems to pull up and let them get closer to her. When Black Mike, who is leading the other two, gets within maybe fifty yards of her, the red cap bounces away again, always going farther out. It strikes me that Dolores is sort of swimming in wide circles, now half turning as if coming back to the beach, and then taking a swing that carries her seaward again.

When I come to think it over afterwards, I can see that when you are watching her it does not look as if she is swimming away from the beach, and yet all the time she is getting away from it.

One of her circles takes her almost back to Benny, who is a bad last to Black Mike and Scoodles Shea, and in fact she gets so close to Benny that he is lunging for her, when she slides away again, and is off faster than any fish I ever see afloat. Then she does the same to Black Mike and Scoodles. I figure they are playing tag in the water, or some such, and while this may be all right for guys who are full of liquor, and a light-headed doll, I do not consider it a proper amusement at such an hour for guys in their right senses, like Dave the Dude and me.

So I am pleased when he says we better go to bed because by this time Dolores and Black Mike and Scoodles Shea and Benny seem to be very far out in the water indeed. As we are strolling along the Boardwalk, I look back again and there they are, no bigger than pin points on the water, and it seems to me that I can see only three pin points, at that, but I figure Dolores is so far out I cannot see her through the haze.

'They will be good and tuckered out by the time they get back,' I say to Dave the Dude.

'I hope they drown,' Dave says, but a few days later he apologizes for this crack and explains he makes it only because he is tired and disgusted.

*

Well, I often think now that it is strange neither Dave the Dude or me see anything unnatural in the whole play, but we do not even mention Dolores or Black Mike or Scoodles Shea or Benny the Blond Jew until late in the afternoon when we are putting on the old grapefruit and ham and eggs in Dave's room and Dave is looking out over the ocean.

'Say,' he says, as if he just happens to remember it, 'do you know those guys are away out yonder the last we see of them? I wonder if they get back okay?'

And as if answering his question there is a knock on the door, and who walks in but Dolores. She looks all fagged out, but she is so beautiful I will say she seems to light up the room, only I do not wish anybody to think I am getting romantic. Anyway, she is beautiful, but her voice is very tired as she says to Dave the Dude:

'Your friends from St Louis will not return. Mister Dave the Dude. They do not swim so well, but better than I thought. The one that is called Black Mike and Scoodles Shea turn back when we are about three miles out, but they never reach the shore. I see them both go down for the last time. I make sure of this, Mister Dave the Dude. The pale one, Benny, lasts a little farther, although he is the worst swimmer of them all, and he never turns back. He is still trying to follow me when a cramp gets him and he sinks. I guess he loves me the most at that as he always claims.'

Well, naturally, I am greatly horrified by this news, especially as she tells it without batting one of her beautiful eyes.

'Do you mean to tell us you let these poor guys drown out there in all this salt water?' I say, very indignant. 'Why, you are nothing but a cad.'

But Dave the Dude makes a sign for me to shut up, and Dolores says:

'I come within a quarter of a mile of swimming the English Channel in 1927, as you will see by looking up the records,' she says, 'and I can swim the Mississippi one handed, but I cannot pack three big guys such as these on my back. Even,' she says, 'if I care to, which I do not. Benny is the only one who speaks to me before he goes. The last time I circle back to him he waves his hand and says, "I know all along I see you somewhere before. I remember now. You are Frankie Farrone's doll".'

'And you are?' asks Dave the Dude.

'His widow,' says Dolores. 'I promise him as he lays in his coffin that these men will die, and they are dead. I spend my last dollar getting to this town by aeroplane, but I get there, and I get them. Only it is more the hand of Providence,' she says. 'Now I will not need this.'

And she tosses out on the table among our breakfast dishes a little bottle that we find out afterwards is full of enough cyanide to kill forty mules, which always makes me think that this Dolores is a doll who means business.

'There is only one thing I wish to know,' Dave the Dude says.

'Only one thing. How do you coax these fatheads to follow you out in the water?'

'This is the easiest thing of all,' Dolores says. 'It is an inspiration to me as we lay out on the beach. I tell them I will marry the first one who reaches me in the water. I do not wish to seem hard-hearted, but it is a relief to me when I see Black Mike sink. Can you imagine being married to such a bum?'

It is not until we are going home that Dave the Dude has anything to say about the proposition, and then he speaks to me as follows:

'You know,' Dave says, 'I will always consider I get a very lucky break that Dolores does not include me in her offer, or the chances are I will be swimming yet.'

19 'GENTLEMEN, THE KING!'

On Tuesday evenings I always go to Bobby's Chop House to get myself a beef stew, the beef stews in Bobby's being very nourishing, indeed, and quite reasonable. In fact, the beef stews in Bobby's are considered a most fashionable dish by one and all on Broadway on Tuesday evenings.

So on this Tuesday evening I am talking about, I am in Bobby's wrapping myself around a beef stew and reading the race results in the *Journal*, when who comes into the joint but two old friends of mine from Philly, and a third guy I never see before in my life, but who seems to be an old sort of guy, and very fierce looking.

One of these old friends of mine from Philly is a guy by the name of Izzy Cheesecake, who is called Izzy Cheesecake because he is all the time eating cheesecake around delicatessen joints, although of course this is nothing against him, as cheesecake is very popular in some circles, and goes very good with java. Anyway, this Izzy Cheesecake has another name, which is Morris something, and he is slightly Jewish, and has a large beezer, and is considered a handy man in many respects.

The other old friend of mine from Philly is a guy by the name of Kitty Quick, who is maybe thirty-two or -three years old, and who is a lively guy in every way. He is a great hand for wearing good clothes, and he is mobbed up with some very good people in Philly in his day, and at one time has plenty of dough, although I hear that lately things are not going so good for Kitty Quick, or for anybody else in Philly, as far as that is concerned.

Now of course I do not rap to these old friends of mine from Philly at once, and in fact I put the *Journal* up in front of my face, because it is never good policy to rap to visitors in this town, especially visitors from Philly, until you know why they are visiting. But it seems that Kitty Quick spies me before I can get the *Journal* up high enough, and he comes over to my table at once, bringing Izzy Cheesecake and the other guy with him, so naturally I give them a big hello, very cordial, and ask them to sit down and have a few beef stews with me, and as they pull up chairs, Kitty Quick says to me like this:

'Do you know Jo-jo from Chicago?' he says, pointing his thumb at the third guy.

Well, of course I know Jo-jo by his reputation, which is very alarming, but I never meet up with him before, and if it is left to me, I will never meet up with him at all, because Jo-jo is considered a very uncouth character, even in Chicago.

He is an Italian, and a short wide guy, very heavy set, and slow moving, and with jowls you can cut steaks off of, and sleepy eyes, and he somehow reminds me of an old lion I once see in a cage in Ringling's circus. He has a black moustache, and he is an old-timer out in Chicago, and is pointed out to visitors to the city as a very remarkable guy because he lives as long as he does, which is maybe forty years.

His right name is Antonio something, and why he is called Jo-jo I never hear, but I suppose it is because Jo-jo is handier than Antonio. He shakes hands with me, and says he is pleased to meet me, and then he sits down and begins taking on beef stew very rapidly while Kitty Quick says to me as follows:

'Listen,' he says, 'do you know anybody in Europe?'

Well, this is a most unexpected question, and naturally I am not going to reply to unexpected questions by guys from Philly without thinking them over very carefully, so to gain time while I think, I say to Kitty Quick:

'Which Europe do you mean?'

'Why,' Kitty says, greatly surprised, 'is there more than one Europe? I mean the big Europe on the Atlantic Ocean. This is the Europe where we are going, and if you know anybody there we will be glad to go around and say hello to them for you. We are going to Europe on the biggest proposition anybody ever hears of,' he says. 'In fact,' he says, 'it is a proposition which will make us all rich. We are sailing to-night.'

Well, offhand I cannot think of anybody I know in Europe, and if I do know anybody there I will certainly not wish such parties as Kitty Quick, and Izzy Cheesecake, and Jo-jo going around saying hello to them, but of course I do not mention such a thought out loud. I only say I hope and trust that they have a very good *bon voyage* and do not suffer too much from seasickness. Naturally I do not ask what their proposition is, because if I ask such a question they may think I wish to find out, and will consider me a very nosey guy, but I figure the chances are they are going to look after some commercial matter, such as Scotch, or maybe cordials.

Anyway, Kitty Quick and Izzy Cheesecake and Jo-jo eat up quite a few beef stews, and leave me to pay the check, and this is the last I see or hear of any of them for several months. Then one day I am in Philly to see a prizefight, and I run into Kitty Quick on Broad Street, looking pretty much the same as usual, and I ask him how he comes out in Europe.

'It is no good,' Kitty says. 'The trip is something of a bust, although we see many interesting sights, and have quite a few experiences. Maybe,' Kitty says, 'you will like to hear why we go to Europe? It is a very unusual story, indeed, and is by no means a lie, and I will be pleased to tell it to someone I think will believe it.'

So we go into Walter's restaurant, and sit down in a corner, and order up a little java, and Kitty Quick tells me the story as follows:

It all begins [Kitty says] with a certain big lawyer coming to me here in Philly, and wishing to know if I care to take up a proposition which will make me rich, and naturally I say I can think of nothing that will please me more, because at this time things are very bad indeed in Philly, what with investigations going on here and there, and plenty of heat around and about, and I do not have more than a few bobs in my pants pocket, and can think of no way to get any more.

So this lawyer takes me to the Ritz-Carlton hotel, and there he introduces me to a guy by the name of Count Saro, and the lawyer says he will okay anything Saro has to say to me 100 per cent, and then he immediately takes the wind as if he does not care to hear what Saro has to say. But I know this mouthpiece is not putting any proposition away as okay unless he knows it is pretty much okay, because he is a smart guy at his own dodge, and everything else, and has plenty of coconuts.

Now this Count Saro is a little guy with an eyebrow moustache, and he wears striped pants, and white spats, and a cutaway coat, and a monocle in one eye, and he seems to be a foreign nobleman, although he talks English first rate. I do not care much for Count Saro's looks, but I will say one thing for him he is very businesslike, and gets down to cases at once.

He tells me that he is the representative of a political party in his home country in Europe which has a King, and this country wishes to get rid of the King, because Count Saro says Kings are out of style in Europe, and that no country can get anywhere with a King these days. His proposition is for me to take any assistants I figure I may need and go over and get rid of this King, and Count Saro says he will pay two hundred G's for the job in good old American scratch, and will lay twenty-five G's on the line at once, leaving the balance with the lawyer to be paid to me when everything is finished.

Well, this is a most astonishing proposition, indeed, because, while I often hear of propositions to get rid of other guys, I never before hear of a proposition to get rid of a King. Furthermore, it does not sound reasonable to me, as getting rid of a King is apt to attract plenty of attention, and criticism, but Count Saro explains to me that his country is a small, out-of-the-way country, and that his political party will take control of the telegraph wires and everything else as soon as I get rid of the King, so nobody will give the news much of a tumble outside the country.

'Everything will be done very quietly, and in good order,' Count Saro says, 'and there will be no danger to you whatever.'

Well, naturally, I wish to know from Count Saro why he does not get somebody in his own country to do such a job, especially if he can pay so well for it, and he says to me like this:

'Well,' he says, 'in the first place there is no one in our country with enough experience in such matters to be trusted, and in the second place we do not wish anyone in our country to seem to be tangled up with getting rid of the King. It will cause internal complications,' he says. 'An outsider is more logical,' he says, 'because it is quite well known that in the palace of the King there are many valuable jewels, and it will seem a natural play for outsiders, especially Americans, to break into the palace to get these jewels, and if they happen to get rid of the King while getting the jewels, no one will think it is anything more than an accident, such as often occurs in your country.'

Furthermore, Count Saro tells me that everything will be laid out for me in advance by his people, so I will have no great bother getting into the palace to get rid of the King, but he says of course I must not really take the valuable jewels, because his political party wishes to keep them for itself.

Well, I do not care much for the general idea at all, but Count Saro whips out a bundle of scratch, and weeds off twenty-five large coarse notes of a G apiece, and there it is in front of me, and looking at all this dough, and thinking how tough times are, what with banks busting here and there, I am very much tempted indeed, especially as I am commencing to think this Count Saro is some kind of a nut, and is only speaking through his hat about getting rid of a King.

'Listen,' I say to Count Saro, as he sits there watching me, 'how do you know I will not take this dough off of you and then never do anything whatever for it?'

'Why,' he says, much surprised, 'you are recommended to me as an honest man, and I accept your references. Anyway,' he says, 'if you do not carry out your agreement with me, you will only hurt yourself, because you will lose a hundred and seventy-five G's more and the lawyer will make you very hard to catch.'

Well, the upshot of it is I shake hands with Count Saro, and then go out to find Izzy Cheesecake, although I am still thinking Count Saro is a little daffy, and while I am looking for Izzy, who do I see but Jo-jo, and Jo-jo tells me that he is on a vacation from Chicago for awhile, because it seems somebody out there claims he is a public enemy, which Jo-jo says is nothing but a big lie, as he is really very fond of the public at all times.

Naturally I am glad to come across a guy such as Jo-jo, because he is most trustworthy, and naturally Jo-jo is very glad to hear of a proposition that will turn him an honest dollar while he is on his vacation. So Jo-jo and Izzy and I have a meeting, and we agree that I am to have a hundred G's for finding the plant, while Izzy and Jo-jo are to get fifty G's apiece, and this is how we come to go to Europe.

Well, we land at a certain spot in Europe, and who is there to meet us but another guy with a monocle, who states that his name is Baron von Terp, or some such, and who says he is representing Count Saro, and I am commencing to wonder if Count Saro's country is filled with one-eyed guys. Anyway, this Baron von Terp takes us travelling by trains and automobiles for several days, until finally after an extra long hop in an automobile we come to the outskirts of a nice-looking little burg, which seems to be the place we are headed for.

Now Baron von Terp drops us in a little hotel on the outskirts of the town, and says he must leave us because he cannot afford to be seen with us, although he explains he does not mean this as a knock to us. In fact, Baron von Terp says he finds us very nice travelling companions, indeed, except for Jo-jo wishing to engage in target practice along the route with his automatic Roscoe, and using such animals as stray dogs and chickens for his targets. He says he does not even mind Izzy Cheesecake's singing, although personally I will always consider this one of the big drawbacks to the journey.

Before he goes, Baron von Terp draws me a rough diagram of the inside of the palace where we are to get rid of the King, giving me a layout of all the rooms and doors. He says usually there are guards in and about this palace, but that his people arrange it so these guards will not be present around nine o'clock this night, except one guy who may be on guard at the door of the King's bedroom, and Baron von Terp says if we guzzle this guy it will be all right with him, because he does not like the guy, anyway.

But the general idea, he says, is for us to work fast and quietly, so as to be in and out of there inside of an hour or so, leaving no trail behind us, and I say this will suit me and Izzy Cheesecake and Jo-jo very well, indeed, as we are getting tired of travelling, and wish to go somewhere and take a long rest.

Well, after explaining all this, Baron von Terp takes the wind, leaving us a big fast car with an ugly-looking guy driving it who does not talk much English, but is supposed to know all the routes, and it is in this car that we leave the little hotel just before nine o'clock as per instructions, and head for the palace, which turns out to be nothing but a large square old building in the middle of a sort of park, with the town around and about, but some distance off.

Ugly-face drives right into this park and up to what seems to be the front door of the building, and the three of us get out of the car, and Ugly-face pulls the car off into the shadow of some trees to wait for us.

Personally, I am looking for plenty of heat when we start to go into the palace, and I have the old equalizer where I can get at it without too much trouble, while Jo-jo and Izzy Cheesecake also have their rods handy. But just as Baron von Terp tells us, there are no guards around, and in fact there is not a soul in sight as we walk into the palace door, and find ourselves in a big hall with paintings, and armour, and old swords, and one thing and another hanging around and about, and I can see that this is a perfect plant, indeed.

I out with my diagram and see where the King's bedroom is located on the second floor, and when we get there, walking very easy, and ready to start blasting away if necessary, who is at the door but a big tall guy in a uniform, who is very much surprised at seeing us, and who starts to holler something or other, but what it is nobody will ever know, because just as he opens his mouth, Izzy Cheesecake taps him on the noggin with the butt of a forty-five, and knocks him cock-eyed.

Then Jo-jo grabs some cord off a heavy silk curtain which is hanging across the door, and ties the guy up good and tight, and wads a handkerchief into his kisser in case the guy comes to, and wishes to start hollering again, and when all this is done, I quietly turn the knob of the door to the King's bedroom, and we step into a room that looks more like a young convention hall than it does a bedroom, except that it is hung around and about with silk drapes, and there is much gilt furniture here and there.

Well, who is in this room but a nice-looking doll, and a little kid of maybe eight or nine years old, and the kid is in a big bed with a canopy over it like the entrance to a night club, only silk, and the doll is sitting alongside the bed reading to the kid out of a book. It is a very homelike scene, indeed, and causes us to stop and look around in great surprise, for we are certainly not expecting such a scene at all.

As we stand there in the middle of the room somewhat confused the doll turns and looks at us, and the little kid sits up in bed. He is a fat little guy with a chubby face, and a lot of curly hair, and eyes as big as pancakes, and maybe bigger. The doll turns very pale when she sees us, and shakes so the book she is reading falls to the floor, but the kid does not seem scared, and he says to us in very good English like this:

'Who are you?' he says.

Well, this is a fair question, at that, but naturally we do not wish to state who we are at this time, so I say:

'Never mind who we are, where is the King?'

'The King?' the kid says, sitting up straight in the bed, 'why, I am the King.'

Now of course this seems a very nonsensical crack to us, because we have brains enough to know that Kings do not come as small as this little squirt, and anyway we are in no mood to dicker with him, so I say to the doll as follows:

'Listen,' I say, 'we do not care for any kidding at this time, because we are in a great hurry. Where is the King?'

'Why,' she says, her voice trembling quite some, 'this is indeed the King, and I am his governess. Who are you, and what do you want? How do you get in here?' she says. 'Where are the guards?'

'Lady,' I say, and I am greatly surprised at myself for being so patient with her, 'this kid may be a King, but we want the big King. We want the head King himself,' I say.

'There is no other,' she says, and the little kid chips in like this:

'My father dies two years ago, and I am the King in his place,' he says. 'Are you English like Miss Peabody here?' he says. 'Who is the funny looking old man back there?'

Well, of course Jo-jo is funny looking, at that, but no one ever before is impolite enough to speak of it to his face, and Jo-jo begins growling quite some, while Izzy Cheesecake speaks as follows.

'Why,' Izzy says, 'this is a very great outrage. We are sent to get rid of a King, and here the King is nothing but a little punk. Personally,' Izzy says, 'I am not in favour of getting rid of punks, male or female.'

'Well,' Jo-jo says, 'I am against it myself as a rule, but this is a pretty fresh punk.'

'Now,' I say, 'there seems to be some mistake around here, at that. Let us sit down and talk things over quietly, and see if we cannot get this matter straightened out. It looks to me,' I say, 'as if this Count Saro is nothing but a swindler.'

'Count Saro,' the doll says, getting up and coming over to me, and looking very much alarmed. 'Count Saro, do you say? Oh, sir, Count Saro is a very bad man. He is the tool of the Grand Duke Gino of this country, who is this little boy's uncle. The Grand Duke will be king himself if it is not for this boy, and we suspect many plots against the little chap's safety. Oh, gentlemen,' she says, 'you surely do not mean any harm to this poor orphan child?'

Well, this is about the first time in their lives that Jo-jo and Izzy Cheesecake are ever mentioned by anybody as gentlemen, and I can see that it softens them up quite some, especially as the little kid is grinning at them very cheerful, although of course he will not be so cheerful if he knows who he is grinning at.

'Why,' Jo-jo says, 'the Grand Duke is nothing but a rascal for wishing harm to such a little guy as this, although of course,' Jo-jo says, 'if he is a grown-up King it will be a different matter.'

'Who are you?' the little kid says again.

'We are Americans,' I say, very proud to mention my home country. 'We are from Philly and Chicago, two very good towns, at that.'

Well, the little kid's eyes get bigger than ever, and he climbs right out of bed and walks over to us looking very cute in his blue silk pyjamas, and his bare feet.

'Chicago?' he says. 'Do you know Mr Capone?'

'Al?' says Jo-jo. 'Do I know Al? Why, Al and me are just like this,' he says, although personally I do not believe Al Capone will know Jo-jo if he meets him in broad daylight. 'Where do you know Al from?' he asks.

'Oh, I do not know him,' the kid says. 'But I read about him in the magazines, and about the machine guns, and the pineapples. Do you know about the pineapples?' he says.

'Do I know about the pineapples?' Jo-jo says, as if his feelings are hurt by the question. 'He asks me do I know about the pineapples. Why,' he says, 'look here.'

And what does Jo-jo do but out with a little round gadget which I recognize at once as a bomb such as these Guineas like to chuck at people they do not like, especially Guineas from Chicago. Of course I never know Jo-jo is packing this article around and about with him, and Jo-jo can see I am much astonished, and by no means pleased, because he says to me like this:

'I bring this along in case of a bear fight,' he says. 'They are very handy in a bear fight.'

Well, the next thing anybody knows we are all talking about this and that very pleasant, especially the little kid and Jo-jo, who is telling lies faster than a horse can trot, about Chicago and Mr Capone, and I hope and trust that Al never hears some of the lies Jo-jo tells, or he may hold it against me for being with Jo-jo when these lies come off.

I am talking to the doll, whose name seems to be Miss Peabody, and who is not so hard to take, at that, and at the same time I am keeping an eye on Izzy Cheesecake, who is wandering around the room looking things over. The chances are Izzy is trying to find a few of the valuable jewels such as I mention to him when telling him about the proposition of getting rid of the King, and in fact I am taking a stray peek here and there myself, but I do not see anything worth while.

This Miss Peabody is explaining to me about the politics of the country, and it seems the reason the Grand Duke wishes to get rid of the little kid King and be King himself is because he has a business deal on with a big nation near by which wishes to control the kid King's country. I judge from what Miss Peabody tells me that this country is no bigger than Delaware county, Pa., and it seems to me a lot of bother about no more country than this, but Miss Peabody says it is a very nice little country at that.

She says it will be very lovely indeed if it is not for the Grand Duke Gino, because the little kid King stands okay with the people, but it seems the old Grand Duke is pretty much boss of everything, and Miss Peabody says she is personally long afraid that he will finally try to do something very drastic indeed to get rid of the kid King on account of the kid seeming so healthy. Well, naturally I do not state to her that our middle name is drastic, because I do not wish Miss Peabody to have a bad opinion of us.

Now nothing will do but Jo-jo must show the kid his automatic, which is as long as your arm, and maybe longer, and the kid is greatly delighted, and takes the rod and starts pointing it here and there and saying boom-boom, as kids will do. But what happens but he pulls the trigger, and it seems that Jo-jo does not have the safety on, so the Roscoe really goes boom-boom twice before the kid can take his finger off the trigger.

Well, the first shot smashes a big jar over in one corner of the room, which Miss Peabody afterwards tells me is worth fifteen G's if it is worth a dime, and the second slug knocks off Izzy Cheesecake's derby hat, which serves Izzy right, at that, as he is keeping his hat on in the presence of a lady. Naturally these shots are very disturbing to me at the moment, but afterwards I learn they are a very good thing indeed, because it seems a lot of guys who are hanging around outside, including Baron von Terp, and several prominent politicians of the country, watching and listening to see what comes off, hurry right home to bed, figuring the King is got rid of as per contract, and wishing to be found in bed if anybody comes around asking questions.

Well, Jo-jo is finally out of lies about Chicago and Mr Capone, when the little kid seems to get a new idea and goes rummaging around the room looking for something, and just as I am hoping he is about to donate the valuable jewels to us he comes up with a box, and what is in this box but a baseball bat, and a catcher's mitt, and a baseball, and it is very strange indeed to find such homelike articles so far away from home, especially as Babe Ruth's name is on the bat.

'Do you know about these things?' the little kid asks Jo-jo. 'They are from America, and they are sent to me by one of our people when he is visiting there, but nobody here seems to know what they are for.'

'Do I know about them?' Jo-jo says, fondling them very tenderly, indeed. 'He asks me do I know about them. Why,' he says, 'in my time I am the greatest hitter on the West Side Blues back in dear old Chi.'

Well, now nothing will do the kid but we must show him how these baseball articles work, so Izzy Cheesecake, who claims he is once a star back-stopper with the Vine Streets back in Philly, puts on a pad and mask, and Jo-jo takes the bat and lays a small sofa pillow down on the floor for a home plate, and insists that I pitch to him. Now it is years since I handle a baseball, although I wish to say that in my day I am as good as amateur pitcher as there is around Gray's Ferry in Philly, and the chances are I will be with the A's if I do not have other things to do.

So I take off my coat, and get down to the far end of the room, while Jo-jo squares away at the plate, with Izzy Cheesecake behind it. I can see by the way he stands that Jo-jo is bound to be a sucker for a curve, so I take a good windup, and cut loose with the old fadeaway, but of course my arm is not what it used to be, and the ball does not break as I expect, so what happens but Jo-jo belts the old apple right through a high window in what will be right field if the room is laid off like Shibe Park.

Well, Jo-jo starts running as if he is going to first, but of course there is no place in particular for him to run, and he almost knocks his brains out against a wall, and the ball is lost, and the game winds up right there, but the little kid is tickled silly over this business, and even Miss Peabody laughs, and she does not look to me like a doll who gets many laughs out of life, at that.

It is now nearly ten o'clock, and Miss Peabody says if she can find anybody around she will get us something to eat, and this sounds very reasonable, indeed, so I step outside the door and bring in the guy we tie up there, who seems to be wide awake by now, and very much surprised, and quite indignant, and Miss Peabody says something to him in a language which I do not understand. When I come to think it all over afterwards, I am greatly astonished at the way I trust Miss Peabody, because there is no reason why she shall not tell the guy to get the law, but I suppose I trust her because she seems to have an honest face.

Anyway, the guy in the uniform goes away rubbing his noggin, and pretty soon in comes another guy who seems to be a butler, or some such, and who is also greatly surprised at seeing us, and Miss Peabody rattles off something to him and he starts hustling in tables, and dishes, and sandwiches, and coffee, and one thing and another in no time at all.

Well, there we are, the five of us waiting around the table eating and drinking, because what does the butler do but bring in a couple of bottles of good old pre-war champagne, which is very pleasant to the taste, although Izzy Cheesecake embarrasses me no little by telling Miss Peabody that if she can dig up any considerable quantity of this stuff he will make her plenty of bobs by peddling it in our country, and will also cut the King in.

When the butler fills the wine-glasses the first time, Miss Peabody picks hers up, and looks at us, and naturally we have sense enough to pick ours up, too, and then she stands up on her feet and raises her glass high above her head, and says like this:

'Gentlemen, The King!'

Well, I stand up at this, and Jo-jo and Izzy Cheesecake stand up with me, and we say, all together:

'The King!'

And then we swig our champagne, and sit down again and the little kid laughs all over and claps his hands and seems to think it is plenty of fun, which it is, at that, although Miss Peabody does not let him have any wine, and is somewhat indignant when she catches Jo-jo trying to slip him a snort under the table.

Well, finally the kid does not wish us to leave him at all, especially Jo-jo, but Miss Peabody says he must get some sleep, so we tell him we will be back some day, and we take our hats and say good-bye, and leave him standing in the bedroom door with Miss Peabody at his side, and the little kid's arm is around her waist, and I find myself wishing it is my arm, at that.

Of course we never go back again, and in fact we get out of the country this very night, and take the first boat out of the first seaport we hit and return to the United States of America, and the gladdest guy in all the world to see us go is Ugly-face, because he has to drive us about a thousand miles with the muzzle of a rod digging into his ribs.

So [Kitty Quick says] now you know why we go to Europe.

Well, naturally, I am greatly interested in his story, and especially in what Kitty says about the pre-war champagne, because I can see that there may be great business opportunities in such a place if a guy can get in with the right people, but one thing Kitty will never tell me is where the country is located, except that it is located in Europe.

'You see,' Kitty says, 'we are all strong Republicans here in Philly, and I will not get the Republican administration of this country tangled up in any international squabble for the world. You see,' he says, 'when we land back home I find a little item of cable news in a paper which says the Grand Duke Gino dies as a result of injuries received in an accident in his home some weeks before.

'And,' Kitty says, 'I am never sure but what these injuries may be caused by Jo-jo insisting on Ugly-face driving us around to the Grand Duke's house the night we leave and popping his pineapple into the Grand Duke's bedroom window.'

20 THE HOTTEST GUY IN THE WORLD

I WISH to say I am very nervous indeed when Big Jule pops into my hotel room one afternoon, because anybody will tell you that Big Jule is the hottest guy in the whole world at the time I am speaking about.

In fact, it is really surprising how hot he is. They wish to see him in Pittsburgh, Pa., about a matter of a mail truck being robbed, and there is gossip about him in Minneapolis, Minn., where somebody takes a fifty-G pay-roll off a messenger in cash money, and slugs the messenger around somewhat for not holding still.

Furthermore, the Bankers' Association is willing to pay good dough to talk to Big Jule out in Kansas City, Mo., where a jug is knocked off by a stranger, and in the confusion the paying teller, and the cashier, and the second vice-president are clouted about, and the day watchman is hurt, and two coppers are badly bruised, and over fifteen G's is removed from the counters, and never returned.

Then there is something about a department store in Canton, O., and a flour-mill safe in Toledo, and a grocery in Spokane, Wash., and a branch post office in San Francisco, and also something about a shooting match in Chicago, but of course this does not count so much, as only one party is fatally injured. However, you can see that Big Jule is really very hot, what with the coppers all over the country looking for him high and low. In fact, he is practically on fire.

Of course I do not believe Big Jule does all the things the coppers say, because coppers always blame everything no matter where it happens on the most prominent guy they can think of, and Big Jule is quite prominent all over the U.S.A. The chances are he does not do more than half these things, and he probably has a good alibi for the half he does do, at that, but he is certainly hot, and I do not care to have hot guys around me, or even guys who are only just a little bit warm.

But naturally I am not going to say this to Big Jule when he pops in on me, because he may think I am inhospitable, and I do not care to have such a rap going around and about on me, and furthermore, Jule may become indignant if he thinks I am inhospitable, and knock me on my potato, because Big Jule is quick to take offence.

So I say hello to Big Jule, very pleasant, and ask him to have a chair by the window where he can see the citizens walking to and fro down in Eighth Avenue and watch the circus wagons moving into Madison Square Garden by way of the Forty-ninth Street side, for the circus always shows in the Garden in the spring before going out on the road. It is a little warm, and Big Jule takes off his coat, and I can see he has one automatic slung under his arm, and another sticking down in the waist-band of his pants, and I hope and trust that no copper steps into the room while Big Jule is there because it is very much against the law for guys to go around rodded up this way in New York City.

'Well, Jule,' I say, 'this is indeed a very large surprise to me, and I am glad to see you, but I am thinking maybe it is very foolish for you to be popping into New York just now, what with all the heat around here, and the coppers looking to arrest people for very little.'

'I know,' Jule says. 'I know. But they do not have so very much on me around here, no matter what people say, and a guy gets homesick for his old home town, especially a guy who is stuck away where I am for the past few months. I get homesick for the lights and the crowds on Broadway, and for the old neighbourhood. Furthermore, I wish to see my Maw. I hear she is sick and may not live, and I wish to see her before she goes.'

Well, naturally anybody will wish to see their Maw under such circumstances, but Big Jule's Maw lives over in West

Forty-ninth Street near Eleventh Avenue, and who is living in the very same block but Johnny Brannigan, the strong-arm copper, and it is a hundred to one if Big Jule goes nosing around his old neighbourhood, Johnny Brannigan will hear of it, and if there is one guy Johnny Brannigan does not care for, it is Big Jule, although they are kids together.

But it seems that even when they are kids they have very little use for each other, and after they grow up and Johnny gets on the strong-arm squad, he never misses a chance to push Big Jule around, and sometimes trying to boff Big Jule with his black-jack, and it is well known to one and all that before Big Jule leaves town the last time, he takes a punch at Johnny Branni-gan, and Johnny swears he will never rest until he puts Big Jule where he belongs, although where Big Jule belongs, Johnny does not say.

So I speak of Johnny living in the same block with Big Jule's Maw to Big Jule, but it only makes him mad.

'I am not afraid of Johnny Brannigan,' he says. 'In fact,' he says, 'I am thinking for some time lately that maybe I will clip Johnny Brannigan good while I am here. I owe Johnny Bran-nigan a clipping. But I wish to see my Maw first, and then I will go around and see Miss Kitty Clancy. I guess maybe she will be much surprised to see me, and no doubt very glad.'

Well, I figure it is a sure thing Miss Kitty Clancy will be surprised to see Big Jule, but I am not so sure about her being glad, because very often when a guy is away from a doll for a year or more, no matter how ever-loving she may be, she may get to thinking of someone else, for this is the way dolls are, whether they live on Eleventh Avenue or over on Park. Still, I remember hearing that this Miss Kitty Clancy once thinks very well of Big Jule, although her old man, Jack Clancy, who runs a speak-easy, always claims it is a big knock to the Clancy family to have such a character as Big Jule hanging around.

'I often think of Miss Kitty Clancy the past year or so,' Big Jule says, as he sits there by the window, watching the circus wagons, and the crowds. 'I especially think of her the past few months. In fact,' he says, 'thinking of Miss Kitty Clancy is about all I have to do where I am at, which is in an old warehouse on the Bay of Fundy outside of a town that is called St John's, or some such, up in Canada, and thinking of Miss Kitty Clancy all this time, I find out I love her very much indeed.

'I go to this warehouse,' Big Jule says, 'after somebody takes a jewellery store in the town, and the coppers start in blaming me. This warehouse is not such a place as I will choose myself if I am doing the choosing, because it is an old fur warehouse, and full of strange smells, but in the excitement around the jewellery store, somebody puts a slug in my hip, and Leon Pierre carries me to the old warehouse, and there I am until I get well.

'It is very lonesome,' Big Jule says. 'In fact, you will be surprised how lonesome it is, and it is very, very cold, and all I have for company is a lot of rats. Personally, I never care for rats under any circumstances because they carry disease germs, and are apt to bite a guy when he is asleep, if they are hungry, which is what these rats try to do to me.

'The warehouse is away off by itself,' Jule says, 'and nobody ever comes around there except Leon Pierre to bring me grub and dress my hip, and at night it is very still, and all you can hear is the wind howling around outside, and the rats running here and there. Some of them are very, very large rats. In fact, some of them seem about the size of rabbits, and they are pretty fresh, at that. At first I am willing to make friends with these rats, but they seem very hostile, and after they take a few nips at me, I can see there is no use trying to be nice to them, so I have Leon Pierre bring me a lot of ammunition for my rods every day and I practise shooting at the rats.

'The warehouse is so far off there is no danger of anybody hearing the shooting,' Big Jule says, 'and it helps me pass the time away. I get so I can hit a rat sitting, or running, or even flying through the air, because these warehouse rats often leap from place to place like mountain sheep, their idea being generally to take a good nab at me as they fly past.

'Well, sir,' Jule says, 'I keep score on myself one day, and I hit fifty rats hand running without a miss, which I claim makes me the champion rat shooter of the world with a forty-five automatic, although of course,' he says, 'if anybody wishes to challenge me to a rat shooting match I am willing to take them on for a side bet. I get so I can call my shots on the rats, and in fact several times I say to myself, I will hit this one in the right eye, and this one in the left eye, and it always turns out just as I say, although sometimes when you hit a rat with a forty-five up close it is not always possible to tell afterwards just where you hit him, because you seem to hit him all over.

'By and by,' Jule says, 'I seem to discourage the rats somewhat, and they get so they play the chill for me, and do not try to nab me even when I am asleep. They find out that no rat dast poke his whiskers out at me or he will get a very close shave. So I have to look around for other amusement, but there is not much doing in such a place, although I finally find a bunch of doctors' books which turn out to be very interesting reading. It seems these books are left there by some croaker who retires there to think things over after experimenting on his ever-loving wife with a knife. In fact, it seems he cuts his ever-loving wife's head off, and she does not continue living, so he takes his books and goes to the warehouse and remains there until the law finds him, and hangs him up very high, indeed.

'Well, the books are a great comfort to me, and I learn many astonishing things about surgery, but after I read all the books there is nothing for me to do but think, and what I think about is Miss Kitty Clancy, and how much pleasure we have together walking around and about and seeing movie shows, and all this and that, until her old man gets so tough with me. Yes, I will be very glad to see Miss Kitty Clancy, and the old neighbourhood, and my Maw again.'

Well, finally nothing will do Big Jule but he must take a stroll over into his old neighbourhood, and see if he cannot see Miss Kitty Clancy, and also drop in on his Maw, and he asks me to go along with him. I can think of a million things I will rather do than take a stroll with Big Jule, but I do not wish him to think I am snobbish, because as I say, Big Jule is quick to take offence. Furthermore, I figure that at such an hour of the day he is less likely to run into Johnny Brannigan or any other coppers who know him than at any other time, so I say I will go with him, but as we start out, Big Jule puts on his rods.

'Jule,' I say, 'do not take any rods with you on a stroll, because somebody may happen to see them, such as a copper, and you know they will pick you up for carrying a rod in this town quicker than you can say Jack Robinson, whether they know who you are or not. You know the Sullivan law is very strong against guys carrying rods in this town.'

But Big Jule says he is afraid he will catch cold if he goes out without his rods, so we go down into Forty-ninth Street and start west toward Madison Square Garden, and just as we reach Eighth Avenue and are standing there waiting for the traffic to stop, so we can cross the street, I see there is quite some excitement around the Garden on the Forty-ninth Street side, with people running every which way, and yelling no little, and looking up in the air.

So I look up myself, and what do I see sitting up there on the edge of the Garden roof but a big ugly-faced monkey. At first I do not recognize it as a monkey, because it is so big I figure maybe it is just one of the prize-fight managers who stand around on this side of the Garden all afternoon waiting to get a match for their fighters, and while I am somewhat astonished to see a prize-fight manager in such a position, I figure maybe he is doing it on a bet. But when I take a second look I see that it is indeed a big monk, and an exceptionally homely monk at that, although personally I never see any monks I consider so very handsome, anyway.

Well, this big monk is holding something in its arms, and what it is I am not able to make out at first, but then Big Jule and I cross the street to the side opposite the Garden, and now I can see that the monk has a baby in its arms. Naturally I figure it is some kind of advertising dodge put on by the Garden to ballyhoo the circus, or maybe the fight between Sharkey and Risko which is coming off after the circus, but guys are still yelling and running up and down, and dolls are screaming until finally I realize that a most surprising situation prevails.

It seems that the big monk up on the roof is nobody but Bongo, who is a gorilla belonging to the circus, and one of the very few gorillas of any account in this country, or anywhere else, as far as this goes, because good gorillas are very scarce, indeed. Well, it seems that while they are shoving Bongo's cage into the Garden, the door becomes unfastened, and the first thing anybody knows, out pops Bongo, and goes bouncing along the street where a lot of the neighbours' children are playing games on the sidewalk, and a lot of Mammas are sitting out in the sun alongside baby buggies containing their young. This is a very common sight in side streets such as West Forty-ninth on nice days, and by no means unpleasant, if you like Mammas and their young.

Now what does this Bongo do but reach into a baby buggy which a Mamma is pushing past on the sidewalk on the Garden side of the street, and snatch out a baby, though what Bongo wants with this baby nobody knows to this day. It is a very young baby, and not such a baby as is fit to give a gorilla the size of Bongo any kind of struggle, so Bongo has no trouble whatever in handling it. Anyway, I always hear a gorilla will make a sucker out of a grown man in a battle, though I wish to say I never see a battle between a gorilla and a grown man. It ought to be a first-class drawing card, at that.

Well, naturally the baby's Mamma puts up quite a squawk about Bongo grabbing her baby, because no Mamma wishes her baby to keep company with a gorilla, and this Mamma starts in screaming very loud, and trying to take the baby away from Bongo, so what does Bongo do but run right up on the roof of the Garden by way of a big electric sign which hangs down on the Forty-ninth Street side. And there old Bongo sits on the edge of the roof with the baby in his arms, and the baby is squalling quite some, and Bongo is making funny noises, and showing his teeth as the folks commence gathering in the street below.

There is a big guy in his shirt-sleeves running through the crowd waving his hands, and trying to shush everybody, and saying 'Quiet, please' over and over, but nobody pays any attention to him. I figure this guy has something to do with the circus, and maybe with Bongo, too. A traffic copper takes a peek at the situation, and calls for the reserves from the Forty-seventh Street station, and somebody else sends for the fire truck down the street, and pretty soon cops are running from every direction, and the fire engines are coming, and the big guy in his shirt-sleeves is more excited than ever.

'Quiet, please,' he says. 'Everybody keep quiet, because if Bongo becomes disturbed by the noise he will throw the baby down in the street. He throws everything he gets his hands on,' the guy says. 'He acquires this habit from throwing coco-nuts back in his old home country. Let us get a life net, and if you all keep quiet we may be able to save the baby before Bongo starts heaving it like a coco-nut.'

Well, Bongo is sitting up there on the edge of the roof about seven stories above the ground peeking down with the baby in his arms, and he is holding this baby just like a Mamma would, but anybody can see that Bongo does not care for the row below, and once he lifts the baby high above his head as if to bean somebody with it. I see Big Nig, the crap shooter, in the mob, and afterwards I hear he is around offering to lay seven to five against the baby, but everybody is too excited to bet on such a proposition, although it is not a bad price, at that.

I see one doll in the crowd on the sidewalk on the side of the street opposite the Garden who is standing perfectly still staring up at the monk and the baby with a very strange expression on her face, and the way she is looking makes me take a second gander at her, and who is it but Miss Kitty Clancy. Her lips are moving as she stands there staring up, and something tells me Miss Kitty Clancy is saying prayers to herself, because she is such a doll as will know how to say prayers on an occasion like this.

Big Jule sees her about the same time I do, and Big Jule steps up beside Miss Kitty Clancy, and says hello to her, and though it is over a year since Miss Kitty Clancy sees Big Jule she turns to him and speaks to him as if she is talking to him just a minute before. It is very strange indeed the way Miss Kitty Clancy speaks to Big Jule as if he has never been away at all.

'Do something, Julie,' she says. 'You are always the one to do something. Oh, please do something, Julie.'

Well, Big Jule never answers a word, but steps back in the clear of the crowd and reaches for the waistband of his pants, when I grab him by the arm and say to him like this:

'My goodness, Jule,' I say, 'what are you going to do?'

'Why,' Jule says, 'I am going to shoot this thieving monk

before he takes a notion to heave the baby on somebody down here. For all I know,' Jule says, 'he may hit me with it, and I do not care to be hit with anybody's baby.'

'Jule,' I say, very earnestly, 'do not pull a rod in front of all these coppers, because if you do they will nail you sure, if only for having the rod, and if you are nailed you are in a very tough spot, indeed, what with being wanted here and there. Jule,' I say, 'you are hotter than a forty-five all over this country, and I do not wish to see you nailed. Anyway,' I say, 'you may shoot the baby instead of the monk, because anybody can see it will be very difficult to hit the monk up there without hitting the baby. Furthermore, even if you do hit the monk it will fall into the street, and bring the baby with it.'

'You speak great foolishness,' Jule says. 'I never miss what I shoot at. I will shoot the monk right between the eyes, and this will make him fall backwards, not forwards, and the baby will not be hurt because anybody san see it is no fall at all from the ledge to the roof behind. I make a study of such propositions,' Jule says, 'and I know if a guy is in such a position as this monk sitting on a ledge looking down from a high spot, his defensive reflexes tend backwards, so this is the way he is bound to fall if anything unexpected comes up on him, such as a bullet between the eyes. I read all about it in the doctor's books,' Jule says.

Then all of a sudden up comes his hand, and in his hand is one of his rods, and I hear a sound like ker-bap. When I come to think about it afterwards, I do not remember Big Jule even taking aim like a guy will generally do if he is shooting at something sitting, but old Bongo seems to lift up a little bit off the ledge at the crack of the gun, and then he keels over backwards, the baby still in his arms, and squalling more than somewhat, and Big Jule says to me like this:

'Right between the eyes, and I will bet on it,' he says, 'although it is not much of a target, at that.'

Well, nobody can figure what happens for a minute, and there is much silence except from the guy in his shirt-sleeves who is expressing much indignation with Big Jule and saying the circus people will sue him for damages sure if he has hurt

Bongo, because the monk is worth $100,000, or some such. I see Miss Kitty Clancy kneeling on the sidewalk with her hands clasped, and looking upwards, and Big Jule is sticking his rod back in his waistband again.

By this time some guys are out on the roof getting through from the inside of the building with the idea of heading Bongo off from that direction, and they let out a yell, and pretty soon I see one of them holding the baby up so everyone in the street can see it. A couple of other guys get down near the edge of the roof and pick up Bongo and show him to the crowd, as dead as a mackerel, and one of the guys puts a finger between Bongo's eyes to show where the bullet hits the monk, and Miss Kitty Clancy walks over to Big Jule and tries to say something to him, but only busts out crying very loud.

Well, I figure this is a good time for Big Jule and me to take a walk, because everybody is interested in what is going on up on the roof, and I do not wish the circus people to get a chance to serve a summons in a damage suit on Big Jule for shooting the valuable monk. Furthermore, a couple of coppers in harness are looking Big Jule over very critically, and I figure they are apt to put the old sleeve on Jule any second.

All of a sudden a slim young guy steps up to Big Jule and says to him like this:

'Jule,' he says, 'I want to see you,' and who is it but Johnny Brannigan. Naturally Big Jule starts reaching for a rod, but Johnny starts him walking down the street so fast Big Jule does not have time to get in action just then.

'No use getting it out, Jule,' Johnny Brannigan says. 'No use, and no need. Come with me, and hurry.'

Well, Big Jule is somewhat puzzled because Johnny Brannigan is not acting like a copper making a collar, so he goes along with Johnny, and I follow after him, and half-way down the block Johnny stops a Yellow short, and hustles us into it and tells the driver to keep shoving down Eighth Avenue.

'I am trailing you ever since you get in town, Jule,' Johnny Brannigan says. 'You never have a chance around here. I am going over to your Maw's house to put the arm on you, figuring you are sure to go there, when the thing over by the Garden comes off. Now I am getting out of this cab at the next corner, and you go on and see your Maw, and then screw out of town as quick as you can, because you are red hot around here, Jule.

'By the way,' Johnny Brannigan says, 'do you know it is my kid you save, Jule? Mine and Kitty Clancy's? We are married a year ago to-day.'

Well, Big Jule looks very much surprised for a moment, and then he laughs, and says like this: 'Well, I never know it is Kitty Clancy's, but I figure it for yours the minute I see it because it looks like you.'

'Yes,' Johnny Brannigan says, very proud, 'everybody says he does.'

'I can see the resemblance even from a distance,' Big Jule says. 'In fact,' he says, 'it is remarkable how much you look alike. But,' he says, 'for a minute, Johnny, I am afraid I will not be able to pick out the right face between the two on the roof, because it is very hard to tell the monk and your baby apart.'

PENGUIN POPULAR CLASSICS

Published or forthcoming

Aesop	Aesop's Fables
Hans Andersen	Fairy Tales
Louisa May Alcott	Good Wives
	Little Women
Eleanor Atkinson	Greyfriars Bobby
Jane Austen	Emma
	Mansfield Park
	Northanger Abbey
	Persuasion
	Pride and Prejudice
	Sense and Sensibility
R. M. Ballantyne	The Coral Island
J. M. Barrie	Peter Pan
R. D. Blackmore	Lorna Doone
Anne Brontë	Agnes Grey
	The Tenant of Wildfell Hall
Charlotte Brontë	Jane Eyre
	The Professor
	Shirley
	Villette
Emily Brontë	Wuthering Heights
John Buchan	The Thirty-Nine Steps
Frances Hodgson Burnett	A Little Princess
	The Secret Garden
Samuel Butler	The Way of All Flesh
Lewis Carroll	Alice's Adventures in Wonderland
	Through the Looking Glass
Geoffrey Chaucer	The Canterbury Tales
G. K. Chesterton	Father Brown Stories
Erskine Childers	The Riddle of the Sands
John Cleland	Fanny Hill
Wilkie Collins	The Moonstone
	The Woman in White
Sir Arthur Conan Doyle	The Adventures of Sherlock Holmes
	The Hound of the Baskervilles
	A Study in Scarlet

PENGUIN POPULAR CLASSICS

Published or forthcoming

Joseph Conrad	Heart of Darkness
	Lord Jim
	Nostromo
	The Secret Agent
	Victory
James Fenimore Cooper	The Last of the Mohicans
Stephen Crane	The Red Badge of Courage
Daniel Defoe	Moll Flanders
	Robinson Crusoe
Charles Dickens	Bleak House
	The Christmas Books
	David Copperfield
	Great Expectations
	Hard Times
	Little Dorrit
	Martin Chuzzlewit
	Nicholas Nickleby
	The Old Curiosity Shop
	Oliver Twist
	The Pickwick Papers
	A Tale of Two Cities
Charles Darwin	The Origin of Species
Fyodor Dostoyevsky	Crime and Punishment
George Eliot	Adam Bede
	Middlemarch
	The Mill on the Floss
	Silas Marner
John Meade Falkner	Moonfleet
F. Scott Fitzgerald	The Diamond as Big as the Ritz
	The Great Gatsby
Gustave Flaubert	Madame Bovary
Elizabeth Gaskell	Cousin Phillis
	Cranford
	Mary Barton
	North and South

PENGUIN POPULAR CLASSICS

Published or forthcoming

Kenneth Grahame	The Wind in the Willows
George Grossmith	The Diary of a Nobody
Brothers Grimm	Grimm's Fairy Tales
H. Rider Haggard	Allan Quatermain
	King Solomon's Mines
	She
Thomas Hardy	Far from the Madding Crowd
	Jude the Obscure
	The Mayor of Casterbridge
	A Pair of Blue Eyes
	The Return of the Native
	Tess of the D'Urbervilles
	Under the Greenwood Tree
	The Woodlanders
Nathaniel Hawthorne	The Scarlet Letter
Anthony Hope	The Prisoner of Zenda
Thomas Hughes	Tom Brown's Schooldays
Victor Hugo	The Hunchback of Notre-Dame
Washington Irving	Rip Van Winkle
Henry James	The Ambassadors
	The American
	The Aspern Papers
	Daisy Miller
	The Europeans
	The Turn of the Screw
	Washington Square
M. R. James	Ghost Stories
Jerome K. Jerome	Three Men in a Boat
	Three Men on the Bummel
James Joyce	Dubliners
	A Portrait of the Artist as a Young Man
Charles Kingsley	The Water Babies
Rudyard Kipling	Captains Courageous
	The Jungle Books
	Just So Stories
	Kim
	Plain Tales from the Hills
	Puck of Pook's Hill

PENGUIN POPULAR CLASSICS

Published or forthcoming

Charles and Mary Lamb	Tales from Shakespeare
D. H. Lawrence	The Rainbow
	Sons and Lovers
	Women in Love
Edward Lear	Book of Nonsense
Gaston Leroux	The Phantom of the Opera
Jack London	White Fang *and* The Call of the Wild
Captain Marryat	The Children of the New Forest
Herman Melville	Moby Dick
John Milton	Paradise Lost
Edith Nesbit	Five Children and It
	The Railway Children
Francis Turner Palgrave	The Golden Treasury
Edgar Allan Poe	Selected Tales
Sir Walter Scott	Ivanhoe
	Rob Roy
	Waverley
Saki	The Best of Saki
Anna Sewell	Black Beauty
William Shakespeare	Antony and Cleopatra
	As You Like It
	Hamlet
	Henry V
	Julius Caesar
	King Lear
	Macbeth
	The Merchant of Venice
	A Midsummer Night's Dream
	Othello
	Romeo and Juliet
	The Tempest
	Twelfth Night

PENGUIN POPULAR POETRY

Published or forthcoming

The Selected Poems *of:*

Matthew Arnold
William Blake
Robert Browning
Robert Burns
Lord Byron
John Donne
Thomas Hardy
John Keats
Rudyard Kipling
Alexander Pope
Alfred Tennyson
Walt Whitman
William Wordsworth
William Yeats

and collections of:

Sixteenth-Century Poetry
Seventeenth-Century Poetry
Eighteenth-Century Poetry
Poetry of the Romantics
Victorian Poetry
Twentieth-Century Poetry